Tales from

Rudyard Kipling

Rudyard Kipling, son of John Lockwood Kipling and Alice Macdonald, was born in Bombay in 1865. Educated to India to work as a journalist between 1882 and 1889. After a brief period in Vermont, U.S.A., Kipling made his home in England in 1896, travelling abroad frequently to the end of his life. He was awarded a Nobel Prize in 1902 and died in 1936.

Though he is best known for his short stories, Kipling also wrote verse and novels. His writings characteristically combine vivid accounts of action in the external world with searching explorations of the inner self. Among his most famous publications are *Plain Tales from the Hills* (1888), *Barrack-Room Ballads* (1892), *The Jungle Books* (1894-5), *Kim* (1901), *Just So Stories* (1902), *Rewards and Fairies* (1910) and *Debits and Credits* (1926).

Tales from India

Rudyard Kipling

Srishti
PUBLISHERS & DISTRIBUTORS

SRISHTI PUBLISHERS & DISTRIBUTORS
64-A, Adhchini
Sri Aurobindo Marg
New Delhi 110017

Indian paperback published in 1998 by
SRISHTI PUBLISHERS & DISTRIBUTORS
Second impression 1999

ISBN 81-87075-18-X
Rs. 145.00

Cover Design by Arrt Creations
45 Nehru Apartment, New Delhi 110019

Printed and bound in India by
Saurabh Print-O-Pack, Noida

Contents

The Story of Muhammad Din

Who is the happy man? He that sees in his own house at home, little children crowned with dust, leaping and falling and crying.
– *Munichandra*, translated by Professor Peterson.

The polo-ball was an old one, scarred, chipped, and dinted. It stood on the mantelpiece among the pipe-stems which Imam Din, *khitmatgar*, was cleaning for me.

'Does the Heaven-born want this ball?' said Imam Din deferentially.

The Heaven-born set no particular store by it; but of what use was a polo-ball to a *khitmatgar*?

'By Your Honour's favour, I have a little son. He has seen this ball, and desires it to play with. I do not want it for myself.'

No one would for an instant accuse portly old Imam Din of wanting to play with polo-balls. He carried out the battered thing into the verandah; and there followed a hurricane of joyful squeaks, a patter of small feet, and the *thud-thud-thud* of the ball rolling along the ground. Evidently the little son had been waiting outside the door to secure his treasure. But how had he managed to see that polo-ball?

Next day, coming back from office half an hour earlier than usual, I was aware of a small figure in the dining-room – a tiny, plump figure in a ridiculously inadequate shirt which came, perhaps, half-way down the tubby stomach. It wandered round the room, thumb in mouth, crooning to itself as it took stock of the pictures. Undoubtedly this was the 'little son'.

He had no business in my room, of course; but was so deeply absorbed in his discoveries that he never noticed me in the doorway. I stepped into the room and startled him nearly into a fit. He sat down on the ground with a gasp. His eyes opened, and his mouth followed suit. I knew what was coming, and fled, followed by a long, dry howl which reached the servants' quarters far more quickly than any command of mine had ever done. In ten seconds Imam Din was in the dining-room. Then despairing sobs arose, and I returned to find Imam Din admonishing the small sinner who was using most of his shirt as a handkerchief.

'This boy,' said Imam Din judicially, 'is a *budmash* – a big *budmash*. He will, without doubt, go to the *jail-khana* for his behaviour.' Renewed yells from the penitent, and an elaborate apology to myself from Imam Din.

'Tell the baby,' said I, 'that the *Sahib* is not angry, and take him away.' Imam Din conveyed my forgiveness to the offender, who had now gathered all his shirt round his neck, stringwise, and the yell subsided into a sob. The two set off for the door. 'His name,' said Imam Din, as though the name were part of the crime, 'is Muhammad Din, and he is a *budmash*.' Freed from present danger, Muhammad Din turned round in his father's arms, and said gravely, 'It is true that my name is Muhammad Din, *Tahib*, but I am not a *budmash*. I am a *man*!'

From that day dated my acquaintance with Muhammad Din. Never again did he come into my dining-room, but on the neutral ground of the garden, we greeted each other with much state, though our conversation was confined to '*Talaam, Tahib*' from his side, and '*Salaam, Muhammad Din*' from mine. Daily on my return from office, the little white shirt, and the fat little body used to rise from the shade of the creeper-covered trellis where they had been hid; and daily I checked my horse here, that my salutation might not be slurred over or given unseemly.

Muhammad Din never had any companions. He used to trot about the compound, in and out of the castor-oil bushes, on mysterious errands of his own. One day I stumbled upon some of his handiwork far down the grounds. He had half buried the polo-ball in dust, and stuck six shrivelled old marigold flowers in a circle round it. Outside that circle again was a rude square, traced out in bits of red brick alternating with fragments of broken china; the whole bounded by a little bank of dust. The water-man from the well-curb put in a plea for the small architect, saying that it was only the play of a baby and did not much disfigure my garden.

Heaven knows that I had no intention of touching the child's work then or later; but, that evening, a stroll through the garden brought me unawares full on it; so that I trampled, before I knew, marigold-heads, dust-bank, and fragments of broken soap-dish into confusion past all hope of mending. Next morning, I came upon Muhammad Din crying softly to himself over the ruin I had wrought. Some one had cruelly told him that the *Sahib* was very angry with him for spoiling the garden, and had scattered his rubbish, using bad language the while. Muhammad Din laboured for an hour at effacing every trace of the dust-bank and pottery fragments, and it was with a tearful and apologetic face that he said, '*Talaam, Tahib*,' when I came home from office. A hasty inquiry resulted in Imam Din informing Muhammad Din that, by my singular favour, he was permitted to disport himself as he pleased. Whereat the child took heart and fell to tracing the ground-plan of an edifice which was to eclipse the marigold-polo-ball creation.

For some months, the chubby little eccentricity revolved in his humble orbit among the castor-oil bushes and in the dust; always fashioning magnificent palaces from stale flowers thrown away by the bearer, smooth water-worn pebbles, bits of broken glass, and feathers pulled, I fancy, from my fowls – always alone, and always crooning to himself.

A gaily-spotted sea-shell was dropped one day close to the last of his little buildings; and I looked that Muhammad Din should build something more than ordinarily splendid on the strength of it. Nor was I disappointed. He meditated for the better part of an hour, and his crooning rose to a jubilant song. Then he began tracing in the dust. It would certainly be a wondrous palace, this one, for it was two yards long and a yard broad in ground-plan. But the palace was never completed.

Next day there was no Muhammad Din at the head of the carriage-drive, and no '*Talaam, Tahib*' to welcome my return. I had grown accustomed to the greeting, and its omission troubled me. Next day Imam Din told me that the child was suffering slightly from fever and needed quinine. He got the medicine, and an English Doctor.

'They have no stamina, these brats,' said the Doctor, as he left Imam Din's quarters.

A week later, though I would have given much to have avoided it, I met on the road to the Mussulman burying-ground Imam Din, accompanied by one other friend, carrying in his arms, wrapped in a white cloth, all that was left of little Muhammad Din.

In the House of Suddhoo

A stone's throw out on either hand
From that well-ordered road we tread,
  And all the world is wild and strange:
Churel and ghoul and *Djinn* and sprite
Shall bear us company to-night,
For we have reached the Oldest Land
  Wherein the Powers of Darkness range.
From the Dusk to the Dawn

The house of Suddhoo, near the Taksali Gate, is two-storied, with four carved windows of old brown wood, and a flat roof. You may recognise it by five red hand-prints arranged like the Five of Diamonds on the whitewash between the upper windows. Bhagwan Dass the grocer and a man who says he gets his living by seal-cutting live in the lower story with a troop of wives, servants, friends, and retainers. The two upper rooms used to be occupied by Janoo and Azizun and a little black-and-tan terrier that was stolen from an Englishman's house and given to Janoo by a soldier. Today, only Janoo lives in the upper room. Suddhoo sleeps on the roof generally, except when he sleeps in the street. He used to go to Peshawar in the cold weather to visit his son who sells curiosities near the Edwardes' Gate, and then he slept under a real mud roof. Suddhoo is a great friend of mine, because his cousin had a son who secured, thanks to my recommendation, the post of head-messenger to a big firm in the Station. Suddhoo says that God will make me a Lieutenant-Governor one of these days. I daresay his prophecy will come true. He is very, very old with white hair and no teeth worth showing, and he has outlived his wits – outlived nearly everything except his fondness for his son at Peshawar. Janoo and Azizun are Kashmiris, Ladies of the City, and theirs was an ancient and more or less honourable profession; but Azizun has since married a medical student from the North-West and has settled down to a most respectable life somewhere near Bareilly. Bhagwan Dass is an extortionate and an adulterator. He is very rich. The man who is supposed to get his living by seal-cutting pretends to be very poor. This lets you know as much as is necessary of the four principal tenants in the house of Suddhoo. Then there is Me of course; but I am only the chorus that comes in at the end to explain things. So I do not count.

Suddhoo was not clever. The man who pretended to cut seals was the cleverest of them all – Bhagwan Dass only knew how to lie – except Janoo. She was also beautiful, but that was her own affair.

Suddhoo's son at Peshawar was attacked by pleurisy, and old Suddhoo was troubled. The seal-cutter man heard of Suddhoo's anxiety and made capital out of it. He was abreast of the times. He got a friend in Peshawar to telegraph daily accounts of the son's health. And here the story begins.

Suddhoo's cousin's son told me, one evening, that Suddhoo wanted to see me; that he was too old and feeble to come personally, and that I should be conferring an everlasting honour on the House of Suddhoo if I went to him. I went; but I think, seeing how well off Suddhoo was then, that he might have sent something better than an *ekka*, which jolted fearfully, to haul out a future Lieutenant-Governor to the City on a muggy April evening. The *ekka* did not run quickly. It was full dark when we pulled up opposite the door of Ranjit Singh's Tomb near the main gate of the Fort. Here was Suddhoo, and he said that, by reason of my condescension, it was absolutely certain that I should become a Lieutenant-Governor while my hair was yet black. Then we talked about the weather and the state of my health, and the wheat crops, for fifteen minutes, in the Huzuri Bagh, under the stairs.

Suddhoo came to the point at last. He said that Janoo had told him that there was an order of the *Sirkar* against magic, because it was feared that magic might one day kill the Empress of India. I didn't know anything about the state of the law; but I fancied that something interesting was going to happen. I said that so far from magic being discouraged by the Government it was highly commended. The greatest officials of the State practised it themselves. (If the Financial Statement isn't magic, I don't know what is.) Then, to encourage him further, I said that, if there was any *jadoo* afoot, I had not the least objection to giving it my countenance and sanction, and to seeing that it was clean *jadoo* – white magic, as distinguished from the unclean *jadoo* which kills folk. It took a long time before Suddhoo admitted that this was just what he had asked me to come for. Then he told me, in jerks and quavers, that the man who said he cut seals was a sorcerer of the cleanest kind; that every day he gave Suddhoo news of the sick son in Peshawar more quickly than the lightning could fly, and that this news was always corroborated by the letters. Further, that he had told Suddhoo how a great danger was threatening his son, which could be removed by clean *jadoo*; and, of course, heavy payment. I began to see exactly how the land lay, and told Suddhoo that I also understood a little *jadoo* in the Western line, and would go to his house to see that everything was done decently and in order. We set off together; and on the way Suddhoo told me that he had paid the seal-cutter between one hundred and two hundred rupees already; and the *jadoo* of that night would cost two hundred more. Which was cheap, he said, considering the greatness of his son's danger; but I do not think he meant it.

The lights were all cloaked in the front of the house when we arrived. I could hear awful noises from behind the seal-cutter's shop-front, as if some one were groaning his soul out. Suddhoo shook all over, and while we groped our way upstairs told me that the *jadoo* had begun. Janoo and Azizun met us at the stair-head, and told us that the *jadoo*-work was coming off in their rooms, because there was more space there. Janoo is a lady of a freethinking turn of mind. She whispered that the *jadoo* was an invention to get money out of Suddhoo, and that the seal-cutter would go to a hot place when he died. Suddhoo was nearly crying with fear and old age. He kept walking up and down the room in the half-light, repeating his son's name over and over again, and asking Azizun if the seal-cutter ought not to make a reduction in the case of his own landlord. Janoo pulled me over to the shadow in the recess of the carved bow-windows. The boards were up, and the rooms were only lit by one tiny oil-lamp. There was no chance of my being seen if I stayed still.

Presently, the groans below ceased, and we heard steps on the staircase. That was the seal-cutter. He stopped outside the door as the terrier barked and Azizun fumbled at the chain, and he told Suddhoo to blow out the lamp. This left the place in jet darkness, except for the red glow from the two *huqas* that belonged to Janoo and Azizun. The seal-cutter came in, and I heard Suddhoo throw himself down on the floor and groan. Azizun caught her breath, and Janoo backed on to one of the beds with a shudder. There was a clink of something metallic, and then shot up a pale blue-green flame near the ground. The light was just enough to show Azizun, pressed against one corner of the room with the terrier between her knees; Janoo, with her hands clasped, leaning forward as she sat on the bed; Suddhoo, face down, quivering, and the seal-cutter.

I hope I may never see another man like that seal-cutter. He was stripped to the waist, with a wreath of white jasmine as thick as my wrist round his forehead, a salmon coloured loin-cloth round his middle, and a steel bangle on each ankle. This was not awe-inspiring. It was the face of the man that turned me cold. It was blue-gray in the first place. In the second, the eyes were rolled back till you could only see the whites of them; and, in the third, the face was the face of a demon – a ghoul – anything you please except of the sleek, oily old ruffian who sat in the daytime over his turning-lathe downstairs. He was lying on his stomach with his arms turned and crossed behind him, as if he had been thrown down pinioned. His head and neck were the only parts of him off the floor. They were nearly at right angles to the body, like the head of a cobra at spring. It was ghastly. In the centre of the room, on the bare earth floor, stood a big, deep, brass basin, with a pale blue-green light floating in the centre like a night-light. Round that basin the man on the floor wriggled himself three times. How he did it I do not know. I could see the muscles ripple along his spine and fall smooth again; but I could not see any other motion. The head seemed the only thing alive about him, except that slow curl and uncurl of the labouring back-muscles. Janoo from the bed was breathing seventy to the minute; Azizun held her hands before her eyes; and old Suddhoo, fingering at the dirt that had got into his white beard, was crying to himself. The horror of it was that the creeping, crawly thing made no sound – only crawled! And, remember, this lasted for ten minutes, while the terrier whined, and Azizun shuddered, and Janoo gasped, and Suddhoo cried.

I felt the hair lift at the back of my head, and my heart thump like a thermantidote paddle. Luckily, the seal-cutter betrayed himself by his most impressive trick and made me calm again. After he had finished that unspeakable triple crawl, he stretched his head away from the floor as high as he could, and sent out a jet of fire from his nostrils. Now I knew how fire-spouting is done – I can do it myself – so I felt at ease. The business was a fraud. If he had only kept to that crawl without trying to raise the effect, goodness knows what I might not have thought. Both the girls shrieked at the jet of fire and the head dropped, chin-down on the floor, with a thud; the whole body lying then like a corpse with its arms trussed. There was a pause of five full minutes after this, and the blue-green flame died down. Janoo stooped to settle one of her anklets, while Azizun turned her face to the wall and took the terrier in her arms. Suddhoo put out an arm mechanically to Janoo's *huqa*, and she slid it across the floor with her foot. Directly above the body and on the wall, were a couple of flaming portraits, in stamped-paper frames, of the Queen and the Prince of Wales. They looked down on the performance, and to my thinking, seemed to heighten the grotesqueness of it all.

Just when the silence was getting unendurable, the body turned over and rolled away from the basin to the side of the room, where it lay stomach-up. There was a faint 'plop' from the basin – exactly like the noise a fish makes when it takes a fly – and the green light in the centre revived.

I looked at the basin, and saw, bobbing in the water, the dried, shrivelled, black head of a native baby – open eyes, open mouth, and shaved scalp. It was worse, being so very sudden, than the crawling exhibition. We had no time to say anything before it began to speak.

Read Poe's account of the voice that came from the mesmerised dying man, and you will realise less than one half of the horror of that head's voice.

There was an interval of a second or two between each word, and a sort of 'ring, ring, ring,' in the note of the voice, like the timbre of a bell. It pealed slowly, as if talking to itself, for several minutes before I got rid of my cold sweat. Then the blessed solution struck me. I looked at the body lying near the doorway, and saw, just where the hollow of the throat joins on the shoulders, a muscle that had nothing to do with any man's regular breathing twitching away steadily. The whole thing was a careful reproduction of the Egyptian teraphim that one reads about sometimes; and the voice was as clever and as appalling a piece of ventriloquism as one could wish to hear. All this time the head was 'lip-lip-lapping' against the side of the basin, and speaking. It told Suddhoo, on his face again whining, of his son's illness and of the state of the illness up to the evening of that very night. I always shall respect the seal-cutter for keeping so faithfully to the time of the Peshawar telegrams. It went on to say that skilled doctors were night and day watching over the man's life; and that he would eventually recover if the fee to the potent sorcerer, whose servant was the head in the basin, were doubled.

Here the mistake from the artistic point of view came in. To ask for twice your stipulated fee in a voice that Lazarus might have used when he rose from the dead, is absurd. Janoo, who is really a woman of masculine intellect, saw this as quickly as I did. I heard her say '*Asli nahin! Fareib!*' scornfully under her breath; and just as she said so, the light in the basin died out, the head stopped talking, and we heard the room door creak on its hinges. Then Janoo struck a match, lit the lamp, and we saw that head, basin, and seal-cutter were gone. Suddhoo was wringing his hands and explaining to any one who cared to listen, that, if his chances of eternal salvation depended on it, he could not raise another two hundred rupees. Azizun was nearly in hysterics in the corner; while Janoo sat down composedly on one of the beds to discuss the probabilities of the whole thing being a *bunao*, or 'make-up'.

I explained as much as I knew of the seal-cutter's way of *jadoo*; but her argument was much more simple – 'The magic that is always demanding gifts is no true magic,' said she. 'My mother told me that the only potent love-spells are those which are told you for love. This seal-cutter man is a liar and a devil. I dare not tell, do anything, or get anything done, because I am in debt to Bhagwan Dass the *bunnia* for two gold rings and a heavy anklet. I must get my food from his shop. The seal-cutter is the friend of Bhagwan Dass, and he would poison my food.

A fool's *jadoo* has been going on for ten days, and has cost Suddhoo many rupees each night. The seal-cutter used black hens and lemons and *mantras* before. He never showed us anything like this till tonight. Azizun is a fool, and will be a *purdahnashin* soon. Suddhoo has lost his strength and his wits. See now! I had hoped to get from Suddhoo many rupees while he lived, and many more after his death; and behold, he is spending everything on that offspring of a devil and a she-ass, the seal-cutter!'

Here I said, 'But what induced Suddhoo to drag me into the business? Of course I can speak to the seal-cutter, and he shall refund. The whole thing is child's talk – shame – and senseless.'

'Suddhoo *is* an old child,' said Janoo. 'He has lived on the roofs these seventy years and is as senseless as a milch-goat. He brought you here to assure himself that he was not breaking any law of the *Sirkar*, whose salt he ate many years ago. He worships the dust off the feet of the seal-cutter, and that cow-devourer has forbidden him to go and see his son. What does Suddhoo know of your laws or the lightning-post? I have to watch his money going day by day to that lying beast below.'

Janoo stamped her foot on the floor and nearly cried with vexation; while Suddhoo was whimpering under a blanket in the corner, and Azizun was trying to guide the pipe-stem to his foolish old mouth.

Now, the case stands thus. Unthinkingly, I have laid myself open to the charge of aiding and abetting the seal-cutter in obtaining money under false pretences, which is forbidden by Section 420 of the Indian Penal Code. I am helpless in the matter for these reasons. I cannot inform the Police. What witnesses would support my statements? Janoo refuses flatly, and Azizun is a veiled woman somewhere near Bareilly – lost in this big India of ours. I dare not again take the law into my own hands, and speak to the seal-cutter; for certain am I that, not only would Suddhoo disbelieve me, but this step would end in the poisoning of Janoo, who is bound hand and foot by her debt to the *bunnia*. Suddhoo is an old dotard; and whenever we meet mumbles my idiotic joke that the *Sirkar* rather patronises the Black Art than otherwise. His son is well now; but Suddhoo is completely under the influence of the seal-cutter, by whose advice he regulates the affairs of his life. Janoo watches daily the money that she hoped to wheedle out of Suddhoo taken by the seal-cutter, and becomes daily more furious and sullen.

She will never tell, because she dare not; but, unless something happens to prevent her, I am afraid that the seal-cutter will die of cholera – the white arsenic kind – about the middle of May. And thus I shall be privy to a murder in the House of Suddhoo.

Without Benefit of Clergy

Before my Spring I garnered Autumn's gain,
Out of her time my field was white with grain,
The year gave up her secrets to my woe.
Forced and deflowered each sick season lay,
In mystery of increase and decay;
I saw the sunset ere men saw the day,
Who am too wise in that I should not know.

Bitter Waters

I

'But if it be a girl?'

'Lord of my life, it cannot be. I have prayed for so many nights, and sent gifts to Sheikh Badl's shrine so often, that I know God will give us a son – a man-child that shall grow into a man. Think of this and be glad. My mother shall be his mother till I can take him again, and the mullah of the Pattan mosque shall cast his nativity – God send he be born in an auspicious hour! – and then, and then thou wilt never weary of me, thy slave.'

'Since when hast thou been a slave, my queen?'

'Since the beginning – till this mercy came to me. How could I be sure of thy love when I knew that I had been bought with silver?'

'Nay, that was the dowry. I paid it to thy mother.'

'And she has buried it, and sits upon it all day long like a hen. What talk is yours of dower! I was bought as though I had been a Lucknow dancing-girl instead of a child.'

'Art thou sorry for the sale?'

'I have sorrowed; but today I am glad. Thou wilt never cease to love me now? – answer, my king.'

'Never – never. No.'

'Not even though the *mem-log* – the white women of thy own blood – love thee? And remember, I have watched them driving in the evening; they are very fair.'

'I have seen fire-balloons by the hundred. I have seen the moon, and – then I saw no more fire-balloons.'

Ameera clapped her hands and laughed. 'Very good talk,' she

said. Then with an assumption of great stateliness, 'It is enough. Thou hast my permission to depart, – if thou wilt.'

The man did not move. He was sitting on a low red-lacquered couch in a room furnished only with a blue-and-white floor-cloth, some rugs, and a very complete collection of native cushions. At his feet sat a woman of sixteen, and she was all but all the world in his eyes. By every rule and law she should have been otherwise, for he was an Englishman, and she a Mussulman's daughter bought two years before from her mother, who, being left without money, would have sold Ameera shrieking to the Prince of Darkness if the price had been sufficient.

It was a contract entered into with a light heart; but even before the girl had reached her bloom she came to fill the greater portion of John Holden's life. For her, and the withered hag her mother, he had taken a little house overlooking the great red-walled city, and found, – when the marigolds had sprung up by the well in the courtyard, and Ameera had established herself according to her own ideas of comfort, and her mother had ceased grumbling at the inadequacy of the cooking-places, the distance from the daily market, and at matters of house-keeping in general, – that the house was to him his home. Any one could enter his bachelor's bungalow by day or night, and the life that he led there was an unlovely one. In the house in the city his feet only could pass beyond the outer courtyard to the women's rooms; and when the big wooden gate was bolted behind him he was king in his own territory, with Ameera for queen. And there was going to be added to this kingdom a third person whose arrival Holden felt inclined to resent. It interfered with his perfect happiness. It disarranged the orderly peace of the house that was his own. But Ameera was wild with delight at the thought of it, and her mother not less so. The love of a man, and particularly a white man, was at the best an inconstant affair, but it might, both women argued, be held fast by a baby's hands. 'And then,' Amerra would always say, 'then he will never care for the white *mem-log*. I hate them all – I hate them all.'

'He will go back to his own people in time,' said the mother; 'but by the blessing of God that time is yet afar off.'

Holden sat silent on the couch thinking of the future, and his thoughts were not pleasant. The drawbacks of a double life are manifold. The Government, with singular care, had ordered him out of the station for a fortnight on special duty in the place of a man who was watching by the bedside of a sick wife. The verbal notification of the transfer had been edged by a cheerful remark that Holden ought to think himself lucky in being a bachelor and a free man. He came to break the news to Ameera.

'It is not good,' she said slowly, 'but it is not all bad. There is my mother here, and no harm will come to me – unless indeed I die of pure joy. Go thou to thy work and think no troublesome thoughts. When the days are done I believe . . . nay, I am sure. And – and then I shall lay *him* in thy arms, and thou wilt love me for ever. The train goes tonight, at midnight, is it not? Go now, and do not let thy heart by heavy by cause of me. But thou wilt not delay in returning? Thou wilt not stay on the road to talk to the bold white *mem-log*? Come back to me swiftly, my life.'

As he left the courtyard to reach his horse that was tethered to the gate-post, Holden spoke to the white-haired old watchman who guarded the house, and bade him under certain contingencies despatch the filled-up telegraph-form that Holden gave him. It was all that could be done, and with the sensations of a man who has attended his own funeral Holden went away by the night mail to his exile. Every hour of the day he dreaded the arrival of the telegram, and every hour of the night he pictured to himself the death of Ameera. In consequence his work for the State was not of first-rate quality, nor was his temper towards his colleagues of the most amiable. The fortnight ended without a sign from his home, and, torn to pieces by his anxieties, Holden returned to be swallowed up for two precious hours by a dinner at the club, wherein he heard, as a man hears in a swoon, voices telling him how execrably he had performed the other man's duties, and how he had endeared himself to all his associates. Then he fled on horseback through the night with his heart in his mouth. There was no answer at first to his blows on the gate, and he had just wheeled his horse round to kick it in when Pir Khan appeared with a lantern and held his stirrup.

'Has aught occurred?' said Holden.

'The news does not come from my mouth, Protector of the

Poor, but——' He held out his shaking hand as befitted the bearer of good news who is entitled to a reward.

Holden hurried through the courtyard. A light burned in the upper room. His horse neighed in the gateway, and he heard a shrill little wail that sent all the blood into the apple of his throat. It was a new voice, but it did not prove that Ameera was alive.

'Who is there?' he called up the narrow brick staircase.

There was a cry of delight from Ameera, and then the voice of the mother, tremulous with old age and pride – 'We be two women and – the – man – thy – son.'

On the threshold of the room Holden stepped on a naked dagger, that was laid there to avert ill-luck, and it broke at the hilt under his impatient heel.

'God is great!' cooed Ameera in the half-light. 'Thou hast taken his misfortunes on thy head.'

'Ay, but how is it with thee, life of my life? Old woman, how is it with her?'

'She has forgotten her sufferings for joy that the child is born. There is no harm; but speak softly,' said the mother.

'It only needed thy presence to make me all well,' said Ameera. 'My king, thou hast been very long away. What gifts hast thou for me? Ah, ah! It is I that bring gifts this time. Look, my life, look. Was there ever such a babe? Nay, I am too weak even to clear my arm from him.'

'Rest then, and do not talk. I am here, *bachari* [little woman].'

'Well said, for there is a bond and a heel-rope [*peecharee*] between us now that nothing can break. Look – canst thou see in this light? He is without spot or blemish. Never was such a man-child. *Ya illah!* he shall be a pundit – no, a trooper of the Queen. And, my life, dost thou love me as well as ever, though I am faint and sick and worn? Answer truly.'

'Yea. I love as I have loved, with all my soul. Lie still, pearl, and rest.'

'Then do not go. Sit by my side here – so. Mother, the lord of this house needs a cushion. Bring it.' There was an almost imperceptible movement on the part of the new life that lay in the hollow of Ameera's arm. 'Aho!' she said, her voice breaking with love. 'The babe is a champion from his birth. He is kicking me in the side with mighty kicks. Was there ever such a babe! And he is ours to us – thine and mine. Put thy hand on his head, but carefully, for he is very young, and men are unskilled in such matters.'

Very cautiously Holden touched with the tips of his fingers the downy head.

'He is of the Faith,' said Ameera; 'for lying here in the night-watches I whispered the call to prayer and the profession of faith into his ears. And it is most marvellous that he was born upon a Friday, as I was born. Be careful of him, my life; but he can almost grip with his hands.'

Holden found one helpless little hand that closed feebly on his finger. And the clutch ran through his body till it settled about his heart. Till then his sole thought had been for Ameera. He began to realise that there was some one else in the world, but he could not feel that it was a veritable son with a soul. He sat down to think, and Ameera dozed lightly.

'Get hence, *sahib*,' said her mother under her breath. 'It is not good that she should find you here on waking. She must be still.'

'I go,' said Holden submissively. 'Here be rupees. See that my *baba* gets fat and finds all that he needs.'

The chink of the silver roused Ameera. 'I am his mother, and no hireling,' she said weakly. 'Shall I look to him more or less for the sake of money? Mother, give it back. I have borne my lord a son.'

The deep sleep of weakness came upon her almost before the sentence was completed. Holden went down to the courtyard very softly with his heart at ease. Pir Khan, the old watchman, was chuckling with delight. 'This house is now complete,' he said, and without further comment thrust into Holden's hands the hilt of a sabre worn many years ago when he, Pir Khan, served the Queen in the police. The bleat of a tethered goat came from the well-kerb.

'There be two,' said Pir Khan, 'two goats of the best. I bought them, and they cost much money; and since there is no birth-party assembled their flesh will be all mine. Strike craftily, *sahib*! 'Tis an ill-balanced sabre at the best. Wait till they raise their heads from cropping the marigolds.'

'And why?' said Holden, bewildered.

'For the birth-sacrifice. What else? Otherwise the child being unguarded from fate may die. The Protector of the Poor knows the fitting words to be said.'

Holden had learned them once with little thought that he would ever speak them in earnest. The touch of the cold sabre-hilt in his palm turned suddenly to the clinging grip of the child up-stairs – the child that was his own son – and a dread of loss filled him.

'Strike!' said Pir Khan. 'Never life came into the world but life was paid for it. See, the goats have raised their heads. Now! With a drawing cut!'

Hardly knowing what he did, Holden cut twice as he muttered the Mahomedan prayer that runs: 'Almighty! In place of this my son I offer life for life, blood for blood, head for head, bone for bone, hair for hair, skin for skin.' The waiting horse snorted and bounded in his pickets at the smell of the raw blood that spirted over Holden's riding-boots.

'Well smitten!' said Pir Khan wiping the sabre. 'A swordsman was lost in thee. Go with a light heart, Heaven-born. I am thy servant, and the servant of thy son. May the Presence live a thousand years and . . . the flesh of the goats is all mine?' Pir Khan drew back richer by a month's pay. Holden swung himself into the saddle and rode off through the low-hanging wood-smoke of the evening. He was full of riotous exultation, alternating with a vast vague tenderness directed towards no particular object, that made him choke as he bent over the neck of his uneasy horse. 'I never felt like this in my life,' he thought. 'I'll go to the club and pull myself together.'

A game of pool was beginning, and the room was full of men. Holden entered, eager to get to the light and the company of his fellows, singing at the top of his voice –

In Baltimore a-walking, a lady I did meet!

'Did you?' said the club-secretary from his corner. 'Did she happen to tell you that your boots were wringing wet? Great goodness, man, it's blood!'

'Bosh!' said Holden, picking his cue from the rack. 'May I

cut in? It's dew. I've been riding through high crops. My faith! my boots are in a mess though!

'And if it be a girl she shall wear a wedding-ring,
And if it be a boy he shall fight for his king
With his dirk, and his cap, and his little jacket blue,
He shall walk the quarter-deck –'

'Yellow on blue – green next player,' said the marker monotonously.

'*He shall walk the quarter-deck*, – Am I green, marker? *He shall walk the quarter-deck*, – eh! that's a bad shot, – *As his daddy used to do!*'

'I don't see that you have anything to crow about,' said a zealous junior civilian acidly. 'The Government is not exactly pleased with your work when you relieved Sanders.'

'Does that mean a wigging from headquarters?' said Holden with an abstracted smile. 'I think I can stand it.'

The talk beat up round the ever-fresh subject of each man's work, and steadied Holden till it was time to go to his dark empty bungalow, where his butler received him as one who knew all his affairs. Holden remained awake for the greater part of the night, and his dreams were pleasant ones.

II

'How old is he now?'

'*Ya illah!* What a man's question! He is all but six weeks old; and on this night I go up to the house-top with thee, my life, to count the stars. For that is auspicious. And he was born on a Friday under the sign of the Sun, and it has been told to me that he will outlive us both and get wealth. Can we wish for aught better, beloved?'

'There is nothing better. Let us go up to the roof, and thou shalt count the stars – but a few only, for the sky is heavy with cloud.'

'The winter rains are late, and maybe they come out of season. Come, before all the stars are hid. I have put on my richest jewels.'

'Thou hast forgotten the best of all.'

'*Ai!* Ours. He comes also. He has never yet seen the skies.'

Ameera climbed the narrow staircase that led to the flat roof. The child, placid and unwinking, lay in the hollow of her right arm, gorgeous in silver-fringed muslin with a small skull-cap on his head. Ameera wore all that she valued most. The diamond nose-stud that takes the place of the Western patch in drawing attention to the curve of the nostril, the gold ornament in the centre of the forehead studded with tallow-drop emeralds and flawed rubies, the heavy circlet of beaten gold that was fastened round her neck by the softness of the pure metal, and the chinking curb-patterned silver anklets hanging low over the rosy ankle-bone. She was dressed in jade-green muslin as befitted a daughter of the Faith, and from shoulder to elbow and elbow to wrist ran bracelets of silver tied with floss silk, frail glass bangles slipped over the wrist in proof of the slenderness of the hand, and certain heavy gold bracelets that had no part in her country's ornaments, but, since they were Holden's gift and fastened with a cunning European snap, delighted her immensely.

They sat down by the low white parapet of the roof, overlooking the city and its lights.

'They are happy down there,' said Ameera. 'But I do not think that they are as happy as we. Nor do I think the white *mem-log* are as happy. And thou?'

'I know they are not.'

'How dost thou know?'

'They give their children over to the nurses.'

'I have never seen that,' said Ameera with a sigh, 'nor do I wish to see. *Ahi!*' – she dropped her head on Holden's shoulder, – 'I have counted forty stars, and I am tired. Look at the child, love of my life, he is counting too.'

The baby was staring with round eyes at the dark of the heavens. Ameera placed him in Holden's arms, and he lay there without a cry.

'What shall we call him among ourselves?' she said. 'Look! Art thou ever tired of looking? He carries thy very eyes. But the mouth——'

'Is thine, most dear. Who should know better than I?'

''Tis such a feeble mouth. Oh, so small! And yet it holds my heart between its lips. Give him to me now. He has been too long away.'

'Nay, let him lie; he has not yet begun to cry.'

'When he cries thou wilt give him back – eh? What a man of mankind thou art! If he cried he were only the dearer to me. But, my life, what little name shall we give him?'

The small body lay close to Holden's heart. It was utterly helpless and very soft. He scarcely dared to breathe for fear of crushing it. The caged green parrot that is regarded as a sort of guardian-spirit in most native households moved on its perch and fluttered a drowsy wing.

'There is the answer,' said Holden. 'Mian Mittu has spoken. He shall be The Parrot. When he is ready he will talk mightily and run about. Mian Mittu is The Parrot in thy – in the Mussulman tongue, is it not?'

'Why put me so far off?' said Ameera fretfully. 'Let it be like unto some English name – but not wholly. For he is mine.'

'Then call him Tota, for that is likest English.'

'Ay, Tota, and that is still The Parrot. Forgive me, my lord, for a minute ago, but in truth he is too little to wear all the weight of Mian Mittu for name. He shall be Tota – our Tota to us. Hearest thou, oh, small one? Littlest, thou art Tota.' She touched the child's cheek, and he waking wailed, and it was necessary to return him to his mother, who soothed him with the wonderful rhyme of *Aré koko, Faré koko!* which says –

> 'Oh, crow! Go, crow! Baby's sleeping sound,
> And the wild plums grow in the jungle, only a penny a pound.
> Only a penny a pound, *baba*, only a penny a pound.'

Reassured many times as to the price of those plums, Tota cuddled himself down to sleep. The two sleek, white well-bullocks in the courtyard were steadily chewing the cud of their evening meal; old Pir Khan squatted at the head of Holden's horse, his police sabre across his knees, pulling drowsily at a big water-pipe that croaked like a bull-frog in a pond. Ameera's mother sat spinning in the lower verandah, and the wooden gate was shut and barred. The music of a marriage-procession came to the roof above the gentle hum of the city, and a string of flying-foxes crossed the face of the low moon.

'I have prayed,' said Ameera after a long pause, 'I have prayed for two things. First, that I may die in thy stead if thy death is demanded, and in the second, that I may die in the place of the child. I have prayed to the Prophet and to Beebee Miriam [the Virgin Mary]. Thinkest thou either will hear?'

'From thy lips who would not hear the lightest word?'

'I asked for straight talk, and thou hast given me sweet talk. Will my prayers be heard?'

'How can I say? God is very good.'

'Of that I am not sure. Listen now. When I die, or the child dies, what is thy fate? Living, thou wilt return to the bold white *mem-log*, for kind calls to kind.'

'Not always.'

'With a woman, no; with a man it is otherwise. Thou wilt in this life, later on, go back to thine own folk. That I could almost endure, for I should be dead. But in thy very death thou wilt be taken away to a strange place and a paradise that I do not know.'

'Will it be paradise?'

'Surely, for who would harm thee? But we two – I and the child – shall be elsewhere, and we cannot come to thee, nor canst thou come to us. In the old days, before the child was born, I did not think of these things; but now I think of them always. It is very hard talk.'

'It will fall as it will fall. Tomorrow we do not know, but today and love we know well. Surely we are happy now.'

'So happy that it were well to make our happiness assured. And thy Beebee Miriam should listen to me; for she is also a woman. But then she would envy me! It is not seemly for men to worship a woman.'

Holden laughed aloud at Ameera's little spasm of jealousy.

'Is it not seemly? Why didst thou not turn me from worship of thee, then?'

'Thou a worshipper! And of me? My king, for all thy sweet words, well I know that I am thy servant and thy slave, and the dust under thy feet. And I would not have it otherwise. See!'

Before Holden could prevent her she stooped forward and

touched his feet; recovering herself with a little laugh she hugged Tota closer to her bosom. Then, almost savagely –

'Is it true that the bold white *mem-log* live for three times the length of my life? Is it true that they make their marriages not before they are old women?'

'They marry as do others – when they are women.'

'That I know, but they wed when they are twenty-five. Is that true?'

'That is true.'

'*Ya illah!* At twenty-five! Who would of his own will take a wife even of eighteen? She is a woman – aging every hour. Twenty-five! I shall be an old woman at that age, and—— Those *mem-log* remain young for ever. How I hate them!'

'What have they to do with us?'

'I cannot tell. I know only that there may now be alive on this earth a woman ten years older than I who may come to thee and take thy love ten years after I am an old woman, gray-headed, and the nurse of Tota's son. That is unjust and evil. They should die too.'

'Now, for all thy years thou art a child, and shalt be picked up and carried down the staircase.'

'Tota! Have a care for Tota, my lord! Thou at least art as foolish as any babe!' Ameera tucked Tota out of harm's way in the hollow of her neck, and was carried downstairs laughing in Holden's arms, while Tota opened his eyes and smiled after the manner of the lesser angels.

He was a silent infant, and, almost before Holden could realise that he was in the world, developed into a small gold-coloured little god and unquestioned despot of the house overlooking the city. Those were months of absolute happiness to Holden and Ameera – happiness withdrawn from the world, shut in behind the wooden gate that Pir Khan guarded. By day Holden did his work with an immense pity for such as were not so fortunate as himself, and a sympathy for small children that amazed and amused many mothers at the little station-gatherings. At nightfall he returned to Ameera, – Ameera full of the wondrous doings of Tota; how he had been seen to clap his hands together and move his fingers with intention and purpose – which was manifestly a miracle – how later, he had of his own initiative crawled out of his low bedstead on to the floor and swayed on both feet for the space of three breaths.

'And they were long breaths, for my heart stood still with delight,' said Ameera.

Then Tota took the beasts into his councils – the well-bullocks, the little gray squirrels, the mongoose that lived in a hole near the well, and especially Mian Mittu, the parrot, whose tail he grievously pulled, and Mian Mittu screamed till Ameera and Holden arrived.

'Oh, villain! Child of strength! This to thy brother on the house-top! *Tobah, tobah!* Fie! Fie! But I know a charm to make him wise as Suleiman and Aflatoun [Solomon and Plato]. Now look,' said Ameera. She drew from an embroidered bag a handful of almonds. 'See! we count seven. In the name of God!'

She placed Mian Mittu, very angry and rumpled, on the top of his cage, and seating herself between the babe and the bird she cracked and peeled an almond less white than her teeth. 'This is a true charm, my life, and do not laugh. See! I give the parrot one-half and Tota the other.' Mian Mittu with careful beak took his share from between Ameera's lips, and she kissed the other half into the mouth of the child, who ate it slowly with wondering eyes. 'This I will do each day of seven, and without doubt he who is ours will be a bold speaker and wise. Eh, Tota, what wilt thou be when thou art a man and I am gray-headed?' Tota tucked his fat legs into adorable creases. He could crawl, but he was not going to waste the spring of his youth in idle speech. He wanted Mian Mittu's tail to tweak.

When he was advanced to the dignity of a silver belt – which, with a magic square engraved on silver and hung round his neck, made up the greater part of his clothing – he staggered on a perilous journey down the garden to Pir Khan, and proffered him all his jewels in exchange for one little ride on Holden's horse, having seen his mother's mother chaffering with pedlars in the verandah. Pir Khan wept and set the untried feet on his own gray head in sign of fealty, and brought the bold adventurer to his mother's arms, vowing that Tota would be a leader of men ere his beard was grown.

One hot evening, while he sat on the roof between his father and mother watching the never-ending warfare of the kites that the city boys flew, he demanded a kite of his own with Pir Khan to fly it, because he had a fear of dealing with anything larger than himself, and when Holden called him a 'spark', he rose to his feet and answered slowly in defence of his new-found individuality, '*Hum 'park nahin hai. Hum admi hai* [I am no spark, but a man].'

The protest made Holden choke and devote himself very seriously to a consideration of Tota's future. He need hardly have taken the trouble. The delight of that life was too perfect to endure. Therefore it was taken away as many things are taken away in India – suddenly and without warning. The little lord of the house, as Pir Khan called him, grew sorrowful and complained of pains who had never known the meaning of pain. Ameera, wild with terror, watched him through the night, and in the dawning of the second day the life was shaken out of him by fever – the seasonal autumn fever. It seemed altogether impossible that he could die, and neither Ameera nor Holden at first believed the evidence of the little body on the bedstead. Then Ameera beat her head against the wall and would have flung herself down the well in the garden had Holden not restrained her by main force.

One mercy only was granted to Holden. He rode to his office in broad daylight and found waiting him an unusually heavy mail that demanded concentrated attention and hard work. He was not, however, alive to this kindness of the gods.

III

The first shock of a bullet is no more than a brisk pinch. The wrecked body does not send in its protest to the soul till ten or fifteen seconds later. Holden realised his pain slowly, exactly as he had realised his happiness, and with the same imperious necessity for hiding all trace of it. In the beginning he only felt that there had been a loss, and that Ameera needed comforting, where she sat with her head on her knees shivering as Mian Mittu from the house-top called, *Tota! Tota! Tota!* Later all his world and the daily life of it rose up to hurt him. It was an outrage that any one of the children at the band-stand in the evening should be alive and clamorous, when his own child lay dead. It was more than mere pain when one of them touched him, and stories told by over-fond fathers of their children's latest performances cut him to the quick. He could not declare his pain. He had neither help, comfort, nor sympathy; and Ameera at the end of each weary day would lead him through the hell of self-questioning reproach which is reserved for those who have lost a child, and believe that with a little – just a little more care – it might have been saved.

'Perhaps,' Ameera would say, 'I did not take sufficient heed. Did I, or did I not? The sun on the roof that day when he played so long alone and I was – *ahi!* braiding my hair – it may be that the sun then bred the fever. If I had warned him from the sun he might have lived. But, oh, my life, say that I am guiltless! Thou knowest that I loved him as I love thee. Say that there is no blame on me, or I shall die – I shall die!'

'There is no blame, – before God, none. It was written, and how could we do aught to save? What has been, has been. Let it go, beloved.'

'He was all my heart to me. How can I let the thought go when my arm tells me every night that he is not here? *Ahi! Ahi!* Oh, Tota, come back to me – come back again, and let us be all together as it was before!'

'Peace, peace! For thine own sake, and for mine also, if thou lovest me – rest.'

'By this I know thou dost not care; and how shouldst thou? The white men have hearts of stone and souls of iron. Oh, that I had married a man of mine own people – though he beat me – and had never eaten the bread of an alien!'

'Am I an alien – mother of my son?'

'What else – *Sahib*? . . . Oh, forgive me – forgive! The death has driven me mad. Thou art the life of my heart, and the light of my eyes, and the breath of my life, and – and I have put thee from me, though it was but for a moment. If thou goest away, to whom shall I look for help? Do not be angry. Indeed, it was the pain that spoke and not thy slave.'

'I know, I know. We be two who were three. The greater need therefore that we should be one.'

They were sitting on the roof as of custom. The night was a warm one in early spring, and sheet-lightning was dancing on the horizon to a broken tune played by far-off thunder. Ameera settled herself in Holden's arms.

'The dry earth is lowing like a cow for the rain, and I – I am afraid. It was not like this when we counted the stars. But thou lovest me as much as before, though a bond is taken away? Answer!'

'I love more because a new bond has come out of the sorrow that we have eaten together, and that thou knowest.'

'Yea, I knew,' said Ameera in a very small whisper. 'But it is good to hear thee say so, my life, who art so strong to help. I will be a child no more, but a woman and an aid to thee. Listen! Give me my *sitar* and I will sing bravely.'

She took the light silver-studded *sitar* and began a song of the great hero Rajah Rasalu. The hand failed on the strings, the tune halted, checked, and at a low note turned off to the poor little nursery-rhyme about the wicked crow –

'And the wild plums grow in the jungle, only a penny a pound.
Only a penny a pound, *baba* – only . . .'

Then came the tears, and the piteous rebellion against fate till she slept, moaning a little in her sleep, with the right arm thrown clear of the body as though it protected something that was not there. It was after this night that life became a little easier for Holden. The ever-present pain of loss drove him into his work, and the work repaid him by filling up his mind for nine or ten hours a day. Ameera sat alone in the house and brooded, but grew happier when she understood that Holden was more at ease, according to the custom of women. They touched happiness again, but this time with caution.

'It was because we loved Tota that he died. The jealousy of God was upon us,' said Ameera. 'I have hung up a large black jar before our window to turn the evil eye from us, and we must make no protestations of delight, but go softly underneath the stars, lest God find us out. Is that not good talk, worthless one?'

She had shifted the accent on the word that means 'beloved', in proof of the sincerity of her purpose. But the kiss that followed the new christening was a thing that any deity might have envied. They went about henceforward saying, 'It is naught, it is naught'; and hoping that all the Powers heard.

The Powers were busy on other things. They had allowed thirty million people four years of plenty, wherein men fed well and the crops were certain, and the birth-rate rose year by year; the districts reported a purely agricultural population varying from nine hundred to two thousand to the square mile of the overburdened earth; and the Member for Lower Tooting, wandering about India in top-hat and frock-coat, talked largely of the benefits of British rule, and suggested as the one thing needful the establishment of a duly qualified electoral system and a general bestowal of the franchise. His long-suffering hosts smiled and made him welcome, and when he paused to admire, with pretty picked words, the blossom of the blood-red *dhak*-tree that had flowered untimely for a sign of what was coming, they smiled more than ever.

It was the Deputy Commissioner of Kot-Kumharsen, staying at the club for a day, who lightly told a tale that made Holden's blood run cold as he overheard the end.

'He won't bother any one any more. Never saw a man so astonished in my life. By Jove, I thought he meant to ask a question in the House about it. Fellow-passenger in his ship – dined next him – bowled over by cholera and died in eighteen hours. You needn't laugh, you fellows. The Member for Lower Tooting is awfully angry about it; but he's more scared. I think he's going to take his enlightened self out of India.'

'I'd give a good deal if he were knocked over. It might keep a few vestrymen of his kidney to their own parish. But what's this about cholera? It's full early for anything of that kind,' said the warden of an unprofitable salt-lick.

'Don't know,' said the Deputy Commissioner reflectively. 'We've got locusts with us. There's sporadic cholera all along the north – at least we're calling it sporadic for decency's sake. The spring crops are short in five districts, and nobody seems to know where the rains are. It's nearly March now. I don't want to scare anybody, but it seems to me that Nature's going to audit her accounts with a big red pencil this summer.'

'Just when I wanted to take leave, too!' said a voice across the room.

'There won't be much leave this year, but there ought to be a great deal of promotion. I've come in to persuade the Government to put my pet canal on the list of famine-relief works. It's an ill-wind that blows no good. I shall get that canal finished at last.'

'Is it the old programme then,' said Holden; 'famine, fever, and cholera?'

'Oh no. Only local scarcity and an unusual prevalence of seasonal sickness. You'll find it all in the reports if you live till next year. You're a lucky chap. *You* haven't got a wife to send out of harm's way. The hill-stations ought to be full of women this year.'

'I think you're inclined to exaggerate the talk in the *bazars*,' said a young civilian, in the Secretariat. 'Now I have observed——'

'I daresay you have,' said the Deputy Commissioner, 'but you've a great deal more to observe, my son. In the meantime, I wish to observe to you——' and he drew him aside to discuss the construction of the canal that was so dear to his heart. Holden went to his bungalow and began to understand that he was not alone in the world, and also that he was afraid for the sake of another, – which is the most soul-satisfying fear known to man.

Two months later, as the Deputy had foretold, Nature began to audit her accounts with a red pencil. On the heels of the spring-reapings came a cry for bread, and the Government, which had decreed that no man should die of want, sent wheat. Then came the cholera from all four quarters of the compass. It struck a pilgrim-gathering of half a million at a sacred shrine. Many died at the feet of their god; the others broke and ran over the face of the land carrying the pestilence with them. It smote a walled city and killed two hundred a day. The people crowded the trains, hanging on to the footboards and squatting on the roofs of the carriages, and the cholera followed them, for at each station they dragged out the dead and the dying. They died by the roadside, and the horses of the Englishmen shied at the corpses in the grass. The rains did not come, and the earth turned to iron lest man should escape death by hiding in her. The English sent their wives away to the hills and went about their work, coming forward as they were bidden to fill the gaps in the fighting-line. Holden, sick with fear of losing his chiefest treasure on earth, had done his best to persuade Ameera to go away with her mother to the Himalayas.

'Why should I go?' said she, one evening on the roof.

'There is sickness, and people are dying, and all the white *mem-log* have gone.'

'All of them?'

'All – unless perhaps there remain some old scald-head who vexes her husband's heart by running risk of death.'

'Nay; who stays is my sister, and thou must not abuse her, for I will be a scald-head too. I am glad all the bold *mem-log* are gone.'

'Do I speak to a woman or a babe? Go to the hills, and I will see to it that thou goest like a queen's daughter. Think, child. In a red-lacquered bullock cart, veiled and curtained, with brass peacocks upon the pole and red cloth hangings. I will send two orderlies for guard and——'

'Peace! Thou art the babe in speaking thus. What use are those toys to me? *He* would have patted the bullocks and played with the housings. For his sake, perhaps, – thou hast made me very English – I might have gone. Now, I will not. Let the *mem-log* run.'

'Their husbands are sending them, beloved.'

'Very good talk. Since when hast thou been my husband to tell me what to do? I have but borne thee a son. Thou art only all the desire of my soul to me. How shall I depart when I know that if evil befall thee by the breadth of so much as my littlest finger-nail – is that not small? – I should be aware of it though I were in paradise. And here, this summer thou mayest die – *ai, janee*, die! and in dying they might call to tend thee a white woman, and she would rob me in the last of thy love!'

'But love is not born in a moment or on a death-bed!'

'What dost thou know of love, stoneheart? She would take thy thanks at least and, by God and the Prophet and Beebee Miriam the mother of thy Prophet, that I will never endure. My lord and my love, let there be no more foolish talk of going away. Where thou art, I am. It is enough.' She put an arm round his neck and a hand on his mouth.

There are not many happinesses so complete as those that are snatched under the shadow of the sword. They sat together and laughed, calling each other openly by every pet name that could move the wrath of the gods. The city below them was locked up in its own torments. Sulphur fires blazed in the streets; the conches in the Hindu temples screamed and bellowed, for the gods were inattentive in those days. There was a service in the great Mahomedan shrine, and the call to prayer from the minarets was almost unceasing. They heard the wailing in the houses of the dead, and once the shriek of a mother who had lost a child and was calling for its return. In the gray dawn they saw the dead borne out through the city gates, each litter with its own little knot of mourners. Wherefore they kissed each other and shivered.

It was a red and heavy audit, for the land was very sick and needed a little breathing-space ere the torrent of cheap life should flood it anew. The children of immature fathers and undeveloped mothers made no resistance. They were cowed and sat still, waiting till the sword should be sheathed in November if it were so willed. There were gaps among the English, but the gaps were filled. The work of superintending famine-relief, cholera-sheds, medicine-distribution, and what little sanitation was possible, went forward because it was so ordered.

Holden had been told to keep himself in readiness to move to replace the next man who should fall. There were twelve hours in each day when he could not see Ameera, and she might die in three. He was considering what his pain would be if he could not see her for three months, or if she died out of his sight. He was absolutely certain that her death would be demanded – so certain, that when he looked up from the telegram and saw Pir Khan breathless in the doorway, he laughed aloud. 'And?' said he,——

'When there is a cry in the night and the spirit flutters into the throat, who has a charm that will restore? Come swiftly, Heaven-born! It is the black cholera.'

Holden galloped to his home. The sky was heavy with clouds, for the long-deferred rains were near and the heat was stifling. Ameera's mother met him in the courtyard, whimpering, 'She is dying. She is nursing herself into death. She is all but dead. What shall I do, *sahib*?'

Ameera was lying in the room in which Tota had been born. She made no sign when Holden entered, because the human soul is a very lonely thing and, when it is getting ready to go away, hides itself in a misty borderland where the living may not follow. The black cholera does its work quietly and without explanation. Ameera was being thrust out of life as though the Angel of Death had himself put his hand upon her. The quick breathing seemed to show that she was either afraid or in pain, but neither eyes nor mouth gave any answer to Holden's kisses. There was nothing to be said or done. Holden could only wait and suffer. The first drops of the rain began to fall on the roof and he could hear shouts of joy in the parched city.

The soul came back a little and the lips moved. Holden bent down to listen. 'Keep nothing of mine,' said Ameera. 'Take no hair from my head. *She* would make thee burn it later on. That flame I should feel. Lower! Stoop lower! Remember only that I was thine and bore thee a son. Though thou wed a white woman tomorrow, the pleasure of receiving in thy arms thy first son is taken from thee for ever. Remember me when thy son is born – the one that shall carry thy name before all men. His misfortunes be on my head. I bear witness – I bear witness' – the lips were forming the words on his ear – 'that there is no God but – thee, beloved!'

Then she died. Holden sat still, and all thought was taken from him, – till he heard Ameera's mother lift the curtain.

'Is she dead, *sahib*?'

'She is dead.'

'Then I will mourn, and afterwards take an inventory of the furniture in this house. For that will be mine. The *sahib* does not mean to resume it? It is so little, so very little, *sahib*, and I am an old woman. I would like to lie softly.'

'For the mercy of God be silent a while. Go out and mourn where I cannot hear.'

'*Sahib*, she will be buried in four hours.'

'I know the custom. I shall go ere she is taken away. That matter is in thy hands. Look to it that the bed on which – on which she lies——'

'Aha! That beautiful red-lacquered bed. I have long desired—'

'That the bed is left here untouched for my disposal. All else in the house is thine. Hire a cart, take everything, go hence, and before sunrise let there be nothing in this house but that which I have ordered thee to respect.'

'I am an old woman. I would stay at least for the days of mourning, and the rains have just broken. Whither shall I go?'

'What is that to me? My order is that there is a going. The house-gear is worth a thousand rupees and my orderly shall bring thee a hundred rupees tonight.'

'That is very little. Think of the cart-hire.'

'It shall be nothing unless thou goest, and with speed. O woman, get hence and leave me with my dead!'

The mother shuffled down the staircase, and in her anxiety to take stock of the house-fittings forgot to mourn. Holden stayed by Ameera's side and the rain roared on the roof. He could not think connectedly by reason of the noise, though he made many attempts to do so. Then four sheeted ghosts glided dripping into the room and stared at him through their veils. They were the washers of the dead. Holden left the room and went out to his horse. He had come in a dead, stifling calm through ankle-deep dust. He found the courtyard a rain-lashed pond alive with frogs; a torrent of yellow water ran under the gate, and a roaring wind drove the bolts of the rain like buckshot against the mud-walls. Pir Khan was shivering in his little hut by the gate, and the horse was stamping uneasily in the water.

'I have been told the *sahib*'s order,' said Pir Khan. 'It is well. This house is now desolate. I go also, for my monkey-face would be a reminder of that which has been. Concerning the bed, I will bring that to thy house yonder in the morning; but remember, *sahib*, it will be to thee a knife turning in a green wound. I go upon a pilgrimage, and I will take no money. I have grown fat in the protection of the Presence whose sorrow is my sorrow. For the last time I hold his stirrup.'

He touched Holden's foot with both hands and the horse sprang out into the road, where the creaking bamboos were whipping the sky and all the frogs were chuckling. Holden could not see for the rain in his face. He put his hands before his eyes and muttered –

'Oh, you brute! You utter brute!'

The news of his trouble was already in his bungalow. He read the knowledge in his butler's eyes when Ahmed Khan brought in food, and for the first and last time in his life laid a hand upon his master's shoulder, saying, 'Eat, *sahib*, eat. Meat is good against sorrow. I also have known. Moreover the shadows come and go, *sahib*; the shadows come and go. These be curried eggs.'

Holden could neither eat nor sleep. The heavens sent down eight inches of rain in that night and washed the earth clean. The waters tore down walls, broke roads, and scoured open the shallow graves on the Mahomedan burying-ground. All next day it rained, and Holden sat still in his house considering his sorrow. On the morning of the third day he received a telegram which said only, 'Ricketts, Myndonie. Dying. Holden relieve. Immediate.' Then he thought that before he departed he would look at the house wherein he had been master and lord. There was a break in the weather, and the rank earth steamed with vapour.

He found that the rains had torn down the mud pillars of the gateway, and the heavy wooden gate that had guarded his life hung lazily from one hinge. There was grass three inches high in the courtyard; Pir Khan's lodge was empty, and the sodden thatch sagged between the beams. A gray squirrel was in possession of the verandah, as if the house had been untenanted for thirty years instead of three days. Ameera's mother had removed everything except some mildewed matting. The *tick-tick* of the little scorpions as they hurried across the floor was the only sound in the house. Ameera's room and the other one where Tota had lived were heavy with mildew; and the narrow staircase leading to the roof was streaked and stained with rain-borne mud. Holden saw all these things, and came out again to meet in the road Durga Dass, his landlord, – portly, affable, clothed in white muslin, and driving a Cee-spring buggy. He was overlooking his property to see how the roofs stood the stress of the first rains.

'I have heard,' said he, 'you will not take this place any more, *sahib*?'

'What are you going to do with it?'

'Perhaps I shall let it again.'

'Then I will keep it on while I am away.'

Durga Dass was silent for some time. 'You shall not take it on, *sahib*,' he said. 'When I was a young man I also——, but today I am a member of the Municipality. Ho! Ho! No. When the birds have gone what need to keep the nest? I will have it pulled down – the timber will sell for something always. It shall be pulled down, and the Municipality shall make a road across, as they desire, from the burning-ghaut to the city wall, so that no man may say where this house stood.'

On Greenhow Hill

To Love's low voice she lent a careless ear;
Her hand within his rosy fingers lay,
A chilling weight. She would not turn or hear;
But with averted face went on her way.
But when pale Death, all featureless and grim,
Lifted his bony hand, and beckoning
Held out his cypress-wreath, she followed him,
And Love was left forlorn and wondering,
That she who for his bidding would not stay,
At Death's first whisper rose and went away.
Rivals

'*Ohê, Ahmed Din! Shafiz Ullah ahoo!* Bahadur Khan, where are you? Come out of the tents, as I have done, and fight against the English. Don't kill your own kin! Come out to me!'

The deserter from a native corps was crawling round the outskirts of the camp, firing at intervals, and shouting invitations to his old comrades. Misled by the rain and the darkness, he came to the English wing of the camp, and with his yelping and rifle-practice disturbed the men. They had been making roads all day, and were tired.

Ortheris was sleeping at Learoyd's feet. 'Wot's all that?' he said thickly. Learoyd snored, and a Snider bullet ripped its way through the tent wall. The men swore. 'It's that bloomin' deserter from the Aurangabadis,' said Ortheris. 'Git up, some one, an' tell 'im 'e's come to the wrong shop.'

'Go to sleep, little man,' said Mulvaney, who was steaming nearest the door. 'I can't arise an' expaytiate with him. 'Tis rainin' entrenchin' tools outside.'

''Tain't because you bloomin' can't. It's 'cause you bloomin' won't, ye long, limp, lousy, lazy beggar, you. 'Ark to 'im 'owlin'!'

'Wot's the good of argifying? Put a bullet into the swine! 'E's keepin' us awake!' said another voice.

A subaltern shouted angrily, and a dripping sentry whined from the darkness –

''Tain't no good, sir. I can't see 'im. 'E's 'idin' somewhere down 'ill.'

Ortheris tumbled out of his blanket. 'Shall I try to get 'im, sir?' said he.

'No,' was the answer. 'Lie down. I won't have the whole camp shooting all round the clock. Tell him to go and pot his friends.'

Ortheris considered for a moment. Then, putting his head under the tent wall, he called, as a 'bus conductor calls in a block, ''Igher up, there! 'Igher up!'

The men laughed, and the laughter was carried down wind to the deserter, who, hearing that he had made a mistake, went off to worry his own regiment half a mile away. He was received with shots; the Aurangabadis were very angry with him for disgracing their colours.

'An' that's all right,' said Ortheris, withdrawing his head as he heard the hiccough of the Sniders in the distance. 'S'elp me Gawd, tho', that man's not fit to live – messin' with my beauty-sleep this way.'

'Go out and shoot him in the morning, then,' said the subaltern incautiously. 'Silence in the tents now. Get your rest, men.'

Ortheris lay down with a happy little sigh, and in two minutes there was no sound except the rain on the canvas and the all-embracing and elemental snoring of Learoyd.

The camp lay on a bare ridge of the Himalayas, and for a week had been waiting for a flying column to make connection. The nightly rounds of the deserter and his friends had become a nuisance.

In the morning the men dried themselves in hot sunshine and cleaned their grimy accoutrements. The native regiment was to take its turn of road-making that day while the Old Regiment loafed.

'I'm goin' to lay for a shot at that man,' said Ortheris, when he had finished washing out his rifle. ''E comes up the water-course every evenin' about five o'clock. If we go and lie out on the north 'ill a bit this afternoon we'll get 'im.'

'You're a bloodthirsty little mosquito,' said Mulvaney, blowing blue clouds into the air. 'But I suppose I will have to come wid you. Fwhere's Jock?'

'Gone out with the Mixed Pickles, 'cause 'e thinks 'isself a bloomin' marksman,' said Ortheris with scorn.

The 'Mixed Pickles' were a detachment of picked shots, generally employed in clearing spurs of hills when the enemy were too impertinent. This taught the young officers how to handle men, and did not do the enemy much harm. Mulvaney and Ortheris strolled out of camp, and passed the Aurangabadis going to their road-making.

'You've got to sweat today,' said Ortheris genially. 'We're going to get your man. You didn't knock 'im out last night by any chance, any of you?'

'No. The pig went away mocking us. I had one shot at him,' said a private. 'He's my cousin, and *I* ought to have cleared our dishonour. But good luck to you.'

They went cautiously to the north hill, Ortheris leading, because, as he explained, 'this is a long-range show, an' I've got to do it.' His was an almost passionate devotion to his rifle, which, by barrack-room report, he was supposed to kiss every night before turning in. Charges and scuffles he held in contempt, and, when they were inevitable, slipped between Mulvaney and Learoyd, bidding them to fight for his skin as well as their own. They never failed him. He trotted along, questing like a hound on a broken trail, through the wood of the north hill. At last he was satisfied, and threw himself down on the soft pine-needled slope that commanded a clear view of the watercourse and a brown, bare hillside beyond it. The trees made a scented darkness in which an army corps could have hidden from the sun-glare without.

''Ere's the tail o' the wood,' said Ortheris. ''E's got to come up the watercourse, 'cause it gives 'im cover. We'll lay 'ere. 'Tain't not arf so bloomin' dusty neither.'

He buried his nose in a clump of scentless white violets. No one had come to tell the flowers that the season of their strength was long past, and they had bloomed merrily in the twilight of the pines.

'This is something like,' he said luxuriously. 'Wot a 'evinly clear drop for a bullet acrost. How much d'you make it, Mulvaney?'

'Seven hunder. Maybe a trifle less, bekaze the air's so thin.'

Wop! wop! wop! went a volley of musketry on the rear face of the north hill.

'Curse them Mixed Pickles firin' at nothin'! They'll scare arf the country.'

'Thry a sightin' shot in the middle of the row,' said Mulvaney, the man of many wiles. 'There's a red rock yonder he'll be sure to pass. Quick!'

Ortheris ran his sight up to six hundred yards and fired. The bullet threw up a feather of dust by a clump of gentians at the base of the rock.

'Good enough!' said Ortheris, snapping the scale down. 'You snick your sights to mine or a little lower. You're always firin' high. But remember, first shot to me. O Lordy! but it's a lovely afternoon.'

The noise of the firing grew louder, and there was a tramping of men in the wood. The two lay very quiet, for they knew that the British soldier is desperately prone to fire at anything that moves or calls. Then Learoyd appeared, his tunic ripped across the breast by a bullet, looking ashamed of himself. He flung down on the pine-needles, breathing in snorts.

'One o' them damned gardeners o' th' Pickles,' said he, fingering the rent. 'Firin' to th' right flank, when he knowed I was there. If I knew who he was I'd 'a' rippen the hide offan him. Look at ma tunic!'

'That's the spishil trustability av a marksman. Train him to hit a fly wid a stiddy rest at seven hunder, an' he'll loose on anythin' he sees or hears up to th' mile. You're well out av that fancy-firin' gang, Jock. Stay here.'

'Bin firin' at the bloomin' wind in the bloomin' treetops,' said Ortheris with a chuckle. 'I'll show you some firin' later on.'

They wallowed in the pine-needles, and the sun warmed them where they lay. The Mixed Pickles ceased firing, and returned to camp, and left the wood to a few scared apes. The water-course lifted up its voice in the silence, and talked foolishly to the rocks. Now and again the dull thump of a blasting charge three miles away told that the Aurangabadis were in difficulties with their road-making. The men smiled as they listened and lay still, soaking in the warm leisure. Presently Learoyd, between the whiffs of his pipe –

'Seems queer – about 'im yonder – desertin' at all.'

''E'll be a bloomin' side queerer when I've done with 'im,' said Ortheris. They were talking in whispers, for the stillness of the wood and the desire of slaughter lay heavy upon them.

'I make no doubt he had his reasons for desertin'; but, my faith! I make less doubt ivry man has good reason for killin' him,' said Mulvaney.

'Happen there was a lass tewed up wi' it. Men do more than more for th' sake of a lass.'

'They make most av us 'list. They've no manner av right to make us desert.'

'Ah; they make us 'list, or their fathers do,' said Learoyd softly, his helmet over his eyes.

Ortheris's brows contracted savagely. He was watching the valley. 'If it's a girl I'll shoot the beggar twice over, an' second time for bein' a fool. You're blasted sentimental all of a sudden. Thinkin' o' your last near shave?'

'Nay, lad; ah was but thinkin' o' what has happened.'

'An' fwhat has happened, ye lumberin' child av calamity, that you're lowing like a cow-calf at the back av the pasture, an' suggestin' invidious excuses for the man Stanley's goin' to kill. Ye'll have to wait another hour yet, little man. Spit it out, Jock, an' bellow melojus to the moon. It takes an earthquake or a bullet graze to fetch aught out av you. Discourse, Don Juan! The a-moors av Lotharius Learoyd! Stanley, kape a rowlin' rig'mental eye on the valley.'

'It's along o' yon hill there,' said Learoyd, watching the bare sub-Himalayan spur that reminded him of his Yorkshire moors. He was speaking more to himself than his fellows. 'Ay,' said he, 'Rumbolds Moor stands up ower Skipton town, an' Greenhow Hill stands up ower Pately Brig. I reckon you've never heeard tell o' Greenhow Hill, but yon bit o' bare stuff if there was nobbut a white road windin' is like ut; strangely like. Moors an' moors an' moors, wi' never a tree for shelter, an' gray houses wi' flagstone rooves, and pewits cryin', an' a windhover goin' to and fro just like these kites. And cold! A wind that cuts you like a knife. You could tell Greenhow Hill folk by the red-apple colour o' their cheeks an' nose tips, and their blue eyes, driven into pin-points by the wind. Miners mostly, burrowin' for lead i' th' hillsides, followin' the trail of th' ore vein same as a field-rat. It was the roughest minin' I ever seen. Yo'd come on a bit o' creakin' wood windlass like a well-head, an' you was let down i' th' bight of a rope, fendin' yoursen off the side wi' one hand, carryin' a candle stuck in a lump o' clay with t'other, an' clickin' hold of a rope with t'other hand.'

'An' that's three of them,' said Mulvaney. 'Must be a good climate in those parts.'

Learoyd took no heed.

'An' then yo' came to a level, where you crept on your hands and knees through a mile o' windin' drift, an' you come out into a cave-place as big as Leeds Townhall, with a engine pumpin' water from workin's 'at went deeper still. It's a queer country, let alone minin', for the hill is full of those natural caves, an' the rivers an' the becks drops into what they call pot-holes, an' come out again miles away.'

'Wot was you doin' there?' said Ortheris.

'I was a young chap then, an' mostly went wi' 'osses, leadin' coal and lead ore; but at th' time I'm tellin' on I was drivin' the waggon-team i' th' big sumph. I didn't belong to that country-side by rights. I went there because of a little difference at home, an' at fust I took up wi' a rough lot. One night we'd been drinkin', an' I must ha' hed more than I could stand, or happen th' ale was none so good. Though i' them days, By for God, I never seed bad ale.' He flung his arms over his head, and gripped a vast handful of white violets. 'Nah,' said he, 'I never seed the ale I could not drink, the bacca I could not smoke, nor the lass I could not kiss. Well, we mun have a race home, the lot on us. I lost all th' others, an' when I was climbin' ower one of them walls built o' loose stones, I comes down into the ditch, stones and all, an' broke my arm. Not as I knawed much about it, for I fell on th' back of my head, an' was knocked stupid like. An' when I come to mysen it were mornin', an' I were lyin' on the settle i' Jesse Roantree's house-place, an' 'Liza Roantree was settin' sewin'. I ached all ovver, and my mouth were like a lime-kiln. She gave me a drink out of a china mug wi' gold letters – "A Present from Leeds" – as I looked at many and many a time at after. "Yo're to lie still while Dr Warbottom comes, because your arm's broken, and father has sent a lad to fetch him. He found yo' when he was goin' to work, an' carried you here on his back," sez she. "Oa!" sez I; an' I shet my eyes, for I felt ashamed o' mysen. "Father's gone to his work these three hours, an' he said he'd tell 'em to get somebody to drive the tram." The clock ticked, an' a bee comed in the house, an' they rung i' my head like mill-wheels. An' she give me another drink an' settled the pillow. "Eh, but yo're young to be getten drunk an' such like, but yo' won't do it again, will yo'?" – "Noa," sez I, "I wouldn't if she'd nobbut stop they mill-wheels clatterin'." '

'Faith, it's a good thing to be nursed by a woman when you're sick!' said Mulvaney. 'Dir' cheap at the price av twenty broken heads.'

Ortheris turned to frown across the valley. He had not been nursed by many women in his life.

'An' then Dr Warbottom comes ridin' up, an' Jesse Roantree along with 'im. He was a high-larned doctor, but he talked wi' poor folk same as theirsens. "What's ta bin agaate on naa?" he sings out. "Brekkin' tha thick head?" An' he felt me all ovver. "That's none broken. Tha's nobbut knocked a bit sillier than ordinary, an' that's daaft eneaf." An' soa he went on, callin' me all the names he could think on, but settin' my arm, wi' Jesse's help, as careful as could be. "Yo' mun let the big oaf bide here a bit, Jesse," he says, when he hed strapped me up an' given me a dose o' physic; "an' you an' 'Liza will tend him, though he's scarcelins worth the trouble. An' tha'll lose tha work," sez he, "an' tha'll be upon th' Sick Club for a couple o' months an' more. Doesn't tha think tha's a fool?" '

'But whin was a young man, high or low, the other av a fool, I'd like to know?' said Mulvaney. 'Sure, folly's the only safe way to wisdom, for I've thried it.'

'Wisdom!' grinned Ortheris, scanning his comrades with uplifted chin. 'You're bloomin' Solomons, you two, ain't you?'

Learoyd went calmly on, with a steady eye like an ox chewing the cud.

'And that was how I comed to know 'Liza Roantree. There's some tunes as she used to sing – aw, she were always singin' – that fetches Greenhow Hill before my eyes as fair as yon brow across there. And she would learn me to sing bass, an' I was to go to th' chapel wi' 'em, where Jesse and she led the singin', th' old man playin' the fiddle. He was a strange chap, old Jesse, fair mad wi' music, an' he made me promise to learn the big fiddle when my arm was better. It belonged to him, and it stood up in a big case alongside o' th' eight-day clock, but Willie Satterthwaite, as played it in the chapel, had getten deaf as a doorpost, and it vexed Jesse, as he had to rap him ower his head wi' th' fiddle-stick to make him give ower sawin' at th' right time.

'But there was a black drop in it all, an' it was a man in a black coat that brought it. When th' Primitive Methodist preacher came to Greenhow, he would always stop wi' Jesse Roantree, an' he laid hold of me from th' beginning. It seemed I wor a soul to be saved, and he meaned to do it. At th' same time I jealoused 'at he were keen o' savin' 'Liza Roantree's soul as well, and I could ha' killed him many a time. An' this went on till one day I broke out, an' borrowed th' brass for a drink from 'Liza. After fower days I come back, wi' my tail between my legs, just to see 'Liza again. But Jesse were at home an' th' preacher – th' Reverend Amos Barraclough. 'Liza said naught, but a bit o' red come into her face as were white of a regular thing. Says Jesse, tryin' his best to be civil, "Nay, lad, it's like this. You've getten to choose which way it's goin' to be. I'll ha' nobody across ma doorstep as goes a-drinkin', an' borrows my lass's money to spend i' their drink. Ho'd tha tongue, 'Liza," sez he, when she wanted to put in a word 'at I were welcome to th' brass, and she were none afraid that I wouldn't pay it back. Then the Reverend cuts in, seein' as Jesse were losin' his temper, an' they fair beat me among them. But it were 'Liza, as looked an' said naught, as did more than either o' their tongues, an' soa I concluded to get converted.'

'Fwhat!' shouted Mulvaney. Then, checking himself, he said softly, 'Let be! Let be! Sure the Blessed Virgin is the mother of all religion an' most women; an' there's a dale av piety in a girl if the men would only let ut stay there. I'd ha' been converted myself under the circumstances.'

'Nay, but,' pursued Learoyd with a blush, 'I meaned it.'

Ortheris laughed as loudly as he dared, having regard to his business at the time.

'Ay, Ortheris, you may laugh, but you didn't know yon preacher Barraclough – a little white-faced chap, wi' a voice as 'ud wile a bird offan a bush, and a way o' layin' hold of folks as made them think they'd never had a live man for a friend before. You never saw him, an' – an' – you never seed 'Liza Roantree – never seed 'Liza Roantree. . . . Happen it was as muchs 'Liza as th' preacher and her father, but anyways they all meaned it, an' I was fair shamed o' mysen, an' so I become what they called a changed character. And when I think on, it's hard to believe as yon chap going to prayer-meetin's, chapel, and class-meetin's were me. But I never had naught to say for mysen, though there was a deal o' shoutin', and old Sammy Strother, as were almost clemmed to death and doubled up with the rheumatics, would sing out, "Joyful! Joyful!" and 'at it were better to go up to heaven in a coal-basket than down to hell i' a coach an' six. And he would put his poor old claw on my shoulder, sayin', "Doesn't tha feel it, tha great lump? Doesn't tha feel it?" An' sometimes I thought I did, and then again I thought I didn't, an' how was that?'

'The iverlastin' nature av mankind,' said Mulvaney. 'An', furthermore, I misdoubt you were built for the Primitive Methodians. They're a new corps anyways. I hold by the Ould Church, for she's the mother of them all – ay, an' the father, too. I like her bekaze she's most remarkable regimental in her fittings. I may die in Honolulu, Nova Zambra, or Cape Cayenne, but wherever I die, me bein' fwhat I am, an' a priest handy, I go under the same orders an' the same words an' the same unction as tho' the Pope himself come down from the roof av St Peter's to see me off. There's neither high nor low, nor broad nor deep, nor betwixt nor between wid her, an' that's what I like. But mark you, she's no manner av Church for a wake man, bekaze she takes the body and the soul av him, onless he has his proper work to do. I remember when my father died that was three months comin' to his grave; begad he'd ha' sold the shebeen above our heads for ten minutes' quittance of purgathory. An' he did all he could. That's why I say ut takes a strong man to deal with the Ould Church, an' for that reason you'll find so many women go there. An' that sames a conundrum.'

'Wot's the use o' worrittin' 'bout these things?' said Ortheris.

'You're bound to find all out quicker nor you want to, any'ow.' He jerked the cartridge out of the breech-block into the palm of his hand. ''Ere's my chaplain,' he said, and made the venomous black-headed bullet bow like a marionette. ''E's goin' to teach a man all about which is which, an' wot's true, after all, before sundown. But wot 'appened after that, Jock?'

'There was one thing they boggled at, and almost shut th' gate i' my face for, and that were my dog Blast, th' only one saved out o' a litter o' pups as was blowed up when a keg o' minin' powder loosed off in th' store-keeper's hut. They liked his name no better than his business, which were fightin' every dog he comed across; a rare good dog, wi' spots o' black and pink on his face, one ear gone, and lame o' one side wi' being driven in a basket through an iron roof, a matter of half a mile.

'They said I mun give him up 'cause he were worldly and low; and would I let mysen be shut out of heaven for the sake on a dog? "Nay," says I, "if th' door isn't wide enough for th' pair on us, we'll stop outside, for we'll none be parted." And th' preacher spoke up for Blast, as had a likin' for him from th' first – I reckon that was why I come to like th' preacher – and wouldn't hear o' changin' his name to Bless, as some o' them wanted. So th' pair on us became reg'lar chapel-members. But it's hard for a young chap o' my build to cut traces from the world, th' flesh, an' the devil all uv a heap. Yet I stuck to it for a long time, while th' lads as used to stand about th' town-end an' lean ower th' bridge, spittin' into th' beck o' a Sunday, would call after me, "Sitha, Learoyd, when's ta bean to preach, 'cause we're comin' to hear tha." – "Ho'd tha jaw. He hasn't getten th' white choaker on ta morn," another lad would say, and I had to double my fists hard i' th' bottom of my Sunday coat, and say to mysen, "If 'twere Monday and I warn't a member o' the Primitive Methodists, I'd leather all th' lot of yond'." That was th' hardest of all – to know that I could fight and I mustn't fight.'

Sympathetic grunts from Mulvaney.

'So what wi' singin', practisin', and class-meetin's, and th' big fiddle, as he made me take between my knees, I spent a deal o' time i' Jesse Roantree's house-place. But often as I was there, th' pracher fared to me to go oftener, and both th' old man an' th' young woman were pleased to have him. He lived i' Pately Brig, as were a goodish step off, but he come. He come all the same. I liked him as well or better as any man I'd ever seen i' one way, and yet I hated him wi' all my heart i' t'other, and we watched each other like cat and mouse, but civil as you please, for I was on my best behaviour, and he was that fair and open that I was bound to be fair with him. Rare good company he was, if I hadn't wanted to wring his cliver little neck half of the time. Often and often when he was goin' from Jesse's I'd set him a bit on the road.'

'See 'im 'ome, you mean?' said Ortheris.

'Ay. It's a way we have i' Yorkshire o' seein' friends off. Yon was a friend as I didn't want to come back, and he didn't want me to come back neither, and so we'd walk together towards Pately, and then he'd set me back again, and there we'd be wal two o'clock i' the mornin' settin' each other to an' fro like a blasted pair o' pendulums twixt hill and valley, long after th' light had gone out i' 'Liza's window, as both on us had been looking at, pretending to watch the moon.'

'Ah!' broke in Mulvaney, 'ye'd no chanst against the maraudin' psalm-singer. They'll take the airs an' the graces instid av the man nine times out av ten, an' they only find the blunder later – the wimmen.'

'That's just where yo're wrong,' said Learoyd, reddening under the freckled tan of his cheeks. 'I was th' first wi' 'Liza, an' yo'd think that were enough. But th' parson were a steady-gaited sort o' chap, and Jesse were strong o' his side, and all th' women i' the congregation dinned it to 'Liza 'at she were fair fond to take up wi' a wastrel ne'er-do-weel like me, as was scarcelins respectable an' a fighting dog at his heels. It was all very well for her to be doing me good and saving my soul, but she must mind as she didn't do herself harm. They talk o' rich folk bein' stuck up an' genteel, but for cast-iron pride o' respectability there's naught like poor chapel folk. It's as cold as th' wind o' Greenhow Hill – ay, and colder, for 'twill never change. And now I come to think on it, one at strangest things I know is 'at they couldn't abide th' thought o' soldiering. There's a vast o' fightin' i' th' Bible, and there's a deal of Methodists i' th' army; but to hear chapel folk talk yo'd think that soldierin' were next door, an' t'other side, to hangin'. I' their meetin's all their talk is o' fightin'. When Sammy Strother were stuck for summat to say in his prayers, he'd sing out, "Th' sword o' th' Lord and o' Gideon." They were allus at it about puttin' on th' whole armour o' righteousness, an' fightin' the good fight o' faith. And then, atop o' 't all, they held a prayer-meetin' ower a young chap as wanted to 'list, and nearly deafened him, till he picked up his hat and fair ran away. And they'd tell tales in th' Sunday-school o' bad lads as had been thumped and brayed for bird-nesting o' Sundays and playin' truant o' week-days, and how they took to wrestlin', dog-fightin', rabbit-runnin', and drinkin', till at last, as if 'twere a hepitaph on a gravestone, they damned him across th' moors wi', "an' then he went and 'listed for a soldier", an' they'd all fetch a deep breath, and throw up their eyes like a hen drinkin'.'

'Fwhy is ut?' said Mulvaney, bringing down his hand on his thigh with a crack. 'In the name av God, fwhy is ut? I've seen ut, tu. They cheat an' they swindle an' they lie an' they slander, an' fifty things fifty times worse; but the last an' the worst by their reckonin' is to serve the Widdy honest. It's like the talk av childer – seein' things all round.'

'Plucky lot of fightin' good fights of whatsername they'd do if we didn't see they had a quiet place to fight in. And such fightin' as theirs is! Cats on the tiles. T'other callin' to which to come on. I'd give a month's pay to get some o' them broad-backed beggars in London sweatin' through a day's road-makin' an' a night's rain. They'd carry on a deal afterwards – same as we're supposed to carry on. I've bin turned out of a measly arf-licence pub down Lambeth way, full o' greasy kebmen, 'fore now,' said Ortheris with an oath.

'Maybe you were dhrunk,' said Mulvaney soothingly.

'Worse nor that. The Forders were drunk. *I* was wearin' the Queen's uniform.'

'I'd no particular thought to be a soldier i' them days,' said Learoyd, still keeping his eye on the bare hill opposite, 'but this sort o' talk put it i' my head. They was so good, th' chapel folk, that they tumbled ower t'other side. But I stuck to it for 'Liza's sake, specially as she was learning me to sing the bass part in a horotorio as Jesse were gettin' up. She sung like a throstle hersen, and we had practisin's night after night for a matter of three months.'

'I know what a horotorio is,' said Ortheris pertly. 'It's a sort of chaplain's sing-song – words all out of the Bible, and hullabaloojah choruses.'

'Most Greenhow Hill folks played some instrument or t'other, an' they all sung so you might have heard them miles away, and they were so pleased wi' the noise they made they didn't fare to want anybody to listen. The preacher sung high seconds when he wasn't playin' the flute, an' they set me, as hadn't got far with big fiddle, again Willie Satterthwaite, to jog his elbow when he had to get agate playin'. Old Jesse was happy if ever a man was, for he were th' conductor an' th' first fiddle an' th' leadin' singer, beatin' time wi' his fiddle-stick, till at times he'd rap with it on the table, and cry out, "Now, you mun all stop; it's my turn." And he'd face round to his front, fair sweating wi' pride, to sing th' tenor solos. But he were grandest i' th' choruses, waggin' his head, flinging his arms round like a windmill, and singin' hisself black in the face. A rare singer were Jesse.

'Yo' see, I was not o' much account wi' 'em all exceptin' to 'Liza Roantree, and I had a deal o' time settin' quiet at meetings and horotorio practices to hearken their talk, and if it were strange to me at beginnin', it got stranger still at after, when I was shut on it, and could study what it meaned.

'Just after th' horotorios came off, 'Liza, as had allus been weakly like, was took very bad. I walked Dr Warbottom's horse up and down a deal of times while he were inside, where they wouldn't let me go, though I fair ached to see her.

' "She'll be better i' noo, lad – better i' noo," he used to say. "Tha mun ha' patience." Then they said if I was quiet I might go in, and th' Reverend Amos Barraclough used to read to her lyin' propped up among th' pillows. Then she began to mend a bit, and they let me carry her on to th' settle, and when it got warm again she went about same as afore. Th' preacher and me and Blast was a deal together i' them days, and i' one way we was rare good comrades. But I could ha' stretched him time and again with a good will. I mind one day he said he would like to go down into th' bowels o' th' earth, and see how th' Lord had builded th' framework o' th' everlastin' hills. He were one of them chaps as had a gift o' sayin' things. They rolled off the tip of his clever tongue, same as Mulvaney here, as would ha' made a rare good preacher if he had nobbut given his mind to it. I lent him a suit o' miner's kit as almost buried th' little man, and his white face down i' th' coat-collar and hat-flap looked like the face of a boggart, and he cowered down i' th' bottom o' the waggon. I was drivin' a tram as led up a bit of an incline up to th' cave where the engine was pumpin', and where th' ore was brought up and put into th' waggons as went down o' themselves, me puttin' th' brake on and th' horses a-trottin' after. Long as it was daylight we were good friends, but when we got fair into th' dark, and could nobbut see th' day shinin' at the hole like a lamp at a street-end, I feeled downright wicked. Ma religion dropped all away from me when I looked back at him as were always comin' between me and 'Liza. The talk was 'at they were to be wed when she got better, an' I couldn't get her to say yes or nay to it. He began to sing a hymn in his thin voice, and I came out wi' a chorus that was all cussin' an' swearin' at my horses, an' I began to know how I hated him. He were such a little chap, too. I could drop him wi' one hand down Garstang's Copper-hole – a place where th' beck slithered ower th' edge on a rock, and fell wi' a bit of a whisper into a pit as no rope i' Greenhow could plump.'

Again Learoyd rooted up the innocent violets. 'Ay, he should see th' bowels o' th' earth an' never naught else. I could take him a mile or two along th' drift, and leave him wi' his candle doused to cry hallelujah, wi' none to hear him and say amen. I was to lead him down th' ladder-way to th' drift where Jesse Roantree was workin', and why shouldn't he slip on th' ladder, wi' my feet on his fingers till they loosed grip, and I put him down wi' my heel? If I went fust down th' ladder I could click hold on him and chuck him over my head, so as he should go squshin' down the shaft, breakin' his bones at ev'ry timberin' as Bill Appleton did when he was fresh, and hadn't a bone left when he wrought to th' bottom. Niver a blasted leg to walk from Pately. Niver an arm to put round 'Liza Roantree's waist. Niver no more – niver no more.'

The thick lips curled back over the yellow teeth, and that flushed face was not pretty to look upon. Mulvaney nodded sympathy, and Ortheris, moved by his comrade's passion, brought up the rifle to his shoulder, and searched the hillside for his quarry, muttering ribaldry about a sparrow, a spout, and a thunder-storm. The voice of the watercourse supplied the necessary small talk till Learoyd picked up his story.

'But it's none so easy to kill a man like yon. When I'd given up my horses to th' lad as took my place and I was showin' th' preacher th' workin's, shoutin' into his ear across th' clang o' th' pumpin' engines, I saw he were afraid o' naught; and when the lamplight showed his black eyes, I could feel as he was masterin' me again. I were no better nor Blast chained up short and growlin' i' the depths of him while a strange dog went safe past.

' "Th'art a coward and a fool," I said to mysen; an' I wrestled i' my mind again' him till, when we come to Garstang's Copper-hole, I laid hold o' the preacher and lifted him up over my head and held him into the darkest on it. "Now, lad," I says, "it's to be one or t'other on us – thee or me – for 'Liza Roantree. Why, isn't thee afraid for thysen?" I says, for he were still i' my arms as a sack. "Nay; I'm but afraid for thee, my poor lad, as knows naught," says he. I set him down on th' edge, an' th' beck run stiller, an' there was no more buzzin' in my head like when th' bee come through th' window o' Jesse's house. "What dost tha mean?" says I.

' "I've often thought as thou ought to know," says he, "but 'twas hard to tell thee. 'Liza Roantree's for neither on us, nor for nobody o' this earth. Dr Warbottom says – and he knows her, and her mother before her – that she is in a decline, and she cannot live six months longer. He's known it for many a day. Steady, John! Steady!" says he. And that weak little man pulled me further back and set me again' him, and talked it all over quiet and still, me turnin' a bunch o' candles in my hand, and counting them ower and ower again as I listened. A deal on it were th' regular preachin' talk, but there were a vast lot as made me begin to think as he were more of a man than I'd ever given him credit for, till I were cut as deep for him as I were for mysen.

'Six candles we had, and we crawled and climbed all that day while they lasted, and I said to mysen, " 'Liza Roantree hasn't six months to live." And when we came into th' daylight again we were like dead men to look at, an' Blast come behind us without so much as waggin' his tail. When I saw 'Liza again she looked at me a minute and says, "Who's telled tha? For I see tha knows." And she tried to smile as she kissed me, and I fair broke down.

'Yo'see, I was a young chap i' them days, and had seen naught o' life, let alone death, as is allus a-waitin'. She telled me as Dr Warbottom said as Greenhow air was too keen, and they were goin' to Bradford, to Jesse's brother David, as worked i' a mill, and I mun hold up like a man and a Christian, and she'd pray for me. Well, and they went away, and the preacher that same back end o' th' year were appointed to another circuit, as they call it, and I were left alone on Greenhow Hill.

'I tried, and I tried hard, to stick to th' chapel, but 'tweren't th' same thing at after. I hadn't 'Liza's voice to follow i' th' singin', nor her eyes a'shinin' acrost their heads. And i' th' class-meetings they said as I mun have some experiences to tell, and I hadn't a word to say for mysen.

'Blast and me moped a good deal, and happen we didn't behave ourselves over well, for they dropped us and wondered however they'd come to take us up. I can't tell how we got through th' time, while i' th' winter I gave up my job and went to Bradford. Old Jesse were at th' door o' th' house, in a long street o' little houses. He'd been sendin' th' children 'way as were clatterin' their clogs in th' causeway, for she were asleep.

' "Is it thee?" he says; "but you're not to see her. I'll none have her wakened for a nowt like thee. She's goin' fast, and she mun go in peace. Thou'lt never be good for naught i' th' world, and as long as thou lives thou'll never play the big fiddle. Get away, lad, get away!" So he shut the door softly i' my face.

'Nobody never made Jesse my master, but it seemed to me he was about right, and I went away into the town and knocked up against a recruiting sergeant. The old tales o' th' chapel folk came buzzin' into my head. I was to get away, and this were th' regular road for the likes o' me. I 'listed there and then, took th' Widow's shillin', and had a bunch o' ribbons pinned i' my hat.

'But next day I found my way to David Roantree's door, and

Jesse came to open it. Says he, "Thou's come back again wi' th' devil's colours flyin' – thy true colours, as I always telled thee."

'But I begged and prayed of him to let me see her nobbut to say goodbye, till a woman calls down th' stair-way, "She says John Learoyd's to come up." Th' old man shifts aside in a flash, and lays his hand on my arm, quite gentle like. "But thou'lt be quiet, John," says he, "for she's rare and weak. Thou was allus a good lad."

'Her eyes were all alive wi' light, and her hair was thick on the pillow round her, but her cheeks were thin – thin to frighten a man that's strong. "Nay, father, yo' mayn't say th' devil's colours. Them ribbons is pretty." An' she held out her hands for th' hat, an' she put all straight as a woman will wi' ribbons. "Nay, but what they're pretty," she says. "Eh, but I'd ha' liked to see thee i' thy red coat, John, for thou was allus my own lad – my very own lad, and none else."

'She lifted up her arms, and they come round my neck i' a gentle grip, and they slacked away, and she seemed fainting. "Now yo' mun get away, lad," says Jesse, and I picked up my hat and I came downstairs.

'Th' recruiting sergeant were waitin' for me at th' corner public-house. "Yo've seen your sweet-heart?" says he. "Yes, I've seen her," says I. "Well, we'll have a quart now, and you'll do your best to forget her," says he, bein' one o' them smart, bustlin' chaps. "Ay, sergeant," says I. "Forget her." And I've been forgettin' her ever since.'

He threw away the wilted clump of white violets as he spoke. Ortheris suddenly rose to his knees, his rifle at his shoulder, and peered across the valley in the clear afternoon light. His chin cuddled the stock, and there was a twitching of the muscles of the right cheek as he sighted; Private Stanley Ortheris was engaged on his business. A speck of white crawled up the water-course.

'See that beggar? . . . Got 'im.'

Seven hundred yards away, and a full two hundred down the hillside, the deserter of the Aurangabadis pitched forward, rolled down a red rock, and lay very still, with his face in a clump of blue gentians, while a big raven flapped out of the pine wood to make investigation.

'That's a clean shot, little man,' said Mulvaney.

Learoyd thoughtfully watched the smoke clear away. 'Happen there was a lass tewed up wi' him, too,' said he.

Ortheris did not reply. He was staring across the valley, with the smile of the artist who looks on the completed work.

'The Finest Story in the World'

'Or ever the knightly years were gone
  With the old world to the grave,
I was a king in Babylon
  And you were a Christian slave.'

W. E. Henley

His name was Charlie Mears; he was the only son of his mother who was a widow, and he lived in the north of London, coming into the City every day to work in a bank. He was twenty years old and was full of aspirations. I met him in a public billiard-saloon where the marker called him by his first name, and he called the marker 'Bullseye'. Charlie explained, a little nervously, that he had only come to the place to look on, and since looking on at games of skill is not a cheap amusement for the young, I suggested that Charlie should go back to his mother.

That was our first step towards better acquaintance. He would call on me sometimes in the evenings instead of running about London with his fellow-clerks; and before long, speaking of himself as a young man must, he told me of his aspirations, which were all literary. He desired to make himself an undying name chiefly through verse, though he was not above sending stories of love and death to the penny-in-the-slot journals. It was my fate to sit still while Charlie read me poems of many hundred lines, and bulky fragments of plays that would surely shake the world. My reward was his unreserved confidence, and the self-revelations and troubles of a young man are almost as holy as those of a maiden. Charlie had never fallen in love, but was anxious to do so on the first opportunity; he believed in all things good and all things honourable, but at the same time, was curiously careful to let me see that he knew his way about the world as befitted a bank-clerk on twenty-five shillings a week. He rhymed 'dove' with 'love' and 'moon' with 'June', and devoutly believed that they had never so been rhymed before. The long lame gaps in his plays he filled up with hasty words of apology and description, and swept on, seeing all that he intended to do so clearly that he esteemed it already done, and turned to me for applause.

I fancy that his mother did not encourage his aspirations; and I know that his writing-table at home was the edge of his washstand. This he told me almost at the outset of our acquaintance – when he was ravaging my bookshelves, and a little before I was implored to speak the truth as to his chances of 'writing something really great, you know'. Maybe I encouraged him too much, for, one night, he called on me, his eyes flaming with excitement, and said breathlessly:

'Do you mind – can you let me stay here and write all this evening? I won't interrupt you, I won't really. There's no place for me to write in at my mother's.'

'What's the trouble?' I said, knowing well what that trouble was.

'I've a notion in my head that would make the most splendid story that was ever written. Do let me write it out here. It's *such* a notion!'

There was no resisting the appeal. I set him a table; he hardly thanked me, but plunged into his work at once. For half an hour the pen scratched without stopping. Then Charlie sighed and tugged his hair. The scratching grew slower, there were more erasures, and at last ceased. The finest story in the world would not come forth.

'It looks such awful rot now,' he said mournfully. 'And yet it seemed so good when I was thinking about it. What's wrong?'

I could not dishearten him by saying the truth. So I answered: 'Perhaps you don't feel in the mood for writing.'

'Yes I do – except when I look at this stuff. Ugh!'

'Read me what you've done,' I said,

He read, and it was wondrous bad, and he paused at all the specially turgid sentences, expecting a little approval; for he was proud of those sentences, as I knew he would be.

'It needs compression,' I suggested cautiously.

'I hate cutting my things down. I don't think you could alter a word here without spoiling the sense. It reads better aloud than when I was writing it.'

'Charlie, you're suffering from an alarming disease afflicting a numerous class. Put the thing by, and tackle it again in a week.'

'I want to do it at once. What do you think of it?'

'How can I judge from a half-written tale? Tell me the story as it lies in your head.'

Charlie told, and in the telling there was everything that his ignorance had so carefully prevented from escaping into the written word. I looked at him, wondering whether it were possible that he did not know the originality, the power of the notion that had come in his way? It was distinctly a Notion among notions. Men had been puffed up with pride by ideas not a tithe as excellent and practicable. But Charlie babbled on serenely, interrupting the current of pure fancy with samples of horrible sentences that he purposed to use. I heard him out to the end. It would be folly to allow his thought to remain in his own inept hands, when I could do so much with it. Not all that could be done indeed; but, oh so much!

'What do you think?' he said at last. 'I fancy I shall call it "The Story of a Ship".'

'I think the idea's pretty good; but you won't be able to handle it for ever so long. Now I——'

'Would it be of any use to you? Would you care to take it? I should be proud,' said Charlie promptly.

There are few things sweeter in this world than the guileless, hot-headed, intemperate, open admiration of a junior. Even a woman in her blindest devotion does not fall into the gait of the man she adores, tilt her bonnet to the angle at which he wears his hat, or interlard her speech with his pet oaths. And Charlie did all these things. Still it was necessary to salve my conscience before I possessed myself of Charlie's thoughts.

'Let's make a bargain. I'll give you a fiver for the notion,' I said.

Charlie became a bank-clerk at once.

'Oh, that's impossible. Between two pals, you know, if I may call you so, and speaking as a man of the world, I couldn't. Take the notion if it's any use to you. I've heaps more.'

He had – none knew this better than I – but they were the notions of other men.

'Look at it as a matter of business – between men of the

world,' I returned. 'Five pounds will buy you any number of poetry-books. Business is business, and you may be sure I shouldn't give that price unless——'

'Oh, if you put it *that* way,' said Charlie, visibly moved by the thought of the books. The bargain was clinched with an agreement that he should at unstated intervals come to me with all the notions that he possessed, should have a table of his own to write at, and unquestioned right to inflict upon me all his poems and fragments of poems. Then I said, 'Now tell me how you came by this idea.'

'It came by itself.' Charlie's eyes opened a little.

'Yes, but you told me a great deal about the hero that you must have read before somewhere.'

'I haven't any time for reading, except when you let me sit here, and on Sundays I'm on my bicycle or down the river all day. There's nothing wrong about the hero, is there?'

'Tell me again and I shall understand clearly. You say that your hero went pirating. How did he live?'

'He was on the lower deck of this ship-thing that I was telling you about.'

'What sort of ship?'

'It was the kind rowed with oars, and the sea spurts through the oar-holes, and the men row sitting up to their knees in water. Then there's a bench running down between the two lines of oars, and an overseer with a whip walks up and down the bench to make the men work.'

'How do you know that?'

'It's in the tale. There's a rope running overhead, looped to the upper-deck, for the overseer to catch hold of when the ship rolls. When the overseer misses the rope once and falls among the rowers, remember the hero laughs at him and gets licked for it. He's chained to his oar of course – the hero.'

'How is he chained?'

'With an iron band round his waist fixed to the bench he sits on, and a sort of handcuff on his left wrist chaining him to the oar. He's on the lower deck where the worst men are sent, and the only light comes from the hatchways and through the oar-holes. Can't you imagine the sunlight just squeezing through between the handle and the hole and wobbling about as the ship moves?'

'I can, but I can't imagine your imagining it.'

'How could it be any other way? Now you listen to me. The long oars on the upper deck are managed by four men to each bench, the lower ones by three, and the lowest of all by two. Remember it's quite dark on the lowest deck and all the men there go mad. When a man dies at his oar on that deck he isn't thrown overboard, but cut up in his chains and stuffed through the oar-hole in little pieces.'

'Why?' I demanded amazed, not so much at the information as the tone of command in which it was flung out.

'To save trouble and to frighten the others. It needs two overseers to drag a man's body up to the top deck; and if the men at the lower deck oars were left alone, of course they'd stop rowing and try to pull up the benches by all standing up together in their chains.'

'You've a most provident imagination. Where have you been reading about galleys and galley-slaves?'

'Nowhere that I remember. I row a little when I get the chance. But, perhaps, if you say so, I may have read something.'

He went away shortly afterwards to deal with booksellers, and I wondered how a bank-clerk aged twenty could put into my hands with a profligate abundance of detail, all given with absolute assurance, the story of extravagant and bloodthirsty adventure, riot, piracy, and death in unnamed seas. He had led his hero a desperate dance through revolt against the overseers, to command of a ship of his own, and at last to the establishment of a kingdom on an island 'somewhere in the sea, you know'; and, delighted with my paltry five pounds, had gone out to buy the notions of other men, that these might teach him how to write. I had the consolation of knowing that this notion was mine by right of purchase, and I thought that I could make something of it.

When next he came to me he was drunk – royally drunk on many poets for the first time revealed to him. His pupils were dilated, his words tumbled over each other, and he wrapped himself in quotations – as a beggar would enfold himself in the purple of emperors. Most of all was he drunk with Longfellow.

'Isn't it splendid? Isn't it superb?' he cried, after hasty greetings. 'Listen to this –

' "Wouldst thou," – so the helmsman answered,
"Know the secret of the sea?
Only those who brave its dangers
Comprehend its mystery."

By gum!

' "Only those who brave its dangers
Comprehend its mystery," '

he repeated twenty times, walking up and down the room and forgetting me. 'But *I* can understand it too,' he said to himself. 'I don't know how to thank you for that fiver. And this; listen –

' "I remember the black wharves and the slips
And the sea-tides tossing free;
And the Spanish sailors with bearded lips,
And the beauty and mystery of the ships,
And the magic of the sea."

I haven't braved any dangers, but I feel as if I knew all about it.'

'You certainly seem to have a grip of the sea. Have you ever seen it?'

'When I was a little chap I went to Brighton once; we used to live in Coventry, though, before we came to London. I never saw it,

' "When descends on the Atlantic
The gigantic
Storm-wind of the Equinox." '

He shook me by the shoulder to make me understand the passion that was shaking himself.

'When that storm comes,' he continued, 'I think that all the oars in the ship that I was talking about get broken, and the rowers have their chests smashed in by the oar-heads bucking.

By the way, have you done anything with that notion of mine yet?'

'No. I was waiting to hear more of it from you. Tell me how in the world you're so certain about the fittings of the ship. You know nothing of ships.'

'I don't know. It's as real as anything to me until I try to write it down. I was thinking about it only last night in bed, after you had lent me *Treasure Island*; and I made up a whole lot of new things to go into the story.'

'What sort of things?'

'About the food the men ate; rotten figs and black beans and wine in a skin bag, passed from bench to bench.'

'Was the ship built so long ago as *that*?'

'As what? I don't know whether it was long ago or not. It's only a notion, but sometimes it seems just as real as if it was true. Do I bother you with talking about it?'

'Not in the least. Did you make up anything else?'

'Yes, but it's nonsense.' Charlie flushed a little.

'Never mind; let's hear about it.'

'Well, I was thinking over the story, and after awhile I got out of bed and wrote down on a piece of paper the sort of stuff the men might be supposed to scratch on their oars with the edges of their handcuffs. It seemed to make the thing more life-like. It *is* so real to me, y'know.'

'Have you the paper on you?'

'Y – es, but what's the use of showing it? It's only a lot of scratches. All the same, we might have 'em reproduced in the book on the front page.'

'I'll attend to those details. Show me what your men wrote.'

He pulled out of his pocket a sheet of notepaper, with a single line of scratches upon it, and I put this carefully away.

'What is it supposed to mean in English?' I said.

'Oh, I don't know. I mean it to mean "I'm beastly tired". It's great nonsense,' he repeated, 'but all those men in the ship seem as real as real people to me. Do do something to the notion soon; I should like to see it written and printed.'

'But all you've told me would make a long book.'

'Make it then. You've only to sit down and write it out.'

'Give me a little time. Have you any more notions?'

'Not just now. I'm reading all the books I've bought. They're splendid.'

When he had left I looked at the sheet of notepaper with the inscription upon it. Then I took my head tenderly between both hands, to make certain that it was not coming off or turning round. Then . . . but there seemed to be no interval between quitting my rooms and finding myself arguing with a policeman outside a door marked *Private* in a corridor of the British Museum. All I demanded, as politely as possible, was 'the Greek antiquity man'. The policeman knew nothing except the rules of the Museum, and it became necessary to forage through all the houses and offices inside the gates. An elderly gentleman called away from his lunch put an end to my search by holding the notepaper between finger and thumb and sniffing at it scornfully.

'What does this mean? H'mm,' said he. 'So far as I can ascertain it is an attempt to write extremely corrupt Greek on the part' – here he glared at me with intention – 'of an extremely illiterate – ah – person.' He read slowly from the paper, '*Pollock, Erckmann, Tauchnitz, Henniker*' – four names familiar to me.

'Can you tell me what the corruption is supposed to mean – the gist of the thing?' I asked.

'I have been – many times – overcome with weariness in this particular employment. That is the meaning.' He returned me the paper, and I fled without a word of thanks, explanation, or apology.

I might have been excused for forgetting much. To me of all men had been given the chance to write the most marvellous tale in the world, nothing less than the story of a Greek galley-slave, as told by himself. Small wonder that his dreaming had seemed real to Charlie. The Fates that are so careful to shut the doors of each successive life behind us had, in this case, been neglectful, and Charlie was looking, though that he did not know, where never man had been permitted to look with full knowledge since Time began. Above all, he was absolutely ignorant of the knowledge sold to me for five pounds; and he would retain that ignorance, for bank-clerks do not understand metempsychosis, and a sound commercial education does not include Greek. He would supply me – here I capered among the dumb gods of Egypt and laughed in their battered faces – with material to make my tale sure – so sure that the world would hail it as an impudent and vamped fiction. And I – I alone would know that it was absolutely and literally true. I – I alone held this jewel to my hand for the cutting and polishing! Therefore I danced again among the gods of the Egyptian court till a policeman saw me and took steps in my direction.

It remained now only to encourage Charlie to talk, and here there was no difficulty. But I had forgotten those accursed books of poetry. He came to me time after time, as useless as a surcharged phonograph – drunk on Byron, Shelley, or Keats. Knowing now what the boy had been in his past lives, and desperately anxious not to lose one word of his babble, I could not hide from him my respect and interest. He misconstrued both into respect for the present soul of Charlie Mears, to whom life was as new as it was to Adam, and interest in his readings; and stretched my patience to breaking point by reciting poetry – not his own now, but that of others. I wished every English poet blotted out of the memory of mankind. I blasphemed the mightiest names of song because they had drawn Charlie from the path of direct narrative, and would, later, spur him to imitate them; but I choked down my impatience until the first flood of enthusiasm should have spent itself and the boy returned to his dreams.

'What's the use of my telling you what *I* think, when these chaps wrote things for the angels to read?' he growled, one evening. 'Why don't you write something like theirs?'

'I don't think you're treating me quite fairly,' I said, speaking under strong restraint.

'I've given you the story,' he said shortly, replunging into 'Lara'.

'But I want the details.'

'The things I make up about that damned ship that you call a galley? They're quite easy. You can just make 'em up for yourself. Turn up the gas a little, I want to go on reading.'

I could have broken the gas globe over his head for his amazing stupidity. I could indeed make up things for myself did I only know what Charlie did not know that he knew. But since the doors were shut behind me I could only wait his youthful pleasure and strive to keep him in good temper. One minute's want of guard might spoil a priceless revelation: now and again he would toss his books aside – he kept them in my rooms, for his mother would have been shocked at the waste of good money had she seen them – and launched into his sea-dreams. Again I cursed all the poets of England. The plastic mind of the bank-clerk had been overlaid, coloured, and distorted by that which he had read, and the result as delivered was a confused tangle of other voices most like the mutter and hum through a City telephone in the busiest part of the day.

He talked of the galley – his own galley had he but known it – with illustrations borrowed from the 'Bride of Abydos'. He pointed the experiences of his hero with quotations from 'The Corsair', and threw in deep and desperate moral reflections from 'Cain' and 'Manfred', expecting me to use them all. Only when the talk turned on Longfellow were the jarring cross-currents dumb, and I knew that Charlie was speaking the truth as he remembered it.

'What do you think of this?' I said one evening, as soon as I understood the medium in which his memory worked best, and, before he could expostulate, read him nearly the whole of 'The Saga of King Olaf!'

He listened open-mouthed, flushed, his hands drumming on the back of the sofa where he lay, till I came to the Song of Einar Tamberskelver and the verse:–

'Einar then, the arrow taking
   From the loosened string,
Answered, "That was Norway breaking
   'Neath thy hand, O King." '

He gasped with pure delight of sound.

'That's better than Byron, a little?' I ventured.

'Better! Why it's *true*! How could he have known?'

I went back and repeated:-

' "What was that?" said Olaf, standing
   On the quarter-deck,
"Something heard I like the stranding
   Of a shattered wreck." '

'How could he have known how the ships crash and the oars rip out and go *z-zzp* all along the line? Why only the other night . . . But go back, please, and read "The Skerry of Shrieks" again.'

'No, I'm tired. Let's talk. What happened the other night?'

'I had an awful dream about that galley of ours. I dreamed I was drowned in a fight. You see we ran alongside another ship in harbour. The water was dead still except where our oars whipped it up. You know where I always sit in the galley?' He spoke haltingly at first, under a fine English fear of being laughed at.

'No. That's news to me,' I answered meekly, my heart beginning to beat.

'On the fourth oar from the bow on the right side on the upper deck. There were four of us at that oar, all chained. I remember watching the water and trying to get my handcuffs off before the row began. Then we closed up on the other ship, and all their fighting men jumped over our bulwarks, and my bench broke and I was pinned down with the three other fellows on top of me, and the big oar jammed across our backs.'

'Well?' Charlie's eyes were alive and alight. He was looking at the wall behind my chair.

'I don't know how we fought. The men were trampling all over my back, and I lay low. Then our rowers on the left side – tied to their oars, you know – began to yell and back water. I could hear the water sizzle, and we spun round like a cockchafer, and I knew, lying where I was, that there was a galley coming up bow-on to ram us on the left side. I could just lift up my head and see her sail over the bulwarks. We wanted to meet her bow to bow, but it was too late. We could only turn a little bit because the galley on our right had hooked herself on to us and stopped our moving. Then, by gum! there was a crash! Our left oars began to break as the other galley, the moving one y'know, stuck her nose into them. Then the lower-deck oars shot up through the deck planking, butt first, and one of them jumped clear up into the air and came down again close at my head.'

'How was that managed?'

'The moving galley's bow was plunking them back through

their own oar-holes, and I could hear no end of a shindy in the decks below. Then her nose caught us nearly in the middle, and we tilted sideways, and the fellows in the right-hand galley unhitched their hooks and ropes, and threw things on to our upper deck – arrows, and hot pitch or something that stung, and we went up and up and up on the left side, and the right side dipped, and I twisted my head round and saw the water stand still as it topped the right bulwarks, and then it curled over and crashed down on the whole lot of us on the right side, and I felt it hit my back, and I woke.'

'One minute, Charlie. When the sea topped the bulwarks, what did it look like?' I had my reasons for asking. A man of my acquaintance had once gone down with a leaking ship in a still sea, and had seen the water-level pause for an instant ere it fell on the deck.

'It looked just like a banjo-string drawn tight, and it seemed to stay there for years,' said Charlie.

Exactly! The other man had said: 'It looked like a silver wire laid down along the bulwarks, and I thought it was never going to break.' He had paid everything except the bare life for this little valueless piece of knowledge, and I had travelled ten thousand weary miles to meet him and take his knowledge at second hand. But Charlie, the bank-clerk on twenty-five shillings a week, who had never been out of sight of a made road, knew it all. It was no consolation to me that once in his lives he had been forced to die for his gains. I also must have died scores of times, but behind me, because I could have used my knowledge, the doors were shut.

'And then?' I said, trying to put away the devil of envy.

'The funny thing was, though, in all the row I didn't feel a bit astonished or frightened. It seemed as if I'd been in a good many fights, because I told my next man so when the row began. But that cad of an overseer on my deck wouldn't unloose our chains and give us a chance. He always said that we'd all be set free after a battle, but we never were; we neve were.' Charlie shook his head mournfully.

'What a scoundrel!'

'I should say he was. He never gave us enough to eat, and

sometimes we were so thirsty that we used to drink salt-water. I can taste that salt-water still.'

'Now tell me something about the harbour where the fight was fought.'

'I didn't dream about that. I know it was a harbour, though; because we were tied up to a ring on a white wall and all the face of the stone under water was covered with wood to prevent our ram getting chipped when the tide made us rock.'

'That's curious. Our hero commanded the galley, didn't he?'

'Didn't he just! He stood by the bows and shouted like a good 'un. He was the man who killed the overseer.'

'But you were all drowned together, Charlie, weren't you?'

'I can't make that fit quite,' he said, with a puzzled look. 'The galley must have gone down with all hands, and yet I fancy that the hero went on living afterwards. Perhaps he climbed into the attacking ship. I wouldn't see that, of course. I was dead, you know.'

He shivered slightly and protested that he could remember no more.

I did not press him further, but to satisfy myself that he lay in ignorance of the workings of his own mind, deliberately introduced him to Mortimer Collins's *Transmigration*, and gave him a sketch of the plot before he opened the pages.

'What rot it all is!' he said frankly, at the end of an hour. 'I don't understand his nonsense about the Red Planet Mars and the King, and the rest of it. Chuck me the Longfellow again.'

I handed him the book and wrote out as much as I could remember of his description of the sea-fight, appealing to him from time to time for confirmation of fact or detail. He would answer without raising his eyes from the book, as assuredly as though all his knowledge lay before him on the printed page. I spoke under the normal key of my voice that the current might not be broken, and I knew that he was not aware of what he was saying, for his thoughts were out on the sea with Longfellow.

'Charlie,' I asked, 'when the rowers on the galleys mutinied how did they kill their overseers?'

'Tore up the benches and brained 'em. That happened when a heavy sea was running. An overseer on the lower deck slipped from the centre plank and fell among the rowers. They choked him to death against the side of the ship with their chained hands quite quietly, and it was too dark for the other overseer to see what had happened. When he asked, he was pulled down too and choked, and the lower deck fought their way up deck by deck, with the pieces of the broken benches banging behind 'em. How they howled!'

'And what happened after that?'

'I don't know. The hero went away – red hair and red beard and all. That was after he had captured our galley, I think.'

The sound of my voice irritated him, and he motioned slightly with his left hand as a man does when interruption jars.

'You never told me he was red-headed before, or that he captured your galley,' I said, after a discreet interval.

Charlie did not raise his eyes.

'He was as red as a red bear,' said he abstractedly. 'He came from the north; they said so in the galley when he looked for rowers – not slaves, but free men. Afterwards – years and years afterwards – news came from another ship, or else he came back——'

His lips moved in silence. He was rapturously retasting some poem before him.

'Where had he been, then?' I was almost whispering that the sentence might come gently to whichever section of Charlie's brain was working on my behalf.

'To the Beaches – the Long and Wonderful Beaches!' was the reply after a minute of silence.

'To Furdurstrandi?' I asked, tingling from head to foot.

'Yes, to Furdurstrandi,' he pronounced the word in a new fashion. 'And I too saw——' The voice failed.

'Do you know what you have said?' I shouted incautiously.

He lifted his eyes, fully roused now. 'No!' he snapped. 'I wish you'd let a chap go on reading. Hark to this:–

' "But Othere, the old sea captain,
He neither paused nor stirred
Till the king listened, and then
Once more took up his pen
And wrote down every word.

' "And to the King of the Saxons
In witness of the truth,
Raising his noble head,
He stretched his brown hand and said,
'Behold this walrus tooth.' "

By Jove, what chaps those must have been, to go sailing all over the shop never knowing where they'd fetch the land! Hah!'

'Charlie,' I pleaded, 'if you'll only be sensible for a minute or two I'll make our hero in our tale every inch as good as Othere.'

'Umph! Longfellow wrote that poem. I don't care about writing things any more. I want to read.' He was thoroughly out of tune now, and raging over my own ill-luck, I left him.

Conceive yourself at the door of the world's treasure-house guarded by a child – an idle, irresponsible child playing knuckle-bones – on whose favour depends the gift of the key, and you will imagine one-half my torment. Till that evening Charlie had spoken nothing that might not lie within the experiences of a Greek galley-slave. But now, or there was no virtue in books, he had talked of some desperate adventure of the Vikings, of Thorfin Karlsefne's sailing to Wineland, which is America, in the ninth or tenth century. The battle in the harbour he had seen; and his own death he had described. But this was a much more startling plunge into the past. Was it possible that he had skipped half-a-dozen lives, and was then dimly remembering some episode of a thousand years later? It was a maddening jumble, and the worst of it was that Charlie Mears in his normal condition was the last person in the world to clear it up. I could only wait and watch, but I went to bed that night full of the wildest imaginings. There was nothing that was not possible if Charlie's detestable memory only held good.

I might rewrite the Saga of Thorfin Karlsefne as it had never been written before, might tell the story of the first discovery of America, myself the discoverer. But I was entirely at Charlie's mercy, and so long as there was a three-and-sixpenny Bohn volume within his reach Charlie would not tell. I dared not curse him openly; I hardly dared jog his memory, for I was dealing with the experiences of a thousand years ago, told through the mouth of a boy of today; and a boy of today is affected by every change of tone and gust of opinion, so that he must lie even when he most desires to speak the truth.

I saw no more of Charlie for nearly a week. When next I met him it was in Gracechurch Street with a bill-book chained to his waist. Business took him over London Bridge, and I accompanied him. He was very full of the importance of that book and magnified it. As we passed over the Thames we paused to look at a steamer unloading great slabs of white and brown marble. A barge drifted under the steamer's stern and a lonely ship's cow in that barge bellowed. Charlie's face changed from the face of the bank-clerk to that of an unknown and – though he would not have believed this – a much shrewder man. He flung out his arm across the parapet of the bridge and laughing very loudly, said:–

'When they heard *our* bulls bellow the Skrœlings ran away!'

I waited only for an instant, but the barge and the cow had disappeared under the bows of the steamer before I answered.

'Charlie, what do you suppose are Skrœlings?'

'Never heard of 'em before. They sound like a new kind of sea-gull. What a chap you are for asking questions!' he replied. 'I have to go to the cashier of the Omnibus Company yonder. Will you wait for me and we can lunch somewhere together? I've a notion for a poem.'

'No, thanks. I'm off. You're sure you know nothing about Skrœlings?'

'Not unless he's been entered for the Liverpool Handicap.' He nodded and disappeared in the crowd.

Now it is written in the Saga of Eric the Red or that of Thorfin Karlsefne, that nine hundred years ago when Karlsefne's galleys came to Leif's booths, which Leif had erected in the unknown land called Markland, which may or may not have been Rhode Island, the Skrœlings – and the Lord He knows who these may or may not have been – came to trade with the Vikings, and ran away because they were frightened at the bellowing of the cattle which Thorfin had brought with him in the ships. But what in the world could a Greek slave know of that affair? I wandered up and down among the streets trying to unravel the mystery, and the more I considered it the more baffling it grew. One thing only seemed certain, and that certainty took away my breath for the moment. If I came to full knowledge of anything at all, it would not be one life of the soul in Charlie Mears's body, but half a dozen – half a dozen several and separate existences spent on blue water in the morning of the world!

Then I reviewed the situation.

Obviously if I used my knowledge I should stand alone and unapproachable until all men were as wise as myself. That would be something, but, manlike, I was ungrateful. It seemed bitterly unfair that Charlie's memory should fail me when I needed it most. Great Powers Above – I looked up at them through the fog-smoke – did the Lords of Life and Death know what this meant to me? Nothing less than eternal fame of the best kind, that comes from One, and is shared by one alone. I would be content – remembering Clive, I stood astounded at my own moderation – with the mere right to tell one story, to work out one little contribution to the light literature of the day. If Charlie were permitted full recollection for one hour – for sixty short minutes – of existences that had extended over a thousand years – I would forego all profit and honour from all that I should make of his speech. I would take no share in the commotion that would follow throughout the particular corner of the earth that calls itself 'the world'. The thing should be put forth anonymously. Nay, I would make other men believe that they had written it. They would hire bull-hided self-advertising Englishmen to bellow it abroad. Preachers would found a fresh conduct of life upon it, swearing that it was new and that they had lifted the fear of death from all mankind. Every Orientalist in Europe would patronise it discursively with Sanskrit and Pali texts. Terrible women would invent unclean variants of the men's belief for the elevation of their sisters. Churches and religions would war over it. Between the hailing and restarting of an omnibus I foresaw the scuffles that would arise among half a dozen denominations all professing 'the doctrine of the True Metempsychosis as applied to the world and the New Era'; and saw, too, the respectable English newspapers shying, like frightened kine, over the beautiful simplicity of the tale. The mind leaped forward a hundred – two hundred – a thousand years. I saw with sorrow that men would mutilate and garble the story; that rival creeds would turn it upside down till, at last, the western world which clings to the dread of death more closely than the hope of life, would set it aside as an interesting superstition and stampede after some faith so long forgotten that it seemed altogether new. Upon this I changed the terms of the bargain that I would make with the Lords of Life and Death. Only let me know, let me write, the story with sure knowledge that I wrote the truth, and I would burn the manuscript as a solemn sacrifice. Five minutes after the last line was written I would destroy it all. But I must be allowed to write it with absolute certainty.

There was no answer. The flaming colours of an Aquarium poster caught my eye, and I wondered whether it would be wise or prudent to lure Charlie into the hands of the professional mesmerist then, and whether, if he were under his power, he would speak of his past lives. If he did, and if people believed him . . . but Charlie would be frightened and flustered, or made conceited by the interviews. In either case he would begin to lie through fear or vanity. He was safest in my own hands.

'They are very funny fools, your English,' said a voice at my elbow, and turning round I recognised a casual acquaintance, a young Bengali law student, called Grish Chunder, whose father had sent him to England to become civilised. The old man was a retired native official, and on an income of five pounds a month contrived to allow his son two hundred pounds a year, and the run of his teeth in a city where he could pretend to be the cadet of a royal house, and tell stories of the brutal Indian bureaucrats who ground the faces of the poor.

Grish Chunder was a young, fat, full-bodied Bengali, dressed with scrupulous care in frock coat, tall hat, light trousers, and tan gloves. But I had known him in the days when the brutal Indian Government paid for his university education, and he contributed cheap sedition to the *Sachi Durpan*, and intrigued with the wives of his fourteen-year-old schoolmates.

'That is very funny and very foolish,' he said, nodding at the poster. 'I am going down to the Northbrook Club. Will you come too?'

I walked with him for some time. 'You are not well,' he said. 'What is there on your mind? You do not talk.'

'Grish Chunder, you've been too well educated to believe in a God, haven't you?'

'Oah, yes, *here*! But when I go home I must conciliate popular superstition, and make ceremonies of purification, and my women will anoint idols.'

'And hang up *tulsi* and feast the *purohit*, and take you back into caste again, and make a good *khuttri* of you again, you advanced Freethinker. And you'll eat *desi* food, and like it all, from the smell in the courtyard to the mustard oil over you.'

'I shall very much like it,' said Grish Chunder unguardedly. 'Once a Hindu – always a Hindu. But I like to know what the English think they know.'

'I'll tell you something that one Englishman knows. It's an old tale to you.'

I began to tell the story of Charlie in English, but Grish Chunder put a question in the vernacular, and the history went forward naturally in the tongue best suited for its telling. After all, it could never have been told in English. Grish Chunder heard me, nodding from time to time, and then came up to my rooms, where I finished the tale.

'*Beshak*,' he said philosophically. '*Lekin darwaza band hai.* [Without doubt; but the door is shut.] I have heard of this remembering of previous existences among my people. It is of course an old tale with us, but, to happen to an Englishman – a cow-fed *Mlechh* – an outcast. By Jove, that is *most* peculiar!'

'Outcast yourself, Grish Chunder! You eat cow-beef every day. Let's think the thing over. The boy remembers his incarnations.'

'Does he know that?' said Grish Chunder quietly, swinging his legs as he sat on my table. He was speaking in his English now.

'He does not know anything. Would I speak to you if he did? Go on!'

'There is no going on at all. If you tell that to your friends they will say you are mad and put it in the papers. Suppose, now, you prosecute for libel.'

'Let's leave that out of the question entirely. Is there any chance of his being made to speak?'

'There is a chance. Oah, yess! But *if* he spoke it would mean that all this world would end now – *instanto* – fall down on your head. These things are not allowed, you know. As I said, the door is shut.'

'Not a ghost of a chance?'

'How can there be? You are a Christi-án, and it is forbidden to eat, in your books, of the Tree of Life, or else you would never die. How shall you all fear death if you all know what your friend does not know that he knows? I am afraid to be kicked, but I am not afraid to die, because I know what I know. You are not afraid to be kicked, but you are afraid to die. If you were not, by God! you English would be all over the shop in an hour, upsetting the balances of power, and making commotions. It would not be good. But no fear. He will remember a little and a little less, and he will call it dreams. Then he will forget altogether. When I passed my First Arts Examination in Calcutta that was all in the cram-book on Wordsworth. "Trailing clouds of glory", you know.'

'This seems to be an exception to the rule.'

'There are no exceptions to rules. Some are not so hard-looking as others, but they are all the same when you touch. If this friend of yours said so-and-so and so-and-so, indicating that he remembered all his lost lives, or one piece of a lost life, he would not be in the bank another hour. He would be what you call sacked because he was mad, and they would send him to an asylum for lunatics. You can see that, my friend.'

'Of course I can, but I wasn't thinking of him. His name need never appear in the story.'

'Ah! I see. That story will never be written. You can try.'

'I am going to.'

'For your own credit and for the sake of money, *of* course?'

'No. For the sake of writing the story. On my honour that will be all.'

'Even then there is no chance. You cannot play with the gods. It is a very pretty story now. As they say, Let it go on that – I mean at that. Be quick; he will not last long.'

'How do you mean?'

'What I say. He has never, so far, thought about a woman.'

'Hasn't he, though!' I remembered some of Charlie's confidences.

'I mean no woman has thought about him. When that comes; *bus* – *hogya* – all up! I know. There are millions of women here. Housemaids, for instance. They kiss you behind doors.'

I winced at the thought of my story being ruined by a housemaid. And yet nothing was more probable.

Grish Chunder grinned.

'Yes – also pretty girls – cousins of his house, and perhaps *not* of his house. One kiss that he gives back again and remembers will cure all this nonsense, or else——'

'Or else what? Remember he does not know that he knows.'

'I know that. Or else, if nothing happens he will become immersed in the trade and the financial speculation like the rest. It must be so. You can see that it must be so. But the woman will come first, *I* think.'

There was a rap at the door, and Charlie charged in impetuously. He had been released from office, and by the look in his eyes I could see that he had come over for a long talk; most probably with poems in his pockets. Charlie's poems were very wearying, but someimes they led him to speak about the galley.

Grish Chunder looked at him keenly for a minute.

'I beg your pardon,' Charlie said uneasily; 'I didn't know you had any one with you.'

'I am going,' said Grish Chunder.

He drew me into the lobby as he departed.

'That is your man,' he said quickly. 'I tell you he will never speak all you wish. That is rot – bosh. But he would be most good to make to see things. Suppose now we pretend that it was only play' – I had never seen Grish Chunder so excited – 'and pour the ink-pool into his hand. Eh, what do you think? I tell you that he could see *anything* that a man could see. Let me get the ink and the camphor. He is a seer and he will tell us very many things.'

'He may be all you say, but I'm not going to trust him to your gods and devils.'

'It will not hurt him. He will only feel a little stupid and dull when he wakes up. You have seen boys look into the ink-pool before.'

'That is the reason why I am not going to see it any more. You'd better go, Grish Chunder.'

He went, insisting far down the staircase that it was throwing away my only chance of looking into the future.

This left me unmoved, for I was concerned for the past, and no peering of hypnotised boys into mirrors and ink-pools would help me to that. But I recognised Grish Chunder's point of view and sympathised with it.

'What a big black brute that was!' said Charlie, when I returned to him. 'Well, look here, I've just done a poem; did it instead of playing dominoes after lunch. May I read it?'

'Let me read it to myself.'

'Then you miss the proper expression. Besides, you always make my things sound as if the rhymes were all wrong.'

'Read it aloud, then. You're like the rest of 'em.'

Charlie mouthed me his poem, and it was not much worse than the average of his verses. He had been reading his books faithfully, but he was not pleased when I told him that I preferred my Longfellow undiluted with Charlie.

Then we began to go through the MS line by line, Charlie parrying every objection and correction with:

'Yes, that may be better, but you don't catch what I'm driving at.'

Charlie was, in one way at least, very like one kind of poet.

There was a pencil scrawl at the back of the paper, and 'What's that?' I said.

'Oh, that's not poetry at all. It's some rot I wrote last night before I went to bed, and it was too much bother to hunt for rhymes; so I made it a sort of blank verse instead.

Here is Charlie's 'blank verse':–

'We pulled for you when the wind was against us and the sails were low.
Will you never let us go?
We ate bread and onions when you took towns, or ran aboard quickly when you were beaten back by the foe,
The captains walked up and down the deck in fair weather singing songs, but we were below.
We fainted with our chins on the oars and you did not see that we were idle for we still swung to and fro.
Will you never let us go?

The salt made the oar-handles like shark-skin; our knees were cut to the bone with salt cracks; our hair was stuck to our foreheads; and our lips were cut to our gums, and you whipped us because we could not row.

Will you never let us go?

But in a little time we shall run out of the portholes as the water runs along the oar-blade, and though you tell the others to row after us you will never catch us till you catch the oar-thresh and tie up the winds in the belly of the sail. Aho!

Will you never let us go?'

'H'm. What's oar-thresh, Charlie?'

'The water washed up by the oars. That's the sort of song they might sing in the galley y'know. Aren't you ever going to finish that story and give me some of the profits?'

'It depends on yourself. If you had only told me more about your hero in the first instance it might have been finished by now. You're so hazy in your notions.'

'I only want to give you the general notion of it – the knocking about from place to place and the fighting and all that. Can't you fill in the rest yourself? Make the hero save a girl on a pirate-galley and marry her or do something.'

'You're a really helpful collaborator. I suppose the hero went through some few adventures before he married.'

'Well then, make him a very artful card – a low sort of man – a sort of political man who went about making treaties and breaking them – a black-haired chap who hid behind the mast when the fighting began.'

'But you said the other day that he was red-haired.'

'I couldn't have. Make him black-haired of course. You've no imagination.'

Seeing that I had just discovered the entire principles upon which the half-memory falsely called imagination is based, I felt entitled to laugh, but forbore for the sake of the tale.

'You're right. *You're* the man with imagination. A black-haired chap in a decked ship,' I said.

'No, an open ship – like a big boat.'

This was maddening.

'Your ship has been built and designed, closed and decked in; you said so yourself,' I protested.

'No, no, not that ship. That was open or half-decked because—— By Jove, you're right. You made me think of the hero as a red-haired chap. Of course if he were red, the ship would be an open one with painted sails.'

Surely, I thought, he would remember now that he had served in two galleys at least – in a three-decked Greek one under the black-haired 'political man', and again in a Viking's open sea-serpent under the man 'red as a red bear' who went to Markland. The devil prompted me to speak.

'Why "of course", Charlie?' said I.

'I don't know. Are you making fun of me?'

The current was broken for the time being. I took up a note-book and pretended to make many entries in it.

'It's a pleasure to work with an imaginative chap like yourself,' I said, after a pause. 'The way that you've brought out the character of the hero is simply wonderful.'

'Do you think so?' he answered, with a pleased flush. 'I often tell myself that there's more in me than my mo—— than people think.'

'There's an enormous amount in you.'

'Then, won't you let me send an essay on The Ways of Bank-Clerks to *Tit-Bits*, and get the guinea prize?'

'That wasn't exactly what I meant, old fellow: perhaps it would be better to wait a little and go ahead with the galley-story.'

'Ah, but I sha'n't get the credit of that. *Tit-Bits* would publish my name and address if I win. What are you grinning at? They *would*.'

'I know it. Suppose you go for a walk. I want to look through my notes about our story.'

Now this reprehensible youth who left me, a little hurt and put back, might for aught he or I knew have been one of the crew of the Argo – had been certainly slave or comrade to Thorfin Karlsefne. Therefore he was deeply interested in guinea competitions. Remembering what Grish Chunder had said I laughed aloud. The Lords of Life and Death would never allow Charlie Mears to speak with full knowledge of his pasts, and I must even piece out what he had told me with my own poor inventions while Charlie wrote of the ways of bank-clerks.

I got together and placed on one file all my notes; and the net result was not cheering. I read them a second time. There was nothing that might not have been compiled at second-hand from other people's books – except, perhaps, the story of the fight in the harbour. The adventures of a Viking had been written many times before; the history of a Greek galley-slave was no new thing, and though I wrote both, who could challenge or confirm the accuracy of my details? I might as well tell a tale of two thousand years hence. The Lords of Life and Death were as cunning as Grish Chunder had hinted. They would allow nothing to escape that might trouble or make easy the minds of men. Though I was convinced of this, yet I could not leave the tale alone. Exaltation followed reaction, not once, but twenty times in the next few weeks. My moods varied with the March sunlight and flying clouds. By night or in the beauty of a spring morning I perceived that I could write that tale and shift continents thereby. In the wet windy afternoons, I saw that the tale might indeed be written, but would be nothing more than a faked, false-varnished, sham-rusted piece of Wardour Street work in the end. Then I blessed Charlie in many ways – though it was no fault of his. He seemed to be busy with prize competitions, and I saw less and less of him as the weeks went by and the earth cracked and grew ripe to spring, and the buds swelled in their sheaths. He did not care to read or talk of what he had read, and there was a new ring of self-assertion in his voice. I hardly cared to remind him of the galley when we met; but Charlie alluded to it on every occasion, always as a story from which money was to be made.

'I think I deserve twenty-five per cent, don't I, at least?' he said, with beautiful frankness. 'I supplied all the ideas, didn't I?'

This greediness for silver was a new side in his nature. I assumed that it had been developed in the City, where Charlie was picking up the curious nasal drawl of the underbred City man.

'When the thing's done we'll talk about it. I can't make anything of it at present. Red-haired or black-haired heroes are equally difficult.'

He was sitting by the fire staring at the red coals. '*I* can't understand what you find so difficult. It's all as clear as mud to me,' he replied. A jet of gas puffed out between the bars, took light, and whistled softly. 'Suppose we take the red-haired hero's adventures first, from the time that he came south to my galley and captured it and sailed to the Beaches.'

I knew better now than to interrupt Charlie. I was out of reach of pen and paper, and dared not move to get them lest I should break the current. The gas-jet puffed and whinnied, Charlie's voice dropped almost to a whisper, and he told a tale of the sailing of an open galley to Furdurstrandi, of sunsets on the open sea, seen under the curve of the one sail evening after evening when the galley's beak was notched into the centre of the sinking disc, and 'we sailed by that for we had no other guide', quoth Charlie. He spoke of a landing on an island and explorations in its woods, where the crew killed three men whom they found asleep under the pines. Their ghosts, Charlie said, followed the galley, swimming and choking in the water, and the crew cast lots and threw one of their number overboard as a sacrifice to the strange gods whom they had offended. Then they ate seaweed when their provisions failed, and their legs swelled, and their leader, the red-haired man, killed two rowers who mutinied, and after a year spent among the woods they set sail for their own country, and a wind that never failed carried them back so safely that they all slept at night. This, and much more Charlie told. Sometimes the voice fell so low that I could not catch the words, though every nerve was on the strain. He spoke of their leader, the red-haired man, as a pagan speaks of his God; for it was he who cheered them and slew them impartially as he thought best for their needs; and it was he who steered them for three days among floating ice, each floe crowded with strange beasts that 'tried to sail with us', said Charlie, 'and we beat them back with the handles of the oars.'

The gas-jet went out, a burnt coal gave way, and the fire settled with a tiny crash to the bottom of the grate. Charlie ceased speaking, and I said no word.

'By Jove!' he said at last, shaking his head. 'I've been staring at the fire till I'm dizzy. What was I going to say?'

'Something about the galley-book.'

'I remember now. It's twenty-five per cent of the profits, isn't it?'

'It's anything you like when I've done the tale.'

'I wanted to be sure of that. I must go now. I've – I've an appointment.' And he left me.

Had not my eyes been held I might have known that that broken muttering over the fire was the swan-song of Charlie Mears. But I thought it the prelude to fuller revelation. At last and at last I should cheat the Lords of Life and Death!

When next Charlie came to me I received him with rapture. He was nervous and embarrassed, but his eyes were very full of light, and his lips a little parted.

'I've done a poem,' he said; and then, quickly: 'It's the best I've ever done. Read it.' He thrust it into my hand and retreated to the window.

I groaned inwardly. It would be the work of half an hour to criticise – that is to say, praise – the poem sufficiently to please Charlie. Then I had good reason to groan, for Charlie, discarding his favourite centipede metres, had launched into shorter and choppier verse, and verse with a motive at the back of it. This is what I read:–

'The day is most fair, the cheery wind
    Halloos behind the hill,
Where he bends the wood as seemeth good,
    And the sapling to his will!
Riot, O wind; there is that in my blood
    That would not have thee still!

'She gave me herself, O Earth, O Sky;
    Gray sea, she is mine alone!
Let the sullen boulders hear my cry,
    And rejoice tho' they be but stone!

'Mine! I have won her, O good brown earth,
    Make merry! 'Tis hard on Spring;
    Make merry; my love is doubly worth
    All worship your fields can bring!
Let the hind that tills you feel my mirth
    At the early harrowing!'

'Yes, it's the early harrowing, past a doubt,' I said, with a dread at my heart. Charlie smiled, but did not answer.

'Red cloud of the sunset, tell it abroad;
I am victor. Greet me, O Sun,
Dominant master and absolute lord
Over the soul of one!'

'Well?' said Charlie, looking over my shoulder.

I thought it far from well, and very evil indeed, when he silently laid a photograph on the paper – the photograph of a girl with a curly head and a foolish slack mouth.

'Isn't it – isn't it wonderful?' he whispered, pink to the tips of his ears, wrapped in the rosy mystery of first love. 'I didn't know; I didn't think – it came like a thunderclap.'

'Yes. It comes like a thunderclap. Are you very happy, Charlie?'

'My God – she – she loves me!' He sat down repeating the last words to himself. I looked at the hairless face, the narrow shoulders already bowed by desk-work, and wondered when, where, and how he had loved in his past lives.

'What will your mother say?' I asked cheerfully.

'I don't care a damn what she says!'

At twenty the things for which one does not care a damn should, properly, be many, but one must not include mothers in the list. I told him this gently; and he described Her, even as Adam must have described to the newly named beasts the glory and tenderness and beauty of Eve. Incidentally I learned that She was a tobacconist's assistant with a weakness for pretty dress, and had told him four or five times already that She had never been kissed by a man before.

Charlie spoke on and on, and on; while I, separated from him by thousands of years, was considering the beginnings of things. Now I understood why the Lords of Life and Death shut the doors so carefully behind us. It is that we may not remember our first and most beautiful wooings. Were this not so, our world would be without inhabitants in a hundred years.

'Now, about that galley-story,' I said still more cheerfully, in a pause in the rush of the speech.

Charlie looked up as though he had been hit. 'The galley – what galley? Good heavens, don't joke, man! This is serious! You don't know how serious it is!'

Grish Chunder was right. Charlie had tasted the love of woman that kills remembrance, and the finest story in the world would never be written.

The Miracle of Purun Bhagat

The night we felt the earth would move
  We stole and plucked him by the hand,
Because we loved him with the love
  That knows but cannot understand.

And when the roaring hillside broke,
  And all our world fell down in rain,
We saved him, we the Little Folk;
  But lo! he does not come again!

Mourn now, we saved him for the sake
  Of such poor love as wild ones may.
Mourn ye! Our brother will not wake,
  And his own kind drive us away!

Dirge of the Langurs

There was once a man in India who was Prime Minister of one of the semi-independent native States in the north-western part of the country. He was a Brahmin, so high-caste that caste ceased to have any particular meaning for him; and his father had been an important official in the gay-coloured tag-rag and bobtail of an old-fashioned Hindu Court. But as Purun Dass grew up he felt that the old order of things was changing, and that if any one wished to get on in the world he must stand well with the English, and imitate all that the English believed to be good. At the same time a native official must keep his own master's favour. This was a difficult game, but the quiet, close-mouthed young Brahmin, helped by a good English education at a Bombay University, played it coolly, and rose, step by step, to be Prime Minister of the kingdom. That is to say, he held more real power than his master, the Maharajah.

When the old king – who was suspicious of the English, their railways and telegraphs – died, Purun Dass stood high with his young successor, who had been tutored by an Englishman; and between them, though he always took care that his master should have the credit, they established schools for little girls, made roads, and started State dispensaries and shows of agricultural implements, and published a yearly blue-book on the 'Moral and Material Progress of the State', and the Foreign

Office and the Government of India were delighted. Very few native States take up English progress altogether, for they will not believe, as Purun Dass showed he did, that what was good for the Englishman must be twice as good for the Asiatic. The Prime Minister became the honoured friend of Viceroys, and Governors, and Lieutenant-Governors, and medical missionaries, and common missionaries, and hard-riding English officers who came to shoot in the State preserves, as well as of whole hosts of tourists who travelled up and down India in the cold weather, showing how things ought to be managed. In his spare time he would endow scholarships for the study of medicine and manufactures on strictly English lines, and write letters to the *Pioneer*, the greatest Indian daily paper, explaining his master's aims and objects.

At last he went to England on a visit, and had to pay enormous sums to the priests when he came back; for even so high-caste a Brahmin as Purun Dass lost caste by crossing the black sea. In London he met and talked with every one worth knowing – men whose names go all over the world – and saw a great deal more than he said. He was given honorary degrees by learned universities, and he made speeches and talked of Hindu social reform to English ladies in evening dress, till all London cried, 'This is the most fascinating man we have ever met at dinner since cloths were first laid.'

When he returned to India there was a blaze of glory, for the Viceroy himself made a special visit to confer upon the Maharajah the Grand Cross of the Star of India – all diamonds and ribbons and enamel; and at the same ceremony, while the cannon boomed, Purun Dass was made a Knight Commander of the Order of the Indian Empire; so that his name stood Sir Purun Dass, KCIE.

That evening, at dinner in the big Viceregal tent, he stood up with the badge and the collar of the Order on his breast, and replying to the toast of his master's health, made a speech few Englishmen could have bettered.

Next month, when the city had returned to its sun-baked quiet, he did a thing no Englishman would have dreamed of doing; for, so far as the world's affairs went, he died. The jewelled order of his knighthood went back to the Indian

Government, and a new Prime Minister was appointed to the charge of affairs, and a great game of General Post began in all the subordinate appointments. The priests knew what had happened, and the people guessed; but India is the one place in the world where a man can do as he pleases and nobody asks why; and the fact that Dewan Sir Purun Dass, KCIE, had resigned position, palace, and power, and taken up the begging-bowl and ochre-coloured dress of a Sunnyasi, or holy man, was considered nothing extraordinary. He had been, as the Old Law recommends, twenty years a youth, twenty years a fighter, – though he had never carried a weapon in his life, – and twenty years head of a household. He had used his wealth and his power for what he knew both to be worth; he had taken honour when it came his way; he had seen men and cities far and near, and men and cities had stood up and honoured him. Now he would let these things go, as a man drops the cloak he no longer needs.

Behind him, as he walked through the city gates, an antelope skin and brass-handled crutch under his arm, and a begging-bowl of polished brown *coco-de-mer* in his hand, barefoot, alone, with eyes cast on the ground – behind him they were firing salutes from the bastions in honour of his happy successor. Purun Dass nodded. All that life was ended; and he bore it no more ill-will or good-will than a man bears to a colourless dream of the night. He was a Sunnyasi – a houseless, wandering mendicant, depending on his neighbours for his daily bread; and so long as there is a morsel to divide in India, neither priest nor beggar starves. He had never in his life tasted meat, and very seldom eaten even fish. A five-pound note would have covered his personal expenses for food through any one of the many years in which he had been absolute master of millions of money. Even when he was being lionised in London he had held before him his dream of peace and quiet – the long, white, dusty Indian road, printed all over with bare feet, the incessant, slow-moving traffic, and the sharp-smelling wood smoke curling up under the fig-trees in the twilight, where the wayfarers sit at their evening meal.

When the time came to make that dream true the Prime Minister took the proper steps, and in three days you might more easily have found a bubble in the trough of the long Atlantic seas than Purun Dass among the roving, gathering, separating millions of India.

At night his antelope skin was spread where the darkness overtook him – sometimes in a Sunnyasi monastery by the roadside; sometimes by a mud-pillar shrine of Kala Pir, where the Jogis, who are another misty division of holy men, would receive him as they do those who know what castes and divisions are worth; sometimes on the outskirts of a little Hindu village, where the children would steal up with the food their parents had prepared; and sometimes on the pitch of the bare grazing-grounds, where the flame of his stick fire waked the drowsy camels. It was all one to Purun Dass – or Purun Bhagat, as he called himself now. Earth, people, and food were all one. But unconsciously his feet drew him away northward and eastward; from the south to Rohtak; from Rohtak to Kurnool; from Kurnool to ruined Samanah, and then up-stream along the dried bed of the Gugger river that fills only when the rain falls in the hills, till one day he saw the far line of the great Himalayas.

Then Purun Bhagat smiled, for he remembered that his mother was of Rajput Brahmin birth, from Kulu way – a Hill-woman, always homesick for the snows – and that the least touch of Hill blood draws a man in the end back to where he belongs.

'Yonder,' said Purun Bhagat, breasting the lower slopes of the Sewaliks, where the cacti stand up like seven-branched candle-sticks – 'yonder I shall sit down and get knowledge'; and the cool wind of the Himalayas whistled about his ears as he trod the road that led to Simla.

The last time he had come that way it had been in state, with a clattering cavalry escort, to visit the gentlest and most affable of Viceroys; and the two had talked for an hour together about mutual friends in London, and what the Indian common folk really thought of things. This time Purun Bhagat paid no calls, but leaned on the rail of the Mall, watching that glorious view of the Plains spread out forty miles below, till a native Mohammedan policeman told him he was obstructing traffic; and Purun Bhagat salaamed reverently to the Law, because he knew the value of it, and was seeking for a Law of his own. Then he moved on, and slept that night in an empty hut at Chota Simla, which looks like the very last end of the earth, but it was only the beginning of his journey.

He followed the Himalaya–Thibet road, the little ten-foot track that is blasted out of solid rock, or strutted out on timbers over gulfs a thousand feet deep; that dips into warm, wet, shut-in valleys, and climbs out across bare, grassy hill-shoulders where the sun strikes like a burning-glass; or turns through dripping, dark forests where the tree-ferns dress the trunks from head to heel, and the pheasant calls to his mate. And he met Thibetan herdsmen with their dogs and flocks of sheep, each sheep with a little bag of borax on his back, and wandering wood-cutters, and cloaked and blanketed Lamas from Thibet, coming into India on pilgrimage, and envoys of little solitary Hill-states, posting furiously on ring-streaked and piebald ponies, or the cavalcade of a Rajah paying a visit; or else for a long, clear day he would see nothing more than a black bear grunting and rooting below in the valley. When he first started, the roar of the world he had left still rang in his ears, as the roar of a tunnel rings long after the train has passed through; but when he had put the Mutteeanee Pass behind him that was all done, and Purun Bhagat was alone with himself, walking, wondering, and thinking, his eyes on the ground, and his thoughts with the clouds.

One evening he crossed the highest pass he had met till then – it had been a two-days' climb – and came out on a line of snow-peaks that banded all the horizon – mountains from fifteen to twenty thousand feet high, looking almost near enough to hit with a stone, though they were fifty or sixty miles away. The pass was crowned with dense, dark forest – deodar, walnut, wild cherry, wild olive, and wild pear, but mostly deodar, which is the Himalayan cedar; and under the shadow of the deodars stood a deserted shrine to Kali – who is Durga, who is Sitala, who is sometimes worshipped against the smallpox.

Purun Dass swept the stone floor clean, smiled at the grinning statue, made himself a little mud fireplace at the back of the shrine, spread his antelope skin on a bed of fresh pine-needles, tucked his *bairagi* – his brass-handled crutch – under his armpit, and sat down to rest.

Immediately below him the hillside fell away, clean and

cleared for fifteen hundred feet, where a little village of stone-walled houses, with roofs of beaten earth, clung to the steep tilt. All round it the tiny terraced fields lay out like aprons of patchwork on the knees of the mountain, and cows no bigger than beetles grazed between the smooth stone circles of the threshing-floors. Looking across the valley, the eye was deceived by the size of things, and could not at first realise that what seemed to be low scrub, on the opposite mountain-flank, was in truth a forest of hundred-foot pines. Purun Bhagat saw an eagle swoop across the gigantic hollow, but the great bird dwindled to a dot ere it was half-way over. A few bands of scattered clouds strung up and down the valley, catching on a shoulder of the hills, or rising up and dying out when they were level with the head of the pass. And 'Here shall I find peace,' said Purun Bhagat.

Now, a Hill-man makes nothing of a few hundred feet up or down, and as soon as the villagers saw the smoke in the deserted shrine, the village priest climbed up the terraced hillside to welcome the stranger.

When he met Purun Bhagat's eyes – the eyes of a man used to control thousands – he bowed to the earth, took the begging-bowl without a word, and returned to the village, saying, 'We have at last a holy man. Never have I seen such a man. He is of the Plains – but pale-coloured – a Brahmin of the Brahmins.' Then all the housewives of the village said, 'Think you he will stay with us?' and each did her best to cook the most savoury meal for the Bhagat. Hill-food is very simple, but with buck-wheat and Indian corn, and rice and red pepper, and little fish out of the stream in the valley, and honey from the flue-like hives built in the stone walls, and dried apricots, and turmeric, and wild ginger, and bannocks of flour, a devout woman can make good things, and it was a full bowl that the priest carried to the Bhagat. Was he going to stay? asked the priest. Would he need a *chela* – a disciple – to beg for him? Had he a blanket against the cold weather? Was the food good?

Purun Bhagat ate, and thanked the giver. It was in his mind to stay. That was sufficient, said the priest. Let the begging-bowl be placed outside the shrine, in the hollow made by those two twisted roots, and daily should the Bhagat be fed; for the village felt honoured that such a man – he looked timidly into the Bhagat's face – should tarry among them.

That day saw the end of Purun Bhagat's wanderings. He had come to the place appointed for him – the silence and the space. After this, time stopped, and he, sitting at the mouth of the shrine, could not tell whether he were alive or dead; a man with control of his limbs, or a part of the hills, and the clouds, and the shifting rain and sunlight. He would repeat a Name softly to himself a hundred hundred times, till, at each repetition, he seemed to move more and more out of his body, sweeping up to the doors of some tremendous discovery; but, just as the door was opening, his body would drag him back, and, with grief, he felt he was locked up again in the flesh and bones of Purun Bhagat.

Every morning the filled begging-bowl was laid silently in the crutch of the roots outside the shrine. Sometimes the priest brought it; sometimes a Ladakhi trader, lodging in the village, and anxious to get merit, trudged up the path; but, more often, it was the woman who had cooked the meal overnight; and she would murmur, hardly above her breath: 'Speak for me before the gods, Bhagat. Speak for such a one, the wife of so-and-so!' Now and then some bold child would be allowed the honour, and Purun Bhagat would hear him drop the bowl and run as fast as his little legs could carry him, but the Bhagat never came down to the village. It was laid out like a map at his feet. He could see the evening gatherings, held on the circle of the threshing-floors, because that was the only level ground; could see the wonderful unnamed green of the young rice, the indigo blues of the Indian corn, the dock-like patches of buckwheat, and, in its season, the red bloom of the amaranth, whose tiny seeds, being neither grain nor pulse, make a food that can be lawfully eaten by Hindus in time of fasts.

When the year turned, the roofs of the huts were all little squares of purest gold, for it was on the roofs that they laid out their cobs of the corn to dry. Hiving and harvest, rice-sowing and husking, passed before his eyes, all embroidered down there on the many-sided plots of fields, and he thought of them all, and wondered what they all led to at the long last.

Even in populated India a man cannot a day sit still before

the wild things run over him as though he were a rock; and in that wilderness very soon the wild things, who knew Kali's Shrine well, came back to look at the intruder. The *langurs*, the big gray-whiskered monkeys of the Himalayas, were, naturally, the first, for they are alive with curiosity; and when they had upset the begging-bowl, and rolled it round the floor, and tried their teeth on the brass-handled crutch, and made faces at the antelope skin, they decided that the human being who sat so still was harmless. At evening, they would leap down from the pines, and beg with their hands for things to eat, and then swing off in graceful curves. They liked the warmth of the fire, too, and huddled round it till Purun Bhagat had to push them aside to throw on more fuel; and in the morning, as often as not, he would find a furry ape sharing his blanket. All day long, one or other of the tribe would sit by his side, staring out at the snows, crooning and looking unspeakably wise and sorrowful.

After the monkeys came the *barasingh*, that big deer which is like our red deer, but stronger. He wished to rub off the velvet of his horns against the cold stones of Kali's statue, and stamped his feet when he saw the man at the shrine. But Purun Bhagat never moved, and, little by little, the royal stag edged up and nuzzled his shoulder. Purun Bhagat slid one cool hand along the hot antlers, and the touch soothed the fretted beast, who bowed his head, and Purun Bhagat very softly rubbed and ravelled off the velvet. Afterward, the *barasingh* brought his doe and fawn – gentle things that mumbled on the holy man's blanket – or would come alone at night, his eyes green in the fire-flicker, to take his share of fresh walnuts. At last, the musk-deer, the shyest and almost the smallest of the deerlets, came, too, her big rabbity ears erect; even brindled, silent *mushick-nabha* must needs find out what the light in the shrine meant, and drop out her moose-like nose into Purun Bhagat's lap, coming and going with the shadows of the fire. Purun Bhagat called them all 'my brothers', and his low call of '*Bhai! Bhai!*' would draw them from the forest at noon if they were within earshot. The Himalayan black bear, moody and suspicious – Sona, who has the V-shaped white mark under his chin – passed that way more than once; and since the Bhagat showed no fear, Sona showed no anger, but watched him, and came closer, and begged a share of the caresses, and a dole of bread or wild berries. Often, in the still dawns, when the Bhagat would climb to the very crest of the pass to watch the red day walking along the peaks of the snows, he would find Sona shuffling and grunting at his heels, thrusting a curious fore-paw under fallen trunks, and bringing it away with a *whoof* of impatience; or his early steps would wake Sona where he lay curled up, and the great brute, rising erect, would think to fight, till he heard the Bhagat's voice and knew his best friend.

Nearly all hermits and holy men who live apart from the big cities have the reputation of being able to work miracles with the wild things, but all the miracle lies in keeping still, in never making a hasty movement, and, for a long time, at least, in never looking directly at a visitor. The villagers saw the outline of the *barasingh* stalking like a shadow through the dark forest behind the shrine; saw the *minaul*, the Himalayan pheasant, blazing in her best colours before Kali's statue; and the *langurs* on their haunches, inside, playing with the walnut shells. Some of the children, too, had heard Sona singing to himself, bear-fashion, behind the fallen rocks, and the Bhagat's reputation as miracle-worker stood firm.

Yet nothing was farther from his mind than miracles. He believed that all things were one big Miracle, and when a man knows that much he knows something to go upon. He knew for a certainty that there was nothing great and nothing little in this world: and day and night he strove to think out his way into the heart of things, back to the place whence his soul had come.

So thinking, his untrimmed hair fell down about his shoulders, the stone slab at the side of the antelope skin was dented into a little hole by the foot of his brass-handled crutch, and the place between the tree-trunks, where the begging-bowl rested day after day, sunk and wore into a hollow almost as smooth as the brown shell itself; and each beast knew his exact place at the fire. The fields changed their colours with the seasons; the threshing-floors filled and emptied, and filled again and again; and again and again, when winter came, the *langurs* frisked among the branches feathered with light snow, till the mother-monkeys brought their sad-eyed little babies up from the warmer valleys with the spring. There were few changes in the village. The priest was older, and many of the little children who used to come with the begging-dish sent their own children now; and when you asked of the villagers how long their holy man had lived in Kali's Shrine at the head of the pass, they answered, 'Always.'

Then came such summer rains as had not been known in the Hills for many seasons. Through three good months the valley was wrapped in cloud and soaking mist – steady, unrelenting downfall, breaking off into thunder-shower after thunder-shower. Kali's Shrine stood above the clouds, for the most part, and there was a whole month in which the Bhagat never caught a glimpse of his village. It was packed away under a white floor of cloud that swayed and shifted and rolled on itself and bulged upward, but never broke from it piers – the streaming flanks of the valley.

All that time he heard nothing but the sound of a million little waters, overhead from the trees, and underfoot along the ground, soaking through the pine-needles, dripping from the tongues of draggled fern, and spouting in newly torn muddy channels down the slopes. Then the sun came out, and drew forth the good incense of the deodars and the rhododendrons, and that far-off, clean smell which the Hill people call 'the smell of the snows'. The hot sunshine lasted for a week, and then the rains gathered together for their last downpour, and the water fell in sheets that flayed off the skin of the ground and leaped back in mud. Purun Bhagat heaped his fire high that night, for he was sure his brothers would need warmth; but never a beast came to the shrine, though he called and called till he dropped asleep, wondering what had happened in the woods.

It was in the black heart of the night, the rain drumming like a thousand drums, that he was roused by a plucking at his blanket, and, stretching out, felt the little hand of a *langur*. 'It is better here than in the trees,' he said sleepily, loosening a fold of blanket; 'take it and be warm.' The monkey caught his hand and pulled hard. 'Is it food, then?' said Purun Bhagat. 'Wait awhile, and I will prepare some.' As he knieeled to throw fuel on the fire the *langur* ran to the door of the shrine, crooned, and ran back again, plucking at the man's knee.

'What is it? What is thy trouble, Brother?' said Purun Bhagat, for the *langur*'s eyes were full of things that he could not tell. 'Unless one of thy caste be in a trap – and none set traps here – I will not go into that weather. Look, Brother, even the *barasingh* comes for shelter!'

The deer's antlers clashed as he strode into the shrine, clashed against the grinning statue of Kali. He lowered them in Purun Bhagat's direction and stamped uneasily, hissing through his half-shut nostrils.

'Hai! Hai! Hai!' said the Bhagat, snapping his fingers. 'Is *this* payment for a night's lodging?' But the deer pushed him toward the door, and as he did so Purun Bhagat heard the sound of something opening with a sigh, and saw two slabs of the floor draw away from each other, while the sticky earth below smacked its lips.

'Now I see,' said Purun Bhagat. 'No blame to my brothers that they did not sit by the fire tonight. The mountain is falling. And yet – why should I go?' His eye fell on the empty begging-bowl, and his face changed. 'They have given me good food daily since – since I came, and, if I am not swift, tomorrow there will not be one mouth in the valley. Indeed, I must go and warn them below. Back there, Brother! Let me get to the fire.'

The *barasingh* backed unwillingly as Purun Bhagat drove a pine torch deep into the flame, twirling it till it was well lit. 'Ah! ye came to warn me,' he said, rising. 'Better than that we shall do; better than that. Out, now, and lend me thy neck, Brother, for I have but two feet.'

He clutched the bristling withers of the *barasingh* with his right hand, held the torch away with his left, and stepped out of the shrine into the desperate night. There was no breath of wind, but the rain nearly drowned the flare as the great deer hurried down the slope, sliding on his haunches. As soon as they were clear of the forest more of the Bhagat's brothers joined them. He heard, though he could not see, the *langurs* pressing about him, and behind them the *uhh! uhh!* of Sona. The rain matted his long white hair into ropes; the water splashed beneath his bare feet, and his yellow robe clung to his frail old body, but he stepped down steadily, leaning against the *bara-singh*. He was no longer a holy man, but Sir Purun Dass, KCIE, Prime Minister of no small State, a man accustomed to command, going out to save life. Down the steep, plashy path they poured all together, the Bhagat and his brothers, down and down till the deer's feet clicked and stumbled on the wall of a threshing-floor, and he snorted because he smelt Man. Now they were at the head of the one crooked village street, and the Bhagat beat with his crutch on the barred windows of the blacksmith's house, as his torch blazed up in the shelter of the eaves. 'Up and out!' cried Purun Bhagat; and he did not know his own voice, for it was years since he had spoken aloud to a man. 'The hill falls! The hill is falling! Up and out, oh, you within!'

'It is our Bhagat,' said the blacksmith's wife. 'He stands among his beasts. Gather the little ones and give the call.'

It ran from house to house, while the beasts, cramped in the narrow way, surged and huddled round the Bhagat, and Sona puffed impatiently.

The people hurried into the street – they were no more than seventy souls all told – and in the glare of the torches they saw their Bhagat holding back the terrified *barasingh*, while the monkeys plucked piteously at his skirts, and Sona sat on his haunches and roared.

'Across the valley and up the next hill!' shouted Purun Bhagat. 'Leave none behind! We follow!'

Then the people ran as only Hill folk can run, for they knew that in a landslip you must climb for the highest ground across the valley. They fled, splashing through the little river at the bottom, and panted up the terraced fields on the far side, while the Bhagat and his brethren followed. Up and up the opposite mountain they climbed, calling to each other by name – the roll-call of the village – and at their heels toiled the big *barasingh*, weighted by the failing strength of Purun Bhagat. At last the deer stopped in the shadow of a deep pine-wood, five hundred feet up the hillside. His instinct, that had warned him of the coming slide, told him he would be safe here.

Purun Bhagat dropped fainting by his side, for the chill of the rain and that fierce climb were killing him; but first he called to the scattered torches ahead, 'Stay and count your numbers'; then, whispering to the deer as he saw the lights gather in a cluster: 'Stay with me, Brother. Stay – till – I – go!'

There was a sigh in the air that grew to a mutter, and a mutter that grew to a roar, and a roar that passed all sense of hearing, and the hillside on which the villagers stood was hit in the darkness, and rocked to the blow. Then a note as steady, deep, and true as the deep C of the organ drowned everything for perhaps five minutes, while the very roots of the pines quivered to it. It died away, and the sound of the rain falling on miles of hard ground and grass changed to the muffled drum of water on soft earth. That told its own tale.

Never a villager – not even the priest – was bold enough to speak to the Bhagat who had saved their lives. They crouched under the pines and waited till the day. When it came they looked across the valley and saw that what had been forest, and terraced field, and track-threaded grazing-ground was one raw, red, fan-shaped smear, with a few trees flung head-down on the scarp. That red ran high up the hill of their refuge, damming back the little river, which had begun to spread into a brick-coloured lake. Of the village, of the road to the shrine, of the shrine itself, and the forest behind, there was no trace. For one mile in width and two thousand feet in sheer depth the mountain-side had come away bodily, planed clean from head to heel.

And the villagers, one by one, crept through the wood to pray before their Bhagat. They saw the *barasingh* standing over him, who fled when they came near, and they heard the *langurs* wailing in the branches, and Sona moaning up the hill; but their Bhagat was dead, sitting cross-legged, his back against a tree, his crutch under his armpit, and his face turned to the north-east.

The priest said: 'Behold a miracle after a miracle, for in this very attitude must all Sunnyasis be buried! Therefore where he now is we will build the temple to our holy man.'

They built the temple before a year was ended – a little stone-and-earth shrine – and they called the hill the Bhagat's Hill, and they worship there with lights and flowers and offerings to this day. But they do not know that the saint of their worship is the late Sir Purun Dass, KCIE, DCL, PH.D, etc., once Prime Minister of the progressive and enlightened State of Mohiniwala, and honorary or corresponding member of more learned and scientific societies than will ever do any good in this world or the next.

A SONG OF KABIR

Oh, light was the world that he weighed in his hands!
Oh, heavy the tale of his fiefs and his lands!
He has gone from the *guddee* and put on the shroud,
And departed in guise of *bairagi* avowed!

Now the white road to Delhi is mat for his feet,
The *sál* and the *kikar* must guard him from heat;
His home is the camp, and the waste, and the crowd –
He is seeking the Way as *bairagi* avowed!

He has looked upon Man, and his eyeballs are clear
(There was One; there is One, and but One, saith Kabir);
The Red Mist of Doing has thinned to a cloud –
He has taken the Path for *bairagi* avowed!

To learn and discern of his brother the clod,
Of his brother the brute, and his brother the God.
He has gone from the council and put on the shroud
('Can ye hear?' saith Kabir), a *bairagi* avowed!

The Bridge-Builders

The least that Findlayson, of the Public Works Department, expected was a CIE; he dreamed of a CSI: indeed his friends told him that he deserved more. For three years he had endured heat and cold, disappointment, discomfort, danger, and disease, with responsibility almost too heavy for one pair of shoulders; and day by day, through that time, the great Kashi Bridge over the Ganges had grown under his charge. Now, in less than three months, if all went well, His Excellency the Viceroy would open the bridge in state, an archbishop would bless it, the first train-load of soldiers would come over it, and there would be speeches.

Findlayson, CE, sat in his trolley on a construction-line that ran along one of the main revetments – the huge stone-faced banks that flared away north and south for three miles on either side of the river – and permitted himself to think of the end. With its approaches, his work was one mile and three-quarters in length; a lattice-girder bridge, trussed with the Findlayson truss, standing on seven-and-twenty brick piers. Each one of those piers was twenty-four feet in diameter, capped with red Agra stone and sunk eighty feet below the shifting sand of the Ganges' bed. Above them ran the railway-line fifteen feet broad; above that, again, a cart-road of eighteen feet, flanked with footpaths. At either end rose towers of red brick, loopholed for musketry and pierced for big guns, and the ramp of the road was being pushed forward to their haunches. The raw earth-ends were crawling and alive with hundreds upon hundreds of tiny asses climbing out of the yawning borrow-pit below with sackfuls of stuff; and the hot afternoon air was filled with the noise of hooves, the rattle of the drivers' sticks, and the swish and roll-down of the dirt. The river was very low, and on the dazzling white sand between the three centre piers stood squat cribs of railway-sleepers, filled within and daubed without with mud, to support the last of the girders as those were riveted up. In the little deep water left by the drought, an overhead-crane travelled to and fro along its spile-pier, jerking sections of iron into place, snorting and backing and grunting as an elephant grunts in the timber-yard. Riveters by the hundred swarmed about the lattice side-work and the iron roof of the railway-line, hung from invisible staging under the bellies of the girders, clustered round the throats of the piers, and rode on the overhang of the footpath-stanchions; their fire-pots and the spurts of flame that answered each hammer-stroke showing no more than pale yellow in the sun's glare. East and west and north and south the construction-trains rattled and shrieked up and down the embankments, the piled trucks of brown and white stone banging behind them till the side-boards were unpinned, and with a roar and a grumble a few thousand tons more material were thrown out to hold the river in place.

Findlayson, CE, turned on his trolley and looked over the face of the country that he had changed for seven miles around. Looked back on the humming village of five thousand workmen; upstream and down, along the vista of spurs and sand; across the river to the far piers, lessening in the haze; overhead to the guard-towers – and only he knew how strong those were – and with a sigh of contentment saw that his work was good. There stood his bridge before him in the sunlight, lacking only a few weeks' work on the girders of the three middle piers – his bridge, raw and ugly as original sin, but *pukka* – permanent – to endure when all memory of the builder, yea, even of the splendid Findlayson truss, had perished. Practically, the thing was done.

Hitchcock, his assistant, cantered along the line on a little switch-tailed Kabuli pony, who, through long practice, could have trotted securely over a trestle, and nodded to his chief.

'All but,' said he, with a smile.

'I've been thinking about it,' the senior answered. 'Not half a bad job for two men, is it?'

'One – and a half. 'Gad, what a Cooper's Hill cub I was when I came on the works!' Hitchcock felt very old in the crowded experiences of the past three years, that had taught him power and responsibility.

'You *were* rather a colt,' said Findlayson. 'I wonder how you'll like going back to office work when this job's over.'

'I shall hate it!' said the young man, and as he went on his eye followed Findlayson's, and he muttered, 'Isn't it damned good?'

'I think we'll go up the service together,' Findlayson said to himself. 'You're too good a youngster to waste on another man. Cub thou wast; assistant thou art. Personal assistant, and at Simla, thou shalt be, if any credit comes to me out of the business!'

Indeed, the burden of the work had fallen altogether on Findlayson and his assistant, the young man whom he had chosen because of his rawness to break to his own needs. There were labour-contractors by the half-hundred – fitters and riveters, European, borrowed from the railway workshops, with perhaps twenty white and half-caste subordinates to direct, under direction, the bevies of workmen – but none knew better than these two, who trusted each other, how the underlings were not to be trusted. They had been tried many times in sudden crises – by slipping of booms, by breaking of tackle, failure of cranes, and the wrath of the river – but no stress had brought to light any man among them whom Findlayson and Hitchcock would have honoured by working as remorselessly as they worked themselves. Findlayson thought it over from the beginning: the months of office work destroyed at a blow when the Government of India, at the last moment, added two feet to the width of the bridge, under the impression that bridges were cut out of paper, and so brought to ruin at least half an acre of calculations – and Hitchcock, new to disappointment, buried his head in his arms and wept; the heart-breaking delays over the filling of the contracts in England; the futile correspondences hinting at great wealth of commission if one, only one, rather doubtful consignment were passed; the war that followed the refusal; the careful, polite obstruction at the other end that followed the war, till young Hitchcock, putting one month's leave to another month, and borrowing ten days from Findlayson, spent his poor little savings of a year in a wild dash to London, and there, as his own tongue asserted and the later consignments proved, put the Fear of God into a man so great that he feared only Parliament, and said so till Hitchcock wrought with him across his own dinner-table, and – he feared the Kashi Bridge and all who spoke in its name. Then there was the cholera that came in the night to the village by the bridge-works; and after the cholera smote the smallpox. The fever they had always with them. Hitchcock had been appointed a magistrate of the third class with whipping powers, for the better government of the community, and Findlayson watched him wield his powers temperately, learning what to overlook and what to look after. It was a long, long reverie, and it covered storm, sudden freshets, death in every manner and shape, violent and awful rage against red tape half frenzying a mind that knows it should be busy on other things; drought, sanitation, finance; birth, wedding, burial, and riot in the village of twenty warring castes; argument, expostulation, persuasion, and the blank despair that a man goes to bed upon, thankful that his rifle is all in pieces in the gun-case. Behind everything rose the black frame of the Kashi Bridge – plate by plate, girder by girder, span by span – and each pier of it recalled Hitchcock, the all-round man, who had stood by his chief without failing from the very first to this last.

So the bridge was two men's work – unless one counted Peroo, as Peroo certainly counted himself. He was a Lascar, a Kharva from Bulsar, familiar with every port between Rockhampton and London, who had risen to the rank of serang on the British India boats, but wearying of routine musters and clean clothes had thrown up the service and gone inland, where men of his calibre were sure of employment. For his knowledge of tackle and the handling of heavy weights, Peroo was worth almost any price he might have chosen to put upon his services; but custom decreed the wage of the overhead-men, and Peroo was not within many silver pieces of his proper value. Neither running water nor extreme heights made him afraid; and, as an ex-serang, he knew how to hold authority. No piece of iron was so big or so badly placed that Peroo could not devise a tackle to lift it – a loose-ended, sagging arrangement, rigged with a scandalous amount of talking, but perfectly equal to the work in hand. It was Peroo who had saved the girder of Number Seven Pier from destruction when the new wire rope jammed in the eye of the crane, and the huge plate tilted in its slings, threatening to slide out sideways. Then the native workmen lost their heads with great shoutings, and Hitchcock's right arm was broken by a falling T-plate, and he buttoned it up in his coat and swooned, and came to and directed for four hours till Peroo, from the top of the crane, reported, 'All's well,' and the plate swung home. There was no one like Peroo, serang, to lash and guy and hold, to control the donkey-engines, to hoist a fallen locomotive craftily out of the borrow-pit into which it had tumbled; to strip and dive, if need be, to see how the concrete blocks round the piers stood the scouring of Mother Gunga, or to adventure upstream on a monsoon night and report on the state of the embankment-facings. He would interrupt the field-councils of Findlayson and Hitchcock without fear, till his wonderful English, or his still more wonderful *lingua-franca*, half Portuguese and half Malay, ran out and he was forced to take string and show the knots that he would recommend. He controlled his own gang of tacklemen – mysterious relatives from Kutch Mandvi gathered month by month and tried to the uttermost. No consideration of family or kin allowed Peroo to keep weak hands or a giddy head on the pay-roll. 'My honour is the honour of this bridge,' he would say to the about-to-be-dismissed. 'What do I care for your honour? Go and work on a steamer. That is all you are fit for.'

The little cluster of huts where he and his gang lived centred round the tattered dwelling of a sea-priest – one who had never set foot on Black Water, but had been chosen as ghostly counsellor by two generations of sea-rovers, all unaffected by port missions or those creeds which are thrust upon sailors by agencies along Thames' bank. The priest of the Lascars had nothing to do with their caste, or indeed with anything at all. He ate the offerings of his church, and slept and smoked, and slept again, 'for', said Peroo, who had haled him a thousand miles inland, 'he is a very holy man. He never cares what you eat so long as you do not eat beef, and that is good, because on land we worship Shiva, we Kharvas; but at sea on the Kumpani's boats we attend strictly to the orders of the Burra Malum (the first mate), and on this bridge we observe what Finlinson Sahib says.'

Findlayson Sahib had that day given orders to clear the scaffolding from the guard-tower on the right bank, and Peroo with his mates was casting loose and lowering down the bamboo poles and planks as swiftly as ever they had whipped the cargo out of a coaster.

From his trolley he could hear the whistle of the serang's silver pipe and the creak and clatter of the pulleys. Peroo was standing on the topmost coping of the tower, clad in the blue dungaree of his abandoned service, and as Findlayson motioned to him to be careful, for his was no life to throw away, he gripped the last pole, and, shading his eyes ship-fashion, answered with the long-drawn wail of the fo'c'sle look-out: '*Ham dekhta hai*' ['I am looking out']. Findlayson laughed, and then sighed. It was years since he had seen a steamer, and he was sick for home. As his trolley passed under the tower, Peroo descended by a rope, ape-fashion, and cried: 'It looks well now, Sahib. Our bridge is all but done. What think you Mother Gunga will say when the rail runs over?'

'She has said little so far. It was never Mother Gunga that delayed us.'

'There is always time for her; and none the less there has been delay. Has the Sahib forgotten last autumn's flood, when the stone-boats were sunk without warning – or only a half-day's warning?'

'Yes, but nothing save a big flood could hurt us now. The spurs are holding well on the west bank.'

'Mother Gunga eats great allowances. There is always room for more stone on the revetments. I tell this to the Chota Sahib' – he meant Hitchcock – 'and he laughs.'

'No matter, Peroo. Another year thou wilt be able to build a bridge in thine own fashion.'

The Lascar grinned. 'Then it will not be in this way – with stonework sunk under water, as the *Quetta* was sunk. I like sus-sus-pen-sheen bridges that fly from bank to bank, with one big step, like a gang-plank. Then no water can hurt. When does the Lord Sahib come to open the bridge?'

'In three months, when the weather is cooler.'

'Ho! ho! He is like the Burra Malum. He sleeps below while the work is being done. Then he comes upon the quarter-deck and touches with his finger, and says: "This is not clean! Dam jiboonwallah!" '

'But the Lord Sahib does not call me a dam jiboonwallah, Peroo.'

'No, Sahib; but he does not come on deck till the work is all finished. Even the Burra Malum of the *Nerbudda* said once at Tuticorin——'

'Bah! Go! I am busy.'

'I, also!' said Peroo, with an unshaken countenance. 'May I take the light dinghy now and row along the spurs?'

'To hold them with thy hands? They are, I think, sufficiently heavy.'

'Nay, Sahib. It is thus. At sea, on the Black Water, we have room to be blown up and down without care. Here we have no room at all. Look you, we have put the river into a dock, and run her between stone sills.'

Findlayson smiled at the 'we'.

'We have bitted and bridled her. She is not like the sea, that can beat against a soft beach. She is Mother Gunga – in irons.' His voice fell a little.

'Peroo, thou hast been up and down the world more even than I. Speak true talk, now. How much dost thou in thy heart believe of Mother Gunga?'

'All that our priest says. London is London, Sahib. Sydney is Sydney, and Port Darwin is Port Darwin. Also Mother Gunga is Mother Gunga, and when I come back to her banks I know this and worship. In London I did poojah to the big temple by the river for the sake of the God within. . . . Yes, I will not take the cushions in the dinghy.'

Findlayson mounted his horse and trotted to the shed of a bungalow that he shared with his assistant. The place had become home to him in the last three years. He had grilled in the heat, sweated in the rains, and shivered with fever under the rude thatch roof; the limewash beside the door was covered with rough drawings and formulæ, and the sentry-path trodden in the matting of the verandah showed where he had walked alone. There is no eight-hour limit to an engineer's work, and the evening meal with Hitchcock was eaten booted and spurred: over their cigars they listened to the hum of the village as the gangs came up from the river-bed and the lights began to twinkle.

'Peroo has gone up the spurs in your dinghy. He's taken a couple of nephews with him, and he's lolling in the stern like a commodore,' said Hitchcock.

'That's all right. He's got something on his mind. You'd think that ten years in the British India boats would have knocked most of his religion out of him.'

'So it has,' said Hitchcock, chuckling. 'I overheard him the other day in the middle of a most atheistical talk with that fat old *guru* of theirs. Peroo denied the efficacy of prayer; and wanted the *guru* to go to sea and watch a gale out with him, and see if he could stop a monsoon.'

'All the same, if you carried off his *guru* he'd leave us like a shot. He was yarning away to me about praying to the dome of St Paul's when he was in London.'

'He told me that the first time he went into the engine-room of a steamer, when he was a boy, he prayed to the low-pressure cylinder.'

'Not half a bad thing to pray to, either. He's propitiating his own Gods now, and he wants to know what Mother Gunga will think of a bridge being run across her. Who's there?' A shadow darkened the doorway, and a telegram was put into Hitchcock's hand.

'She ought to be pretty well used to it by this time. Only a *tar*. It ought to be Ralli's answer about the new rivets. . . . Great Heavens!' Hitchcock jumped to his feet.

'What is it?' said the senior, and took the form. '*That's* what Mother Gunga thinks, is it,' he said, reading. 'Keep cool, young 'un. We've got all our work cut for us. Let's see. Muir wires, half an hour ago: "*Floods on the Ramgunga. Look out.*" Well, that gives us – one, two – nine and a half for the flood to reach Melipur Ghaut and seven's sixteen and a half to Latodi – say fifteen hours before it comes down to us.'

'Curse that hill-fed sewer of a Ramgunga! Findlayson, this is two months before anything could have been expected, and the left bank is littered up with stuff still. Two full months before the time!'

'That's why it happens. I've only known Indian rivers for five and twenty years, and I don't pretend to understand. Here comes another *tar*.' Findlayson opened the telegram. 'Cockran, this time, from the Ganges Canal: "*Heavy rains here. Bad.*" He might have saved the last word. Well, we don't want to know any more. We've got to work the gangs all night and clean up the river-bed. You'll take the east bank and work out to meet me in the middle. Get everything that floats below the bridge: we shall have quite enough river-craft coming down adrift anyhow, without letting the stone-boats ram the piers. What have you got on the east bank that needs looking after?'

'Pontoon, one big pontoon with the overhead crane on it. T'other overhead crane on the mended pontoon, with the cart-road rivets from Twenty to Twenty-three piers – two construction lines, and a turning-spur. The pile-work must take its chance,' said Hitchcock.

'All right. Roll up everything you can lay hands on. We'll give the gang fifteen minutes more to eat their grub.'

Close to the verandah stood a big night-gong, never used except for flood, or fire in the village. Hitchcock had called for a fresh horse, and was off to his side of the bridge when Findlayson took the cloth-bound stick and smote with the rubbing stroke that brings out the full thunder of the metal.

Long before the last rumble ceased every night-gong in the village had taken up the warning. To these were added the hoarse screaming of conchs in the little temples; the throbbing of drums and tomtoms; and from the European quarters, where the riveters lived, M'Cartney's bugle, a weapon of offence on Sundays and festivals, brayed desperately, calling to 'Stables'. Engine after engine toiling home along the spurs after her day's work whistled in answer till the whistles were answered from the far bank. Then the big gong thundered thrice for a sign that it was flood and not fire; conch, drum, and whistle echoed the call, and the village quivered to the sound of bare feet running upon soft earth. The order in all cases was to stand by the day's work and wait instructions. The gangs poured by in the dusk; men stopping to knot a loin-cloth or fasten a sandal; gang-foremen shouting to their subordinates as they ran or paused by the tool-issue sheds for bars and mattocks; locomotives creeping down their tracks wheel-deep in the crowd, till the brown torrent disappeared into the dusk of the river-bed, raced over the pile-work, swarmed along the lattices, clustered by the cranes, and stood still, each man in his place.

Then the troubled beating of the gong carried the order to take up everything and bear it beyond high-water mark, and the flare-lamps broke out by the hundred between the webs of dull-iron as the riveters began a night's work racing against the flood that was to come. The girders of the three centre piers – those that stood on the cribs – were all but in position. They needed just as many rivets as could be driven into them, for the flood would assuredly wash out the supports, and the iron-work would settle down on the caps of stone if they were not blocked at the ends. A hundred crowbars strained at the sleepers of the temporary line that fed the unfinished piers. It was heaved up in lengths, loaded into trucks, and backed up the bank beyond flood-level by the groaning locomotives. The tool-sheds on the sands melted away before the attack of shouting armies, and with them went the stacked ranks of Government stores, iron-bound boxes of rivets, pliers, cutters, duplicate parts of the riveting-machines, spare pumps and chains. The big crane would be the last to be shifted, for she was hoisting all the heavy stuff up to the main structure of the bridge. The concrete blocks on the fleet of stone-boats were dropped overside, where there was any depth of water, to guard the piers, and the empty boats themselves were poled under the bridge downstream. It was here that Peroo's pipe shrilled loudest, for the first stroke of the big gong had brought back the dinghy at racing speed, and Peroo and his people were stripped to the waist, working for the honour and credit which are better than life.

'I knew she would speak,' he cried. '*I* knew, but the telegraph gave us good warning. O sons of unthinkable begetting – children of unspeakable shame – are we here for the look of the thing?' It was two feet of wire rope frayed at the ends, and it did wonders as Peroo leaped from gunnel to gunnel, shouting the language of the sea.

Findlayson was more troubled for the stone-boats than anything else. M'Cartney, with his gangs, was blocking up the ends of the three doubtful spans, but boats adrift, if the flood chanced to be a high one, might endanger the girders; and there was a very fleet in the shrunken channels.

'Get them behind the swell of the guard-tower,' he shouted to Peroo. 'It will be dead-water there; get them below the bridge.'

'*Accha*! [Very good.] *I* know. We are mooring them with wire rope,' was the answer. 'Heh! Listen to the Chota Sahib. He is working hard.'

From across the river came an almost continuous whistling of locomotives, backed by the rumble of stone. Hitchcock at the last minute was spending a few hundred more trucks of Tarakee stone in reinforcing his spurs and embankments.

'The bridge challenges Mother Gunga,' said Peroo, with a laugh. 'But when *she* talks I know whose voice will be the loudest.'

For hours the naked men worked, screaming and shouting under the lights. It was a hot, moonless night; the end of it was darkened by clouds and a sudden squall that made Findlayson very grave.

'She moves!' said Peroo, just before the dawn. 'Mother Gunga is awake! Hear!' He dipped his hand over the side of a boat and the current mumbled on it. A little wave hit the side of a pier with a crisp slap.

'Six hours before her time,' said Findlayson, mopping his forehead savagely. 'Now we can't depend on anything. We'd better clear all hands out of the river-bed.'

Again the big gong beat, and a second time there was the rushing of naked feet on earth and ringing iron; the clatter of tools ceased. In the silence, men heard the dry yawn of water crawling over thirsty sand.

Foreman after foreman shouted to Findlayson, who had posted himself by the guard-tower, that his section of the river-bed had been cleaned out, and when the last voice dropped Findlayson hurried over the bridge till the iron plating of the permanent way gave place to the temporary plank-walk over the three centre piers, and there he met Hitchcock.

''All clear your side?' said Findlayson. The whisper rang in the box of latticework.

'Yes, and the east channel's filling now. We're utterly out of our reckoning. When is this thing down on us?'

'There's no saying. She's filling as fast as she can. Look!' Findlayson pointed to the planks below his feet, where the sand, burned and defiled by months of work, was beginning to whisper and fizz.

'What orders?' said Hitchcock.

'Call the roll – count stores – sit on your hunkers – and pray for the bridge. That's all I can think of. Good-night. Don't risk your life trying to fish out anything that may go downstream.'

'Oh, I'll be as prudent as you are! 'Night. Heavens, how she's filling! Here's the rain in earnest!' Findlayson picked his way back to his bank, sweeping the last of M'Cartney's riveters before him. The gangs had spread themselves along the embankments, regardless of the cold rain of the dawn, and there they waited for the flood. Only Peroo kept his men together behind the swell of the guard-tower, where the stone-boats lay tied fore and aft with hawsers, wire-rope, and chains.

A shrill wail ran along the line, growing to a yell, half fear and half wonder: the face of the river whitened from bank to bank between the stone facings, and the far-away spurs went out in spouts of foam. Mother Gunga had come bank-high in haste, and a wall of chocolate-coloured water was her messenger. There was a shriek above the roar of the water, the complaint of the spans coming down on their blocks as the cribs were whirled out from under their bellies. The stone-boats groaned and ground each other in the eddy that swung round the abutment, and their clumsy masts rose higher and higher against the dim sky-line.

'Before she was shut between these walls we knew what she would do. Now she is thus cramped God only knows what she will do!' said Peroo, watching the furious turmoil round the guard-tower. 'Ohé! Fight, then! Fight hard, for it is thus that a woman wears herself out.'

But Mother Gunga would not fight as Peroo desired. After the first downstream plunge there came no more walls of water, but the river lifted herself bodily, as a snake when she drinks in midsummer, plucking and fingering along the revetments, and banking up behind the piers till even Findlayson began to recalculate the strength of his work.

When day came the village gasped. 'Only last night,' men said, turning to each other, 'it was as a town in the river-bed! Look now!'

And they looked and wondered afresh at the deep water, the racing water that licked the throat of the piers. The farther bank was veiled by rain, into which the bridge ran out and vanished;

the spurs upstream were marked by no more than eddies and spoutings, and downstream the pent river, once freed of her guide-lines, had spread like a sea to the horizon. Then hurried by, rolling in the water, dead men and oxen together, with here and there a patch of thatched roof that melted when it touched a pier.

'Big flood,' said Peroo, and Findlayson nodded. It was as big a flood as he had any wish to watch. His bridge would stand what was upon her now, but not very much more; and if by any of a thousand chances there happened to be a weakness in the embankments, Mother Gunga would carry his honour to the sea with the other raffle. Worst of all, there was nothing to do except to sit still; and Findlayson sat still under his macintosh till his helmet became pulp on his head, and his boots were over-ankle in mire. He took no count of time, for the river was marking the hours, inch by inch and foot by foot, along the embankment, and he listened, numb and hungry, to the straining of the stone-boats, the hollow thunder under the piers, and the hundred noises that make the full note of a flood. Once a dripping servant brought him food, but he could not eat; and once he thought that he heard a faint toot from a locomotive across the river, and then he smiled. The bridge's failure would hurt his assistant not a little, but Hitchcock was a young man with his big work yet to do. For himself the crash meant everything – everything that made a hard life worth the living. They would say, the men of his own profession—— he remembered the half-pitying things that he himself had said when Lockhart's big water-works burst and broke down in brick heaps and sludge, and Lockhart's spirit broke in him and he died. He remembered what he himself had said when the Sumao Bridge went out in the big cyclone by the sea; and most he remembered poor Hartopp's face three weeks later, when the shame had marked it. His bridge was twice the size of Hartopp's, and it carried the Findlayson truss as well as the new pier-shoe – the Findlayson bolted shoe. There were no excuses in his service. Government might listen, perhaps, but his own kind would judge him by his bridge, as that stood or fell. He went over it in his head, plate by plate, span by span, brick by brick, pier by pier, remembering, comparing, estimating, and recalculating, lest there should be any mistake; and through the long hours and through the flights of formulæ that danced and wheeled before him a cold fear would come to pinch his heart. His side of the sum was beyond question; but what man knew Mother Gunga's arithmetic? Even as he was making all sure by the multiplication-table, the river might be scooping pot-holes to the very bottom of any one of those eighty-foot piers that carried his reputation. Again a servant came to him with food, but his mouth was dry, and he could only drink and return to the decimals in his brain. And the river was still rising. Peroo, in a mat shelter-coat, crouched at his feet, watching now his face and now the face of the river, but saying nothing.

At last the Lascar rose and floundered through the mud towards the village, but he was careful to leave an ally to watch the boats.

Presently he returned, most irreverently driving before him the priest of his creed – a fat old man, with a grey beard that whipped the wind with the wet cloth that blew over his shoulder. Never was seen so lamentable a *guru*.

'What good are offerings and little kerosene lamps and dry grain,' shouted Peroo, 'if squatting in the mud is all that thou canst do? Thou hast dealt long with the Gods when they were contented and well-wishing. Now they are angry. Speak to them!'

'What is a man against the wrath of Gods?' whined the priest, cowering as the wind took him. 'Let me go to the temple, and I will pray there.'

'Son of a pig, pray *here*! Is there no return for salt fish and curry powder and dried onions? Call aloud! Tell Mother Gunga we have had enough. Bid her be still for the night. I cannot pray, but I have served in the Kumpani's boats, and when men did not obey my orders I——' A flourish of the wire-rope colt rounded the sentence, and the priest, breaking from his disciple, fled to the village.

'Fat pig!' said Peroo. 'After all that we have done for him! When the flood is down I will see to it that we get a new *guru*. Finlinson Sahib, it darkens for night now, and since yesterday nothing has been eaten. Be wise, Sahib. No man can endure watching and great thinking on an empty belly. Lie down, Sahib. The river will do what the river will do.'

'The bridge is mine; I cannot leave it.'

'Wilt thou hold it up with thy hands, then?' said Peroo, laughing. 'I was troubled for my boats and sheers *before* the flood came. Now we are in the hands of the Gods. The Sahib will not eat and lie down? Take these, then. They are meat and good toddy together, and they kill all weariness, besides the fever that follows the rain. I have eaten nothing else today at all.'

He took a small tin tobacco-box from his sodden waist-belt and thrust it into Findlayson's hand, saying, 'Nay, do not be afraid. It is no more than opium – clean Malwa opium!'

Findlayson shook two or three of the dark-brown pellets into his hand, and hardly knowing what he did, swallowed them. The stuff was at least a good guard against fever – the fever that was creeping upon him out of the wet mud – and he had seen what Peroo could do in the stewing mists of autumn on the strength of a dose from the tin box.

Peroo nodded with bright eyes. 'In a little – in a little the Sahib will find that he thinks well again. I too will——' He dived into his treasure-box, resettled the rain-coat over his head, and squatted down to watch the boats. It was too dark now to see beyond the first pier, and the night seemed to have given the river new strength. Findlayson stood with his chin on his chest, thinking. There was one point about one of the piers – the Seventh – that he had not fully settled in his mind. The figures would not shape themselves to the eye except one by one and at enormous intervals of time. There was a sound, rich and mellow in his ears, like the deepest note of a double-bass – an entrancing sound upon which he pondered for several hours, as it seemed. Then Peroo was at his elbow, shouting that a wire hawser had snapped and the stone-boats were loose. Findlayson saw the fleet open and swing out fanwise to a long-drawn shriek of wire straining across gunnels.

'A tree hit them. They will all go,' cried Peroo. 'The main hawser has parted. What does the Sahib do?'

An immensely complex plan had suddenly flashed into Findlayson's mind. He saw the ropes running from boat to boat in straight lines and angles – each rope a line of white fire. But there was one rope which was the master-rope. He could see that rope. If he could pull it once, it was absolutely and mathematically certain that the disordered fleet would reassemble itself in the backwater behind the guard-tower. But why, he wondered, was Peroo clinging so desperately to his waist as he hastened down the bank? It was necessary to put the Lascar aside, gently and slowly, because it was necessary to save the boats, and, further, to demonstrate the extreme ease of the problem that looked so difficult. And then – but it was of no conceivable importance – a wire rope raced through his hand, burning it, the high bank disappeared, and with it all the slowly dispersing factors of the problem. He was sitting in the rainy darkness – sitting in a boat that spun like a top, and Peroo was standing over him.

'I had forgotten,' said the Lascar slowly, 'that to those fasting and unused the opium is worse than any wine. Those who die in Gunga go to the Gods. Still, I have no desire to present myself before such great ones. Can the Sahib swim?'

'What need? He can fly – fly as swiftly as the wind,' was the thick answer.

'He is mad!' muttered Peroo under his breath. 'And he threw me aside like a bundle of dung-cakes. Well, he will not know his death. The boat cannot live an hour here even if she strike nothing. It is not good to look at death with a clear eye.'

He refreshed himself again from the tin box, squatted down in the bows of the reeling, pegged, and stitched craft, staring through the mist at the nothing that was there. A warm drowsiness crept over Findlayson, the Chief Engineer, whose duty was with his bridge. The heavy raindrops struck him with a thousand tingling little thrills, and the weight of all time since time was made hung heavy on his eyelids. He thought and perceived that he was perfectly secure, for the water was so solid that a man could surely step out upon it, and, standing still with his legs apart to keep his balance – this was the most important point – would be borne with great and easy speed to the shore. But yet a better plan came to him. It needed only an exertion of will for the soul to hurl the body ashore as wind drives paper; to waft it kite-fashion to the bank. Thereafter – the boat spun dizzily – suppose the high wind got under the freed body? Would it tower up like a kite and pitch headlong on the far-away sands, or would it duck about beyond control through all eternity? Findlayson gripped the gunnel to anchor himself, for it seemed that he was on the edge of taking the flight before he had settled all his plans. Opium has more effect on the white man than the black. Peroo was only comfortably indifferent to accidents. 'She cannot live,' he grunted. 'Her seams open already. If she were even a dinghy with oars we could have ridden it out; but a box with holes is no good. Finlinson Sahib, she fills.'

'*Accha!* I am going away. Come thou also.'

In his mind Findlayson had already escaped from the boat, and was circling high in air to find a rest for the sole of his foot. His body – he was really sorry for its gross helplessness – lay in the stern, the water rushing about its knees.

'How very ridiculous!' he said to himself, from his eyrie; 'that – is Findlayson – chief of the Kashi Bridge. The poor beast is going to be drowned, too. Drowned when it's close to shore. I'm – I'm on shore already. Why doesn't it come along?'

To his intense disgust, he found his soul back in his body again, and that body spluttering and choking in deep water. The pain of the reunion was atrocious, but it was necessary, also, to fight for the body. He was conscious of grasping wildly at wet sand, and striding prodigiously, as one strides in a dream, to keep foot-hold in the swirling water, till at last he hauled himself clear of the hold of the river, and dropped, panting, on wet earth.

'Not this night,' said Peroo in his ear. 'The Gods have protected us.' The Lascar moved his feet cautiously, and they rustled among dried stumps. 'This is some island of last year's indigo crop,' he went on. 'We shall find no men here; but have great care, Sahib; all the snakes of a hundred miles have been flooded out. Here comes the lightning, on the heels of the wind. Now we shall be able to look; but walk carefully.'

Findlayson was far and far beyond any fear of snakes, or indeed any merely human emotion. He saw, after he had rubbed the water from his eyes, with an immense clearness, and trod, so it seemed to himself, with world-encompassing strides.

Somewhere in the night of time he had built a bridge – a bridge that spanned illimitable levels of shining seas; but the Deluge had swept it away, leaving this one island under heaven for Findlayson and his companion, sole survivors of the breed of man.

An incessant lightning, forked and blue, showed all that there was to be seen on the little patch in the flood – a clump of thorn, a clump of swaying creaking bamboos, and a grey gnarled peepul overshadowing a Hindoo shrine, from whose dome floated a tattered red flag. The holy man whose summer resting-place it was had long since abandoned it, and the weather had broken the red-daubed image of his God. The two men stumbled, heavy-limbed and heavy-eyed, over the ashes of a brick-set cooking-place, and dropped down under the shelter of the branches, while the rain and river roared together.

The stumps of the indigo crackled, and there was a smell of cattle, as a huge and dripping Brahminee Bull shouldered his way under the tree. The flashes revealed the trident mark of Shiva on his flank, the insolence of head and hump, the luminous stag-like eyes, the brow crowned with a wreath of sodden marigold blooms, and the silky dewlap that nigh swept the ground.. There was a noise behind him of other beasts coming up from the flood-line through the thicket, a sound of heavy feet and deep breathing.

'Here be more beside ourselves,' said Findlayson, his head against the tree-pole, looking through half-shut eyes, wholly at ease.

'Truly,' said Peroo thickly, 'and no small ones.'

'What are they, then? I do not see clearly.'

'The Gods. Who else? Look!'

'Ah, true! The Gods surely – the Gods.' Findlayson smiled as his head fell forward on his chest. Peroo was eminently right. After the Flood, who should be alive in the land except the Gods that made it – the Gods to whom his village prayed nightly – the Gods who were in all men's mouths and about all men's ways? He could not raise his head or stir a finger for the trance that held him, and Peroo was smiling vacantly at the lightning.

The Bull paused by the shrine, his head lowered to the damp earth. A green Parrot in the branches preened his wet wings and screamed against the thunder as the circle under the tree filled with the shifting shadows of beasts. There was a Black-buck at the Bull's heels – such a buck as Findlayson in his far-away life upon earth might have seen in dreams – a buck with a royal head, ebon back, silver belly, and gleaming straight horns. Beside him, her head bowed to the ground, the green eyes burning under the heavy brows, with restless tail switching the dead grass, paced a Tigress, full-bellied and deep-jowled.

The Bull crouched beside the shrine, and there leaped from the darkness a monstrous grey Ape, who seated himself man-wise in the place of the fallen image, and the rain spilled like jewels from the hair of his neck and shoulders.

Other shadows came and went behind the circle, among them a drunken Man flourishing staff and drinking-bottle. Then a hoarse bellow broke out from near the ground. 'The flood lessens even now,' it cried. 'Hour by hour the water falls, and their bridge still stands!'

'My bridge,' said Findlayson to himself. 'That must be very old work now. What have the Gods to do with my bridge?'

His eyes rolled in the darkness following the roar. A Crocodile – the blunt-nosed, ford-haunting Mugger of the Ganges – draggled herself before the beasts, lashing furiously to right and left with her tail.

'They have made it too strong for me. In all this night I have only torn away a handful of planks. The walls stand! The towers stand! They have chained my flood, and my river is not free any more. Heavenly Ones, take this yoke away! Give me clear water between bank and bank! It is I, Mother Gunga, that speak. The Justice of the Gods! Deal me the Justice of the Gods!'

'What said I?' whispered Peroo. 'This is in truth a Punchayet of the Gods. Now we know that all the world is dead, save you and I, Sahib.'

The Parrot screamed and fluttered again, and the Tigress, her ears flat to her head, snarled wickedly.

Somewhere in the shadow a great trunk and gleaming tusks swayed to and fro, and a low gurgle broke the silence that followed on the snarl.

'We be here,' said a deep voice, 'the Great Ones. One only

and very many. Shiv, my father, is here, with Indra. Kali has spoken already. Hanuman listens also.'

'Kashi is without her Kotwal tonight,' shouted the Man with the drinking-bottle, flinging his staff to the ground, while the island rang to the baying of hounds. 'Give her the Justice of the Gods.'

'Ye were still when they polluted my waters,' the great Crocodile bellowed. 'Ye made no sign when my river was trapped between the walls. I had no help save my own strength, and that failed – the strength of Mother Gunga failed – before their guard-towers. What could I do? I have done everything. Finish now, Heavenly Ones!'

'I brought the death; I rode the spotted sickness from hut to hut of their workmen, and yet they would not cease.' A nose-slitten, hide-worn Ass, lame, scissor-legged, and galled, limped forward. 'I cast the death at them out of my nostrils, but they would not cease.'

Peroo would have moved, but the opium lay heavy upon him.

'Bah!' he said, spitting. 'Here is Sitala herself; Mata – the small-pox. Has the Sahib a handkerchief to put over his face?'

'Small help! They fed me the corpses for a month, and I flung them out on my sand-bars, but their work went forward. Demons they are, and sons of demons! And ye left Mother Gunga alone for their fire-carriage to make a mock of. The Justice of the Gods on the bridge-builders!'

The Bull turned the cud in his mouth and answered slowly, 'If the Justice of the Gods caught all who made a mock of holy things, there would be many dark altars in the land, mother.'

'But this goes beyond a mock,' said the Tigress, darting forward a griping paw. 'Thou knowest, Shiv, and ye too, Heavenly Ones; ye know that they have defiled Gunga. Surely they must come to the Destroyer. Let Indra judge.'

The Buck made no movement as he answered, 'How long has this evil been?'

'Three years, as men count years,' said the Mugger, close pressed to the earth.

'Does Mother Gunga die, then, in a year, that she is so anxious to see vengeance now? The deep sea was where she runs but yesterday, and tomorrow the sea shall cover her again as the

Gods count that which men call time. Can any say that this their bridge endures till tomorrow?' said the Buck.

There was a long hush, and in the clearing of the storm the full moon stood up above the dripping trees.

'Judge ye, then,' said the River sullenly. 'I have spoken my shame. The flood falls still. I can do no more.'

'For my own part' – it was the voice of the great Ape seated within the shrine – 'it pleases me well to watch these men, remembering that I also builded no small bridge in the world's youth.'

'They say, too,' snarled the Tiger, 'that these men came of the wreck of thy armies, Hanuman, and therefore thou hast aided——'

'They toil as my armies toiled in Lanka, and they believe that their toil endures. Indra is too high, but Shiv, thou knowest how the land is threaded with their fire-carriages.'

'Yea, I know,' said the Bull. 'Their Gods instructed them in the matter.'

A laugh ran round the circle.

'Their Gods! What should their Gods know? They were born yesterday, and those that made them are scarcely yet cold,' said the Mugger. 'Tomorrow their Gods will die.'

'Ho!' said Peroo. 'Mother Gunga talks good talk. I told that to the padre-sahib who preached on the *Mombassa*, and he asked the Burra Malum to put me in irons for a great rudeness.'

'Surely they make these things to please their Gods,' said the Bull again.

'Not altogether,' the Elephant rolled forth. 'It is for the profit of my mahajuns – my fat money-lenders that worship me at each new year, when they draw my image at the head of the account-books. I, looking over their shoulders by lamplight, see that the names in the books are those of men in far places – for all the towns are drawn together by the fire-carriage, and the money comes and goes swiftly, and the account-books grow as fat as – myself. And I, who am Ganesh of Good Luck, I bless my peoples.'

'They have changed the face of the land – which is my land. They have killed and made new towns on my banks,' said the Mugger.

'It is but the shifting of a little dirt. Let the dirt dig in the dirt if it pleases the dirt,' answered the Elephant.

'But afterwards?' said the Tiger. 'Afterwards they will see that Mother Gunga can avenge no insult, and they fall away from her first, and later from us all, one by one. In the end, Ganesh, we are left with naked altars.'

The drunken Man staggered to his feet, and hiccupped vehemently in the face of the assembled Gods.

'Kali lies. My sister lies. Also this my stick is the Kotwal of Kashi, and he keeps tally of my pilgrims. When the time comes to worship Bhairon – and it is always time – the fire-carriages move one by one, and each bears a thousand pilgrims. They do not come afoot any more, but rolling upon wheels, and my honour is increased.'

'Gunga, I have seen thy bed at Pryag black with the pilgrims,' said the Ape, leaning forward, 'and but for the fire-carriage they would have come slowly and in fewer numbers. Remember.'

'They come to me always,' Bhairon went on thickly. 'By day and night they pray to me, all the Common People in the fields and the roads. Who is like Bhairon today? What talk is this of changing faiths? Is my staff Kotwal of Kashi for nothing? He keeps the tally, and he says that never were so many altars as today, and the fire-carriage serves them well. Bhairon am I – Bhairon of the Common People, and the chiefest of the Heavenly Ones today. Also my staff says——'

'Peace, thou!' lowed the Bull. 'The worship of the schools is mine, and they talk very wisely, asking whether I be one or many, as is the delight of my people, and ye know what I am. Kali, my wife, thou knowest also.'

'Yea, I know,' said the Tigress, with lowered head.

'Greater am I than Gunga also. For ye know who moved the minds of men that they should count Gunga holy among the rivers. Who die in that water – ye know how men say – come to us without punishment, and Gunga knows that the fire-carriage has borne to her scores upon scores of such anxious ones; and Kali knows that she has held her chiefest festivals among the pilgrimages that are fed by the fire-carriage. Who smote at Pooree, under the Image there, her thousands in a day and a night, and bound the sickness to the wheels of the fire-carriages, so that it ran from one end of the land to the other? Who but Kali? Before the fire-carriage came it was a heavy toil. The fire-carriages have served thee well, Mother of Death. But I speak for mine own altars, who am not Bhairon of the Common Folk, but Shiv. Men go to and fro, making words and telling talk of strange Gods, and I listen. Faith follows faith among my people in the schools, and I have no anger; for when the words are said, and the new talk is ended, to Shiv men return at the last.'

'True. It is true,' murmured Hanuman. 'To Shiv and to the others, mother, they return. I creep from temple to temple in the North, where they worship one God and His Prophet; and presently my image is alone within their shrines.'

'Small thanks,' said the Buck, turning his head slowly. 'I am that One and His Prophet also.'

'Even so, father,' said Hanuman. 'And to the South I go who am the oldest of the Gods as men know the Gods, and presently I touch the shrines of the new faith and the Woman whom we know is hewn twelve-armed, and still they call her Mary.'

'Small thanks, brother,' said the Tigress. 'I am that Woman.'

'Even so, sister; and I go West among the fire-carriages, and stand before the bridge-builders in many shapes, and because of me they change their faiths and are very wise. Ho! ho! I am the builder of bridges indeed – bridges between this and that, and each bridge leads surely to Us in the end. Be content, Gunga. Neither these men nor those that follow them mock thee at all.'

'Am I alone, then, Heavenly Ones? Shall I smooth out my flood lest unhappily I bear away their walls? Will Indra dry my springs in the hills and make me crawl humbly between their wharfs? Shall I bury me in the sand ere I offend?'

'And all for the sake of a little iron bar with the fire-carriage atop. Truly, Mother Gunga is always young!' said Ganesh the Elephant. 'A child had not spoken more foolishly. Let the dirt dig in the dirt ere it return to the dirt. I know only that my people grow rich and praise me. Shiv has said that the men of the schools do not forget; Bhairon is content for his crowd of the Common People: and Hanuman laughs.'

'Surely I laugh,' said the Ape. 'My altars are few beside those of Ganesh or Bhairon, but the fire-carriages bring me new worshippers from beyond the Black Water – the men who believe that their God is toil. I run before them beckoning, and they follow Hanuman.'

'Give them the toil that they desire, then,' said the River. 'Make a bar across my flood and throw the water back upon the bridge. Once thou wast strong in Lanka, Hanuman. Stoop and lift my bed.'

'Who gives life can take life.' The Ape scratched in the mud with a long forefinger. 'And yet, who would profit by the killing? Very many would die.'

There came up from the water a snatch of a love-song such as the boys sing when they watch their cattle in the noon heats of late spring. The Parrot screamed joyously, sidling along his branch with lowered head as the song grew louder, and in a patch of clear moonlight stood revealed the young herd, the darling of the Gopis, the idol of dreaming maids and of mothers ere their children are born – Krishna the Well-beloved. He stooped to knot up his long wet hair, and the Parrot fluttered to his shoulder.

'Fleeting and singing, and singing and fleeting,' hiccupped Bhairon. 'Those make thee late for the council, brother.'

'And then?' said Krishna, with a laugh, throwing back his head. 'Ye can do little without me or Karma here. He fondled the Parrot's plumage and laughed again. 'What is this sitting and talking together? I heard Mother Gunga roaring in the dark, and so came quickly from a hut where I lay warm. And what have ye done to Karma, that he is so wet and silent? And what does Mother Gunga here? Are the heavens full that ye must come paddling in the mud beast-wise? Karma, what do they do?'

'Gunga has prayed for a vengeance on the bridge-builders, and Kali is with her. Now she bids Hanuman whelm the bridge, that her honour may be made great,' cried the Parrot. 'I waited here, knowing that thou wouldst come, O my master!'

'And the Heavenly Ones said nothing? Did Gunga and the Mother of Sorrows out-talk them? Did none speak for my people?'

'Nay,' said Ganesh, moving uneasily from foot to foot; 'I said it was but dirt at play, and why should we stamp it flat?'

'I was content to let them toil – well content,' said Hanuman.

'What had I to do with Gunga's anger?' said the Bull.

'I am Bhairon of the Common Folk, and this my staff is Kotwal of all Kashi. I spoke for the Common People.'

'Thou?' The young God's eyes sparkled.

'Am I not the first of the Gods in their mouths today?' returned Bhairon, unabashed. 'For the sake of the Common People I said – very many wise things which I have now forgotten – but this my staff——'

Krishna turned impatiently, saw the Mugger at his feet, and kneeling, slipped an arm round the cold neck. 'Mother,' he said gently, 'get thee to thy flood again. The matter is not for thee. What harm shall thy honour take of this live dirt? Thou hast given them their fields new year after year, and by thy flood they are made strong. They come all to thee at the last. What need to slay them now? Have pity, mother, for a little – and it is only for a little.'

'If it be only for a little——' the slow beast began.

'Are they Gods, then?' Krishna returned with a laugh, his eyes looking into the dull eyes of the River. 'Be certain that it is only for a little. The Heavenly Ones have heard thee, and presently justice will be done. Go now, mother, to the flood again. Men and cattle are thick on the waters – the banks fall – the villages melt because of thee.'

'But the bridge – the bridge stands.' The Mugger turned grunting into the undergrowth as Krishna rose.

'It is ended,' said the Tigress, viciously. 'There is no more justice from the Heavenly Ones. Ye have made shame and sport of Gunga, who asked no more than a few score lives.'

'Of *my* people – who lie under the leaf-roofs of the village yonder – of the young girls, and the young men who sing to them in the dark – of the child that will be born next morn – of that which was begotten tonight,' said Krishna. 'And when all is done, what profit? Tomorrow sees them at work. Ay, if ye swept the bridge out from end to end they would begin anew. Hear me! Bhairon is drunk always. Hanuman mocks his people with new riddles.'

'Nay, but they are very old ones,' the Ape said, laughing.

'Shiv hears the talk of the schools and the dreams of the holy men; Ganesh thinks only of his fat traders; but I – I live with these my people, asking for no gifts, and so receiving them hourly.'

'And very tender art thou of thy people,' said the Tigress.

'They are my own. The old women dream of me, turning in their sleep; the maids look and listen for me when they go to fill their lotahs by the river. I walk by the young men waiting without the gates at dusk, and I call over my shoulder to the white-beards. Ye know, Heavenly Ones, that I alone of us all walk upon the earth continually, and have no pleasure in our heavens so long as a green blade springs here, or there are two voices at twilight in the standing crops. Wise are ye, but ye live far off, forgetting whence ye came. So do I not forget. And the fire-carriage feeds your shrines, ye say? And the fire-carriages bring a thousand pilgrimages where but ten came in the old years? True. That is true today.'

'But tomorrow they are dead, brother,' said Ganesh.

'Peace!' said the Bull, as Hanuman leaned forward again. 'And tomorrow, beloved – what of tomorrow?'

'This only. A new word creeping from mouth to mouth among the Common Folk – a word that neither man nor God can lay hold of – an evil word – a little lazy word among the Common Folk, saying (and none know who set that word afoot) that they weary of ye, Heavenly Ones.'

The Gods laughed together softly. 'And then, beloved?' they said.

'And to cover that weariness they, my people, will bring to thee, Shiv, and to thee, Ganesh, at first greater offerings and a louder noise of worship. But the word has gone abroad, and, after, they will pay fewer dues to your fat Brahmins. Next they will forget your altars, but so slowly that no man can say how his forgetfulness began.'

'I knew – I knew! I spoke this also, but they would not hear,' said the Tigress. 'We should have slain – we should have slain!'

'It is too late now. Ye should have slain at the beginning, when the men from across the water had taught our folk nothing. Now my people see their work, and go away thinking. They do not think of the Heavenly Ones altogether. They think of the fire-carriage and the other things that the bridge-builders have done, and when your priests thrust forward hands asking alms, they give unwillingly a little. That is the beginning, among one or two, or five or ten – for I, moving among my people, know what is in their hearts.'

'And the end, Jester of the Gods? What shall the end be?' said Ganesh.

'The end shall be as it was in the beginning, O slothful son of Shiv! The flame shall die upon the altars and the prayer upon the tongue till ye become little Gods again – Gods of the jungle – names that the hunters of rats and noosers of dogs whisper in the thicket and among the caves – rag-Gods, pot Godlings of the tree, and the village-mark, as ye were at the beginning. That is the end, Ganesh, for thee, and for Bhairon – Bhairon of the Common People.'

'It is very far away,' grunted Bhairon. 'Also, it is a lie.'

'Many women have kissed Krishna. They told him this to cheer their own hearts when the grey hairs came, and he has told us the tale,' said the Bull, below his breath.

'Their Gods came, and we changed them. I took the Woman and made her twelve-armed. So shall we twist all their Gods,' said Hanuman.

'Their Gods! This is no question of their Gods – one or three – man or woman. The matter is with the people. *They* move, and not the Gods of the bridge-builders,' said Krishna.

'So be it. I have made a man worship the fire-carriage as it stood still breathing smoke, and he knew not that he worshipped me,' said Hanuman the Ape. 'They will only change a little the names of their Gods. I shall lead the builders of the bridges as of old; Shiv shall be worshipped in the schools by such as doubt and despise their fellows; Ganesh shall have his mahajuns, and Bhairon the donkey-drivers, the pilgrims, and the sellers of toys. Beloved, they will do no more than change the names, and that we have seen a thousand times.'

'Surely they will do no more than change the names,' echoed Ganesh: but there was an uneasy movement among the Gods.

'They will change more than the names. Me alone they cannot kill, so long as maiden and man meet together or the spring follows the winter rains. Heavenly Ones, not for nothing have I walked upon the earth. My people know not now what they know; but I, who live with them, I read their hearts. Great Kings, the beginning of the end is born already. The fire-carriages shout the names of new Gods that are *not* the old under new names. Drink now and eat greatly! Bathe your faces in the smoke of the altars before they grow cold! Take dues and listen to the cymbals and the drums, Heavenly Ones, while yet there are flowers and songs. As men count time the end is far off; but as we who know reckon it is today. I have spoken.'

The young God ceased, and his brethren looked at each other long in silence.

'This I have not heard before,' Peroo whispered in his companion's ear. 'And yet sometimes, when I oiled the brasses in the engine-room of the *Goorkha*, I have wondered if our priests were so wise – so wise. The day is coming, Sahib. They will be gone by the morning.'

A yellow light broadened in the sky, and the tone of the river changed as the darkness withdrew.

Suddenly the Elephant trumpeted aloud as though man had goaded him.

'Let Indra judge. Father of all, speak thou! What of the things we have heard? Has Krishna lied indeed? Or—'

'Ye know,' said the Buck, rising to his feet. 'Ye know the Riddle of the Gods. When Brahm ceases to dream the Heavens and the Hells and Earth disappear. Be content. Brahm dreams still. The dreams come and go, and the nature of the dreams changes, but still Brahm dreams. Krishna has walked too long upon earth, and yet I love him the more for the tale he has told. The Gods change, beloved – all save One!'

'Ay, all save one that makes love in the hearts of men,' said Krishna, knotting his girdle. 'It is but a little time to wait, and ye shall know if I lie.'

'Truly it is but a little time, as thou sayest, and we shall know. Get thee to thy huts again, beloved, and make sport for the young things, for still Brahm dreams. Go, my children! Brahm dreams – and till He wakes the Gods die not.'

'Whither went they?' said the Lascar, awe-struck, shivering a little with the cold.

'God knows!' said Findlayson. The river and the island lay in full daylight now, and there was never mark of hoof or pug on the wet earth under the peepul. Only a parrot screamed in the branches, bringing down showers of water-drops as he fluttered his wings.

'Up! We are cramped with cold! Has the opium died out? Canst thou move, Sahib?'

Findlayson staggered to his feet and shook himself. His head swam and ached, but the work of the opium was over, and, as he sluiced his forehead in a pool, the Chief Engineer of the Kashi Bridge was wondering how he had managed to fall upon the island, what chances the day offered of return, and, above all, how his work stood.

'Peroo, I have forgotten much. I was under the guard-tower watching the river; and then—— Did the flood sweep us away?'

'No. The boats broke loose, Sahib, and' (if the Sahib had forgotten about the opium, decidedly Peroo would not remind him) 'in striving to retie them, so it seemed to me – but it was dark – a rope caught the Sahib and threw him upon a boat. Considering that we two, with Hitchcock Sahib, built, as it were, that bridge, I came also upon the boat, which came riding on horseback, as it were, on the nose of this island, and so, splitting, cast us ashore. I made a great cry when the boat left the wharf, and without doubt Hitchcock Sahib will come for us. As for the bridge, so many have died in the building that it cannot fall.'

A fierce sun, that drew out all the smell of the sodden land, had followed the storm, and in that clear light there was no room for a man to think of dreams of the dark. Findlayson stared upstream, across the blaze of moving water, till his eyes ached. There was no sign of any bank to the Ganges, much less of a bridge-line.

'We came down far,' he said. 'It was wonderful that we were not drowned a hundred times.'

'That was the least of the wonder, for no man dies before his time. I have seen Sydney, I have seen London, and twenty great ports, but' – Peroo looked at the damp, discoloured shrine under the peepul – 'never man has seen that we saw here.'

'What?'

'Has the Sahib forgotten; or do we black men only see the Gods?'

'There was a fever upon me.' Findlayson was still looking uneasily across the water. 'It seemed that the island was full of beasts and men talking, but I do not remember. A boat could live in this water now, I think.'

'Oho! Then it *is* true. "When Brahm ceases to dream, the Gods die." Now I know, indeed, what he meant. Once, too, the *guru* said as much to me; but then I did not understand. Now I am wise.'

'What?' said Findlayson over his shoulder.

Peroo went on as if he were talking to himself. 'Six – seven – ten monsoons since, I was watch on the fo'c'sle of the *Rewah* – the Kumpani's big boat – and there was a big *tufan*, green and black water beating; and I held fast to the life-lines, choking under the waters. Then I thought of the Gods – of Those whom we saw tonight' – he stared curiously at Findlayson's back, but the white man was looking across the flood. 'Yes, I say of Those whom we saw this night past, and I called upon Them to protect me. And while I prayed, still keeping my look-out, a big wave came and threw me forward upon the ring of the great black bow-anchor, and the *Rewah* rose high and high, leaning towards the left-hand side, and the water drew away from beneath her nose, and I lay upon my belly, holding the ring, and looking down into those great deeps. Then I thought, even in the face of death, if I lose hold I die, and for me neither the *Rewah* nor my place by the galley where the rice is cooked, nor Bombay, nor Calcutta, nor even London, will be any more for me. "How shall I be sure," I said, "that the Gods to whom I pray will abide at all?" This I thought, and the *Rewah* dropped her nose as a hammer falls, and all the sea came in and slid me backwards along the fo'c'sle and over the break of the fo'c'sle, and I very badly bruised my shin against the donkey-engine: but I did not die, and I have seen the Gods. They are good for live men, but for the dead—— They have spoken Themselves. Therefore, when I come to the village I will beat the *guru* for talking riddles which are no riddles. When Brahm ceases to dream, the Gods go.

'Look upstream. The light blinds. Is there smoke yonder?'

Peroo shaded his eyes with his hands. 'He is a wise man and quick. Hitchcock Sahib would not trust a rowboat. He has borrowed the Rao Sahib's steam-launch, and comes to look for us. I have always said that there should have been a steam-launch on the bridge-works for us.'

The territory of the Rao of Baraon lay within ten miles of the bridge; and Findlayson and Hitchcock had spent a fair portion of their scanty leisure in playing billiards and shooting Black-buck with the young man. He had been bear-led by an English tutor of sporting tastes for some five or six years, and was now royally wasting the revenues accumulated during his minority by the Indian Government. His steam-launch, with its silver-plated rails, striped silk awning, and mahogany decks, was a new toy which Findlayson had found horribly in the way when the Rao came to look at the bridge-works.

'It's great luck,' murmured Findlayson, but he was none the less afraid, wondering what news might be of the bridge.

The gaudy blue-and-white funnel came downstream swiftly. They could see Hitchcock in the bows, with a pair of opera-glasses, and his face was unusually white. Then Peroo hailed, and the launch made for the tail of the island. The Rao Sahib, in tweed shooting-suit and a seven-hued turban, waved his royal hand, and Hitchcock shouted. But he need have asked no questions, for Findlayson's first demand was for his bridge.

'All serene! 'Gad, I never expected to see you again, Findlayson. You're seven koss downstream. Yes, there's not a stone shifted anywhere; but how are you? I borrowed the Rao Sahib's launch, and he was good enough to come along. Jump in.'

'Ah, Finlinson, you are very well, eh? That was most unprecedented calamity last night, eh? My royal palace, too, it leaks like the devil, and the crops will also be short all about my country. Now you shall back her out, Hitchcock. I – I do not understand steam-engines. You are wet? You are cold, Finlinson? I have some things to eat here, and you will take a good drink.'

'I'm immensely grateful, Rao Sahib. I believe you've saved my life. How did Hitchcock——'

'Oho! His hair was upon end. He rode to me in the middle of the night and woke me up in the arms of Morphus. I was most truly concerned, Finlinson, so I came too. My head-priest he is very angry just now. We will go quick, Mister Hitchcock. I am due to attend at twelve forty-five in the state temple, where we sanctify some new idol. If not so I would have asked you to spend the day with me. They are dam-bore, these religious ceremonies, Finlinson, eh?'

Peroo, well known to the crew, had possessed himself of the wheel, and was taking the launch craftily upstream. But while he steered he was, in his mind, handling two feet of partially untwisted wire-rope; and the back upon which he beat was the back of his *guru*.

The Cat that Walked by Himself

Hear and attend and listen; for this befell and behappened and became and was, O my Best Beloved, when the Tame animals were wild. The Dog was wild, and the Horse was wild, and the Cow was wild, and the Sheep was wild, and the Pig was wild – as wild as wild could be – and they walked in the Wet Wild Woods by their wild lones. But the wildest of all the wild animals was the Cat. He walked by himself, and all places were alike to him.

Of course the Man was wild too. He was dreadfully wild. He didn't even begin to be tame till he met the Woman, and she told him that she did not like living in his wild ways. She picked out a nice dry Cave, instead of a heap of wet leaves, to lie down in; and she strewed clean sand on the floor; and she lit a nice fire of wood at the back of the Cave; and she hung a dried wild-horse skin, tail-down, across the opening of the Cave; and she said, 'Wipe your feet, dear, when you come in, and now we'll keep house.'

That night, Best Beloved, they ate wild sheep roasted on the hot stones, and flavoured with wild garlic and wild pepper; and wild duck stuffed with wild rice and wild fenugreek and wild coriander; and marrow-bones of wild oxen; and wild cherries, and wild grenadillas. Then the Man went to sleep in front of the fire ever so happy; but the Woman sat up, combing her hair. She took the bone of the shoulder of mutton – the big flat blade-bone – and she looked at the wonderful marks on it, and she threw more wood on the fire, and she made a Magic. She made the First Singing Magic in the world.

Out in the Wet Wild Woods all the wild animals gathered

together where they could see the light of the fire a long way off, and they wondered what it meant.

Then Wild Horse stamped with his wild foot and said, 'O my Friends and O my Enemies, why have the Man and the Woman made that great light in that great Cave, and what harm will it do us?'

Wild Dog lifted up his wild nose and smelled the smell of the roast mutton, and said, 'I will go up and see and look, and say; for I think it is good. Cat, come with me.'

'Nenni!' said the Cat. 'I am the Cat who walks by himself, and all places are alike to me. I will not come.'

'Then we can never be friends again,' said Wild Dog, and he trotted off to the Cave. But when he had gone a little way the Cat said to himself, 'All places are alike to me. Why should I not go too and see and look and come away at my own liking?' So he slipped after Wild Dog softly, very softly, and hid himself where he could hear everything.

When Wild Dog reached the mouth of the Cave he lifted up the dried horse-skin with his nose and sniffed the beautiful smell of the roast mutton, and the Woman, looking at the blade-bone, heard him, and laughed, and said, 'Here comes the first. Wild Thing out of the Wild Woods, what do you want?'

Wild Dog said, 'O my Enemy and Wife of my Enemy, what is this that smells so good in the Wild Woods?'

Then the Woman picked up a roasted mutton-bone and threw it to Wild Dog, and said, 'Wild Thing out of the Wild Woods, taste and try.' Wild Dog gnawed the bone, and it was more delicious than anything he had ever tasted, and he said, 'O my Enemy and Wife of my Enemy, give me another.'

The Woman said, 'Wild Thing out of the Wild Woods, help my Man to hunt through the day and guard this Cave at night, and I will give you as many roast bones as you need.'

'Ah!' said the Cat, listening. 'This is a very wise Woman, but she is not so wise as I am.'

Wild Dog crawled into the Cave and laid his head on the Woman's lap, and said, 'O my Friend and Wife of my Friend, I will help your Man to hunt through the day, and at night I will guard your Cave.'

'Ah!' said the Cat, listening. 'That is a very foolish Dog.' And he went back through the Wet Wild Woods waving his wild tail, and walking by his wild lone. But he never told anybody.

When the Man waked up he said, 'What is Wild Dog doing here?' And the Woman said, 'His name is not Wild Dog any more, but the First Friend, because he will be our friend for always and always and always. Take him with you when you go hunting.'

Next night the Woman cut great green armfuls of fresh grass from the water-meadows, and dried it before the fire, so that it smelt like new-mown hay, and she sat at the mouth of the Cave and plaited a halter out of horse-hide, and she looked at the shoulder-of-mutton bone – at the big broad blade-bone – and she made a Magic. She made the Second Singing Magic in the world.

Out in the Wild Woods all the wild animals wondered what had happened to Wild Dog, and at last Wild Horse stamped with his foot and said, 'I will go and see and say why Wild Dog has not returned. Cat, come with me.'

'Nenni!' said the Cat. 'I am the Cat who walks by himself, and all places are alike to me. I will not come.' But all the same he followed Wild Horse softly, very softly, and hid himself where he could hear everything.

When the Woman heard Wild Horse tripping and stumbling on his long mane, she laughed and said, 'Here comes the second. Wild Thing out of the Wild Woods, what do you want?'

Wild Horse said, 'O my Enemy and Wife of my Enemy, where is Wild Dog?'

The Woman laughed, and picked up the blade-bone and looked at it, and said, 'Wild Thing out of the Wild Woods, you did not come here for Wild Dog, but for the sake of this good grass.'

And Wild Horse, tripping and stumbling on his long mane, said, 'That is true; give it me to eat.'

The Woman said, 'Wild Thing out of the Wild Woods, bend your wild head and wear what I give you, and you shall eat the wonderful grass three times a day.'

'Ah!' said the Cat, listening. 'This is a clever Woman, but she is not so clever as I am.'

Wild Horse bent his wild head, and the Woman slipped the

This is the picture of the Cave where the Man and the Woman lived first of all. It was really a very nice Cave, and much warmer than it looks. The Man had a canoe. It is on the edge of the river, being soaked in water to make it swell up. The tattery-looking thing across the river is the Man's salmon-net to catch salmon with. There are nice clean stones leading up from the river to the mouth of the Cave, so that the Man and the Woman could go down for water without getting sand between their toes. The things like blackbeetles far down the beach are really trunks of dead trees that floated down the river from the Wet Wild Woods on the other bank. The Man and the Woman used to drag them out and dry them and cut them up for firewood. I haven't drawn the horse-hide curtain at the mouth of the Cave, because the Woman has just taken it down to be cleaned. All those little smudges on the sand between the Cave and the river are the marks of the Woman's feet and the Man's feet.

The Man and the Woman are both inside the Cave eating their dinner. They went to another cosier Cave when the Baby came, because the Baby used to crawl down to the river and fall in, and the Dog had to pull him out.

plaited-hide halter over it, and Wild Horse breathed on the Woman's feet and said, 'O my Mistress, and Wife of my Master, I will be your servant for the sake of the wonderful grass.'

'Ah!' said the Cat, listening. 'That is a very foolish Horse.' And he went back through the Wet Wild Woods, waving his wild tail and walking by his wild lone. But he never told anybody.

When the Man and the Dog came back from hunting, the Man said, 'What is Wild Horse doing here?' And the Woman said, 'His name is not Wild Horse any more, but the First Servant, because he will carry us from place to place for always and always and always. Ride on his back when you go hunting.'

Next day, holding her wild head high that her wild horns should not catch in the wild trees, Wild Cow came up to the Cave, and the Cat followed, and hid himself just the same as before; and everything happened just the same as before; and the Cat said the same things as before; and when Wild Cow had promised to give her milk to the Woman every day in exchange for the wonderful grass, the Cat went back through the Wet Wild Woods waving his wild tail and walking by his wild lone, just the same as before. But he never told anybody. And when the Man and the Horse and the Dog came home from hunting and asked the same questions same as before, the Woman said, 'Her name is not Wild Cow any more, but the Giver of Good Food. She will give us the warm white milk for always and always and always, and I will take care of her while you and the First Friend and the First Servant go hunting.'

Next day the Cat waited to see if any other Wild Thing would go up to the Cave, but no one moved in the Wet Wild Woods, so the Cat walked there by himself; and he saw the Woman milking the Cow, and he saw the light of the fire in the Cave, and he smelt the smell of the warm white milk.

Cat said, 'O my Enemy and Wife of my Enemy, where did Wild Cow go?'

The Woman laughed and said, 'Wild Thing out of the Wild Woods, go back to the Woods again, for I have braided up my hair, and I have put away the magic blade-bone, and we have no more need of either friends or servants in our Cave.'

Cat said, 'I am not a friend, and I am not a servant. I am the Cat who walks by himself, and I wish to come into your Cave.'

Woman said, 'Then why did you not come with First Friend on the first night?'

Cat grew very angry and said, 'Has Wild Dog told tales of me?'

Then the Woman laughed and said, 'You are the Cat who walks by himself, and all places are alike to you. You are neither a friend nor a servant. You have said it yourself. Go away and walk by yourself in all places alike.'

Then Cat pretended to be sorry and said, 'Must I never come into the Cave? Must I never sit by the warm fire? Must I never drink the warm white milk? You are very wise and very beautiful. You should not be cruel even to a Cat.'

Woman said, 'I knew I was wise, but I did not know I was beautiful. So I will make a bargain with you. If ever I say one word in your praise, you may come into the Cave.'

'And if you say two words in my praise?' said the Cat.

'I never shall,' said the Woman, 'but if I say two words in your praise, you may sit by the fire in the Cave.'

'And if you say three words?' said the Cat.

'I never shall,' said the Woman, 'but if I say three words in your praise, you may drink the warm white milk three times a day for always and always and always.'

Then the Cat arched his back and said, 'Now let the Curtain at the mouth of the Cave, and the Fire at the back of the Cave, and the Milk-pots that stand beside the Fire, remember what my Enemy and the Wife of my Enemy has said.' And he went away through the Wet Wild Woods waving his wild tail and walking by his wild lone.

That night when the Man and the Horse and the Dog came home from hunting, the Woman did not tell them of the bargain that she had made with the Cat, because she was afraid that they might not like it.

Cat went far and far away and hid himself in the Wet Wild Woods by his wild lone for a long time till the Woman forgot all about him. Only the Bat – the little upside-down Bat – that hung inside the Cave knew where Cat hid; and every evening Bat would fly to Cat with news of what was happening.

This is the picture of the Cat that Walked by Himself, walking by his wild lone through the Wet Wild Woods and waving his wild tail. There is nothing else in the picture except some toadstools. They had to grow there because the Woods were so wet. The lumpy thing on the low branch isn't a bird. It is moss that grew there because the Wild Woods were so wet.

Underneath the truly picture is a picture of the cosy Cave that the Man and the Woman went to after the Baby came. It was their summer Cave, and they planted wheat in front of it. The man is riding on the Horse to find the Cow and bring her back to the Cave to be milked He is holding up his hand to call the Dog, who has swum across to the other side of the river, looking for rabbits.

One evening Bat said, 'There is a Baby in the Cave. He is new and pink and fat and small, and the Woman is very fond of him.'

'Ah,' said the Cat, listening. 'But what is the Baby fond of?'

'He is fond of things that are soft and tickle,' said the Bat. 'He is fond of warm things to hold in his arms when he goes to sleep. He is fond of being played with. He is fond of all those things.'

'Ah,' said the Cat, listening. 'Then my time has come.'

Next night Cat walked through the Wet Wild Woods and hid very near the Cave till morning-time, and Man and Dog and Horse went hunting. The Woman was busy cooking that morning, and the Baby cried and interrupted. So she carried him outside the Cave and gave him a handful of pebbles to play with. But still the Baby cried.

Then the Cat put out his paddy paw and patted the Baby on the cheek, and it cooed; and the Cat rubbed against its fat knees and tickled it under its fat chin with his tail. And the Baby laughed; and the Woman heard him and smiled.

Then the Bat – the little upside-down Bat – that hung in the mouth of the Cave said, 'O my Hostess and Wife of my Host and Mother of my Host's Son, a Wild Thing from the Wild Woods is most beautifully playing with your Baby.'

'A blessing on that Wild Thing whoever he may be,' said the Woman, straightening her back, 'for I was a busy woman this morning and he has done me a service.'

That very minute and second, Best Beloved, the dried horse-skin Curtain that was stretched tail-down at the mouth of the Cave fell down – *woosh!* – because it remembered the bargain she had made with the Cat; and when the Woman went to pick it up – lo and behold! – the Cat was sitting quite comfy inside the Cave.

'O my Enemy and Wife of my Enemy and Mother of my Enemy,' said the Cat, 'it is I: for you have spoken a word in my praise, and now I can sit within the Cave for always and always and always. But still I am the Cat who walks by himself, and all places are alike to me.'

The Woman was very angry, and shut her lips tight and took up her spinning-wheel and began to spin.

But the Baby cried because the Cat had gone away, and the Woman could not hush it, for it struggled and kicked and grew black in the face.

'O my Enemy and Wife of my Enemy and Mother of my Enemy,' said the Cat, 'take a strand of the thread that you are spinning and tie it to your spindle-whorl and drag it along the floor, and I will show you a Magic that shall make your Baby laugh as loudly as he is now crying.'

'I will do so,' said the Woman, 'because I am at my wits' end; but I will not thank you for it.'

She tied the thread to the little clay spindle-whorl and drew it across the floor, and the Cat ran after it and patted it with his paws and rolled head over heels, and tossed it backward over his shoulder and chased it between his hind legs and pretended to lose it, and pounced down upon it again, till the Baby laughed as loudly as it had been crying, and scrambled after the Cat and frolicked all over the Cave till it grew tired and settled down to sleep with the Cat in its arms.

'Now,' said Cat, 'I will sing the Baby a song that shall keep him asleep for an hour.' And he began to purr, loud and low, low and loud, till the Baby fell fast asleep. The Woman smiled as she looked down upon the two of them, and said, 'That was wonderfully done. No question but you are very clever, O Cat.'

That very minute and second, Best Beloved, the smoke of the Fire at the back of the Cave came down in clouds from the roof – *puff!* – because it remembered the bargain she had made with the Cat; and when it had cleared away – lo and behold! – the Cat was sitting quite comfy close to the fire.

'O my Enemy and Wife of my Enemy and Mother of my Enemy,' said the Cat, 'it is I: for you have spoken a second word in my praise, and now I can sit by the warm fire at the back of the Cave for always and always and always. But still I am the Cat who walks by himself, and all places are alike to me.'

Then the Woman was very very angry, and let down her hair and put more wood on the fire and brought out the broad blade-bone of the shoulder of mutton and began to make a Magic that should prevent her from saying a third word in praise of the Cat. It was not a Singing Magic, Best Beloved, it was a Still

Magic; and by and by the Cave grew so still that a little wee-wee mouse crept out of a corner and ran across the floor.

'O my Enemy and Wife of my Enemy and Mother of my Enemy,' said the Cat, 'is that little mouse part of your Magic?'

'Ouh! Chee! No indeed!' said the Woman, and she dropped the blade-bone and jumped upon the footstool in front of the fire and braided up her hair very quick for fear that the mouse should run up it.

'Ah,' said the Cat, watching. 'Then the mouse will do me no harm if I eat it?'

'No,' said the Woman, braiding up her hair, 'eat it quickly and I will ever be grateful to you.'

Cat made one jump and caught the little mouse, and the Woman said, 'A hundred thanks. Even the First Friend is not quick enough to catch little mice as you have done. You must be very wise.'

That very minute and second, O Best Beloved, the Milk-pot that stood by the fire cracked in two piece – *ffft!* – because it remembered the bargain she had made with the Cat; and when the Woman jumped down from the footstool – lo and behold! – the Cat was lapping up the warm white milk that lay in one of the broken pieces.

'O my Enemy and Wife of my Enemy and Mother of my Enemy,' said the Cat, 'it is I: for you have spoken three words in my praise, and now I can drink the warm white milk three times a day for always and always and always. But *still* I am the Cat who walks by himself, and all places are alike to me.'

Then the Woman laughed and set the Cat a bowl of the warm white milk and said, 'O Cat, you are as clever as a man, but remember that your bargain was not made with the Man or the Dog, and I do not know what they will do when they come home.'

'What is that to me?' said the Cat. 'If I have my place in the Cave by the fire and my warm white milk three times a day I do not care what the Man or the Dog can do.'

That evening when the Man and the Dog came into the Cave, the Woman told them all the story of the bargain, while the Cat sat by the fire and smiled. Then the Man said, 'Yes, but he has not made a bargain with *me* or with all proper Men after me.'

Then he took off his two leather boots and he took up his little stone axe (that makes three) and he fetched a piece of wood and a hatchet (that is five altogether), and he set them out in a row and he said, 'Now we will make *our* bargain. If you do not catch mice when you are in the Cave for always and always and always, I will throw these five things at you whenever I see you, and so shall all proper Men do after me.'

'Ah!' said the Woman, listening. 'This is a very clever Cat, but he is not so clever as my Man.'

The Cat counted the five things (and they looked very knobby) and he said, 'I will catch mice when I am in the Cave for always and always and always; but *still* I am the Cat who walks by himself, and all places are alike to me.'

'Not when I am near,' said the Man. 'If you had not said that last I would have put all these things away for always and always and always; but now I am going to throw my two boots and my little stone axe (that makes three) at you whenever I meet you. And so shall all proper Men do after me!'

Then the Dog said, 'Wait a minute. He has not made a bargain with *me* or with all proper Dogs after me.' And he showed his teeth and said, 'If you are not kind to the Baby while I am in the Cave for always and always and always, I will hunt you till I catch you, and when I catch you I will bite you. And so shall all proper Dogs do after me.'

'Ah!' said the Woman, listening. 'This is a very clever Cat, but he is not so clever as the Dog.'

Cat counted the Dog's teeth (and they looked very pointed) and he said, 'I will be kind to the Baby while I am in the Cave, as long as he does not pull my tail too hard, for always and always and always. But *still* I am the Cat who walks by himself, and all places are alike to me.'

'Not when I am near,' said the Dog. 'If you had not said that last I would have shut my mouth for always and always and always; but *now* I am going to hunt you up a tree whenever I meet you. And so shall all proper Dogs do after me.'

Then the Man threw his two boots and his little stone axe (that makes three) at the Cat, and the Cat ran out of the Cave and the Dog chased him up a tree; and from that day to this, Best Beloved, three proper Men out of five will always throw things at a Cat whenever they meet him, and all proper Dogs will chase him up a tree. But the Cat keeps his side of the bargain too. He will kill mice, and he will be kind to Babies when he is in the house, just as long as they do not pull his tail too hard. But when he has done that, and between times, and when the moon gets up and night comes, he is the Cat that walks by himself, and all places are alike to him. Then he goes out to the Wet Wild Woods or up the Wet Wild Trees or on the Wet Wild Roofs, waving his wild tail and walking by his wild lone.

Pussy can sit by the fire and sing,
 Pussy can climb a tree,
Or play with a silly old cork and string
 To 'muse herself, not me.
But I like *Binkie* my dog, because
 He knows how to behave;
So, *Binkie's* the same as the First Friend was,
 And I am the Man in the Cave!

Pussy will play Man Friday till
 It's time to wet her paw
And make her walk on the window-sill
 (For the footprint Crusoe saw);
Then she fluffles her tail and mews,
 And scratches and won't attend.
But *Binkie* will play whatever I choose,
 And he is my true First Friend!

Pussy will rub my knees with her head
 Pretending she loves me hard;
But the very minute I go to my bed
 Pussy runs out in the yard,
And there she stays till the morning-light;
 So I know it is only pretend;
But *Binkie*, he snores at my feet all night,
 And he is my Firstest Friend!

'They'

THE RETURN OF THE CHILDREN

Neither the harps nor the crowns amused, nor the cherubs' dove-winged races –
Holding hands forlornly the Children wandered beneath the Dome;
Plucking the radiant robes of the passers-by, and with pitiful faces
Begging what Princes and Powers refused:– 'Ah, please will you let us go home?'

Over the jewelled floor, nigh weeping, ran to them Mary the Mother,
Kneeled and caressed and made promise with kisses, and drew them along to the gateway –
Yea, the all-iron unbribeable Door which Peter must guard and none other.
Straightway She took the Keys from his keeping, and opened and freed them straightway.

Then to Her Son, Who had seen and smiled, She said: 'On the night that I bore Thee
What didst Thou care for a love beyond mine or a heaven that was not my arm?
Didst Thou push from the nipple, O Child, to hear the angels adore Thee?
When we two lay in the breath of the kine?' And He said:– 'Thou hast done no harm.'

So through the Void the Children ran homeward merrily hand in hand,
Looking neither to left nor right where the breathless Heavens stood still;
And the Guards of the Void resheathed their swords, for they heard the Command:
'Shall I that have suffered the children to come to me hold them against their will?'

One view called me to another; one hill top to its fellow, half across the county, and since I could answer at no more trouble than the snapping forward of a lever, I let the county flow under my wheels. The orchid-studded flats of the East gave way to the thyme, ilex, and grey grass of the Downs; these again to the rich cornland and fig-trees of the lower coast, where you carry the beat of the tide on your left hand for fifteen level miles; and when at last I turned inland through a huddle of rounded hills and woods I had run myself clean out of my known marks. Beyond that precise hamlet which stands godmother to the capital of the United States, I found hidden villages where bees, the only things awake, boomed in eighty-foot lindens that overhung grey Norman churches; miraculous brooks diving under stone bridges built for heavier traffic than would ever vex them again; tithe-barns larger than their churches, and an old smithy that cried out aloud how it had once been a hall of the Knights of the Temple. Gipsies I found on a common where the gorse, bracken, and heath fought it out together up a mile of Roman road; and a little farther on I disturbed a red fox rolling dog-fashion in the naked sunlight.

As the wooded hills closed about me I stood up in the car to take the bearings of that great Down whose ringed head is a landmark for fifty miles across the low countries. I judged that the lie of the country would bring me across some westward-running road that went to his feet, but I did not allow for the confusing veils of the woods. A quick turn plunged me first into a green cutting brim-full of liquid sunshine, next into a gloomy tunnel where last year's dead leaves whispered and scuffled about my tyres. The strong hazel stuff meeting overhead had not been cut for a couple of generations at least, nor had any axe helped the moss-cankered oak and beech to spring above them. Here the road changed frankly into a carpeted ride on whose brown velvet spent primrose-clumps showed like jade, and a few sickly, white-stalked bluebells nodded together. As the slope favoured I shut off the power and slid over the whirled leaves, expecting every moment to meet a keeper; but I only heard a jay, far off, arguing against the silence under the twilight of the trees.

Still the track descended. I was on the point of reversing and working my way back on the second speed ere I ended in some swamp, when I saw sunshine through the tangle ahead and lifted the brake.

It was down again at once. As the light beat across my face

my fore-wheels took the turf of a great still lawn from which sprang horsemen ten feet high with levelled lances, monstrous peacocks, and sleek round-headed maids of honour – blue, black, and glistening – all of clipped yew. Across the lawn – the marshalled woods besieged it on three sides – stood an ancient house of lichened and weather-worn stone, with mullioned windows and roofs of rose-red tile. It was flanked by semicircular walls, also rose-red, that closed the lawn on the fourth side, and at their feet a box hedge grew man-high. There were doves on the roof about the slim brick chimneys, and I caught a glimpse of an octagonal dove-house behind the screening wall.

Here, then, I stayed; a horseman's green spear laid at my breast; held by the exceeding beauty of that jewel in that setting.

'If I am not packed off for a trespasser, or if this knight does not ride a wallop at me,' thought I, 'Shakespeare and Queen Elizabeth at least must come out of that half-open garden door and ask me to tea.'

A child appeared at an upper window, and I thought the little thing waved a friendly hand. But it was to call a companion, for presently another bright head showed. Then I heard a laugh among the yew-peacocks, and turning to make sure (till then I had been watching the house only) I saw the silver of a fountain behind a hedge thrown up against the sun. The doves on the roof cooed to the cooing water; but between the two notes I caught the utterly happy chuckle of a child absorbed in some light mischief.

The garden door – heavy oak sunk deep in the thickness of the wall – opened further: a woman in a big garden hat set her foot slowly on the time-hollowed stone step and as slowly walked across the turf. I was forming some apology when she lifted up her head and I saw that she was blind.

'I heard you,' she said. 'Isn't that a motor car?'

'I'm afraid I've made a mistake in my road. I should have turned off up above – I never dreamed——' I began.

'But I'm very glad. Fancy a motor car coming into the garden! It will be such a treat——' She turned and made as though looking about her. 'You – you haven't seen anyone, have you – perhaps?'

'No one to speak to, but the children seemed interested at a distance.'

'Which?'

'I saw a couple up at the window just now, and I think I heard a little chap in the grounds.'

'Oh, lucky you!' she cried, and her face brightened. 'I hear them, of course, but that's all. You've seen them and heard them?'

'Yes,' I answered. 'And if I know anything of children, one of them's having a beautiful time by the fountain yonder. Escaped, I should imagine.'

'You're fond of children?'

I gave her one or two reasons why I did not altogether hate them.

'Of course, of course,' she said. 'Then you understand. Then you won't think it foolish if I ask you to take your car through the gardens, once or twice – quite slowly. I'm sure they'd like to see it. They see so little, poor things. One tries to make their life pleasant, but——' she threw out her hands towards the woods. 'We're so out of the world here.'

'That will be splendid,' I said. 'But I can't cut up your grass.'

She faced to the right. 'Wait a minute,' she said. 'We're at the South gate, aren't we? Behind those peacocks there's a flagged path. We call it the Peacocks' Walk. You can't see it from here, they tell me, but if you squeeze along by the edge of the wood you can turn at the first peacock and get on to the flags.

It was sacrilege to wake that dreaming house-front with the clatter of machinery, but I swung the car to clear the turf, brushed along the edge of the wood and turned in on the broad stone path where the fountain-basin lay like one star-sapphire.

'May I come too?' she cried. 'No, please don't help me. They'll like it better if they see me.'

She felt her way lightly to the front of the car, and with one foot on the step she called: 'Children, oh, children! Look and see what's going to happen!'

The voice would have drawn lost souls from the Pit, for the yearning that underlay its sweetness, and I was not surprised to hear an answering shout behind the yews. It must have been the child by the fountain, but he fled at our approach, leaving a little toy boat in the water. I saw the glint of his blue blouse among the still horsemen.

Very disposedly we paraded the length of the walk and at her request backed again. This time the child had got the better of his panic, but stood far off and doubting.

'The little fellow's watching us,' I said. 'I wonder if he'd like a ride.'

'They're very shy still. Very shy. But, oh, lucky you to be able to see them! Let's listen.'

I stopped the machine at once, and the humid stillness, heavy with the scent of box, cloaked us deep. Shears I could hear where some gardener was clipping; a mumble of bees and broken voices that might have been the doves.

'Oh, unkind!' she said weariedly.

'Perhaps they're only shy of the motor. The little maid at the window looks tremendously interested.'

'Yes?' She raised her head. 'It was wrong of me to say that. They are really fond of me. It's the only thing that makes life worth living – when they're fond of you, isn't it? I daren't think what the place would be without them. By the way, is it beautiful?'

'I think it is the most beautiful place I have ever seen.'

'So they all tell me. I can feel it, of course, but that isn't quite the same thing.'

'Then have you never——?' I began, but stopped abashed.

'Not since I can remember. It happened when I was only a few months old, they tell me. And yet I must remember something, else how could I dream about colours. I see light in my dreams, and colours, but I never see *them*. I only hear them just as I do when I'm awake.'

'It's difficult to see faces in dreams. Some people can, but most of us haven't the gift,' I went on, looking up at the window where the child stood all but hidden.

'I've heard that too,' she said. 'And they tell me that one never sees a dead person's face in a dream. Is that true?'

'I believe it is – now I come to think of it.'

'But how is it with yourself – yourself?' The blind eyes turned towards me.

'I have never seen the faces of my dead in any dream,' I answered.

'Then it must be as bad as being blind.'

The sun had dipped behind the woods and the long shades were possessing the insolent horsemen one by one. I saw the light die from off the top of a glossy-leaved lance and all the brave hard green turn to soft black. The house, accepting another day at end, as it had accepted an hundred thousand gone, seemed to settle deeper into its rest among the shadows.

'Have you ever wanted to?' she said after the silence.

'Very much sometimes,' I replied. The child had left the window as the shadows closed upon it.

'Ah! So've I, but I don't suppose it's allowed. . . . Where d'you live?'

'Quite the other side of the county – sixty miles and more, and I must be going back. I've come without my big lamp.'

'But it's not dark yet. I can feel it.'

'I'm afraid it will be by the time I get home. Could you lend me someone to set me on my road at first? I've utterly lost myself.'

'I'll send Madden with you to the crossroads. We are so out of the world, I don't wonder you were lost! I'll guide you round to the front of the house; but you will go slowly, won't you, till you're out of the grounds? It isn't foolish, do you think?

'I promise you I'll go like this,' I said, and let the car start herself down the flagged path.

We skirted the left wing of the house, whose elaborately cast lead guttering alone was worth a day's journey; passed under a great rose-grown gate in the red wall, and so round to the high front of the house which in beauty and stateliness as much excelled the back as that all others I had seen.

'Is it so very beautiful?' she said wistfully when she heard my raptures. 'And you like the lead-figures too? There's the old azalea garden behind. They say that this place must have been made for children. Will you help me out, please? I should like to come with you as far as the crossroads, but I mustn't leave them. Is that you, Madden? I want you to show this gentleman the way to the crossroads. He has lost his way but – he has seen them.'

A butler appeared noiselessly at the miracle of old oak that must be called the front door, and slipped aside to put on his hat. She stood looking at me with open blue eyes in which no sight lay, and I saw for the first time that she was beautiful.

'Remember,' she said quietly, 'if you are fond of them you will come again,' and disappeared within the house.

The butler in the car said nothing till we were nearly at the lodge gates, where catching a glimpse of a blue blouse in a shrubbery I swerved amply lest the devil that leads little boys to play should drag me into child-murder.

'Excuse me,' he asked of a sudden, 'but why did you do that, Sir?'

'The child yonder.'

'Our young gentleman in blue?'

'Of course.'

'He runs about a good deal. Did you see him by the fountain, Sir?'

'Oh, yes, several times. Do we turn here?'

'Yes, Sir. And did you 'appen to see them upstairs too?'

'At the upper window? Yes.'

'Was that before the mistress come out to speak to you, Sir?'

'A little before that. Why d'you want to know?'

He paused a little. 'Only to make sure that – that they had seen the car, Sir, because with children running about, though I'm sure you're driving particularly careful, there might be an accident. That was all, Sir. Here are the crossroads. You can't miss your way from now on. Thank you, Sir, but that isn't *our* custom, not with——'

'I beg your pardon,' I said, and thrust away the British silver.

'Oh, it's quite right with the rest of 'em as a rule. Goodbye, Sir.'

He retired into the armour-plated conning tower of his caste and walked away. Evidently a butler solicitous for the honour of his house, and interested, probably through a maid, in the nursery.

Once beyond the signposts at the crossroads I looked back, but the crumpled hills interlaced so jealously that I could not see where the house had lain. When I asked its name at a cottage along the road, the fat woman who sold sweetmeats there gave me to understand that people with motor cars had small right to live – much less to 'go about talking like carriage folk'. They were not a pleasant-mannered community.

When I retraced my route on the map that evening I was little wiser. Hawkin's Old Farm appeared to be the Survey title of the place, and the old County Gazetteer, generally so ample, did not allude to it. The big house of those parts was Hodnington Hall, Georgian with early Victorian embellishments, as an atrocious steel engraving attested. I carried my difficulty to a neighbour – a deep-rooted tree of that soil – and he gave me a name of a family which conveyed no meaning.

A month or so later – I went again, or it may have been that my car took the road of her own volition. She over-ran the fruitless Downs, threaded every turn of the maze of lanes below the hills, drew through the high-walled woods, impenetrable in their full leaf, came out at the crossroads where the butler had left me, and a little farther on developed an internal trouble which forced me to turn her in on a grass way-waste that cut into a summer-silent hazel wood. So far as I could make sure by the sun and a six-inch Ordnance map, this should be the road flank of that wood which I had first explored from the heights above. I made a mighty serious business of my repairs and a glittering shop of my repair kit, spanners, pump, and the like, which I spread out orderly upon a rug. It was a trap to catch all childhood, for on such a day, I argued, the children would not be far off. When I paused in my work I listened, but the wood was so full of the noises of summer (though the birds had mated) that I could not at first distinguish these from the tread of small cautious feet stealing across the dead leaves. I rang my bell in an alluring manner, but the feet fled, and I repented, for to a child a sudden noise is very real terror. I must have been at work half an hour when I heard in the wood the voice of the blind woman crying: 'Children, oh, children! Where are you?' and the stillness made slow to close on the perfection of that cry. She came towards me, half feeling her way between the tree boles, and though a child it seemed clung to her skirt, it swerved into the leafage like a rabbit as she drew nearer.

'Is that you?' she said, 'from the other side of the county?'

'Yes, it's me from the other side of the county.'

'Then why didn't you come through the upper woods? They were there just now.'

'They were here a few minutes ago. I expect they knew my car had broken down, and came to see the fun.'

'Nothing serious, I hope? How do cars break down?'

'In fifty different ways. Only mine has chosen the fifty-first.'

She laughed merrily at the tiny joke, cooed with delicious laughter, and pushed her hat back.

'Let me hear,' she said.

'Wait a moment,' I cried, 'and I'll get you a cushion.'

She set her foot on the rug all covered with spare parts, and stooped above it eagerly. 'What delightful things!' The hands through which she saw glanced in the chequered sunlight. 'A box here – another box! Why, you've arranged them like playing shop!'

'I confess now that I put it out to attract them. I don't need half those things really.'

'How nice of you! I heard your bell in the upper wood. You say they were here before that?'

'I'm sure of it. Why are they so shy? That little fellow in blue who was with you just now ought to have got over his fright. He's been watching me like a Red Indian.'

'It must have been your bell,' she said. 'I heard one of them go past me in trouble when I was coming down. They're shy – so shy even with me.' She turned her face over her shoulder and cried again: 'Children, oh, children! Look and see!'

'They must have gone off together on their own affairs,' I suggested, for there was a murmur behind us of lowered voices broken by the sudden squeaking giggles of childhood. I returned to my tinkerings and she leaned forward, her chin on her hand, listening interestedly.

'How many are they?' I said at last. The work was finished, but I saw no reason to go.

Her forehead puckered a little in thought. 'I don't quite know,' she said simply. 'Sometimes more – sometimes less. They come and stay with me because I love them, you see.'

'That must be very jolly,' I said, replacing a drawer, and as I spoke I heard the inanity of my answer.

'You – you aren't laughing at me?' she cried. 'I – I haven't any of my own. I never married. People laugh at me sometimes about them because – because –'

'Because they're savages,' I returned. 'It's nothing to fret for. That sort laugh at everything that isn't in their own fat lives.'

'I don't know. How should I? I only don't like being laughed at about *them*. It hurts; and when one can't see. . . . I don't want to seem silly,' her chin quivered like a child's as she spoke, 'but we blindies have only one skin, I think. Everything outside hits straight at our souls. It's different with you. You've such good defences in your eyes – looking out – before anyone can really pain you in your soul. People forget that with us.'

I was silent reviewing that inexhaustible matter – the more than inherited (since it is also carefully taught) brutality of the Christian peoples, beside which the mere heathendom of the West Coast nigger is clean and restrained. It led me a long distance into myself.

'Don't do that!' she said of a sudden, putting her hands before her eyes.

'What?'

She made a gesture with her hand.

'That! It's – it's all purple and black. Don't! That colour hurts.'

'But, how in the world do you know about colours?' I exclaimed, for here was a revelation indeed.

'Colours as colours?' she asked.

'No. *Those* Colours which you saw just now.'

'You know as well as I do,' she laughed, 'else you wouldn't have asked that question. They aren't in the world at all. They're in *you* – when you went so angry.'

'D'you mean a dull purplish patch, like port wine mixed with ink?' I said.

'I've never seen ink or port wine, but the colours aren't mixed. They are separate – all separate.'

'Do you mean black streaks and jags across the purple?'

She nodded. 'Yes – if they are like this,' and zig-zagged her finger again, 'but it's more red than purple – that bad colour.'

'And what are the colours at the top of the – whatever you see?'

Slowly she leaned forward and traced on the rug the figure of the Egg itself.

'I see them so,' she said, pointing with a grass stem, 'white, green, yellow, red, purple, and when people are angry or bad, black across the red – as you were just now.'

'Who told you anything about it – in the beginning?' I demanded.

'About the colours? No one. I used to ask what colours were when I was little – in table-covers and curtains and carpets, you see – because some colours hurt me and some made me happy. People told me; and when I got older that was how I saw people.' Again she traced the outline of the Egg which it is given to very few of us to see.

'All by yourself?' I repeated.

'All by myself. There wasn't anyone else. I only found out afterwards that other people did not see the Colours.'

She leaned against the tree-bole plaiting and unplaiting chance-plucked grass stems. The children in the wood had drawn nearer. I could see them with the tail of my eye frolicking like squirrels.

'Now I am sure you will never laugh at me,' she went on after a long silence. 'Nor at *them*.'

'Goodness! No!' I cried, jolted out of my train of thought. 'A man who laughs at a child – unless the child is laughing too – is a heathen!'

'I didn't mean that, of course. You'd never laugh *at* children, but I thought – I used to think – that perhaps you might laugh about *them*. So now I beg your pardon. . . . What are you going to laugh at?'

I had made no sound, but she knew.

'At the notion of your begging my pardon. If you had done your duty as a pillar of the State and a landed proprietress you ought to have summoned me for trespass when I barged through your woods the other day. It was disgraceful of me – inexcusable.'

She looked at me, her head against the tree trunk – long and steadfastly – this woman who could see the naked soul.

'How curious,' she half whispered. 'How very curious.'

'Why, what have I done?'

'You don't understand . . . and yet you understood about the Colours. Don't you understand?'

She spoke with a passion that nothing had justified, and I faced her bewilderedly as she rose. The children had gathered themselves in a roundel behind a bramble bush. One sleek head bent over something smaller, and the set of the little shoulders told me that fingers were on lips. They, too, had some child's tremendous secret. I alone was hopelessly astray there in the broad sunlight.

'No,' I said, and shook my head as though the dead eyes could note. 'Whatever it is, I don't understand yet. Perhaps I shall later – if you'll let me come again.'

'You will come again,' she answered. 'You will surely come again and walk in the wood.'

'Perhaps the children will know me well enough by that time to let me play with them – as a favour. You know what children are like.'

'It isn't a matter of favour but of right,' she replied, and while I wondered what she meant, a dishevelled woman plunged round the bend of the road, loose-haired, purple, almost lowing with agony as she ran. It was my rude, fat friend of the sweetmeat shop. The blind woman heard and stepped forward. 'What is it, Mrs Madehurst?' she asked.

The woman flung her apron over her head and literally grovelled in the dust, crying that her grandchild was sick to death, that the local doctor was away fishing, that Jenny the mother was at her wits' end, and so forth, with repetitions and bellowings.

'Where's the next nearest doctor?' I asked between paroxysms.

'Madden will tell you. Go round to the house and take him with you. I'll attend to this. By quick!' She half supported the fat woman into the shade. In two minutes I was blowing all the horns of Jericho under the front of the House Beautiful, and Madden, in the pantry, rose to the crisis like a butler and a man.

A quarter of an hour at illegal speeds caught us a doctor five miles away. Within the half-hour we had decanted him, much interested in motors, at the door of the sweetmeat shop, and drew up the road to await the verdict.

'Useful things cars,' said Madden, all man and no butler. 'If I'd had one when mine took sick she wouldn't have died.'

'How was it?' I asked.

'Croup. Mrs Madden was away. No one knew what to do. I drove eight miles in a tax cart for the doctor. She was choked when we came back. This car 'd ha' saved her. She'd have been close on ten now.'

'I'm sorry,' I said. 'I thought you were rather fond of children from what you told me going to the crossroads the other day.'

'Have you seen 'em again, Sir – this mornin'?'

'Yes, but they're well broke to cars. I couldn't get any of them within twenty yards of it.'

He looked at me carefully as a scout considers a stranger – not as a menial should lift his eyes to his divinely appointed superior.

'I wonder why,' he said just above the breath that he drew.

We waited on. A light wind from the sea wandered up and down the long lines of the woods, and the wayside grasses, whitened already with summer dust, rose and bowed in sallow waves.

A woman, wiping the suds off her arms, came out of the cottage next the sweetmeat shop.

'I've be'n listenin' in de back-yard,' she said cheerily. 'He says Arthur's unaccountable bad. Did ye hear him shruck just now? Unaccountable bad. I reckon t'will come Jenny's turn to walk in de wood nex' week along, Mr Madden.'

'Excuse me, Sir, but your lap-robe is slipping,' said Madden deferentially. The woman started, dropped a curtsey, and hurried away.

'What does she mean by "walking in the wood"?' I asked.

'It must be some saying they use hereabouts. I'm from Norfolk myself,' said Madden. 'They're an independent lot in this county. She took you for a chauffeur, Sir.'

I saw the Doctor come out of the cottage followed by a draggle-tailed wench who clung to his arm as though he could make treaty for her with Death. 'Dat sort,' she wailed – 'dey're just as much to us dat has 'em as if dey was lawful born. Just as much – just as much! An' God he'd be just as pleased if you saved 'un, Doctor. Don't take it from me. Miss Florence will tell ye de very same. Don't leave 'im, Doctor!'

'I know, I know,' said the man; 'but he'll be quiet for a while now. We'll get the nurse and the medicine as fast as we can.' He signalled me to come forward with the car, and I strove not to be privy to what followed; but I saw the girl's face, blotched and frozen with grief, and I felt the hand without a ring clutching at my knees when we moved away.

The Doctor was a man of some humour, for I remember he claimed my car under the Oath of Æsculapius, and used it and me without mercy. First we convoyed Mrs Madehurst and the blind woman to wait by the sick bed till the nurse should come. Next we invaded a neat county town for prescriptions (the Doctor said the trouble was cerebro-spinal meningitis), and when the County Institute, banked and flanked with scared market cattle, reported itself out of nurses for the moment we literally flung ourselves loose upon the county. We conferred with the owners of great houses – magnates at the ends of overarching avenues whose big-boned womenfolk strode away from their tea-tables to listen to the imperious Doctor. At last a white-haired lady sitting under a cedar of Lebanon and surrounded by a court of magnificent Borzois – all hostile to motors – gave the Doctor, who received them as from a princess, written orders which we bore many miles at top speed, through a park, to a French nunnery, where we took over in exchange a pallid-faced and trembling Sister. She knelt at the bottom of the tonneau telling her beads without pause till, by short cuts of the Doctor's invention, we had her to the sweetmeat shop once more. It was a long afternoon crowded with mad episodes that rose and dissolved like the dust of our wheels; cross-sections of remote and incomprehensible lives through which we raced at right angles; and I went home in the dusk, wearied out, to dream of the clashing horns of cattle; round-eyed nuns walking in a garden of graves; pleasant tea-parties beneath shaded trees; the carbolic-scented, grey-painted corridors of the County Institute; the steps of shy children in the wood, and the hands that clung to my knees as the motor began to move.

I had intended to return in a day or two, but it pleased Fate to hold me from that side of the county, on many pretexts, till the elder and the wild rose had fruited. There came at last a brilliant day, swept clear from the south-west, that brought the hills within hand's reach – a day of unstable airs and high filmy clouds. Through no merit of my own I was free, and set the car for the third time on that known road. As I reached the crest of the Downs I felt the soft air change, saw it glaze under the sun; and, looking down at the sea, in that instant beheld the blue of the Channel turn through polished silver and dulled steel to dingy pewter. A laden collier hugging the coast steered outward for deeper water, and, across copper-coloured haze, I saw sails rise one by one on the anchored fishing-fleet. In a deep dene behind me an eddy of sudden wind drummed through sheltered oaks, and spun aloft the first dry sample of autumn leaves. When I reached the beach road the sea-fog fumed over the brickfields, and the tide was telling all the groins of the gale beyond Ushant. In less than an hour summer England vanished in chill grey. We were again the shut island of the North, all the ships of the world bellowing at our perilous gates; and between their outcries ran the piping of bewildered gulls. My cap dripped moisture, the folds of the rug held it in pools or sluiced it away in runnels, and the salt-rime stuck to my lips.

Inland the smell of autumn loaded the thickened fog among the trees, and the drip became a continuous shower. Yet the late flowers – mallow of the wayside, scabious of the field, and dahlia of the garden – showed gay in the mist, and beyond the sea's breath there was little sign of decay in the leaf. Yet in the villages the house doors were all open, and bare-legged, bare-headed children sat at ease on the damp doorsteps to shout 'pip-pip' at the stranger.

I made bold to call at the sweetmeat shop, where Mrs Madehurst met me with a fat woman's hospitable tears. Jenny's child, she said, had died two days after the nun had come. It was, she felt, best out of the way, even though insurance offices, for reasons which she did not pretend to follow, would not willingly insure such stray lives. 'Not but what Jenny didn't tend to Arthur as though he'd come all proper at de end of de first year – like Jenny herself.' Thanks to Miss Florence, the child had been buried with a pomp which, in Mrs Madehurst's opinion, more than covered the small irregularity of its birth. She described the coffin, within and without, the glass hearse, and the evergreen lining of the grave.

'But how's the mother?' I asked.

'Jenny? Oh, she'll get over it. I've felt dat way with one or two o' my own. She'll get over. She's walkin' in de wood now.'

'In this weather?'

Mrs Madehurst looked at me with narrowed eyes across the counter.

'I dunno but it opens de 'eart like. Yes, it opens de 'eart. Dat's where losin' and bearin' comes so alike in de long run, we do say.'

Now the wisdom of the old wives is greater than that of all the Fathers, and this last oracle sent me thinking so extendedly as I went up the road, that I nearly ran over a woman and a child at the wooded corner by the lodge gates of the House Beautiful.

'Awful weather!' I cried, as I slowed dead for the turn.

'Not so bad,' she answered placidly out of the fog. 'Mine's used to 'un. You'll find yours indoors, I reckon.'

Indoors, Madden received me with professional courtesy, and kind inquiries for the health of the motor, which he would put under cover.

I waited in a still, nut-brown hall, pleasant with late flowers and warmed with a delicious wood fire – a place of good influence and great peace. (Men and women may sometimes, after great effort, achieve a creditable lie; but the house, which is their temple, cannot say anything save the truth of those who have lived in it.) A child's cart and a doll lay on the black-and-white floor, where a rug had been kicked back. I felt that the children had only just hurried away – to hide themselves, most like – in the many turns of the great adzed staircase that climbed statelily out of the hall, or to crouch at gaze behind the lions and roses of the carven gallery above. Then I heard her voice above me, singing as the blind sing – from the soul:–

> In the pleasant orchard-closes.

And all my early summer came back at the call.

In the pleasant orchard-closes,
God bless all our gains say we –
But may God bless all our losses,
Better suits with our degree.

She dropped the marring fifth line, and repeated –

Better suits with our degree!

I saw her lean over the gallery, her linked hands white as pearl against the oak.

'Is that you – from the other side of the county?' she called.

'Yes, me – from the other side of the county,' I answered, laughing.

'What a long time before you had to come here again.' She ran down the stairs, one hand lightly touching the broad rail. 'It's two months and four days. Summer's gone!'

'I meant to come before, but Fate prevented.'

'I knew it. Please do something to that fire. They won't let me play with it, but I can feel it's behaving badly. Hit it!'

I looked on either side of the deep fireplace, and found but a half-charred hedge-stake with which I punched a black log into flame.

'It never goes out, day or night,' she said, as though explaining. 'In case anyone comes in with cold toes, you see.'

'It's even lovelier inside than it was out,' I murmured. The red light poured itself along the age-polished dusky panels till the Tudor roses and lions of the gallery took colour and motion. An old eagle-topped convex mirror gathered the picture into its mysterious heart, distorting afresh the distorted shadows, and curving the gallery lines into the curves of a ship. The day was shutting down in half a gale as the fog turned to stringy scud. Through the uncurtained mullions of the broad window I could see valiant horsemen of the lawn rear and recover against the wind that taunted them with legions of dead leaves.

'Yes, it must be beautiful,' she said. 'Would you like to go over it? There's still light enough upstairs.'

I followed her up the unflinching, wagon-wide staircase to the gallery whence opened the thin fluted Elizabethan doors.

'Feel how they put the latch low down for the sake of the children.' She swung a light door inward.

'By the way, where are they?' I asked. 'I haven't even heard them today.'

She did not answer at once. Then, 'I can only hear them,' she replied softly. 'This is one of their rooms – everything ready, you see.'

She pointed into a heavily-timbered room. There were little low gate tables and children's chairs. A doll's house, its hooked front half open, faced a great dappled rocking-horse, from whose padded saddle it was but a child's scramble to the broad window-seat overlooking the lawn. A toy gun lay in a corner beside a gilt wooden cannon.

'Surely they've only just gone,' I whispered. In the failing light a door creaked cautiously. I heard the rustle of a frock and the patter of feet – quick feet through a room beyond.

'I heard that,' she cried triumphantly. 'Did you? Children, oh, children! Where are you?'

The voice filled the walls that held it lovingly to the last perfect note, but there came no answering shout such as I had heard in the garden. We hurried on from room to oak-floored room; up a step here, down three steps there; among a maze of passages; always mocked by our quarry. One might as well have tried to work an unstopped warren with a single ferret. There were bolt-holes innumerable – recesses in walls, embrasures of deep slitten windows now darkened, whence they could start up behind us; and abandoned fireplaces, six feet deep in the masonry, as well as the tangle of communicating doors. Above all, they had the twilight for their helper in our game. I had caught one or two joyous chuckles of evasion, and once or twice had seen the silhouette of a child's frock against some darkening window at the end of a passage; but we returned empty-handed to the gallery, just as a middle-aged woman was setting a lamp in its niche.

'No, I haven't seen her either this evening, Miss Florence,' I heard her say, 'but that Turpin he says he wants to see you about his shed.'

'Oh, Mr Turpin must want to see me very badly. Tell him to come to the hall, Mrs Madden.'

I looked down into the hall whose only light was the dulled fire, and deep in the shadow I saw them at last. They must have slipped down while we were in the passages, and now thought themselves perfectly hidden behind an old gilt leather screen. By child's law, my fruitless chase was as good as an introduction, but since I had taken so much trouble I resolved to force them to come forward later by the simple trick, which children detest, of pretending not to notice them. They lay close, in a little huddle, no more than shadows except when a quick flame betrayed an outline.

'And now we'll have some tea,' she said. 'I believe I ought to have offered it you at first, but one doesn't arrive at manners somehow when one lives alone and is considered – h'm – peculiar.' Then with very pretty scorn, 'Would you like a lamp to see to eat by?'

'The firelight's much pleasanter, I think.' We descended into that delicious gloom and Madden brought tea.

I took my chair in the direction of the screen ready to surprise or be surprised as the game should go, and at her permission, since a hearth is always sacred, bent forward to play with the fire.

'Where do you get these beautiful short faggots from?' I asked idly. 'Why, they are tallies!'

'Of course,' she said. 'As I can't read or write I'm driven back on the early English tally for my accounts. Give me one and I'll tell you what it meant.'

I passed her an unburned hazel-tally, about a foot long, and she ran her thumb down the nicks.

'This is the milk-record for the home farm for the month of April last year, in gallons,' said she. 'I don't know what I should have done without tallies. An old forester of mine taught me the system. It's out of date now for everyone else; but my tenants respect it. One of them's coming now to see me. Oh, it doesn't matter. He has no business here out of office hours. He's a greedy, ignorant man – very greedy or – he wouldn't come here after dark.'

'Have you much land then?'

'Only a couple of hundred acres in hand, thank goodness. The other six hundred are nearly all let to folk who knew my folk before me, but this Turpin is quite a new man – and a highway robber.'

'But are you sure I shan't be——?'

'Certainly not. You have the right. He hasn't any children.'

'Ah, the children!' I said, and slid my low chair back till it nearly touched the screen that hid them. 'I wonder whether they'll come out for me.'

There was a murmur of voices – Madden's and a deeper note – at the low, dark side door, and a ginger-headed, canvas-gaitered giant of the unmistakable tenant-farmer type stumbled or was pushed in.

'Come to the fire, Mr Turpin,' she said.

'If – if you please, Miss, I'll – I'll be quite as well by the door.' He clung to the latch as he spoke like a frightened child. Of a sudden I realised that he was in the grip of some almost over-powering fear.

'Well?'

'About that new shed for the young stock – that was all. These first autumn storms settin' in . . . but I'll come again, Miss.' His teeth did not chatter much more than the door latch.

'I think not,' she answered levelly. 'The new shed – m'm. What did my agent write you on the 15th?'

'I – fancied p'raps that if I came to see you – ma – man to man like, Miss. But——'

His eyes rolled into every corner of the room wide with horror. He half opened the door through which he had entered, but I noticed it shut again – from without and firmly.

'He wrote what I told him,' she went on. 'You are overstocked already. Dunnett's Farm never carried more than fifty bullocks – even in Mr Wright's time. And *he* used cake. You've sixty-seven and you don't cake. You've broken the lease in that respect. You're dragging the heart out of the farm.'

'I'm – I'm getting some minerals – superphosphates – next week. I've as good as ordered a truck-load already. I'll go down to the station tomorrow about 'em. Then I can come and see you man to man like, Miss, in the daylight. . . . That gentleman's not going away, is he?' He almost shrieked.

I had only slid the chair a little farther back, reaching behind me to tap on the leather of the screen, but he jumped like a rat.

'No. Please attend to me, Mr Turpin.' She turned in her chair and faced him with his back to the door. It was an old and sordid little piece of scheming that she forced from him – his plea for the new cowshed at his landlady's expense, that he might with the covered manure pay his next year's rent out of the valuation after, as she made clear, he had bled the enriched pastures to the bone. I could not but admire the intensity of his greed, when I saw him out-facing for its sake whatever terror it was that ran wet on his forehead.

I ceased to tap the leather – was, indeed, calculating the cost of the shed – when I felt my relaxed hand taken and turned softly between the soft hands of a child. So at last I had triumphed. In a moment I would turn and acquaint myself with those quick-footed wanderers. . . .

The little brushing kiss fell in the centre of my palm – as a gift on which the fingers were, once, expected to close: as the all-faithful half-reproachful signal of a waiting child not used to neglect even when grown-ups were busiest – a fragment of the mute code devised very long ago.

Then I knew. And it was as though I had known from the first day when I looked across the lawn at the high window.

I heard the door shut. The woman turned to me in silence, and I felt that she knew.

What time passed after this I cannot say. I was roused by the fall of a log, and mechanically rose to put it back. Then I returned to my place in the chair very close to the screen.

'Now you understand,' she whispered, across the packed shadows.

'Yes, I understand – now. Thank you.'

'I – I only hear them.' She bowed her head in her hands. 'I have no right, you know – no other right. I have neither borne nor lost – neither borne nor lost!'

'Be very glad then,' said I, for my soul was torn open within me.

'Forgive me!'

She was still, and I went back to my sorrow and my joy.

'It was because I loved them so,' she said at last, brokenly. '*That* was why it was, even from the first – even before I knew that they – they were all I should ever have. And I loved them so!'

She stretched out her arms to the shadows and the shadows within the shadow.

'They came because I loved them – because I needed them. I – I must have made them come. Was that wrong, think you?'

'No – no.'

'I – I grant you that the toys and – and all that sort of thing were nonsense, but – but I used to so hate empty rooms myself when I was little.' She pointed to the gallery. 'And the passages all empty. . . . And how could I ever bear the garden door shut? Suppose——'

'Don't! For pity's sake, don't!' I cried. The twilight had brought a cold rain with gusty squalls that plucked at the leaded windows.

'And the same thing with keeping the fire in all night. *I* don't think it so foolish – do you?'

I looked at the broad brick hearth, saw, through tears I believe, that there was no unpassable iron on or near it, and bowed my head.

'I did all that and lots of other things – just to make believe. Then they came. I heard them, but I didn't know that they were not mine by right till Mrs Madden told me——'

'The butler's wife? What?'

'One of them – I heard – she saw. And knew. Hers! *Not* for me. I didn't know at first. Perhaps I was jealous. Afterwards, I began to understand that it was only because I loved them, not because—— . . . Oh, you *must* bear or lose,' she said piteously. 'There is no other way – and yet they love me. They must! Don't they?'

There was no sound in the room except the lapping voices of the fire, but we two listened intently, and she at least took comfort from what she heard. She recovered herself and half rose. I sat still in my chair by the screen.

'Don't think me a wretch to whine about myself like this, but – but I'm all in the dark, you know, and *you* can see.'

In truth I could see, and my vision confirmed me in my resolve, though that was like the very parting of spirit and flesh. Yet a little longer I would stay since it was the last time.

'You think it is wrong, then?' she cried sharply, though I had said nothing.

'Not for you. A thousand times no. For you it is right. . . . I am grateful to you beyond words. For me it would be wrong. For me only. . . .'

'Why?' she said, but passed her hand before her face as she had done at our second meeting in the wood. 'Oh, I see,' she went on simply as a child. 'For you it would be wrong.' Then with a little indrawn laugh, 'and, d'you remember I called you lucky – once – at first. You who must never come here again!'

She left me to sit a little longer by the screen, and I heard the sound of her feet die out along the gallery above.

The House Surgeon

On an evening after Easter Day, I sat at a table in a homeward bound steamer's smoking-room, where half a dozen of us told ghost stories. As our party broke up, a man, playing Patience in the next alcove, said to me: 'I didn't quite catch the end of that last story about the Curse on the family's first-born.'

'It turned out to be drains,' I explained. 'As soon as new ones were put into the house the Curse was lifted, I believe. I never knew the people myself.'

'Ah! I've had *my* drains up twice; I'm on gravel too.'

'You don't mean to say you've a ghost in your house? Why didn't you join our party?'

'Any more orders, gentlemen, before the bar closes?' the steward interrupted.

'Sit down again and have one with me,' said the Patience player. 'No, it isn't a ghost. Our trouble is more depression than anything else.'

'How interesting! Then it's nothing any one can see?'

'It's – it's nothing worse than a little depression. And the odd part is that there hasn't been a death in the house since it was built – in 1863. The lawyer said so. That decided me – my good lady, rather – and he made me pay an extra thousand for it.'

'How curious. Unusual, too!' I said.

'Yes, ain't it? It was built for three sisters – Moultrie was the name – three old maids. They all lived together; the eldest owned it. I bought it from her lawyer a few years ago, and if I've spent a pound on the place first and last, I must have spent five thousand. Electric light, new servants' wing, garden – all that sort of thing. A man and his family ought to be happy after so much expense, ain't it?' He looked at me through the bottom of his glass.

'Does it affect your family much?'

'My good lady – she's a Greek by the way – and myself are middle-aged. We can bear up against depression; but it's hard on my little girl. I say 'little; but she's twenty. We send her visiting to escape it. She almost lived at hotels and hydros last year, but that isn't pleasant for her. She used to be a canary –

a perfect canary – always singing. You ought to hear her. She doesn't sing now. That sort of thing's unwholesome for the young, ain't it?'

'Can you get rid of the place?' I suggested.

'Not except at a sacrifice, and we are fond of it. Just suits us three. We'd love it if we were allowed.'

'What do you mean by not being allowed?'

'I mean because of the depression. It spoils everything.'

'What's it like exactly?'

'I couldn't very well explain. It must be seen to be appreciated, as the auctioneers say. Now, I was much impressed by the story you were telling just now.'

'It wasn't true,' I said.

'My tale is true. If you would do me the pleasure to come down and spend a night at my little place, you'd learn more than you would if I talked till morning. Very likely 'twouldn't touch your good self at all. You might be – immune, ain't it? On the other hand, if this influenza-influence *does* happen to affect you, why, I think it will be an experience.'

While he talked he gave me his card, and I read his name was L. Maxwell M'Leod, Esq., of Holmescroft. A City address was tucked away in a corner.

'My business,' he added, 'used to be furs. If you are interested in furs – I've given thirty years of my life to 'em.'

'You're very kind,' I murmured.

'Far from it, I assure you. I can meet you next Saturday afternoon anywhere in London you choose to name, and I'll be only too happy to motor you down. It ought to be a delightful run at this time of year – the rhododendrons will be out. I mean it. You don't know how truly I mean it. Very probably – it won't affect you at all. And – I think I may say I have the finest collection of narwhal tusks in the world. All the best skins and horns have to go through London, and L. Maxwell M'Leod, he knows where they come from, and where they go to. That's his business.'

For the rest of the voyage up-channel Mr M'Leod talked to me of the assembling, preparation, and sale of the rarer furs; and told me things about the manufacture of fur-lined coats which quite shocked me. Somehow or other, when we landed on Wednesday, I found myself pledged to spend that week-end with him at Holmescroft.

On Saturday he met me with a well-groomed motor, and ran me out in an hour-and-a-half to an exclusive residential district of dustless roads and elegantly designed country villas, each standing in from three to five acres of perfectly appointed land. He told me land was selling at eight hundred pounds the acre, and the new golf links, whose Queen Anne pavilion we passed, had cost nearly twenty-four thousand pounds to create.

Holmescroft was a large, two-storied, low, creeper-covered residence. A verandah at the south side gave on to a garden and two tennis courts, separated by a tasteful iron fence from a most park-like meadow of five or six acres, where two Jersey cows grazed. Tea was ready in the shade of a promising copper beech, and I could see groups on the lawn of young men and maidens appropriately clothed, playing lawn tennis in the sunshine.

'A pretty scene, ain't it?' said Mr M'Leod. 'My good lady's sitting under the tree, and that's my little girl in pink on the far court. But I'll take you to your room, and you can see 'em all later.'

He led me through a wide parquet-floored hall furnished in pale lemon, with huge cloisonné vases, an ebonised and gold grand piano, and banks of pot flowers in Benares brass bowls, up a pale oak staircase to a spacious landing, where there was a green velvet settee trimmed with silver. The blinds were down, and the light lay in parallel lines on the floors.

He showed me my room, saying cheerfully: 'You may be a little tired. One often is without knowing it after a run through traffic. Don't come down till you feel quite restored. We shall all be in the garden.'

My room was rather close, and smelt of perfumed soap. I threw up the window at once, but it opened so close to the floor and worked so clumsily that I came within an ace of pitching out, where I should certainly have ruined a rather lop-sided laburnum below. As I set about washing off the journey's dust, I began to feel a little tired. But, I reflected, I had not come down here in this weather and among these new surroundings to be depressed, so I began to whistle.

And it was just then that I was aware of a little grey shadow, as it might have been a snow-flake seen against the light, floating at an immense distance in the background of my brain. It annoyed me, and I shook my head to get rid of it. Then my brain telegraphed that it was the forerunner of a swift-striding gloom which there was yet time to escape if I would force my thoughts away from it, as a man leaping for life forces his body forward and away from the fall of a wall. But the gloom overtook me before I could take in the meaning of the message. I moved toward the bed, every nerve already aching with the foreknowledge of the pain that was to be dealt it, and sat down, while my amazed and angry soul dropped, gulf by gulf, into that horror of great darkness which is spoken of in the Bible, and which, as auctioneers say, must be experienced to be appreciated.

Despair upon despair, misery upon misery, fear after fear, each causing their distinct and separate woe, packed in upon me for an unrecorded length of time, until at last they blurred together, and I heard a click in my brain like the click in the ear when one descends in a diving bell, and I knew that the pressures were equalised within and without, and that, for the moment, the worst was at an end. But I knew also that at any moment the darkness might come down anew; and while I dwelt on this speculation precisely as a man torments a raging tooth with his tongue, it ebbed away into the little grey shadow on the brain of its first coming, and once more I heard my brain, which knew what would recur, telegraph to every quarter for help, release, or diversion.

The door opened, and M'Leod reappeared. I thanked him politely, saying I was charmed with my room, anxious to meet Mrs M'Leod, much refreshed with my wash, and so on and so forth. Beyond a little stickiness at the corners of my mouth, it seemed to me that I was managing my words admirably, the while that I myself cowered at the bottom of unclimbable pits. M'Leod laid his hand on my shoulder, and said: 'You've got it now already, ain't it?'

'Yes,' I answered, 'it's making me sick!'

'It will pass off when you come outside. I give you my word it will then pass off. Come!'

I shambled out behind him, and wiped my forehead in the hall.

'You mustn't mind,' he said. 'I expect the run tired you. My good lady is sitting there under the copper beech.'

She was a fat woman in an apricot-coloured gown, with a heavily powdered face, against which her black long-lashed eyes showed like currants in dough. I was introduced to many fine ladies and gentlemen of those parts. Magnificently appointed landaus and covered motors swept in and out of the drive, and the air was gay with the merry outcries of the tennis players.

As twilight drew on they all went away, and I was left alone with Mr and Mrs M'Leod, while tall men-servants and maid-servants took away the tennis and tea things. Miss M'Leod had walked a little down the drive with a light-haired young man, who apparently knew everything about every South American railway stock. He had told me at tea that these were the days of financial specialisation.

'I think it went off beautifully, my dear,' said Mr M'Leod to his wife; and to me: 'You feel all right now, ain't it? Of course you do.'

Mrs M'Leod surged across the gravel. Her husband skipped nimbly before her into the south verandah, turned a switch, and all Holmescroft was flooded with light.

'You can do that from your room also,' he said as they went in. 'There is something in money, ain't it?'

Miss M'Leod came up behind me in the dusk. 'We have not yet been introduced,' she said, 'but I suppose you are staying the night?'

'Your father was kind enough to ask me,' I replied.

She nodded. 'Yes, *I* know; and you know too, don't you? I saw your face when you came to shake hands with mamma. You felt the depression very soon. It is simply frightful in that bedroom sometimes. What do you think it is – bewitchment? In Greece, where I was a little girl, it might have been; but not in England, do you think? Or *do* you?'

'I don't know what to think,' I replied. 'I never felt anything like it. Does it happen often?'

'Yes, sometimes. It comes and goes.'

'Pleasant!' I said, as we walked up and down the gravel at the lawn edge. 'What has been your experience of it?'

'That is difficult to say, but – sometimes that – that depression is like as it were' – she gesticulated in most un-English fashion – 'a light. Yes, like a light turned into a room – only a light of blackness, do you understand? – into a happy room. For sometimes we are so happy, all we three, – so very happy. Then this blackness, it is turned on us just like – ah, I know what I mean now – like the head-lamp of a motor, and we are eclip-sed. And there is another thing——'

The dressing gong roared, and we entered the over-lighted hall. My dressing was a brisk athletic performance, varied with outbursts of song – careful attention paid to articulation and expression. But nothing happened. As I hurried downstairs, I thanked Heaven that nothing had happened.

Dinner was served breakfast fashion; the dishes were placed on the sideboard over heaters, and we helped ourselves.

'We always do this when we are alone, so we talk better,' said Mr M'Leod.

'And we are always alone,' said the daughter.

'Cheer up, Thea. It will all come right,' he insisted.

'No, papa.' She shook her dark head. 'Nothing is right while *it* comes.'

'It is nothing that we ourselves have ever done in our lives – that I will swear to you,' said Mrs M'Leod suddenly. 'And we have changed our servants several times. So we know it is not *them*.'

'Never mind. Let us enjoy ourselves while we can,' said Mr M'Leod, opening the champagne.

But we did not enjoy ourselves. The talk failed. There were long silences.

'I beg your pardon,' I said, for I thought someone at my elbow was about to speak.

'Ah! That is the other thing!' said Miss M'Leod. Her mother groaned.

We were silent again, and, in a few seconds it must have been, a live grief beyond words – not ghostly dread or horror, but aching, helpless grief – overwhelmed us, each, I felt, according to his or her nature, and held steady like the beam of a burning-glass. Behind that pain I was conscious there was a desire on somebody's part to explain something on which some tremendously important issue hung.

Meantime I rolled bread pills and remembered my sins; M'Leod considered his own reflection in a spoon; his wife seemed to be praying, and the girl fidgeted desperately with hands and feet, till the darkness passed on – as though the malignant rays of a burning glass had been shifted from us.

'There,' said Miss M'Leod, half rising. 'Now you see what makes a happy home. Oh, sell it – sell it, father mine, and let us go away!'

'But I've spent thousands on it. You shall go to Harrogate next week, Thea dear.'

'I'm only just back from hotels. I am *so* tired of packing.'

'Cheer up, Thea. It is over. You know it does not often come here twice in the same night. I think we shall dare now to be comfortable.'

He lifted a dish-cover, and helped his wife and daughter. His face was lined and fallen like an old man's after debauch, but his hand did not shake, and his voice was clear. As he worked to restore us by speech and action, he reminded me of a grey-muzzled collie herding demoralised sheep.

After dinner we sat round the dining-room fire – the drawing-room might have been under the Shadow for aught we knew – talking with the intimacy of gipsies by the wayside, or of wounded comparing notes after a skirmish. By eleven o'clock the three between them had given me every name and detail they could recall that in any way bore on the house, and what they knew of its history.

We went to bed in a fortifying blaze of electric light. My one fear was that the blasting gust of depression would return – the surest way, of course, to bring it. I lay awake till dawn, breathing quickly and sweating lightly, beneath what De Quincey inadequately describes as 'the oppression of inexpiable guilt'. Now as soon as the lovely day was broken, I fell into the most terrible of all dreams – that joyous one in which all past evil has not only been wiped out of our lives, but has never been committed; and in the very bliss of our assured innocence, before our loves shriek and change countenance, we wake to the day we have earned.

It was a coolish morning, but we preferred to breakfast in the south verandah. The forenoon we spent in the garden, pretending to play games that come out of boxes, such as croquet and clock golf. But most of the time we drew together and talked. The young man who knew all about South American railways took Miss M'Leod for a walk in the afternoon, and at five M'Leod thoughtfully whirled us all up to dine in town.

'Now, don't say you will tell the Psychological Society, and that you will come again,' said Miss M'Leod, as we parted. 'Because I know you will not.'

'You should not say that,' said her mother. 'You should say, "Goodbye, Mr Perseus. Come again." '

'Not him!' the girl cried. 'He has seen the Medusa's head!'

Looking at myself in the restaurant's mirrors, it seemed to me that I had not much benefited by my weekend. Next morning I wrote out all my Holmescroft notes at fullest length, in the hope that by so doing I could put it all behind me. But the experience worked on my mind, as they say certain imperfectly understood rays work on the body.

I am less calculated to make a Sherlock Holmes than any man I know, for I lack both method and patience, yet the idea of following up the trouble to its source fascinated me. I had no theory to go on, except a vague idea that I had come between two poles of a discharge, and had taken a shock meant for someone else. This was followed by a feeling of intense irritation. I waited cautiously on myself, expecting to be overtaken by horror of the supernatural, but my self persisted in being humanly indignant, exactly as though it had been the victim of a practical joke. It was in great pains and upheavals – that I felt in every fibre – but its dominant idea, to put it coarsely, was to get back a bit of its own. By this I knew that I might go forward if I could find the way.

After a few days it occurred to me to go to the office of Mr J. M. M. Baxter – the solicitor who had sold Holmescroft to M'Leod. I explained I had some notion of buying the place. Would he act for me in the matter?

Mr Baxter, a large, greyish, throaty-voiced man, showed no

enthusiasm. 'I sold it to Mr M'Leod,' he said. 'It 'ud scarcely do for me to start on the running-down tack now. But I can recommend—'

'I know he's asking an awful price,' I interrupted, 'and atop of it he wants an extra thousand for what he calls your clean bill of health.'

Mr Baxter sat up in his chair. I had all his attention.

'Your guarantee with the house. Don't you remember it?'

'Yes, yes. That no death had taken place in the house since it was built. I remember perfectly.'

He did not gulp as untrained men do when they lie, but his jaws moved stickily, and his eyes, turning towards the deed boxes on the wall, dulled. I counted seconds, one, two, three – one, two, three – up to ten. A man, I knew, can live through ages of mental depression in that time.

'I remember perfectly.' His mouth opened a little as though it had tasted old bitterness.

'Of course *that* sort of thing doesn't appeal to me,' I went on. '*I* don't expect to buy a house free from death.'

'Certainly not. No one does. But it was Mr M'Leod's fancy – his wife's rather, I believe; and since we could meet it – it was my duty to my clients – at whatever cost to my own feelings – to make him pay.'

'That's really why I came to you. I understood from him you knew the place well.'

'Oh yes. Always did. It originally belonged to some connections of mine.'

'The Misses Moultrie, I suppose. How interesting! They must have loved the place before the country round about was built up.'

'They were very fond of it indeed.'

'I don't wonder. So restful and sunny. I don't see how they could have brought themselves to part with it.'

Now it is one of the most constant peculiarities of the English that in polite conversation – and I had striven to be polite – no one ever does or sells anything for mere money's sake.

'Miss Agnes – the youngest – fell ill' (he spaced his words a little), 'and, as they were very much attached to each other, that broke up the home.'

'Naturally. I fancied it must have been something of that kind. One doesn't associate the Staffordshire Moultries' (my Demon of Irresponsibility at that instant created 'em), 'with – with being hard up.'

'I don't know whether we're related to them,' he answered importantly. 'We may be, for our branch of the family comes from the Midlands.'

I give this talk at length, because I am so proud of my first attempt at detective work. When I left him, twenty minutes later, with instructions to move against the owner of Holmescroft with a view to purchase, I was more bewildered than any Doctor Watson at the opening of a story.

Why should a middle-aged solicitor turn plover's egg colour and drop his jaw when reminded of so innocent and festal a matter as that no death had ever occurred in a house that he had sold? If I knew my English vocabulary at all, the tone in which he said the youngest sister 'fell ill' meant that she had gone out of her mind. That might explain his change of countenance, and it was just possible that her demented influence still hung about Holmescroft; but the rest was beyond me.

I was relieved when I reached M'Leod's City office, and could tell him what I had done – not what I thought.

M'Leod was quite willing to enter into the game of the pretended purchase, but did not see how it would help if I knew Baxter.

'He's the only living soul I can get at who was connected with Holmescroft,' I said.

'Ah! Living soul is good,' said M'Leod. 'At any rate our little girl will be pleased that you are still interested in us. Won't you come down some day this week?'

'How is it there now?' I asked.

He screwed up his face. 'Simply frightful!' he said. 'Thea is at Droitwich.'

'I should like it immensely, but I must cultivate Baxter for the present. You'll be sure and keep him busy your end, won't you?'

He looked at me with quiet contempt. 'Do not be afraid. I shall be a good Jew. I shall be my own solicitor.'

Before a fortnight was over, Baxter admitted ruefully that M'Leod was better than most firms in the business. We buyers were coy, argumentative, shocked at the price of Holmescroft, inquisitive, and cold by turns, but Mr M'Leod the seller easily met and surpassed us; and Mr Baxter entered every letter, telegram, and consultation at the proper rates in a cinematograph-film of a bill. At the end of a month he said it looked as though M'Leod, thanks to him, were really going to listen to reason. I was many pounds out of pocket, but I had learned something of Mr Baxter on the human side. I deserved it. Never in my life have I worked to conciliate, amuse, and flatter a human being as I worked over my solicitor.

It appeared that he golfed. Therefore, I was an enthusiastic beginner, anxious to learn. Twice I invaded his office with a bag (M'Leod lent it) full of the spelicans needed in this detestable game, and a vocabulary to match. The third time the ice broke, and Mr Baxter took me to his links, quite ten miles off, where in a maze of tramway lines, railroads, and nursery-maids, we skelped our divoted way round nine holes like barges plunging through head seas. He played vilely and had never expected to meet anyone worse; but as he realised my form, I think he began to like me, for he took me in hand by the two hours together. After a fortnight he could give me no more than a stroke a hole, and when, with this allowance, I once managed to beat him by one, he was honestly glad, and assured me that I should be a golfer if I stuck to it. I was sticking to it for my own ends, but now and again my conscience pricked me; for the man was a nice man. Between games he supplied me with odd pieces of evidence, such as that he had known the Moultries all his life, being their cousin, and that Miss Mary, the eldest, was an unforgiving woman who would never let bygones be. I naturally wondered what she might have against him; and somehow connected him unfavourably with mad Agnes.

'People ought to forgive and forget,' he volunteered one day between rounds. 'Specially where, in the nature of things, they can't be sure of their deductions. Don't you think so?'

'It all depends on the nature of the evidence on which one forms one's judgment,' I answered.

'Nonsense!' he cried. 'I'm lawyer enough to know that there's nothing in the world so misleading as circumstantial evidence. Never was.'

'Why? Have you ever seen men hanged on it?'

'Hanged? People have been supposed to be eternally lost on it,' his face turned grey again. 'I don't know how it is with you, but my consolation is that God must know. He *must*! Things that seem on the face of 'em like murder, or say suicide, may appear different to God. Heh?'

'That's what the murderer and the suicide can always hope – I suppose.'

'I have expressed myself clumsily as usual. The facts as God knows 'em – may *be* different – even after the most clinching evidence. I've always said that – both as a lawyer and a man, but some people won't – I don't want to judge 'em – we'll say they can't – believe it; whereas *I* say there's always a working chance – a certainty – that the worst hasn't happened.' He stopped and cleared his throat. 'Now, let's come on! This time next week I shall be taking my holiday.'

'What links?' I asked carelessly, while twins in a perambulator got out of our line of fire.

'A potty little nine-hole affair at a Hydro in the Midlands. My cousins stay there. Always will. Not but what the fourth and the seventh holes take some doing. You could manage it, though,' he said encouragingly. 'You're doing much better. It's only your approach shots that are weak.'

'You're right. I can't approach for nuts! I shall go to pieces while you're away – with no one to coach me,' I said mournfully.

'I haven't taught you anything,' he said, delighted with the compliment.

'I owe all I've learned to you, anyhow. When will you come back?'

'Look here,' he began. 'I don't know your engagements, but I've no one to play with at Burry Mills. Never have. Why couldn't you take a few days off and join me there? I warn you it will be rather dull. It's a throat and gout place – baths, massage, electricity, and so forth. But the fourth and the seventh holes really take some doing.'

'I'm for the game,' I answered valiantly, Heaven well knowing that I hated every stroke and word of it.

'That's the proper spirit. As their lawyer I must ask you not to say anything to my cousins about Holmescroft. It upsets 'em.

Always did. But speaking as man to man, it would be very pleasant for me if you could see your way to—'

I saw it as soon as decency permitted, and thanked him sincerely. According to my now well-developed theory he had certainly misappropriated his aged cousins' monies under power of attorney, and had probably driven poor Agnes Moultrie out of her wits, but I wished that he was not so gentle, and good-tempered, and innocent-eyed.

Before I joined him at Burry Mills Hydro, I spent a night at Holmescroft. Miss M'Leod had returned from her Hydro, and first we made very merry on the open lawn in the sunshine over the manners and customs of the English resorting to such places. She knew dozens of hydros, and warned me how to behave in them, while Mr and Mrs M'Leod stood aside and adored her.

'Ah! That's the way she always comes back to us,' he said. 'Pity it wears off so soon, ain't it? You ought to hear her sing "With mirth, thou pretty bird".'

We had the house to face through the evening, and there we neither laughed nor sang. The gloom fell on us as we entered, and did not shift till ten o'clock, when we crawled out, as it were, from beneath it.

'It has been bad this summer,' said Mrs M'Leod in a whisper after we realised that we were freed. 'Sometimes I think the house will get up and cry out – it is so bad.'

'How?'

'Have you forgotten what comes after the depression?'

So then we waited about the small fire, and the dead air in the room presently filled and pressed down upon us with the sensation (but words are useless here) as though some dumb and bound power were striving against gag and bond to deliver its soul of an articulate word. It passed in a few minutes, and I fell to thinking about Mr Baxter's conscience and Agnes Moultrie, gone mad in the well-lit bedroom that waited me. These reflections secured me a night during which I rediscovered how, from purely mental causes, a man can be physically sick; but the sickness was bliss compared to my dreams when the birds waked. On my departure, M'Leod gave me a beautiful narwhal's horn, much as a nurse gives a child sweets for being brave at a dentist's.

'There's no duplicate of it in the world,' he said, 'else it would have come to old Max M'Leod,' and he tucked it into the motor. Miss M'Leod on the far side of the car whispered, 'Have you found out anything, Mr Perseus?'

I shook my head.

'Then I shall be chained to my rock all my life,' she went on. 'Only don't tell papa.'

I supposed she was thinking of the young gentleman who specialised in South American rails, for I noticed a ring on the third finger of her left hand.

I went straight from that house to Burry Mills Hydro, keen for the first time in my life on playing golf, which is guaranteed to occupy the mind. Baxter had taken me a room communicating with his own, and after lunch introduced me to a tall, horse-headed elderly lady of decided manners, whom a white-haired maid pushed along in a bath-chair through the park-like grounds of the Hydro. She was Miss Mary Moultrie, and she coughed and cleared her throat just like Baxter. She suffered – she told me it was the Moultrie caste-mark – from some obscure form of chronic bronchitis, complicated with spasm of the glottis; and, in a dead flat voice, with a sunken eye that looked and saw not, told me what washes, gargles, pastilles, and inhalations she had proved most beneficial. From her I was passed on to her younger sister, Miss Elizabeth, a small and withered thing with twitching lips, victim, she told me, to very much the same sort of throat, but secretly devoted to another set of medicines. When she went away with Baxter and the bath-chair, I fell across a major of the Indian army with gout in his glassy eyes, and a stomach which he had taken all round the Continent. He laid everything before me; and him I escaped only to be confided in by a matron with a tendency to follicular tonsilitis and eczema. Baxter waited hand and foot on his cousins till five o'clock, trying, as I saw, to atone for his treatment of the dead sister. Miss Mary ordered him about like a dog.

'I warned you it would be dull,' he said when we met in the smoking-room.

'It's tremendously interesting,' I said. 'But how about a look round the links?'

'Unluckily damp always affects my eldest cousin. I've got to buy her a new bronchitis-kettle. Arthurs broke her old one yesterday.'

We slipped out to the chemist's shop in the town, and he bought a large glittering tin thing whose workings he explained.

'I'm used to this sort of work. I come up here pretty often,' he said. 'I've the family throat too.'

'You're a good man,' I said. 'A very good man.'

He turned towards me in the evening light among the beeches, and his face was changed to what it might have been a generation before.

'You see,' he said huskily, 'there was the youngest – Agnes. Before she fell ill, you know. But she didn't like leaving her sisters. Never would.' He hurried on with his odd-shaped load and left me among the ruins of my black theories. The man with that face had done Agnes Moultrie no wrong.

We never played our game. I was waked between two and three in the morning from my hygienic bed by Baxter in an ulster over orange and white pyjamas, which I should never have suspected from his character.

'My cousin has had some sort of a seizure,' he said. 'Will you come? I don't want to wake the doctor. Don't want to make a scandal. Quick!'

So I came quickly, and led by the white-haired Arthurs in a jacket and petticoat, entered a double-bedded room reeking with steam and Friar's Balsam. The electrics were all on. Miss Mary – I knew her by her height – was at the open window, wrestling with Miss Elizabeth, who gripped her round the knees. Her hand was at her throat, which was streaked with blood.

'She's done it. She's done it too!' Miss Elizabeth panted. 'Hold her! Help me!'

'Oh, I say! Women don't cut their throats,' Baxter whispered.

'My God! Has she cut her throat?' the maid cried, and with no warning rolled over in a faint. Baxter pushed her under the wash-basins, and leaped to hold the gaunt woman who crowed and whistled as she struggled towards the window. He took her by the shoulder, and she struck out wildly.

'All right! She's only cut her hand,' he said. 'Wet towel – quick!'

While I got that he pushed her backward. Her strength seemed almost as great as his. I swabbed at her throat when I could, and found no mark; then helped him to control her a little. Miss Elizabeth leaped back to bed, wailing like a child.

'Tie up her hand somehow,' said Baxter. 'Don't let it drip about the place. She' – he stepped on broken glass in his slippers, 'she must have smashed a pane.'

Miss Mary lurched towards the open window again, dropped on her knees, her head on the sill, and lay quiet, surrendering the cut hand to me.

'What did she do?' Baxter turned towards Miss Elizabeth in the far bed.

'She was going to throw herself out of the window,' was the answer. 'I stopped her, and sent Arthurs for you. Oh, we can never hold up our heads again!'

Miss Mary writhed and fought for breath. Baxter found a shawl which he threw over her shoulders.

'Nonsense!' said he. 'That isn't like Mary'; but his face worked when he said it.

'You wouldn't believe about Aggie, John. Perhaps you will now!' said Miss Elizabeth. 'I *saw* her do it, and she's cut her throat too!'

'She hasn't,' I said. 'It's only her hand.'

Miss Mary suddenly broke from us with an indescribable grunt, flew, rather than ran, to her sister's bed, and there shook her as one furious schoolgirl would shake another.

'No such thing,' she croaked. 'How dare you think so, you wicked little fool?'

'Get into bed, Mary,' said Baxter. 'You'll catch a chill.'

She obeyed, but sat up with the grey shawl round her lean shoulders, glaring at her sister. 'I'm better now,' she crowed. 'Arthurs let me sit out too long. Where's Arthurs? The kettle.'

'Never mind Arthurs,' said Baxter. '*You* get the kettle.' I hastened to bring it from the side table. 'Now Mary, as God sees you, tell me what you've done.'

His lips were dry, and he could not moisten them with his tongue.

Miss Mary applied herself to the mouth of the kettle, and between indraws of steam said: 'The spasm came on just now, while I was asleep. I was nearly choking to death. So I went to the window. I've done it often before, without waking anyone. Bessie's such an old maid about draughts. I tell you I was choking to death. I couldn't manage the catch, and I nearly fell out. That window opens too low. I cut my hand trying to save myself. Who has tied it up in this filthy handkerchief? I wish you had had my throat, Bessie. I never was nearer dying!' She scowled on us all impartially, while her sister sobbed.

From the bottom of the bed we heard a quivering voice: 'Is she dead? Have they took her away? Oh, I never could bear the sight o' blood!'

'Arthurs,' said Miss Mary, 'you are an hireling. Go away!'

It is my belief that Arthurs crawled out on all fours, but I was busy picking up broken glass from the carpet.

Then Baxter, seated by the side of the bed, began to cross-examine in a voice I scarcely recognised. No one could for an instant have doubted the genuine rage of Miss Mary against her sister, her cousin, or her maid; and that the doctor should have been called in – for she did me the honour of calling me doctor – was the last drop. She was choking with her throat; had rushed to the window for air; had near pitched out, and in catching at the window bars had cut her hand. Over and over she made this clear to the intent Baxter. Then she turned on her sister and tongue-lashed her savagely.

'You mustn't blame me,' Miss Bessie faltered at last. 'You know what we think of night and day.'

'I'm coming to that,' said Baxter. 'Listen to me. What *you* did, Mary, misled four people into thinking you – you meant to do away with yourself.'

'Isn't one suicide in the family enough? Oh God, help and pity us! You *couldn't* have believed that!' she cried.

'The evidence was complete. Now, don't you think,' Baxter's finger wagged under her nose – '*can't* you think that poor Aggie did the same thing at Holmescroft when she fell out of the window?'

'She had the same throat,' said Miss Elizabeth. 'Exactly the same symptoms. Don't you remember, Mary?'

'Which was her bedroom?' I asked of Baxter in an undertone.

'Over the south verandah, looking on to the tennis lawn.'

'I nearly fell out of that very window when I was at Holmescroft – opening it to get some air. The sill doesn't come much above your knees,' I said.

'You hear that, Mary? Mary, do you hear what this gentleman says? Won't you believe that what nearly happened to you must have happened to poor Aggie that night? For God's sake – for her sake – Mary, *won't* you believe?'

There was a long silence while the steam kettle puffed.

'If I could have proof – if I could have proof,' said she, and broke into most horrible tears.

Baxter motioned to me, and I crept away to my room, and lay awake till morning, thinking more specially of the dumb Thing at Holmescroft which wished to explain itself. I hated Miss Mary as perfectly as though I had known her for twenty years, but I felt that, alive or dead, I should not like her to condemn me.

Yet at midday, when I saw Miss Mary in her bath-chair, Arthurs behind and Baxter and Miss Elizabeth on either side, in the park-like grounds of the Hydro, I found it difficult to arrange my words.

'Now that you know all about it,' said Baxter aside, after the first strangeness of our meeting was over, 'it's only fair to tell you that my poor cousin did not die in Holmescroft at all. She was dead when they found her under the window in the morning. Just dead.'

'Under that laburnum outside the window?' I asked, for I suddenly remembered the crooked evil thing.

'Exactly. She broke the tree in falling. But no death has ever taken place *in* the house, so far as we were concerned. You can make yourself quite easy on that point. Mr M'Leod's extra thousand for what you called the "clean bill of health" was something towards my cousins' estate when we sold. It was my duty as their lawyer to get it for them – at any cost to my own feelings.'

I know better than to argue when the English talk about their duty. So I agreed with my solicitor.

'Their sister's death must have been a great blow to your cousins,' I went on. The bath-chair was behind me.

'Unspeakable,' Baxter whispered. 'They brooded on it day

and night. No wonder. If their theory of poor Aggie making away with herself was correct, she was eternally lost!'

'Do you believe that she made away with herself?'

'No, thank God! Never have! And after what happened to Mary last night, I see perfectly what happened to poor Aggie. She had the family throat too. By the way, Mary thinks you are a doctor. Otherwise she wouldn't like your having been in her room.'

'Very good. Is she convinced now about her sister's death?'

'She'd give anything to be able to believe it, but she's a hard woman, and brooding along certain lines makes one groovy. I have sometimes been afraid for her reason – on the religious side, don't you know. Elizabeth doesn't matter. Brain of a hen. Always had.'

Here Arthurs summoned me to the bath-chair, and the ravaged face, beneath its knitted Shetland wool hood, of Miss Mary Moultrie.

'I need not remind you, I hope, of the seal of secrecy – absolute secrecy – in your profession,' she began. 'Thanks to my cousin's and my sister's stupidity, you have found out——' she blew her nose.

'Please don't excite her, sir,' said Arthurs at the back.

'But, my dear Miss Moultrie, I only know what I've seen, of course, but it seems to me that what you thought was a tragedy in your sister's case, turns out, on your own evidence, so to speak, to have been an accident – a dreadfully sad one – but absolutely an accident.'

'Do you believe that too?' she cried. 'Or are you only saying it to comfort me?'

'I believe it from the bottom of my heart. Come down to Holmescroft for an hour – for half an hour – and satisfy yourself.'

'Of what? You don't understand. I see the house every day – every night. I am always there in spirit – waking or sleeping. I couldn't face it in reality.'

'But you must,' I said. 'If you go there in the spirit the greater need for you to go there in the flesh. Go to your sister's room once more, and see the window – I nearly fell out of it myself.

It's – it's awfully low and dangerous. That would convince you,' I pleaded.

'Yet Aggie had slept in that room for years,' she interrupted.

'You've slept in your room here for a long time, haven't you? But you nearly fell out of the window when you were choking.'

'That is true. That is one thing true,' she nodded. 'And I might have been killed as – perhaps – Aggie was killed.'

'In that case your own sister and cousin and maid would have said you had committed suicide, Miss Moultrie. Come down to Holmescroft, and go over the place just once.'

'You are lying,' she said quite quietly. 'You don't want me to come down to see a window. It is something else. I warn you we are Evangelicals. We don't believe in prayers for the dead. "As the tree falls——" '

'Yes. I daresay. But you persist in thinking that your sister committed suicide——'

'No! No! I have always prayed that I might have misjudged her.'

Arthurs at the bath-chair spoke up: 'Oh, Miss Mary! you *would* 'ave it from the first that poor Miss Aggie 'ad made away with herself; an', of course, Miss Bessie took the notion from you. Only Master – Mister John stood out, and – and I'd 'ave taken my Bible oath *you* was making away with yourself last night.'

Miss Mary leaned towards me, one finger on my sleeve.

'If going to Holmescroft kills me,' she said, 'you will have the murder of a fellow-creature on your conscience for all eternity.'

'I'll risk it,' I answered. Remembering what torment the mere reflection of her torments had cast on Holmescroft, and remembering, above all, the dumb Thing that filled the house with its desire to speak, I felt that there might be worse things.

Baxter was amazed at the proposed visit, but at a nod from that terrible woman went off to make arrangements. Then I sent a telegram to M'Leod bidding him and his vacate Holmescroft for that afternoon. Miss Mary should be alone with her dead, as I had been alone.

I expected untold trouble in transporting her, but to do her justice, the promise given for the journey, she underwent it without murmur, spasm, or unnecessary word. Miss Bessie, pressed in a corner by the window, wept behind her veil and from time to time tried to take hold of her sister's hand. Baxter wrapped himself in his newly-found happiness as selfishly as a bridegroom, for he sat still and smiled.

'So long as I know that Aggie didn't make away with herself,' he explained, 'I tell you frankly I don't care what happened. She's as hard as a rock – Mary. Always was. *She* won't die.'

We led her out on to the platform like a blind woman, and so got her into the fly. The half-hour crawl to Holmescroft was the most racking experience of the day. M'Leod had obeyed my instructions. There was no one visible in the house or the gardens; and the front door stood open.

Miss Mary rose from beside her sister, stepped forth first, and entered the hall.

'Come, Bessie,' she cried.

'I daren't. Oh, I daren't.'

'Come!' Her voice had altered. I felt Baxter start. 'There's nothing to be afraid of.'

'Good heavens!' said Baxter. 'She's running up the stairs. We'd better follow.'

'Let's wait below. She's going to the room.'

We heard the door of the bedroom I knew open and shut, and we waited in the lemon-coloured hall, heavy with the scent of flowers.

'I've never been into it since it was sold,' Baxter sighed. 'What a lovely restful place it is! Poor Aggie used to arrange the flowers.'

'Restful?' I began, but stopped of a sudden, for I felt all over my bruised soul that Baxter was speaking truth. It was a light, spacious, airy house, full of the sense of well-being and peace – above all things, of peace. I ventured into the dining-room where the thoughtful M'Leods had left a small fire. There was no terror there, present or lurking; and in the drawing-room, which for good reasons we had never cared to enter, the sun and the peace and the scent of the flowers worked together as is fit in an inhabited house. When I returned to the hall, Baxter was sweetly asleep on a couch, looking most unlike a middle-aged solicitor who had spent a broken night with an exacting cousin.

There was ample time for me to review it all – to felicitate myself upon my magnificent acumen (barring some errors about Baxter as a thief and possibly a murderer), before the door above opened, and Baxter, evidently a light sleeper, sprang awake.

'I've had a heavenly little nap,' he said, rubbing his eyes with the backs of his hands like a child. 'Good Lord! That's not *their* step!'

But it was. I had never before been privileged to see the Shadow turned backward on the dial – the years ripped bodily off poor human shoulders – old sunken eyes filled and alight – harsh lips moistened and human.

'John,' Miss Mary called, 'I know now. Aggie didn't do it!' and 'She didn't do it!' echoed Miss Bessie, and giggled.

'I did not think it wrong to say a prayer,' Miss Mary continued. 'Not for her soul, but for our peace. Then I was convinced.'

'Then we got conviction,' the younger sister piped.

'We've misjudged poor Aggie, John. But I feel she knows now. Wherever she is, she knows that we know she is guiltless.'

'Yes, she knows. I felt it too,' said Miss Elizabeth.

'I never doubted,' said John Baxter, whose face was beautiful at that hour. 'Not from the first. Never have!'

'You never offered me proof, John. Now, thank God, it will not be the same any more. I can think henceforward of Aggie without sorrow.' She tripped, absolutely tripped, across the hall. 'What ideas these Jews have of arranging furniture!' She spied me behind a big cloisonné vase.

'I've seen the window,' she said remotely. 'You took a great risk in advising me to undertake such a journey. However, as it turns out . . . I forgive you, and I pray you may never know what mental anguish means! Bessie! Look at this peculiar piano! Do you suppose, Doctor, these people would offer one tea? I miss mine.'

'I will go and see,' I said, and explored M'Leod's new-built servants' wing. It was in the servants' hall that I unearthed the M'Leod family, bursting with anxiety.

'Tea for three, quick,' I said. 'If you ask me any questions now, I shall have a fit!' So Mrs M'Leod got it, and I was butler, amid murmured apologies from Baxter, still smiling and self-absorbed, and the cold disapproval of Miss Mary, who thought the pattern of the china vulgar. However, she ate well, and even asked me whether I would not like a cup of tea for myself.

They went away in the twilight – the twilight that I had once feared. They were going to an hotel in London to rest after the fatigues of the day, and as their fly turned down the drive, I capered on the doorstep, with the all-darkened house behind me.

Then I heard the uncertain feet of the M'Leods, and bade them not to turn on the lights, but to feel – to feel what I had done; for the Shadow was gone, with the dumb desire in the air. They drew short, but afterwards deeper, breaths, like bathers entering chill water, separated one from the other, moved about the hall, tiptoed upstairs, raced down, and then Miss M'Leod, and I believe her mother, though she denies this, embraced me. I know M'Leod did.

It was a disgraceful evening. To say we rioted through the house is to put it mildly. We played a sort of Blind Man's Buff along the darkest passages, in the unlighted drawing-room, and little dining-room, calling cheerily to each other after each exploration that here, and here, and here, the trouble had removed itself. We came up to *the* bedroom – mine for the night again – and sat, the women on the bed, and we men on chairs, drinking in blessed draughts of peace and comfort and cleanliness of soul, while I told them my tale in full, and received fresh praise, thanks, and blessings.

When the servants, returned from their day's outing, gave us a supper of cold fried fish, M'Leod had sense enough to open no wine. We had been practically drunk since nightfall, and grew incoherent on water and milk.

'I like that Baxter,' said M'Leod. 'He's a sharp man. The death wasn't in the house, but he ran it pretty close, ain't it?'

'And the joke of it is that he supposes I want to buy the place from you,' I said. 'Are you selling?'

'Not for twice what I paid for it – now,' said M'Leod. 'I'll keep you in furs all your life, but not our Holmescroft.'

'No – never our Holmescroft,' said Miss M'Leod. 'We'll ask *him* here on Tuesday, mamma.' They squeezed each other's hands.

'Now tell me,' said Mrs M'Leod – 'that tall one I saw out of the scullery window – did *she* tell you she was always here in the spirit? I hate her. She made all this trouble. It was not her house after she had sold it. What do you think?'

'I suppose,' I answered, 'she brooded over what she believed was her sister's suicide night and day – she confessed she did – and her thoughts being concentrated on this place, they felt like a – like a burning glass.'

'Burning glass is good,' said M'Leod.

'I said it was like a light of blackness turned on us,' cried the girl, twiddling her ring. 'That must have been when the tall one thought worst about her sister and the house.'

'Ah, the poor Aggie!' said Mrs M'Leod. 'The poor Aggie, trying to tell everyone it was not so! No wonder we felt Something wished to say Something. Thea, Max, do you remember that night——'

'We need not remember any more,' M'Leod interrupted. 'It is not our trouble. They have told each other now.'

'Do you think, then,' said Miss M'Leod, 'that those two, the living ones, were actually told something – upstairs – in your – in the room?'

'I can't say. At any rate they were made happy, and they ate a big tea afterwards. As your father says, it is not our trouble any longer – thank God!'

'Amen!' said M'Leod. 'Now, Thea, let us have some music after all these months. "With mirth, thou pretty bird", ain't it? You ought to hear that.'

And in the half-lighted hall, Thea sang an old English song that I had never heard before.

With mirth, thou pretty bird, rejoice
   Thy Maker's praise enhanced;
Lift up thy shrill and pleasant voice,
   Thy God is high advanced!

Thy food before He did provide,
And gives it in a fitting side,
   Wherewith be thou sufficed!
Why shouldst thou now unpleasant be,
   Thy wrath against God venting,
That He a little bird made thee,
   Thy silly head tormenting,

Because He made thee not a man?
Oh, Peace! He hath well thought thereon,
  Therewith be thou sufficied!

THE RABBI'S SONG

If Thought can reach to Heaven,
  On Heaven let it dwell,
For fear that Thought be given
  Like power to reach to Hell.
For fear the desolation
  And darkness of thy mind,
Perplex an habitation
  Which thou hast left behind.

Let nothing linger after –
  No whispering ghost remain,
In wall, or beam, or rafter,
  Of any hate or pain.
Cleanse and call home thy spirit,
  Deny her leave to cast,
On aught thy heirs inherit,
  The shadow of her past.

For think, in all thy sadness,
  What road our grief may take;
Whose brain reflect our madness,
  Or whom our terrors shake.
For think, lest any languish
  By cause of thy distress –
The arrows of our anguish
  Fly farther than we guess.

Our lives, our tears, as water,
  Are poured upon the ground;
God giveth no man quarter,
  Yet God a means hath found;
Though faith and hope have vanished,
  And even love grows dim,
A means whereby His banished
  Be not expelled from Him!

The Tree of Justice

THE BALLAD OF MINEPIT SHAW

About the time that taverns shut
  And men can buy no beer,
Two lads went up by the keepers' hut
  To steal Lord Pelham's deer.

Night and the liquor was in their heads –
  They laughed and talked no bounds,
Till they waked the keepers on their beds,
  And the keepers loosed the hounds.

They had killed a hart, they had killed a hind,
  Ready to carry away,
When they heard a whimper down the wind
  And they heard a bloodhound bay.

They took and ran across the fern,
  Their crossbows in their hand,
Till they met a man with a green lantern
  That called and bade 'em stand.

'What are ye doing, O Flesh and Blood,
  And what's your foolish will,
That you must break into Minepit Wood
  And wake the Folk of the Hill?'

'Oh, we've broke into Lord Pelham's park,
  And killed Lord Pelham's deer,
And if ever you heard a little dog bark
  You'll know why we come here!

'We ask you let us go our way,
  As fast as we can flee,
For if ever you heard a bloodhound bay,
  You'll know how pressed we be.'

'Oh, lay your crossbows on the bank
  And drop the knife from your hand,
And though the hounds are at your flank
  I'll save you where you stand!'

They laid their crossbows on the bank,
  They threw their knives in the wood,
And the ground before them opened and sank
  And saved 'em where they stood.

'Oh, what's the roaring in our ears
  That strikes us well-nigh dumb?'
'Oh, that is just how things appears
  According as they come.'

'What are the stars before our eyes
  That strike us well-nigh blind?'
'Oh, that is just how things arise
  According as you find.'

'And why's our bed so hard to the bones
  Excepting where it's cold?'
'Oh, that's because it is precious stones
  Excepting where 'tis gold.'

'Think it over as you stand,
  For I tell you without fail,
If you haven't got into Fairyland
  You're not in Lewes Gaol.'

All night long they thought of it,
  And, come the dawn, they saw
They'd tumbled into a great old pit,
  At the bottom of Minepit Shaw.

And the keepers' hound had followed 'em close
  And broke her neck in the fall;
So they picked up their knives and their crossbows
  And buried the dog. That's all.

But whether the man was a poacher too
  Or a Pharisee so bold –
I reckon there's more things told than are true,
  And more things true than are told.

It was a warm, dark winter day with the Sou'-West wind singing through Dallington Forest, and the woods below the Beacon. The children set out after dinner to find old Hobden, who had a three months' job in the Rough at the back of Pound's Wood. He had promised to get them a dormouse in its nest. The bright leaf still clung to the beech coppice; the long chestnut leaves lay orange on the ground, and the rides were speckled with scarlet-lipped sprouting acorns. They worked their way by their own short cuts to the edge of Pound's Wood, and heard a horse's feet just as they came to the beech where Ridley the keeper hangs up the vermin. The poor little fluffy bodies dangled from the branches – some perfectly good, but most of them dried to twisted strips.

'Three more owls,' said Dan, counting. 'Two stoats, four jays, and a kestrel. That's ten since last week. Ridley's a beast.'

'In my time this sort of tree bore heavier fruit.' Sir Richard Dalyngridge reined up his grey horse, Swallow, in the ride behind them. 'What play do you make?' he asked.

'Nothing, sir. We're looking for old Hobden,' Dan replied. 'He promised to get us a sleeper.'

'Sleeper? A *dormeuse* do you say?'

'Yes, a dormouse, sir.'

'I understand. I passed a woodman on the low grounds. Come!'

He wheeled up the ride again, and pointed through an opening to the patch of beech-stubs, chestnut, hazel, and birch that old Hobden would turn into firewood, hop-poles, pea-boughs, and house-faggots before spring. The old man was as busy as a beaver.

Something laughed beneath a thorn, and Puck stole out, his finger on his lip.

'Look!' he whispered. 'Along between the spindle trees. Ridley has been there this half-hour.'

The children followed his point, and saw Ridley the keeper in an old dry ditch, watching Hobden as a cat watches a mouse.

'Huhh!' cried Una. 'Hobden always 'tends to his wires before breakfast. He puts his rabbits into the faggots he's allowed to take home. He'll tell us about 'em tomorrow.'

'We had the same breed in my day,' Sir Richard replied, and moved off quietly, Puck at his bridle, the children on either side between the close-trimmed beech stuff.

'What did you do to them?' said Dan, as they repassed Ridley's terrible tree.

'That!' Sir Richard jerked his head toward the dangling owls.

'Not he,' said Puck. 'There was never enough brute Norman in you to hang a man for taking a buck.'

'I – I cannot abide to hear their widows screech. But why am

I on horseback while you are afoot?' He dismounted lightly, tapped Swallow on the chest, so that the wise thing backed instead of turning in the narrow ride, and put himself at the head of the little procession. He walked as though all the woods belonged to him. 'I have often told my friends,' he went on, 'that Red William the King was not the only Norman found dead in a forest while he hunted.'

'D'you mean William Rufus?' said Dan.

'Yes,' said Puck, kicking a clump of red toadstools off a dead log.

'For example, there was a knight new from Normandy,' Sir Richard went on, 'to whom Henry our King granted a manor in Kent near by. He chose to hang his forester's son the day before a deer-hunt that he gave to pleasure the King.'

'Now when would that be?' said Puck, and scratched an ear thoughtfully.

'The summer of the year King Henry broke his brother Robert of Normandy at Tenchebrai fight. Our ships were even then at Pevensey loading for the war.'

'What happened to the knight?' Dan asked.

'They found him pinned to an ash, three arrows through his leather coat. *I* should have worn mail that day.'

'And did you see him all bloody?' Dan continued.

'Nay, I was with De Aquila at Pevensey, counting horse-shoes, and arrow sheaves, and ale-barrels into the holds of the ships. The army only waited for our King to lead them against Robert in Normandy, but he sent word to De Aquila that he would hunt with him here before he set out for France.'

'Why did the King want to hunt so particularly?' Una demanded.

'If he had gone straight to France after the Kentish knight was killed, men would have said he feared being slain like the knight. It was his duty to show himself debonair to his English people as it was De Aquila's duty to see that he took no harm while he did it. But it was a great burden! De Aquila, Hugh, and I ceased work on the ships, and scoured all the Honour of the Eagle – all De Aquila's lands – to make a fit, and, above all, a safe sport for our King. Look!'

The ride twisted, and came out on the top of Pound's Hill

Wood. Sir Richard pointed to the swells of beautiful, dappled Dallington, that showed like a woodcock's breast up the valley. 'Ye know the forest?' said he.

'You ought to see the bluebells there in Spring!' said Una.

'I have seen,' said Sir Richard, gazing, and stretched out his hand. 'Hugh's work and mine was first to move the deer gently from all parts into Dallington yonder, and there to hold them till the King came. Next, we must choose some three hundred beaters to drive the deer to the stands within bowshot of the King. Here was our trouble! In the mellay of a deer-drive a Saxon peasant and a Norman King may come over close to each other. The conquered do not love their conquerors all at once. So we needed sure men, for whom their village or kindred would answer in life, cattle, and land if any harm come to the King. Ye see?'

'If one of the beaters shot the King,' said Puck, 'Sir Richard wanted to be able to punish that man's village. Then the village would take care to send a good man.'

'So! So it was. But, lest our work should be too easy, the King had done such a dread justice over at Salehurst, for the killing of the Kentish knight (twenty-six men he hanged, as I heard), that our folk were half-mad with fear before we began. It is easier to dig out a badger gone to earth than a Saxon gone dumb-sullen. And atop of their misery the old rumour waked that Harold the Saxon was alive and would bring them deliverance from us Normans. This has happened every autumn since Senlac fight.'

'But King Harold was killed at Hastings,' said Una.

'So it was said, and so it was believed by us Normans, but our Saxons always believed he would come again. *That* rumour did not make our work any more easy.'

Sir Richard strode on down the far slope of the wood, where the trees thin out. It was fascinating to watch how he managed his long spurs among the lumps of blackened ling.

'But we did it!' he said. 'After all, a woman is as good as a man to beat the woods, and the mere word that deer are afoot makes cripples and crones young again. De Aquila laughed when Hugh told him over the list of beaters. Half were women; and many of the rest were clerks – Saxon and Norman priests.

'Hugh and I had not time to laugh for eight days, till De Aquila, as Lord of Pevensey, met our King and led him to the first shooting stand – by the Mill on the edge of the forest. Hugh and I – it was no work for hot heads or heavy hands – lay with our beaters on the skirts of Dallington to watch both them and the deer. When De Aquila's great horn blew we went forward, a line half a league long. Oh, to see the fat clerks, their gowns tucked up, puffing and roaring, and the sober millers dusting the undergrowth with their staves; and, like as not, between them a Saxon wench, hand in hand with her man, shrilling like a kite as she ran, and leaping high through the fern, all for joy of the sport.'

'*Ah! How! Ah! How! How-ah! Sa-how-ah!*' Puck bellowed without warning, and Swallow bounded forward, ears cocked, and nostrils cracking.

'*Hal-lal-lal-lal-la-hai-ie!*' Sir Richard answered in a high clear shout.

The two voices joined in swooping circles of sound, and a heron rose out of a red osier bed below them, circling as though he kept time to the outcry. Swallow quivered and swished his glorious tail. They stopped together on the same note.

A hoarse shout answered them across the bare woods.

'That's old Hobden,' said Una.

'Small blame to him. It is in his blood,' said Puck. 'Did your beaters cry so, Sir Richard?'

'My faith, they forgot all else. (Steady, Swallow, steady!) They forgot where the King and his people waited to shoot. They followed the deer to the very edge of the open till the first flight of wild arrows from the stands flew fair over them.

'I cried, "'Ware shot! 'Ware shot!" and a knot of young knights new from Normandy, that had strayed away from the Grand Stand, turned about, and in mere sport loosed off at our line shouting: "'Ware Senlac arrows! 'Ware Senlac arrows!" A jest, I grant you, but too sharp. One of our beaters answered in Saxon: "'Ware New Forest arrows! 'Ware Red William's arrow!" so I judged it time to end the jests, and when the boys saw my old mail gown (for, to shoot with strangers *I* count the same as war), they ceased shooting. So *that* was smoothed over, and we gave our beaters ale to wash down their anger. They were excusable! We – they had sweated to show our guests good sport, and our reward was a flight of hunting-arrows which no man loves, and worse, a churl's jibe over hard-fought, fair-lost Hastings fight. So, before the next beat, Hugh and I assembled and called the beaters over by name, to steady them. The greater part we knew, but among the Netherfield men I saw an old, old man, in the dress of a pilgrim.

'The Clerk of Netherfield said he was well known by repute for twenty years as a witless man that journeyed without rest to all the shrines of England. The old man sits, Saxon fashion, head between fists. We Normans rest our chin on our left palm.

' "Who answers for him?" said I. "If he fails in his duty, who will pay his fine?"

' "Who will pay my fine?" the pilgrim said. "I have asked that of all the Saints in England these forty years, less three months and nine days! They have not answered!" When he lifted his thin face I saw he was one-eyed, and frail as a rushlight.

' "Nay but, Father," I said, "to whom hast thou commended thyself?" He shook his head, so I spoke in Saxon: "Whose man art thou?"

' "I think I have a writing from Rahere, the King's Jester," said he after a while. "I am, as I suppose, Rahere's man."

'He pulled a writing from his scrip, and Hugh coming up, read it.

'It set out that the pilgrim was Rahere's man, and that Rahere was the King's Jester. There was Latin writ at the back.

' "What a plague conjuration's here?" said Hugh, turning it over. "*Pum-quum-sum oc-occ.* Magic?"

' "Black Magic," said the Clerk of Netherfield (he had been a monk at Battle). "They say Rahere is more of a priest than a fool and more of a wizard than either. Here's Rahere's name writ, and there's Rahere's red cockscomb sign drawn below for such as cannot read." He looked slyly at me.

' "Then read it," said I, "and show thy learning." He was a vain little man, and he gave it us after much mouthing.

' "The charm, which I think is from Virgilius the Sorcerer, says: 'When thou art once dead, and Minos (which is a heathen judge) has doomed thee, neither cunning, nor speechcraft, nor good works will restore thee!' A terrible thing! It denies any mercy to a man's soul!"

' "Does it serve?" said the pilgrim, plucking at Hugh's cloak. "Oh, man of the King's blood, does it cover me?"

'Hugh was of Earl Godwin's blood, and all Sussex knew it, though no Saxon dared call him kingly in a Norman's hearing. There can be but one King.

' "It serves," said Hugh. "But the day will be long and hot. Better rest here. We go forward now."

' "No, I will keep with thee, my kinsman," he answered like a child. He was indeed childish through great age.

'The line had not moved a bowshot when De Aquila's great horn blew for a halt, and soon young Fulke – our false Fulke's son – yes, the imp that lit the straw in Pevensey Castle – came thundering up a woodway.

' "Uncle," said he (though he was a man grown, he called me Uncle), "those young Norman fools who shot at you this morn are saying that your beaters cried treason against the King. It has come to Harry's long ears, and he bids you give account of it. There are heavy fines in his eye, but I am with you to the hilt, Uncle."

'When the boy had fled back, Hugh said to me: "It was Rahere's witless man cried, "Ware Red William's arrow!' I heard him, and so did the Clerk of Netherfield."

' "Then Rahere must answer to the King for his man," said I. "Keep him by you till I send," and I hastened down.

'The King was with De Aquila in the Grand Stand above Welansford down in the valley yonder. His Court – knights and dames – lay glittering on the edge of the glade. I made my homage, and Henry took it coldly.

' "How came your beaters to shout threats against me?" said he.

' "The tale has grown," I answered. "One old witless man cried out, "Ware Red William's arrow,' when the young knights shot at our line. We had two beaters hit."

' "I will do justice on that man," he answered. "Who is his master?"

' "He is Rahere's man," said I.

' "Rahere's?" said Henry. "Has my fool a fool?"

'I heard the bells jingle at the back of the stand, and a red leg waved over it, then a black one. So, very slowly, Rahere the King's Jester straddled the edge of the planks, and looked down on us, rubbing his chin. Loose-knit, with cropped hair, and a sad priest's face, under his cockscomb cap, that he could twist like a strip of wet leather. His eyes were hollow-set.

' "Nay, nay, Brother," said he. "If I suffer you to keep your fool, you must e'en suffer me to keep mine."

'This he delivered slowly into the King's angry face! My faith, a King's Jester must be bolder than lions!

' "Now we will judge the matter," said Rahere. "Let these two brave knights go hang my fool because he warned King Henry against running after Saxon deer through woods full of Saxons. 'Faith, Brother, if *thy* Brother, Red William, now among the Saints as we hope, had been timely warned against a certain arrow in New Forest, one fool of us four would not be crowned fool of England this morning. Therefore, hang the fool's fool, knights!"

'Mark the fool's cunning! Rahere had himself given us order to hang the man. No king dare confirm a fool's command to such a great baron as De Aquila; and the helpless King knew it.

' "What? No hanging?" said Rahere, after a silence. "A God's Gracious Name, kill something, then! Go forward with the hunt!"

'He splits his face ear to ear in a yawn like a fish-pond. "Henry," says he, "the next time I sleep, do not pester me with thy fooleries." Then he throws himself out of sight behind the back of the stand.

'I have seen courage with mirth in De Aquila and Hugh, but stark mad courage of Rahere's sort I had never even guessed at.'

'What did the King say?' cried Dan.

'He had opened his mouth to speak, when young Fulke, who had come into the stand with us, laughed, and, boy like, once begun, could not check himself. He kneeled on the instant for pardon, but fell sideways, crying: "His legs! Oh, his long, waving red legs as he went backward!"

'Like a storm breaking, our grave King laughed, – stamped and reeled with laughter till the stand shook. So, like a storm, this strange thing passed!

'He wiped his eyes, and signed to De Aquila to let the drive come on.

'When the deer broke, we were pleased that the King shot from the shelter of the stand, and did not ride out after the hurt beasts as Red William would have done. Most vilely his knights and barons shot!

'De Aquila kept me beside him, and I saw no more of Hugh till evening. We two had a little hut of boughs by the camp, where I went to wash me before the great supper, and in the dusk I heard Hugh on the couch.

' "Wearied, Hugh?" said I.

' "A little," he says. "I have driven Saxon deer all day for a Norman King, and there is enough of Earl Godwin's blood left in me to sicken at the work. Wait awhile with the torch."

'I waited then, and I thought I heard him sob.'

'Poor Hugh! Was he so tired?' said Una. 'Hobden says beating is hard work sometimes.'

'I think this tale is getting like the woods,' said Dan, 'darker and twistier every minute.'

Sir Richard had walked as he talked, and though the children thought they knew the woods well enough, they felt a little lost.

'A dark tale enough,' says Sir Richard, 'but the end was not all black. When we had washed, we went to wait on the King at meat in the great pavilion. Just before the trumpets blew for the Entry – all the guests upstanding – long Rahere comes posturing up to Hugh, and strikes him with his bauble-bladder.

' "Here's a heavy heart for a joyous meal!" he says. "But each man must have his black hour or where would be the merit of laughing? Take a fool's advice, and sit it out with my man. I'll make a jest to excuse you to the King if he remember to ask for you. That's more than I would do for Archbishop Anselm."

'Hugh looked at him heavy-eyed. "Rahere?" said he. "The King's Jester? Oh, Saints, what punishment for my King!" and smites his hands together.

' "Go – go fight it out in the dark," says Rahere, "and thy Saxon Saints reward thee for thy pity to my fool." He pushed him from the pavilion, and Hugh lurched away like one drunk.'

'But why?' said Una. 'I don't understand.'

'Ah, why indeed? Live you long enough, maiden, and you shall know the meaning of many whys.' Sir Richard smiled. 'I wondered too, but it was my duty to wait on the King at the High Table in all that glitter and stir.

'He spoke me his thanks for the sport I had helped show him, and he had learned from De Aquila enough of my folk and my castle in Normandy to graciously feign that he knew and had loved my brother there. (This, also, is part of a king's work.) Many great men sat at the High Table – chosen by the King for their wits, not for their birth. I have forgotten their names, and their faces I only saw that one night. But' – Sir Richard turned in his stride – 'but Rahere, flaming in black and scarlet among our guests, the hollow of his dark cheek flushed with wine – long, laughing Rahere, and the stricken sadness of his face when he was not twisting it about – Rahere I shall never forget.

'At the King's outgoing De Aquila bade me follow him, with his great bishops and two great barons, to the little pavilion. We had devised jugglers and dances for the Court's sport; but Henry loved to talk gravely with grave men, and De Aquila had told him of my travels to the world's end. We had a fire of apple-wood, sweet as incense, – and the curtains at the door being looped up, we could hear the music and see the lights shining on mail and dresses.

'Rahere lay behind the King's chair. The questions he darted forth at me were as shrewd as the flames. I was telling of our fight with the apes, as ye called them, at the world's end.

' "But where is the Saxon knight that went with you?" said Henry. "He must confirm these miracles."

' "He is busy," said Rahere, "confirming a new miracle."

' "Enough miracles for today," said the King. "Rahere, you have saved your long neck. Fetch the Saxon knight."

' "Pest on it," said Rahere. "Who would be a King's Jester? I'll bring him, Brother, if you'll see that none of your home-brewed bishops taste my wine while I am away." So he jingled forth between the men-at-arms at the door.

'Henry had made many bishops in England without the Pope's leave. I know not the rights of the matter, but only Rahere dared jest about it. We waited on the King's next word.

' "I think Rahere is jealous of you," said he, smiling, to Nigel of Ely. He was one bishop; and William of Exeter, the other – Wel-Wast the Saxons called him – laughed long. "Rahere is a priest at heart. Shall I make him a bishop, De Aquila?" says the King.

' "There might be worse," said our Lord of Pevensey. "Rahere would never do what Anselm has done."

'This Anselm, Archbishop of Canterbury, had gone off raging to the Pope at Rome, because Henry would make bishops without *his* leave either. I knew not the rights of it, but De Aquila did, and the King laughed.

' "Anselm means no harm. He should have been a monk, not a bishop," said the King. "I'll never quarrel with Anselm or his Pope till they quarrel with my England. If we can keep the King's peace till my son comes to rule, no man will lightly quarrel with our England."

' "Amen," said De Aquila. "But the King's peace ends when the King dies."

'That is true. The King's peace dies with the King. The custom then is that all laws are outlaw, and men do what they will till the new king is chosen.

' "I will amend that," said the King hotly. "I will have it so that though King, son, and grandson were all slain in one day, *still* the King's peace should hold over all England! What is a man that his mere death must upheave a people? We must have the Law."

' "Truth," said William of Exeter; but that he would have said to any word of the King.

'The two great barons behind said nothing. This teaching was clean against their stomachs, for when the King's peace ends, the great barons go to war and increase their lands. At that instant we heard Rahere's voice returning, in a scurril Saxon rhyme against William of Exeter:

"Well wist Wal-wist where lay his fortune
When that he fawned on the King for his crozier,"

—

and amid our laughter he burst in, with one arm round Hugh, and one round the old pilgrim of Netherfield.

' "Here is your knight, Brother," said he, "and for the better disport of the company, here is my fool. Hold up, Saxon Samson, the gates of Gaza are clean carried away!"

'Hugh broke loose, white and sick, and staggered to my side; the old man blinked upon the company.

'We looked at the King, but he smiled.

' "Rahere promised he would show me some sport after supper to cover his morning's offence," said he to De Aquila. "So this is thy man, Rahere?"

' "Even so," said Rahere. "My man he has been, and my protection he has taken, ever since I found him under the gallows at Stamford Bridge telling the kites atop of it that he was – Harold of England!"

'There was a great silence upon these last strange words, and Hugh hid his face on my shoulder, woman-fashion.

' "It is most cruel true," he whispered to me. "The old man proved it to me at the beat after you left, and again in our hut even now. It is Harold, my King!"

'De Aquila crept forward. He walked about the man and swallowed.

' "Bones of the Saints!" said he, staring.

' "Many a stray shot goes too well home," said Rahere.

'The old man flinched as at an arrow. "Why do you hurt me still?" he said in Saxon. "It was on some bones of some Saints that I promised I would give my England to the Great Duke." He turns on us all crying, shrilly: "Thanes, he had caught me at Rouen – a lifetime ago. If I had not promised, I should have lain there all my life. What else could I have done? I have lain in a strait prison all my life none the less. There is no need to throw stones at me." He guarded his face with his arms, and shivered.

' "Now his madness will strike him down," said Rahere. "Cast out the evil spirit, one of you new bishops."

'Said William of Exeter: "Harold was slain at Santlache fight. All the world knows it."

' "I think this man must have forgotten," said Rahere. "Be comforted, Father. Thou wast well slain at Hastings forty years gone, less three months and nine days. Tell the King."

'The man uncovered his face. "I thought they would stone me," he said. "I did not know I spoke before a King." He came to his full towering height – no mean man, but frail beyond belief.

'The King turned to the tables, and held him out his own cup of wine. The old man drank, and beckoned behind him, and, before all the Normans, my Hugh bore away the empty cup, Saxon fashion, upon the knee.

' "It is Harold!" said De Aquila. "His own stiff-necked blood kneels to serve him."

' "Be it so," said Henry. "Sit, then, thou that hast been Harold of England."

'The madman sat, and hard, dark Henry looked at him between half-shut eyes. We others stared like oxen, all but De Aquila, who watched Rahere as I have seen him watch a far sail on the sea.

'The wine and the warmth cast the old man into a dream. His white head bowed; his hands hung. His eye indeed was opened, but the mind was shut. When he stretched his feet, they were scurfed and road-cut like a slave's.

' "Ah, Rahere," cried Hugh, "why hast thou shown him thus? Better have let him die than shame him – and me!"

' "Shame thee?" said the King. "Would any baron of mine kneel to me if I were witless, discrowned, and alone, and Harold had my throne?"

' "No," said Rahere. "I am the sole fool that might do it, Brother, unless" – he pointed at De Aquila, whom he had only met that day – "yonder tough Norman crab kept me company. But, Sir Hugh, I did not mean to shame him. He hath been somewhat punished through, maybe, little fault of his own."

' "Yet he lied to my Father, the Conqueror," said the King, and the old man flinched in his sleep.

' "Maybe," said Rahere, "but thy Brother Robert, whose throat we purpose soon to slit with our own hands——"

' "Hutt!" said the King, laughing. "I'll keep Robert at my table for a life's guest when I catch him. Robert means no harm. It is all his cursed barons."

' "None the less," said Rahere, "Robert may say that thou hast not always spoken the stark truth to him about England. I should not hang too many men on *that* bough, Brother."

' "And it is certain," said Hugh, "that" – he pointed to the old man – "Harold was forced to make his promise to the Great Duke."

' "Very strongly forced," said De Aquila. He had never any pride in the Duke William's dealings with Harold before Hastings. Yet, as he said, one cannot build a house all of straight sticks.

' "No matter how he was forced," said Henry, "England was promised to my Father William by Edward the Confessor. Is it not so?" William of Exeter nodded. "Harold confirmed that promise to my Father on the bones of the Saints. Afterwards he broke his oath and would have taken England by the strong hand."

' "Oh! La! La!" Rahere rolled up his eyes like a girl. "That ever England should be taken by the strong hand!"

'Seeing that Red William and Henry after him had each in just that fashion snatched England from Robert of Normandy, we others knew not where to look; but De Aquila saved us quickly.

' "Promise kept or promise broken," he said, "Harold came near enough to breaking us Normans at Senlac."

' "Was it so close a fight, then?" said Henry.

' "A hair would have turned it either way," De Aquila answered. "His house-carles stood like rocks against rain. Where wast thou, Hugh, in it?"

' "Among Godwin's folk beneath the Golden Dragon till your front gave back, and we broke our ranks to follow," said Hugh.

' "But I bade you stand! I bade you stand! I knew it was all a deceit!" Harold had waked, and leaned forward as one crying from the grave.

' "Ah, now we see how the traitor himself was betrayed!" said William of Exeter, and looked for a smile from the King.

' "I made thee Bishop to preach at *my* bidding," said Henry;

and turning to Harold, "Tell us here how thy people fought us?" said he. "Their sons serve me now against my Brother Robert!"

'The old man shook his head cunningly. "Na – Na – Na," he cried. "I know better. Every time I tell my tale men stone me. But, Thanes, I will tell you a greater thing. Listen!" He told us how many paces it was from some Saxon Saint's shrine to another shrine, and how many more back to the Abbey of the Battle.

' "Ay," said he. "I have trodden it too often to be out even ten paces. I move very swiftly. Harold of Norway knows that, and so does Tostig my brother. They lie at ease at Stamford Bridge, and from Stamford Bridge to the Battle Abbey it is——" he muttered over many numbers and forgot us.

' "Ay," said De Aquila, all in a muse. "That man broke Harold of Norway at Stamford Bridge, and came near to breaking us at Santlache – all within one month."

' "But how did he come alive from Santlache fight?" asked the King. "Ask him! Hast thou heard it, Rahere?"

' "Never. He says he has been stoned too often for telling the tale. But he can count you off Saxon and Norman shrines till daylight," said Rahere, and the old man nodded proudly.

' "My faith," said Henry after a while, "I think even my Father the Great Duke would pity if he could see him."

' "How if he *does* see?" said Rahere.

'Hugh covered his face with his sound hand. "Ah, why hast thou shamed him?" he cried again to Rahere.

' "No – no," says the old man, reaching to pluck at Rahere's cape. "I am Rahere's man. None stone me now," and he played with the bells on the scollops of it.

' "How if he had been brought to me when you found him?" said the King to Rahere.

' "You would have held him prisoner again – as the Great Duke did," Rahere answered.

' "True," said our King. "He is nothing except his name. Yet that name might have been used by stronger men to trouble my England. Yes. I must have made him my life's guest – as I shall make Robert."

' "I knew it," said Rahere. "But while this man wandered mad by the wayside, none cared what he called himself."

' "I learned to cease talking before the stones flew," says the old man, and Hugh groaned.

' "Ye have heard!" said Rahere. "Witless, landless, nameless, and, but for my protection, masterless, he can still make shift to bide his doom under the open sky."

' "Then wherefore didst thou bring him here for a mock and a shame?" cried Hugh, beside himself with woe.

' "A right mock and a just shame!" said William of Exeter.

' "Not to me," said Nigel of Ely. "I see and I tremble, but I neither mock nor judge."

' "Well spoken, Ely." Rahere falls into the pure fool again. "I'll pray for thee when I turn monk. Thou hast given thy blessing on a war between two most Christian brothers." He meant the war forward 'twixt Henry and Robert of Normandy. "I charge you, Brother," he says, wheeling on the King, "dost thou mock my fool?"

'The King shook his head, and so then did smooth William of Exeter.

' "De Aquila, dost thou mock him?" Rahere jingled from one to another, and the old man smiled.

' "By the Bones of the Saints, not I," said our Lord of Pevensey. "I know how dooms near he broke us at Santlache."

' "Sir Hugh, you are excused the question. But you, valiant, loyal, honourable, and devout barons, Lords of Man's Justice in your own bounds, do *you* mock my fool?"

'He shook his bauble in the very faces of those two barons whose names I have forgotten. "Na – Na!" they said, and waved him back foolishly enough.

'He hies him across to staring, nodding Harold, and speaks from behind his chair.

' "No man mocks thee. Who here judges this man? Henry of England – Nigel – De Aquila! On your souls, swift with the answer!" he cried.

'None answered. We were all – the King not least – overborne by that terrible scarlet and black wizard-jester.

' "Well for your souls," he said, wiping his brow. Next, shrill like a woman: "Oh, come to me!" and Hugh ran forward to hold Harold, that had slidden down in the chair.

' "Hearken," said Rahere, his arm round Harold's neck. "The King – his bishops – the knights – all the world's crazy chess-board neither mock nor judge thee. Take that comfort with thee, Harold of England!"

'Hugh heaved the old man up and he smiled.

' "Good comfort," said Harold. "Tell me again! I have been somewhat punished——"

'Rahere hallooed it once more into his ear as the head rolled. We heard him sigh, and Nigel of Ely stood forth, praying aloud.

' "Out! I will have no Norman!" Harold said as clearly as I speak now, and he refuged himself on Hugh's sound shoulder, and stretched out, and lay all still.'

'Dead?' said Una, turning up a white face in the dusk.

'That was his good fortune. To die in the King's presence, and on the breast of the most gentlest, truest knight of his own house. Some of us envied him,' said Sir Richard, and fell back to take Swallow's bridle.

'Turn left here,' Puck called ahead of them from under an oak. They ducked down a narrow path through close ash plantation.

The children hurried forward, but cutting a corner charged full breast into the thorn-faggot that old Hobden was carrying home on his back.

'My! My!' said he. 'Have you scratted your face, Miss Una?'

'Sorry! It's all right,' said Una, rubbing her nose. 'How many rabbits did you get today?'

'That's tellin's,' the old man grinned as he re-hoisted his faggot. 'I reckon Mus' Ridley he've got rheumatism along o' lyin' in the dik to see I didn't snap up any. Think o' that now!'

They laughed a good deal while he told them the tale.

'An' just as he crawled away I heard someone hollerin' to the hounds in our woods,' said he. 'Didn't you hear? You must ha' been asleep sure-ly.'

'Oh, what about the sleeper you promised to show us?' Dan cried.

''Ere he be – house an' all!' Hobden dived into the prickly heart of the faggot and took out a dormouse's wonderfully woven nest of grass and leaves. His blunt fingers parted it as if it had been precious lace, and tilting it toward the last of the light he showed the little, red, furry chap curled up inside, his tail between his eyes that were shut for their winter sleep.

'Let's take him home. Don't breathe on him,' said Una. 'It'll make him warm and he'll wake up and die straight off. Won't he, Hobby?'

'That's a heap better by my reckonin' than wakin' up and findin' himself in a cage for life. No! We'll lay him into the bottom o' this hedge. Dat's jus' right! No more trouble for him till come Spring. An' now we'll go home.'

A CAROL

Our lord Who did the Ox command
   To kneel to Judah's King,
He binds His frost upon the land
   To ripen it for Spring –
To ripen it for Spring, good sirs,
   According to His word;
Which well must be as ye can see –
   And who shall judge the Lord?

When we poor fenmen skate the ice
   Or shiver on the wold,
We hear the cry of a single tree
   That breaks her heart in the cold –
That breaks her heart in the cold, good sirs,
   And rendeth by the board;
Which well must be as ye can see –
   And who shall judge the Lord?

Her wood is crazed and little worth
   Excepting as to burn,
That we may warm and make our mirth
   Until the Spring return –
Until the Spring return, good sirs,
   When people walk abroad;
Which well must be as ye can see –
   And who shall judge the Lord?

God bless the master of this house,
   And all that sleep therein!
And guard the fens from pirate folk,
   And keep us all from sin,

To walk in honesty, good sirs,
Of thought and deed and word!
Which shall befriend our latter end –
And who shall judge the Lord?

Friendly Brook

The valley was so choked with fog that one could scarcely see a cow's length across a field. Every blade, twig, bracken-frond, and hoof-print carried water, and the air was filled with the noise of rushing ditches and field-drains, all delivering to the brook below. A week's November rain on water-logged land had gorged her to full flood, and she proclaimed it aloud.

Two men in sackcloth aprons were considering an untrimmed hedge that ran down the hillside and disappeared into mist beside those roarings. They stood back and took stock of the neglected growth, tapped an elbow of hedge-oak here, a mossed beech-stub there, swayed a stooled ash back and forth, and looked at each other.

'I reckon she's about two rod thick,' said Jabez the younger, 'an' she hasn't felt iron since – when has she, Jesse?'

'Call it twenty-five year, Jabez, an' you won't be far out.'

'Umm!' Jabez rubbed his wet handbill on his wetter coat-sleeve. 'She ain't a hedge. She's all manner o' trees. We'll just about have to——' He paused, as professional etiquette required.

'Just about have to side her up an' see what she'll bear. But hadn't we best——?' Jesse paused in his turn, both men being artists and equals.

'Get some kind o' line to go by.' Jabez ranged up and down till he found a thinner place, and with clean snicks of the hand-bill revealed the original face of the fence. Jesse took over the dripping stuff as it fell forward, and, with a grasp and a kick, made it to lie orderly on the bank till it should be faggoted.

By noon a length of unclean jungle had turned itself into a cattle-proof barrier, tufted here and there with little plumes of the sacred holly which no woodman touches without orders.

'Now we've a witness-board to go by!' said Jesse at last.

'She won't be as easy as this all along,' Jabez answered. 'She'll need plenty stakes and binders when we come to the brook.'

'Well, ain't we plenty?' Jesse pointed to the ragged perspective ahead of them that plunged downhill into the fog. 'I lay there's a cord an' a half o' firewood, let alone faggots, 'fore we get anywheres anigh the brook.'

'The brook's got up a piece since morning,' said Jabez. 'Sounds like's if she was over Wickenden's door-stones.'

Jesse listened, too. There was a growl in the brook's roar as though she worried something hard.

'Yes. She's over Wickenden's door-stones,' he replied. 'Now she'll flood acrost Alder Bay an' that'll ease her.'

'She won't ease Jim Wickenden's hay none if she do,' Jabez grunted. 'I told Jim he'd set that liddle hay-stack o' his too low down in the medder. I *told* him so when he was drawin' the bottom for it.'

'I told him so, too,' said Jesse. 'I told him 'fore ever you did. I told him when the County Council tarred the roads up along.' He pointed uphill, where unseen automobiles and road-engines droned past continually. 'A tarred road, she shoots every drop o' water into a valley same's a slate roof. 'Tisn't as 'twas in the old days, when the waters soaked in and soaked out in the way o' nature. It rooshes off they tarred roads all of a lump, and naturally every drop is bound to descend into the valley. And there's tar roads both two sides this valley for ten mile. That's what I told Jim Wickenden when they tarred the roads last year. But he's a valley-man. He don't hardly ever journey uphill.'

'What did he say when you told him that?' Jabez demanded, with a little change of voice.

'Why? What did he say to you when *you* told him?' was the answer.

'What he said to you, I reckon, Jesse.'

'Then, you don't need me to say it over again, Jabez.'

'Well, let be how 'twill, what was he gettin' *after* when he said what he said to me?' Jabez insisted.

'*I* dunno; unless you tell me what manner o' words he said to *you*.'

Jabez drew back from the hedge – all hedges are nests of treachery and eavesdropping – and moved to an open cattle-lodge in the centre of the field.

'No need to go ferretin' around,' said Jesse. 'None can't see us here 'fore we see them.'

'What was Jim Wickenden gettin' at when I said he'd set his stack too near anigh the brook?' Jabez dropped his voice. 'He was in his mind.'

'He ain't never been out of it yet to my knowledge,' Jesse drawled, and uncorked his tea-bottle.

'But then Jim says: "I ain't goin' to shift my stack a yard," he says. "The Brook's been good friends to me, and if she be minded," he says, "to take a snatch at my hay, *I* ain't settin' out to withstand her." That's what Jim Wickenden says to me last – last June-end 'twas,' said Jabez.

'Nor he hasn't shifted his stack, neither,' Jesse replied. 'An' if there's more rain, the brook she'll shift it for him.'

'No need tell *me*! But I want to know what Jim was gettin' *at*?'

Jabez opened his clasp-knife very deliberately; Jesse as carefully opened his. They unfolded the newspapers that wrapped their dinners, coiled away and pocketed the string that bound the packages, and sat down on the edge of the lodge manger. The rain began to fall again through the fog, and the brook's voice rose.

'But I always allowed Mary was his lawful child, like,' said Jabez, after Jesse had spoken for a while.

''Tain't so. . . . Jim Wickenden's woman she never made nothing. She come out o' Lewes with her stockin's round her heels, an' she never made nor mended aught till she died. *He* had to light fire an' get breakfast every mornin' except Sundays, while she sowed it abed. Then she took an' died, sixteen, seventeen, year back; but she never had no children.'

'They was valley-folk,' said Jabez apologetically. 'I'd no call to go in among 'em, but I always allowed Mary——'

'No. Mary come out o' one o' those Lunnon Childern Societies. After his woman died, Jim got his mother back from his sister over to Peasmarsh, which she'd gone to house with when Jim married. His mother kept house for Jim after his woman died. They do say 'twas his mother led him on toward adoptin' of Mary – to furnish out the house with a child, like, and to keep him off of gettin' a noo woman. He mostly done what his mother contrived. 'Cardenly, twixt 'em, they asked for a child from one o' those Lunnon societies – same as it might ha' been these Barnardo children – an' Mary was sent down to 'em, in a candle-box, I've heard.'

'Then Mary is chance-born. I never knowed that,' said Jabez. 'Yet I must ha' heard it some time or other . . .'

'No. She ain't. 'Twould ha' been better for some folk if she had been. She come to Jim in a candle-box with all the proper papers – lawful child o' some couple in Lunnon somewheres – mother dead, father drinkin'. *And* there was that Lunnon society's five shillin's a week for her. Jim's mother she wouldn't despise week-end money, but I never heard Jim was much of a muck-grubber. Let be how 'twill, they two mothered up Mary no bounds, till it looked at last like they'd forgot she wasn't their own flesh an' blood. Yes, I reckon they forgot Mary wasn't their'n by rights.'

'That's no new thing,' said Jabez. 'There's more'n one or two in this parish wouldn't surrender back their Bernarders. You ask Mark Copley an' his woman an' that Bernarder cripple-babe o' theirs.'

'Maybe they need the five shillin',' Jesse suggested.

'It's handy,' said Jabez. 'But the child's more. "Dada" he says, an' "Mumma" he says, with his great rollin' head-piece all hurdled up in that iron collar. *He* won't live long – his back-bone's rotten, like. But they Copleys do just about set store by him – five bob or no five bob.'

'Same way with Jim an' his mother,' Jesse went on. 'There was talk betwixt 'em after a few years o' not takin' any more week-end money for Mary; but let alone *she* never passed a farden in the mire 'thout longin's, Jim didn't care, like, to push himself forward into the Society's remembrance. So naun came of it. The week-end money would ha' made no odds to Jim – not after his uncle willed him they four cottages at Eastbourne *an'* money in the bank.'

'That was true, too, then? I heard something in a scadderin' word-o'-mouth way,' said Jabez.

'I'll answer for the house property, because Jim he reequested my signed name at the foot o' some papers concernin' it. Regardin' the money in the bank, he nature-ally wouldn't like such things talked about all round the parish, so he took strangers for witnesses.'

'Then 'twill make Mary worth seekin' after?'

'She'll need it. Her Maker ain't done much for her outside nor yet in.'

'That ain't no odds.' Jabez shook his head till the water showered off his hat-brim. 'If Mary has money, she'll be wed before any likely pore maid. She's cause to be grateful to Jim.'

'She hides it middlin' close, then,' said Jesse. 'It don't sometimes look to me as if Mary has her natural rightful feelin's. She don't put on an apron o' Mondays 'thout being druv to it – in the kitchen *or* the hen-house. She's studyin' to be a school-teacher. She'll make a beauty! I never knowed her show any sort o' kindness to nobody – not even when Jim's mother was took dumb. No! 'Twadn't no stroke. It stifled the old lady in the throat here. First she couldn't shape her words no shape; then she clucked, like, an' lastly she couldn't more than suck down spoon-meat an' hold her peace. Jim took her to Doctor Harding, an' Harding he bundled her off to Brighton Hospital on a ticket, but they couldn't make no stay to her afflictions there; and she was bundled off to Lunnon, an' they lit a great old lamp inside her, and Jim told me they couldn't make out nothing in no sort there; and, along o' one thing an' another, an' all their spyin's and pryin's, she come back a hem sight worse than when she started. Jim said he'd have no more hospitalizin', so he give her a slate, which she tied to her waist-string, and what she was minded to say she writ on it.'

'Now, I never knowed that! But they're valley-folk,' Jabez repeated.

''Twadn't particular noticeable, for she wasn't a talkin' woman any time o' her days. Mary had all three's tongue. . . . Well, then, two years this summer, come what I'm tellin' you. Mary's Lunnon father, which they'd put clean out o' their minds, arrived down from Lunnon with the law on his side, sayin' he'd take his daughter back to Lunnon, after all. I was working for Mus' Dockett at Pounds Farm that summer, but I was obligin' Jim that evenin' muckin' out his pig-pen. I seed a stranger come traipsin' over the bridge agin' Wickenden's door-stones. 'Twadn't the new County Council bridge with the handrail.

They hadn't given it in for a public right o' way then. 'Twas just a bit o' lathy old plank which Jim had throwed acrost the brook for his own conveniences. The man wasn't drunk – only a little concerned in liquor, like – an' his back was a mask where he'd slipped in the muck comin' along. He went up the bricks past Jim's mother, which was feedin' the ducks, an' set himself down at the table inside – Jim was just changin' his socks – an' the man let Jim know all his rights and aims regardin' Mary. Then there just about *was* a hurly-bulloo! Jim's fust mind was to pitch him forth, but he'd done that once in his young days, and got six months up to Lewes jail along o' the man fallin' on his head. So he swallowed his spittle an' let him talk. The law about Mary *was* on the man's side from fust to last, for he showed us all the papers. Then Mary come downstairs – she'd been studyin' for an examination – an' the man tells her who he was, an' she says he had ought to have took proper care of his own flesh and blood while he had it by him, an' not to think he could ree-claim it when it suited. He says somethin' or other, but she looks him up an' down, front an' backwent, an' she just tongues him scadderin' out o' doors, and he went away stuffin' all the papers back into his hat, talkin' most abusefully. Then she come back an' freed her mind against Jim an' his mother for not havin' warned her of her upbringin's, which it come out she hadn't ever been told. They didn't say naun to her. They never did. *I*'d ha' packed her off with any man that would ha' took her – an' God's pity on him!'

'Umm!' said Jabez, and sucked his pipe.

'So then, that was the beginnin'. The man come back again next week or so, an' he catched Jim alone, 'thout his mother this time, an' he fair beazled him with his papers an' his talk – for the law *was* on his side – till Jim went down into his money-purse an' give him ten shillings hush-money – he told me – to withdraw away for a bit an' leave Mary with 'em.'

'But that's no way to get rid o' man or woman,' Jabez said.

'No more 'tis. I told Jim so. "What can I do?" Jim says. "The law's *with* the man. I walk about daytimes thinkin' o' it till I sweats my underclothes wringin', an' I lie abed nights thinkin' o' it till I sweats my sheets all of a sop. 'Tisn't as if I was a young man," he says, "nor yet as if I was a pore man. Maybe he'll drink hisself to death." I e'en a'most told him outright what foolishness he was enterin' into, but he knowed it – he knowed it – because he said next time the man come 'twould be fifteen shillin's. An' next time 'twas. Just fifteen shillin's!'

'An' *was* the man her father?' asked Jabez.

'He had the proofs an' the papers. Jim showed me what that Lunnon Childern's Society had answered when Mary writ up to 'em an' taxed 'em with it. I lay she hadn't been proper polite in her letters to 'em, for they answered middlin' short. They said the matter was out o' their hands, but – let's see if I remember – oh, yes, – they ree-gretted there had been an oversight. I reckon they had sent Mary out in the candle-box as a orphan instead o' havin' a father. Terrible awkward! Then, when he'd drinked up the money, the man come again – in his usuals – an' he kept hammerin' on and hammerin' on about his duty to his pore dear wife, an' what he'd do for his dear daughter in Lunnon, till the tears runned down his two dirty cheeks an' he come away with more money. Jim used to slip it into his hand behind the door; but his mother she heard the chink. She didn't hold with hush-money. She'd write out all her feelin's on the slate, an' Jim 'ud be settin' up half the night answerin' back an' showing that the man had the law with him.'

'Hadn't that man no trade nor business, then?'

'He told me he was a printer. I reckon, though, he lived on the rates like the rest of 'em up there in Lunnon.'

'An' how did Mary take it?'

'She said she'd sooner go into service than go with the man. I reckon a mistress 'ud be middlin' put to it for a maid 'fore she put Mary into cap an' gown. She was studyin' to be a schoo-ool-teacher. A beauty she'll make! . . . Well, that was how things went that fall. Mary's Lunnon father kep' comin' an' comin' 'carden as he'd drinked out the money Jim gave him; an' each time he'd put up his price for not takin' Mary away. Jim's mother, she didn't like partin' with no money, an' bein' obliged to write her feelin's on the slate instead o' givin' 'em vent by mouth, she was just about mad. Just about she *was* mad!

'Come November, I lodged with Jim in the outside room over 'gainst his hen-house. I paid *her* my rent. I was workin' for

Dockett at Pounds – gettin' chestnut-bats out o' Perry Shaw. Just such weather as this be – rain atop o' rain after a wet October. (An' I remember it ended in dry frostes right away up to Christmas.) Dockett he'd sent up to Perry Shaw for me – no, he comes puffin' up to me himself – because a big corner-piece o' the bank had slipped into the brook where she makes that elber at the bottom o' the Seventeen Acre, an' all the rubbishy alders an' sallies which he ought to have cut out when he took the farm, they'd slipped with the slip, an' the brook was comin' rooshin' down atop of 'em, an' they'd just about back an' spill the waters over his winter wheat. The water was lyin' in the flats already. "Gor a-mighty, Jesse!" he bellers out at me, "get that rubbish away all manners you can. Don't stop for no fagottin', but give the brook play or my wheat's past salvation. I can't lend you no help," he says, "but work an' I'll pay ye." '

'You had him there,' Jabez chuckled.

'Yes. I reckon I had ought to have drove my bargain, but the brook was buckin' up on good bread-corn. So 'cardenly, I laid into the mess of it, workin' off the bank where the trees was drownin' themselves head-down in the roosh – just such weather as this – an' the brook creepin' up on me all the time. 'Long toward noon, Jim comes mowchin' along with his toppin' axe over his shoulder.

' "Be you minded for an extra hand at your job?" he says.

' "Be you minded to turn to?" I ses, an' – no more talk to it – Jim laid in alongside o' me. He's no bunger with a toppin' axe.'

'Maybe, but I've seed him at a job o' throwin' in the woods, an' he didn't seem to make out no shape,' said Jabez. 'He haven't got the shoulders, nor yet the judgment – *my* opinion – when he's dealin' with full-girt timber. He don't rightly make up his mind where he's goin' to throw her.'

'We wasn't throwin' nothin'. We was cuttin' out they soft alders, an' haulin' 'em up the bank 'fore they could back the waters on the wheat. Jim didn't say much, 'less it was that he'd had a postcard from Mary's Lunnon father, night before, sayin' he was comin' down that mornin'. Jim, he'd sweated all night, an' he didn't reckon hisself equal to the talkin' an' the swearin' an' the cryin', an' his mother blamin' him afterwards on the slate. "It spiled my day to think of it," he ses, when we was eatin' our pieces. "So I've fair cried dunghill an' run. Mother'll have to tackle him by herself. I lay *she* won't give him no hush-money," he ses. "I lay he'll be surprised by the time he's done with *her*," he ses. An' that was e'en a'most all the talk we had concernin' it. But he's no bunger with the toppin' axe.

'The brook she'd crep' up an' up on us, an' she kep' creepin' upon us till we was workin' knee-deep in the shallers, cuttin' an' pookin' an' pullin' what we could get to o' the rubbish. There was a middlin' lot comin' downstream, too – cattle-bars an' hop-poles and odds-ends bats, all poltin' down together; but they rooshed round the elber good shape by the time we'd backed out they drowned trees. Come four o'clock we reckoned we'd done a proper day's work, an' she'd take no harm if we left her. We couldn't puddle about there in the dark an' wet to no more advantage. Jim he was pourin' the water out of his boots – no, I was doin' that. Jim was kneelin' to unlace his'n. "Damn it all, Jesse," he ses, standin' up; "the flood must be over my doorsteps at home, for here comes my old white-top bee-skep!" '.

'Yes. I allus heard he paints his bee-skeps,' Jabez put in. 'I dunno paint don't tarrify bees more'n it keeps 'em dry.'

' "I'll have a pook at it," he ses, an' he pooks at it as it comes round the elber. The roosh nigh jerked the pooker out of his hand-grips, an' he calls to me, an' I come runnin' barefoot. Then we pulled on the pooker, an' it reared up on eend in the roosh, an' we guessed what 'twas. 'Cardenly we pulled it in into a shaller, an' it rolled a piece, an' a great old stiff man's arm nigh hit me in the face. Then we was sure. " 'Tis a man," ses Jim. But the face was all a mask. "I reckon it's Mary's Lunnon father," he ses presently. "Lend me a match and I'll make sure." He never used baccy. We lit three matches one by another, well's we could in the rain, an' he cleaned off some o' the slob with a tussick o' grass. "Yes," he ses. "It's Mary's Lunnon father. He won't tarrify us no more. D'you want him, Jesse?" he ses.

' "No," I ses. "If this was Eastbourne beach like, he'd be half-a-crown apiece to us 'fore the coroner; but now we'd only lose a day havin' to 'tend the inquest. I lay he fell into the brook."

' "I lay he did," ses Jim. "I wonder if he saw mother." He

turns him over, an' opens his coat and puts his fingers in the waistcoat pocket an' starts laughin'. "He's seen mother, right enough," he ses. "An' he's got the best of her, too. *She* won't be able to crow no more over *me* 'bout givin' him money. *I* never give him more than a sovereign. She's give him two!" an' he trousers 'em, laughin' all the time. "An' now we'll pook him back again, for I've done with him," he ses.

'So we pooked him back into the middle of the brook, an' we saw he went round the elber 'thout balkin', an' we walked quite a piece beside of him to set him on his ways. When we couldn't see no more, we went home by the high road, because we knowed the brook 'u'd be out acrost the medders, an' we wasn't goin' to hunt for Jim's little rotten old bridge in that dark – an' rainin' Heavens' hard, too. I was middlin' pleased to see light an' vittles again when we got home. Jim he pressed me to come insides for a drink. He don't drink in a generality, but he was rid of all his troubles that evenin', d'ye see? "Mother," he ses so soon as the door ope'd, "have you seen him?" She whips out her slate an' writes down – "No." "Oh, no," ses Jim. "You don't get out of it that way, mother. I lay you *have* seen him, an' I lay he's bested you for all your talk, same as he bested me. Make a clean breast of it, mother," he ses. "He got round you too." She was goin' for the slate again, but he stops her. "It's all right, mother," he ses. "I've seen him sense you have, an' he won't trouble us no more." The old lady looks up quick as a robin, an' she writes, "Did he say so?" "No," ses Jim, laughin'. "He didn't say so. That's how I know. But he bested *you*, mother. You can't have it in at *me* for bein' soft-hearted. You're twice as tender-hearted as what I be. Look!" he ses, an' he shows her the two sovereigns. "Put 'em away where they belong," he ses. "He won't never come for no more; an' now we'll have our drink," he ses, "for we've earned it."

'Nature-ally they weren't goin' to let me see where they kep' their monies. She went upstairs with it – for the whisky.'

'I never knowed Jim was a drinkin' man – in his own house, like,' said Jabez.

'No more he isn't; but what he takes he likes good. He won't tech no publican's hogwash acrost the bar. Four shillin's he paid for that bottle o' whisky. I know, because when the old lady brought it down there wasn't more'n jest a liddle few dreenin's an' dregs in it. Nothin' to set before neighbours, I do assure you.'

' "Why, 'twas half full last week, mother," he ses. "You don't mean," he ses, "you've given him all that as well? It's two shillin's worth," he ses. (That's how I knowed he paid four.) "Well, well, mother, you be too tender-'earted to live. But I don't grudge it to him," he ses. "I don't grudge him nothin' he can keep." So, 'cardenly, we drinked up what little sup was left.'

'An' what come to Mary's Lunnon father?' said Jabez, after a full minute's silence.

'I be too tired to go readin' papers of evenin's; but Dockett he told me, that very week, I think, that they'd inquested on a man down at Robertsbridge which had polted and polted up agin' so many bridges an' banks, like, they couldn't make naun out of him.'

'An' what did Mary say to all these doin's?'

'The old lady bundled her off to the village 'fore her Lunnon father come, to buy week-end stuff (an' she forgot the half o' it). When we come in she was upstairs studyin' to be a school-teacher. None told her naun about it. 'Twadn't girls' affairs.'

' 'Reckon *she* knowed?' Jabez went on.

'She? She must have guessed it middlin' close when she saw her money come back. But she never mentioned it in writing so far's I know. She were more worritted that night on account of two-three her chickens bein' drowned, for the flood had skewed their old hen-house round on her postes. I cobbled her up next mornin' when the brook shrinked.'

'An' where did you find the bridge? Some fur downstream, didn't ye?'

'Just where she allus was. She hadn't shifted but very little. The brook had gulled out the bank a piece under one eend o' the plank, so's she was liable to tilt ye sideways if you wasn't careful. But I pooked three-four bricks under her, an' she was all plumb again.'

'Well, I dunno how it *looks* like, but let be how 'twill,' said Jabez, 'he hadn't no business to come down from Lunnon tarrifyin' people, an' threatenin' to take away children which they'd hobbed up for their lawful own – even if 'twas Mary Wickenden.'

'He had the business right enough, an' he had the law with him – no gettin' over that,' said Jesse. 'But he had the drink with him, too, an' that was where he failed, like.'

'Well, well! Let be how 'twill, the brook was a good friend to Jim. I see it now. I allus *did* wonder what he was gettin' at when he said that, when I talked to him about shiftin' the stack. "You dunno everythin'," he ses. "The Brook's been a good friend to me," he ses, "an' if she's minded to have a snatch at my hay, *I* ain't settin' out to withstand her." '

'I reckon she's about shifted it, too, by now,' Jesse chuckled. 'Hark! That ain't any slip off the bank which she's got hold of.'

The Brook had changed her note again. It sounded as though she were mumbling something soft.

THE LAND

When Julius Fabricius, Sub-Prefect of the Weald,
In the days of Diocletian owned our Lower River-
 field,
He called to him Hobdenius – a Briton of the
 Clay,
Saying: 'What about that River-piece for layin' in
 to hay?'

And the aged Hobden answered: 'I remember as
 a lad
My father told your father that she wanted
 dreenin' bad.
An' the more that you neeglect her the less you'll
 get her clean.
Have it jest *as* you've a mind to, but, if I was
 you, I'd dreen.'

So they drained it long and crossways in the lavish
 Roman style.
Still we find among the river-drift their flakes of
 ancient tile,
And in drouthy middle August, when the bones
 of meadows show,
We can trace the lines they followed sixteen
 hundred years ago.

Then Julius Fabricius died as even Prefects do,
And after certain centuries, Imperial Rome died
too.
Then did robbers enter Britain from across the
Northern main
And our Lower River-field was won by Ogier the
Dane.

Well could Ogier work his war-boat – well could
Ogier wield his brand –
Much he knew of foaming waters – not so much
of farming land.
So he called to him a Hobden of the old unaltered
blood,
Saying: 'What about that River-bit, she doesn't
look no good?'

And that aged Hobden answered: ' 'Tain't for *me*
to interfere,
But I've known that bit o' meadow now for five
and fifty year.
Have it *jest* as you've a mind to, but I've proved
it time on time,
If you want to change her nature you have *got* to
give her lime!'

Ogier sent his wains to Lewes, twenty hours'
solemn walk,
And drew back great abundance of the cool, grey,
healing chalk.
And old Hobden spread it broadcast, never
heeding what was in't;
Which is why in cleaning ditches, now and then
we find a flint.

Ogier died. His sons grew English. Anglo-Saxon
was their name,
Till out of blossomed Normandy another pirate
came;
For Duke William conquered England and
divided with his men,
And our Lower River-field he gave to William
of Warenne.

But the Brook (you know her habit) rose one
rainy Autumn night
And tore down sodden flitches of the bank to
left and right.
So, said William to his Bailiff as they rode their
dripping rounds:
'Hob, what about that River-bit – the Brook's
got up no bounds?'

And that aged Hobden answered: ''Tain't my
business to advise,
But ye might ha' known 'twould happen from
the way the valley lies.
When ye can't hold back the water you must try
and save the sile.
Hev it jest as you've a *mind* to, but, if I was you,
I'd spile!'

They spiled along the water-course with trunks
of willow-trees
And planks of elms behind 'em and immortal
oaken knees.
And when the spates of Autumn whirl the gravel-
beds away
You can see their faithful fragments iron-hard in
iron clay.

Georgii Quinti Anno Sexto, I, who own the River-
field,
Am fortified with title-deeds, attested, signed and
sealed,
Guaranteeing me, my assigns, my executors and
heirs
All sorts of powers and profits which – are neither
mine nor theirs.

I have rights of chase and warren, as my dignity
requires.
I can fish – but Hobden tickles. I can shoot – but
Hobden wires.
I repair, but he reopens, certain gaps which, men
allege,
Have been used by every Hobden since a Hobden
swapped a hedge.

Shall I dog his morning progress o'er the track-
    betraying dew?
Demand his dinner-basket into which my pheasant
    flew?
Confiscate his evening faggot into which the
    conies ran,
And summons him to judgment? I would sooner
    summons Pan.

His dead are in the churchyard – thirty generations
    laid.
Their names went down in Domesday Book when
    Domesday Book was made.
And the passion and the piety and prowess of his
    line
Have seeded, rooted, fruited in some land the Law
    calls mine.

Not for any beast that burrows, not for any bird
    that flies,
Would I lose his large sound council, miss his keen
    amending eyes.
He is bailiff, woodman, wheelwright, field-
    surveyor, engineer,
And if flagrantly a poacher – 'tain't for me to
    interfere.

'Hob, what about that River-bit?' I turn to him
    again
With Fabricius and Ogier and William of
    Warenne.
'Hev it jest as you've a mind to, *but*' – and so
    he takes command.
For whoever pays the taxes old Mus' Hobden
    owns the land.

Mary Postgate

Of Miss Mary Postgate, Lady McCausland wrote that she was 'thoroughly conscientious, tidy, companionable, and ladylike. I am very sorry to part with her, and shall always be interested in her welfare.'

Miss Fowler engaged her on this recommendation, and to her surprise, for she had had experience of companions, found that it was true. Miss Fowler was nearer sixty than fifty at the time, but though she needed care she did not exhaust her attendant's vitality. On the contrary, she gave out, stimulatingly and with reminiscences. Her father had been a minor Court official in the days when the Great Exhibition of 1851 had just set its seal on Civilisation made perfect. Some of Miss Fowler's tales, none the less, were not always for the young. Mary was not young, and though her speech was as colourless as her eyes or her hair, she was never shocked. She listened unflinchingly to every one; said at the end, 'How interesting!' or 'How shocking!' as the case might be, and never again referred to it, for she prided herself on a trained mind, which 'did not dwell on these things'. She was, too, a treasure at domestic accounts, for which the village tradesmen, with their weekly books, loved her not. Otherwise she had no enemies; provoked no jealousy even among the plainest; neither gossip nor slander had ever been traced to her; she supplied the odd place at the Rector's or the Doctor's table at half an hour's notice; she was a sort of public aunt to very many small children of the village street, whose parents, while accepting everything, would have been swift to resent what they called 'patronage'; she served on the Village Nursing Committee as Miss Fowler's nominee when Miss Fowler was crippled by rheumatoid arthritis, and came out of six months' fortnightly meetings equally respected by all the cliques.

And when Fate threw Miss Fowler's nephew, an unlovely orphan of eleven, on Miss Fowler's hands, Mary Postgate stood to her share of the business of education as practised in private and public schools. She checked printed clothes-lists, and unitemised bills of extras; wrote to Head and House masters, matrons, nurses and doctors, and grieved or rejoiced over half-term reports. Young Wyndham Fowler repaid her in his holidays by calling her 'Gatepost', 'Postey', or 'Packthread', by thumping her between her narrow shoulders, or by chasing her bleating, round the garden, her large mouth open, her large nose high in air, at a stiff-necked shamble very like a camel's. Later on he filled the house with clamour, argument, and harangues as to his personal needs, likes and dislikes, and the limitations of 'you women', reducing Mary to tears of physical fatigue, or, when he chose to be humorous, of helpless laughter. At crises, which multiplied as he grew older, she was his ambassadress and his interpretress to Miss Fowler, who had no large sympathy with the young; a vote in his interest at the councils on his future; his sewing-woman, strictly accountable for mislaid boots and garments; always his butt and his slave.

And when he decided to become a solicitor, and had entered an office in London; when his greeting had changed from 'Hullo, Postey, you old beast', to 'Mornin', Packthread', there came a war which, unlike all wars that Mary could remember, did not stay decently outside England and in the newspapers, but intruded on the lives of people whom she knew. As she said to Miss Fowler, it was 'most vexatious'. It took the Rector's son who was going into business with his elder brother; it took the Colonel's nephew on the eve of fruit-farming in Canada; it took Mrs Grant's son who, his mother said, was devoted to the ministry; and, very early indeed, it took Wynn Fowler, who announced on a postcard that he had joined the Flying Corps and wanted a cardigan waistcoat.

'He must go, and he must have the waistcoat,' said Miss Fowler. So Mary got the proper-sized needles and wool, while Miss Fowler told the men of her establishment – two gardeners and an odd man, aged sixty – that those who could join the Army had better do so. The gardeners left. Cheape, the odd man, stayed on, and was promoted to the gardener's cottage. The cook, scorning to be limited in luxuries, also left, after a spirited scene with Miss Fowler, and took the housemaid with her. Miss Fowler gazetted Nellie, Cheape's seventeen-year-old daughter, to the vacant post; Mrs Cheape to the rank of cook, with occasional cleaning bouts; and the reduced establishment moved forward smoothly.

Wynn demanded an increase in his allowance. Miss Fowler, who always looked facts in the face, said, 'He must have it. The chances are he won't live long to draw it, and if three hundred makes him happy——'

Wynn was grateful, and came over, in his tight-buttoned uniform, to say so. His training centre was not thirty miles away, and his talk was so technical that it had to be explained by charts of the various types of machines. He gave Mary such a chart.

'And you'd better study it, Postey,' he said. 'You'll be seeing a lot of 'em soon.' So Mary studied the chart, but when Wynn next arrived to swell and exalt himself before his womenfolk, she failed badly in cross-examination, and he rated her as in the old days.

'You *look* more or less like a human being,' he said in his new Service voice. 'You *must* have had a brain at some time in your past. What have you done with it? Where d'you keep it? A sheep would know more than you do, Postey. You're lamentable. You are less use than an empty tin can, you dowey old cassowary.'

'I suppose that's how your superior officer talks to *you*?' said Miss Fowler from her chair.

'But Postey doesn't mind,' Wynn replied. 'Do you, Packthread?'

'Why? Was Wynn saying anything? I shall get this right next time you come,' she muttered, and knitted her pale brows again over the diagrams of Taubes, Farmans, and Zeppelins.

In a few weeks the mere land and sea battles which she read to Miss Fowler after breakfast passed her like idle breath. Her heart and her interest were high in the air with Wynn, who had finished 'rolling' (whatever that might be) and had gone on from a 'taxi' to a machine more or less his own. One morning it circled over their very chimneys, alighted on Vegg's Heath, almost outside the garden gate, and Wynn came in, blue with cold, shouting for food. He and she drew Miss Fowler's bath-chair, as they had often done, along the Heath footpath to look at the biplane. Mary observed that 'it smelt very badly'.

'Postey, I believe you think with your nose,' said Wynn. 'I know you don't with your mind. Now, what type's that?'

'I'll go and get the chart,' said Mary.

'You're hopeless! You haven't the mental capacity of a white mouse,' he cried, and explained the dials and the sockets for bomb-dropping till it was time to mount and ride the wet clouds once more.

'Ah!' said Mary, as the stinking thing flared upward. 'Wait till our Flying Corps gets to work! Wynn says it's much safer than in the trenches.'

'I wonder,' said Miss Fowler. 'Tell Cheape to come and tow me home again.'

'It's all downhill. I can do it,' said Mary, 'if you put the brake on.' She laid her lean self against the pushing-bar and home they trundled.

'Now, be careful you aren't heated and catch a chill,' said overdressed Miss Fowler.

'Nothing makes me perspire,' said Mary. As she bumped the chair under the porch she straightened her long back. The exertion had given her a colour, and the wind had loosened a wisp of hair across her forehead. Miss Fowler glanced at her.

'What do you ever think of, Mary?' she demanded suddenly.

'Oh, Wynn says he wants another three pairs of stockings – as thick as we can make them.'

'Yes. But I mean the things that women think about. Here you are, more than forty——'

'Forty-four,' said truthful Mary.

'Well?'

'Well?' Mary offered Miss Fowler her shoulder as usual.

'And you've been with me ten years now.'

'Let's see,' said Mary. 'Wynn was eleven when he came. He's twenty now, and I came two years before that. It must be eleven.'

'Eleven! And you've never told me anything that matters in all that while. Looking back, it seems to me that *I've* done all the talking.'

'I'm afraid I'm not much of a conversationalist. As Wynn says, I haven't the mind. Let me take your hat.'

Miss Fowler, moving stiffly from the hip, stamped her rubber-tipped stick on the tiled hall floor. 'Mary, aren't you *anything* except a companion? Would you *ever* have been anything except a companion?'

Mary hung up the garden hat on its proper peg. 'No,' she said after consideration. 'I don't imagine I ever should. But I've no imagination, I'm afraid.'

She fetched Miss Fowler her eleven-o'clock glass of Contrexeville.

That was the wet December when it rained six inches to the month, and the women went abroad as little as might be. Wynn's flying chariot visited them several times, and for two mornings (he had warned her by postcard) Mary heard the thresh of his propellers at dawn. The second time she ran to the window, and stared at the whitening sky. A little blur passed overhead. She lifted her lean arms towards it.

That evening at six o'clock there came an announcement in an official envelope that Second Lieutenant W. Fowler had been killed during a trial flight. Death was instantaneous. She read it and carried it to Miss Fowler.

'I never expected anything else,' said Miss Fowler; 'but I'm sorry it happened before he had done anything.'

The room was whirling round Mary Postgate, but she found herself quite steady in the midst of it.

'Yes,' she said. 'It's a great pity he didn't die in action after he had killed somebody.'

'He was killed instantly. That's one comfort,' Miss Fowler went on.

'But Wynn says the shock of a fall kills a man at once – whatever happens to the tanks,' quoted Mary.

The room was coming to rest now. She heard Miss Fowler say impatiently, 'But why can't we cry, Mary?' and herself replying, 'There's nothing to cry for. He has done his duty as much as Mrs Grant's son did.'

'And when he died, *she* came and cried all the morning,' said Miss Fowler. 'This only makes me feel tired – terribly tired. Will you help me to bed, please, Mary? – And I think I'd like the hot-water bottle.'

So Mary helped her and sat beside, talking of Wynn in his riotous youth.

'I believe,' said Miss Fowler suddenly, 'that old people and young people slip from under a stroke like this. The middle-aged feel it most.'

'I expect that's true,' said Mary, rising. 'I'm going to put away the things in his room now. Shall we wear mourning?'

'Certainly not,' said Miss Fowler. 'Except, of course, at the funeral. I can't go. You will. I want you to arrange about his being buried here. What a blessing it didn't happen at Salisbury!'

Everyone, from the Authorities of the Flying Corps to the Rector, was most kind and sympathetic. Mary found herself for the moment in a world where bodies were in the habit of being despatched by all sorts of conveyances to all sorts of places. And at the funeral two young men in buttoned-up uniforms stood beside the grave and spoke to her afterwards.

'You're Miss Postgate, aren't you?' said one. 'Fowler told me about you. He was a good chap – a first-class fellow – a great loss.'

'Great loss!' growled his companion. 'We're all awfully sorry.'

'How high did he fall from?' Mary whispered.

'Pretty nearly four thousand feet, I should think, didn't he? You were up that day, Monkey?'

'All of that,' the other child replied. 'My bar made three thousand, and I wasn't as high as him by a lot.'

'Then *that*'s all right,' said Mary. 'Thank you very much.'

They moved away as Mrs Grant flung herself weeping on Mary's flat chest, under the lych-gate, and cried, '*I* know how it feels! *I* know how it feels!'

'But both his parents are dead,' Mary returned, as she fended her off. 'Perhaps they've all met by now,' she added vaguely as she escaped towards the coach.

'I've thought of that too,' wailed Mrs Grant; 'but then he'll be practically a stranger to them. Quite embarrassing!'

Mary faithfully reported every detail of the ceremony to Miss Fowler, who, when she described Mrs Grant's outburst, laughed aloud.

'Oh, how Wynn would have enjoyed it! He was always utterly unreliable at funerals. D'you remember——' And they talked of him again, each piecing out the other's gaps. 'And now,' said Miss Fowler, 'we'll pull up the blinds and we'll have a general tidy. That always does us good. Have you seen to Wynn's things?'

'Everything – since he first came,' said Mary. 'He was never destructive – even with his toys.'

They faced that neat room.

'It can't be natural not to cry,' Mary said at last. 'I'm *so* afraid you'll have a reaction.'

'As I told you, we old people slip from under the stroke. It's you I'm afraid for. Have you cried yet?'

'I can't. It only makes me angry with the Germans.'

'That's sheer waste of vitality,' said Miss Fowler. 'We must live till the war's finished.' She opened a full wardrobe. 'Now, I've been thinking things over. This is my plan. All his civilian clothes can be given away – Belgian refugees, and so on.'

Mary nodded. 'Boots, collars, and gloves?'

'Yes. We don't need to keep anything except his cap and belt.'

'They came back yesterday with his Flying Corps clothes' – Mary pointed to a roll on the little iron bed.

'Ah, but keep his Service things. Someone may be glad of them later. Do you remember his size?'

'Five feet eight and a half; thirty-six inches round the chest. But he told me he's just put on an inch and a half. I'll mark it on a label and tie it on his sleeping-bag.'

'So that disposes of *that*,' said Miss Fowler, tapping the palm of one hand with the ringed third finger of the other. 'What waste it all is! We'll get his old school trunk tomorrow and pack his civilian clothes.'

'And the rest?' said Mary. 'His books and pictures and the games and the toys – and – and the rest?'

'My plan is to burn every single thing,' said Miss Fowler. 'Then we shall know where they are and no one can handle them afterwards. What do you think?'

'I think that would be much the best,' said Mary. 'But there's such a lot of them.'

'We'll burn them in the destructor,' said Miss Fowler.

This was an open-air furnace for the consumption of refuse; a little circular four-foot tower of pierced brick over an iron grating. Miss Fowler had noticed the design in a gardening journal years ago, and had had it built at the bottom of the garden. It suited her tidy soul, for it saved unsightly rubbish-heaps, and the ashes lightened the stiff clay soil.

Mary considered for a moment, saw her way clear, and nodded again. They spent the evening putting away well-remembered civilian suits, underclothes that Mary had marked, and the regiments of very gaudy socks and ties. A second trunk was needed, and, after that, a little packing-case, and it was late next day when Cheape and the local carrier lifted them to the cart. The Rector luckily knew of a friend's son, about five feet eight and a half inches high, to whom a complete Flying Corps outfit would be most acceptable, and sent his gardener's son down with a barrow to take delivery of it. The cap was hung up in Miss Fowler's bedroom, the belt in Miss Postgate's; for, as Miss Fowler said, they had no desire to make tea-party talk of them.

'That disposes of *that*,' said Miss Fowler. 'I'll leave the rest to you, Mary. I can't run up and down the garden. You'd better take the big clothes-basket and get Nellie to help you.'

'I shall take the wheel-barrow and do it myself,' said Mary, and for once in her life closed her mouth.

Miss Fowler, in moments of irritation, had called Mary deadly methodical. She put on her oldest waterproof and gardening-hat and her ever-slipping goloshes, for the weather was on the edge of more rain. She gathered fire-lighters from the kitchen, a half-scuttle of coals, and a faggot of brushwood. These she wheeled in the barrow down the mossed paths to the dank little laurel shrubbery where the destructor stood under the drip of three oaks. She climbed the wire fence into the Rector's glebe just behind, and from his tenant's rick pulled two large armfuls of good hay, which she spread neatly on the fire-bars. Next, journey by journey, passing Miss Fowler's white face at the morning-room window each time, she brought down in the towel-covered clothes-basket, on the wheelbarrow, thumbed and used Hentys, Marryats, Levers, Stevensons, Baroness Orczys, Garvices, schoolbooks, and atlases, unrelated piles of the *Motor Cyclist*, the *Light Car*, and catalogues of Olympia Exhibitions; the remnants of a fleet of sailing-ships from ninepenny cutters to a three-guinea yacht; a prep-school dressing-gown; bats from three-and-sixpence to twenty-four shillings; cricket and tennis balls; disintegrated steam and clockwork locomotives with their twisted rails; a grey and red tin model of a submarine; a dumb gramophone and cracked records; golf-clubs that had to be broken across the knee, like his walking-sticks, and an assegai; photographs of private and public school cricket and football elevens, and his OTC on the line of march; kodaks, and film-rolls; some pewters, and one real silver cup, for boxing competitions and Junior Hurdles; sheaves of school photographs; Miss Fowler's photograph; her own which he had borne off in fun and (good care she took not to ask!) had never returned; a playbox with a secret drawer; a load of flannels, belts, and jerseys, and a pair of spiked shoes unearthed in the attic; a packet of all the letters that Miss Fowler and she had ever written to him, kept for some absurd reason through all these years; a five-day attempt at a diary; framed pictures of racing motors in full Brooklands career, and load upon load of undistinguishable wreckage of tool-boxes, rabbit-hutches, electric batteries, tin soldiers, fret-saw outfits, and jig-saw puzzles.

Miss Fowler at the window watched her come and go, and said to herself, 'Mary's an old woman. I never realised it before.'

After lunch she recommended her to rest.

'I'm not in the least tired,' said Mary. 'I've got it all arranged. I'm going to the village at two o'clock for some paraffin. Nellie hasn't enough, and the walk will do me good.'

She made one last quest round the house before she started, and found that she had overlooked nothing. It began to mist as soon as she had skirted Vegg's Heath, where Wynn used to descend – it seemed to her that she could almost hear the beat of his propellers overhead, but there was nothing to see. She hoisted her umbrella and lunged into the blind wet till she had reached the shelter of the empty village. As she came out of Mr Kidd's shop with a bottle full of paraffin in her string shopping-bag, she met Nurse Eden, the village nurse, and fell into talk with her, as usual, about the village children. They were just parting opposite the 'Royal Oak', when a gun, they fancied, was fired immediately behind the house. It was followed by a child's shriek dying into a wail.

'Accident!' said Nurse Eden promptly, and dashed through the empty bar, followed by Mary. They found Mrs Gerritt, the publican's wife, who could only gasp and point to the yard, where a little cart-lodge was sliding sideways amid a clatter of tiles. Nurse Eden snatched up a sheet drying before the fire, ran out, lifted something from the ground, and flung the sheet round it. The sheet turned scarlet and half her uniform too, as she bore the load into the kitchen. It was little Edna Gerritt, aged nine, whom Mary had known since her perambulator days.

'Am I hurted bad?' Edna asked, and died between Nurse Eden's dripping hands. The sheet fell aside and for an instant, before she could shut her eyes, Mary saw the ripped and shredded body.

'It's a wonder she spoke at all,' said Nurse Eden. 'What in God's name was it?'

'A bomb,' said Mary.

'One o' the Zeppelins?'

'No. An aeroplane. I thought I heard it on the Heath, but I fancied it was one of ours. It must have shut off its engines as it came down. That's why we didn't notice it.'

'The filthy pigs!' said Nurse Eden, all white and shaken. 'See the pickle I'm in! Go and tell Dr Hennis, Miss Postgate.' Nurse looked at the mother, who had dropped face down on the floor. 'She's only in a fit. Turn her over.'

Mary heaved Mrs Gerritt right side up, and hurried off for the doctor. When she told her tale, he asked her to sit down in the surgery till he got her something.

'But I don't need it, I assure you,' said she. 'I don't think it would be wise to tell Miss Fowler about it, do you? Her heart is so irritable in this weather.'

Dr Hennis looked at her admiringly as he packed up his bag.

'No. Don't tell anybody till we're sure,' he said, and hastened to the 'Royal Oak', while Mary went on with the paraffin. The village behind her was as quiet as usual, for the news had not yet spread. She frowned a little to herself, her large nostrils expanded uglily, and from time to time she muttered a phrase which Wynn, who never restrained himself before his womenfolk, had applied to the enemy. 'Bloody pagans! They *are* bloody pagans. But,' she continued, falling back on the teaching that had made her what she was, 'one mustn't let one's mind dwell on these things.'

Before she reached the house Dr Hennis, who was also a special constable, overtook her in his car.

'Oh, Miss Postgate,' he said, 'I wanted to tell you that that accident at the "Royal Oak" was due to Gerritt's stable tumbling down. It's been dangerous for a long time. It ought to have been condemned.'

'I thought I heard an explosion too,' said Mary.

'You might have been misled by the beams snapping. I've been looking at 'em. They were dry-rotted through and through. Of course, as they broke, they would make a noise just like a gun.'

'Yes?' said Mary politely.

'Poor little Edna was playing underneath it,' he went on, still holding her with his eyes, 'and that and the tiles cut her to pieces, you see?'

'I saw it,' said Mary, shaking her head. 'I heard it too.'

'Well, we cannot be sure.' Dr Hennis changed his tone completely. 'I know both you and Nurse Eden (I've been speaking to her) are perfectly trustworthy, and I can rely on you not to say anything – yet at least. It is no good to stir up people unless——'

'Oh, I never do – anyhow,' said Mary, and Dr Hennis went on to the county town.

After all, she told herself, it might, just possibly, have been the collapse of the old stable that had done all those things to poor little Edna. She was sorry she had even hinted at other things, but Nurse Eden was discretion itself. By the time she reached home the affair seemed increasingly remote by its very monstrosity. As she came in, Miss Fowler told her that a couple of aeroplanes had passed half an hour ago.

'I thought I heard them,' she replied. 'I'm going down to the garden now. I've got the paraffin.'

'Yes, but – what *have* you got on your boots? They're soaking wet. Change them at once.'

Not only did Mary obey but she wrapped the boots in a newspaper, and put them into the string bag with the bottle. So, armed with the longest kitchen poker, she left.

'It's raining again,' was Miss Fowler's last word, 'but – I know you won't be happy till that's disposed of.'

'It won't take long. I've got everything down there, and I've put the lid on the destructor to keep the wet out.'

The shrubbery was filling with twilight by the time she had completed her arrangements and sprinkled the sacrificial oil. As she lit the match that would burn her heart to ashes, she heard a groan or a grunt behind the dense Portugal laurels.

'Cheape?' she called impatiently, but Cheape, with his ancient lumbago, in his comfortable cottage would be the last man to profane the sanctuary. 'Sheep,' she concluded, and threw in the fusee. The pyre went up in a roar, and the immediate flame hastened night around her.

'How Wynn would have loved this!' she thought, stepping back from the blaze.

By its light she saw, half hidden behind a laurel not five paces away, a bareheaded man sitting very stiffly at the foot of one of the oaks. A broken branch lay across his lap – one booted leg protruding from beneath it. His head moved ceaselessly from side to side, but his body was as still as the tree's trunk. He was dressed – she moved sideways to look more closely – in a uniform something like Wynn's, with a flap buttoned across the chest. For an instant, she had some idea that it might be one of the young flying men she had met at the funeral. But their heads were dark and glossy. This man's was as pale as a baby's, and so closely cropped that she could see the disgusting pinky skin beneath. His lips moved.

'What do you say?' Mary moved towards him and stooped.

'Laty! Laty! Laty!' he muttered, while his hands picked at the dead wet leaves. There was no doubt as to his nationality. It made her so angry that she strode back to the destructor, though it was still too hot to use the poker there. Wynn's books seemed to be catching well. She looked up at the oak behind the man; several of the light upper and two or three rotten lower branches had broken and scattered their rubbish on the shrubbery path. On the lowest fork a helmet with dependent strings, showed like a bird's-nest in the light of a long-tongued flame. Evidently this person had fallen through the tree. Wynn had told her that it was quite possible for people to fall out of aeroplanes. Wynn told her too, that trees were useful things to break an aviator's fall, but in this case the aviator must have been broken or he would have moved from his queer position. He seemed helpless except for his horrible rolling head. On the other hand, she could see a pistol case at his belt – and Mary loathed pistols. Months ago, after reading certain Belgian reports together, she and Miss Fowler had had dealings with one – a huge revolver with flat-nosed bullets, which latter, Wynn said, were forbidden by the rules of war to be used against civilised enemies. 'They're good enough for us,' Miss Fowler had replied. 'Show Mary how it works.' And Wynn, laughing at the mere possibility of any such need, had led the craven winking Mary into the Rector's disused quarry, and had shown her how to fire the terrible machine. It lay now in the top-left-hand drawer of her toilet-table – a memento not included in the burning. Wynn would be pleased to see how she was not afraid.

She slipped up to the house to get it. When she came through the rain, the eyes in the head were alive with expectation. The mouth even tried to smile. But at sight of the revolver its corners went down just like Edna Gerritt's. A tear trickled from one eye, and the head rolled from shoulder to shoulder as though trying to point out something.

'Cassée. Tout cassée,' it whimpered.

'What do you say?' said Mary disgustedly, keeping well to one side, though only the head moved.

'Cassée,' it repeated. 'Che me rends. Le médicin! Toctor!'

'Nein!' said she, bringing all her small German to bear with the big pistol. 'Ich haben der todt Kinder gesehn.'

The head was still. Mary's hand dropped. She had been careful to keep her finger off the trigger for fear of accidents. After a few moments' waiting, she returned to the destructor, where the flames were falling, and churned up Wynn's charring books with the poker. Again the head groaned for the doctor.

'Stop that!' said Mary, and stamped her foot. 'Stop that, you bloody pagan!'

The words came quite smoothly and naturally. They were Wynn's own words, and Wynn was a gentleman who for no consideration on earth would have torn little Edna into those vividly coloured strips and strings. But this thing hunched under the oak-tree had done that thing. It was no question of reading horrors out of newspapers to Miss Fowler. Mary had seen it with her own eyes on the 'Royal Oak' kitchen table. She must not allow her mind to dwell upon it. Now Wynn was dead, and everything connected with him was lumping and rustling and tinkling under her busy poker into red black dust and grey leaves of ash. The thing beneath the oak would die too. Mary had seen death more than once. She came of a family that had a knack of dying under, as she told Miss Fowler, 'most distressing circumstances'. She would stay where she was till she was entirely satisfied that It was dead – dead as dear papa in the late 'eighties; aunt Mary in 'eighty-nine; mamma in 'ninety-one; cousin Dick in 'ninety-five; Lady McCausland's housemaid in 'ninety-nine; Lady McCausland's sister in nineteen hundred and one; Wynn buried five days ago; and Edna Gerritt still waiting for decent earth to hide her. As she thought – her under-lip caught up by one faded canine, brows knit and nostrils wide – she wielded the poker with lunges that jarred the grating at the bottom, and careful scrapes round the brick-work above. She looked at her wrist-watch. It was getting on to half-past four, and the rain was coming down in earnest. Tea would be at five. If It did not die before that time, she would be soaked and would have to change. Meantime, and this occupied her, Wynn's things were burning well in spite of the hissing wet, though now and again a book-back with a quite distinguishable title would be heaved up out of the mass. The exercise of stoking had given her a glow which seemed to reach to the marrow of her bones. She hummed – Mary never had a voice – to herself. She had never believed in all those advanced views – though Miss Fowler herself leaned a little that way – of woman's work in the world; but now she saw there was much to be said for them. This, for instance, was *her* work – work which no man, least of all Dr Hennis, would ever have done. A man, at such a crisis, would be what Wynn called a 'sports-man'; would leave everything to fetch help, and would certainly bring It into the house. Now a woman's business was to make a happy home for – for a husband and children. Failing these – it was not a thing one should allow one's mind to dwell upon – but——

'Stop it!' Mary cried once more across the shadows. 'Nein, I tell you! Ich haben der todt Kinder gesehn.'

But it was a fact. A woman who had missed these things could still be useful – more useful than a man in certain respects. She thumped like a pavior through the settling ashes at the secret thrill of it. The rain was damping the fire, but she could feel – it was too dark to see – that her work was done. There was a dull red glow at the bottom of the destructor, not enough to char the wooden lid if she slipped it half over against the driving wet. This arranged, she leaned on the poker and waited, while an increasing rapture laid hold on her. She ceased to think. She gave herself up to feel. Her long pleasure was broken by a sound that she had waited for in agony several times in her life. She leaned forward and listened, smiling. There could be no mistake. She closed her eyes and drank it in. Once it ceased abruptly.

'Go on,' she murmured, half aloud. 'That isn't the end.'

Then the end came very distinctly in a lull between two rain-gusts. Mary Postgate drew her breath short between her teeth and shivered from head to foot. '*That's* all right,' said she contentedly, and went up to the house, where she scandalised the whole routine by taking a luxurious hot bath before tea, and came down looking, as Miss Fowler said when she saw her lying all relaxed on the other sofa, 'quite handsome!'

THE BEGINNINGS

It was not part of their blood,
  It came to them very late
With long arrears to make good,
  When the English began to hate.

They were not easily moved,
  They were icy willing to wait
Till every count should be proved,
  Ere the English began to hate.

Their voices were even and low,
  Their eyes were level and straight.
There was neither sign nor show,
  When the English began to hate.

It was not preached to the crowd,
  It was not taught by the State.
No man spoke it aloud,
  When the English began to hate.

It was not suddenly bred,
  It will not swiftly abate,
Through the chill years ahead,
  When Time shall count from the date
  That the English began to hate.

The Bull that Thought

Westward from a town by the Mouths of the Rhône, runs a road so mathematically straight, so barometrically level, that it ranks among the world's measured miles and motorists use it for records.

I had attacked the distance several times, but always with a Mistral blowing, or the unchancy cattle of those parts on the move. But once, running from the East, into a high-piled, almost Egyptian, sunset, there came a night which it would have been sin to have wasted. It was warm with the breath of summer in advance; moonlit till the shadow of every rounded pebble and pointed cypress wind-break lay solid on that vast flat-floored waste; and my Mr Leggatt, who had slipped out to make sure, reported that the road-surface was unblemished.

'*Now*,' he suggested, 'we might see what she'll do under strict road-conditions. She's been pullin' like the Blue de Luxe all day. Unless I'm all off, it's her night out.'

We arranged the trial for after dinner – thirty kilometres as near as might be; and twenty-two of them without even a level crossing.

There sat beside me at table d'hôte an elderly, bearded Frenchman wearing the rosette of by no means the lowest grade of the Legion of Honour, who had arrived in a talkative Citroën. I gathered that he had spent much of his life in the French Colonial Service in Annam and Tonquin. When the war came, his years barring him from the front line, he had supervised Chinese wood-cutters who, with axe and dynamite, deforested the centre of France for trench-props. He said my chauffeur had told him that I contemplated an experiment. He was interested in cars – had admired mine – would, in short, be greatly indebted to me if I permitted him to assist as an observer. One could not well refuse; and, knowing my Mr Leggatt, it occurred to me there might also be a bet in the background.

While he went to get his coat, I asked the proprietor his name. 'Voiron – Monsieur André Voiron,' was the reply. 'And his business?' 'Mon Dieu! He is Voiron! He is all those things, there!' The proprietor waved his hands at brilliant advertisements on the dining-room walls, which declared that Voiron Frères dealt in wines, agricultural implements, chemical manures, provisions and produce throughout that part of the globe.

He said little for the first five minute of our trip, and nothing at all for the next ten – it being, as Leggatt had guessed, Esmeralda's night out. But, when her indicator climbed to a certain figure and held there for three blinding kilometres, he expressed himself satisfied, and proposed to me that we should celebrate the event at the hotel. 'I keep yonder,' said he, 'a wine on which I should value your opinion.'

On our return, he disappeared for a few minutes, and I heard him rumbling in a cellar. The proprietor presently invited me to the dining-room, where, beneath one frugal light, a table had been set with local dishes of renown. There was, too, a bottle beyond most known sizes, marked black on red, with a date. Monsieur Voiron opened it, and we drank to the health of my car. The velvety, perfumed liquor, between fawn and topaz, neither too sweet nor too dry, creamed in its generous glass. But I knew no wine composed of the whispers of angels' wings, the breath of Eden and the foam and pulse of Youth renewed. So I asked what it might be.

'It is champagne,' he said gravely.

'Then what have I been drinking all my life?'

'If you were lucky, before the War, and paid thirty shillings a bottle, it is possible you may have drunk one of our better-class *tisanes*.'

'And where does one get this?'

'Here, I am happy to say. Elsewhere, perhaps, it is not so easy. We growers exchange these real wines among ourselves.'

I bowed my head in admiration, surrender, and joy. There stood the most ample bottle, and it was not yet eleven o'clock. Doors locked and shutters banged throughout the establishment. Some last servant yawned on his way to bed. Monsieur Voiron opened a window and the moonlight flooded in from a small pebbled court outside. One could almost hear the town of Chambres breathing in its first sleep. Presently, there was a thick noise in the air, the passing of feet and hooves, lowings, and a stifled bark or two. Dust rose over the courtyard wall, followed by the strong smell of cattle.

'They are moving some beasts,' said Monsieur Voiron, cocking an ear. 'Mine, I think. Yes, I hear Christophe. Our beasts do not like automobiles – so we move at night. You do not know our country – the Crau, here, or the Camargue? I was – I am now, again – of it. All France is good; but this is the best.' He spoke, as only a Frenchman can, of his own loved part of his own lovely land.

'For myself, if I were not so involved in all these affairs' – he pointed to the advertisements – 'I would live on our farm with my cattle, and worship them like a Hindu. You know our cattle of the Camargue, Monsieur? No? It is not an acquaintance to rush upon lightly. There are no beasts like them. They have a mentality superior to that of others. They graze and they ruminate, by choice, facing our Mistral, which is more than some automobiles will do. Also they have in them the potentiality of thought – and when cattle think – I have seen what arrives.'

'Are they so clever as all that?' I asked idly.

'Monsieur, when your sportif chauffeur camouflaged your limousine so that she resembled one of your Army lorries, I would not believe her capacities. I bet him – ah – two to one – she would not touch ninety kilometres. It was proved that she could. I can give you no proof, but will you believe me if I tell you what a beast who thinks can achieve?'

'After the War,' said I spaciously, 'everything is credible.'

'That is true! Everything inconceivable has happened; but still we learn nothing and we believe nothing. When I was a child in my father's house – before I became a Colonial Administrator – my interest and my affection were among our cattle. We of the old rock live here – have you seen? – in big farms like castles. Indeed, some of them may have been Saracenic. The barns group round them – great white-walled barns, and yards solid as our houses. One gate shuts all. It is a world apart; an administration of all that concerns beasts. It was there I learned something about cattle. You see, they are our playthings in the Camargue and the Crau. The boy measures his strength against the calf that butts him in play among the manure-heaps. He moves in and out among the cows, who are – not so amiable.

He rides with the herdsmen in the open to shift the herds. Sooner or later, he meets as bulls the little calves that knocked him over. So it was with me – till it became necessary that I should go to our Colonies.' He laughed. 'Very necessary. That is a good time in youth, Monsieur, when one does these things which shock our parents. Why is it always Papa who is so shocked and has never heard of such things – and Mamma who supplies the excuses? . . . And when my brother – my elder who stayed and created the business – begged me to return and help him, I resigned my Colonial career gladly enough. I returned to our own lands, and my well-loved, wicked white and yellow cattle of the Camargue and the Crau. My Faith, I could talk of them all night, for this stuff unlocks the heart, without making repentance in the morning. . . . Yes! It was after the War that this happened. There was a calf, among Heaven knows how many of ours – a bull-calf – an infant indistinguishable from his companions. He was sick, and he had been taken up with his mother into the big farm-yard at home with us. Naturally the children of our herdsmen practised on him from the first. It is in their blood. The Spaniards make a cult of bull-fighting. Our little devils down here bait bulls as automatically as the English child kicks or throws balls. This calf would chase them with his eyes open, like a cow when she hunts a man. They would take refuge behind our tractors and wine-carts in the centre of the yard: he would chase them in and out as a dog hunts rats. More than that, he would study their psychology, his eyes in their eyes. Yes, he watched their faces to divine which way they would run. He himself, also, would pretend sometimes to charge directly at a boy. Then he would wheel right or left – one could never tell – and knock over some child pressed against a wall who thought himself safe. After this, he would stand over him, knowing that his companions must come to his aid; and when they were all together, waving their jackets across his eyes and pulling his tail, he would scatter them – how he would scatter them! He could kick, too, sideways like a cow. He knew his ranges as well as our gunners, and he was as quick on his feet as our Carpentier. I observed him often. Christophe – the man who passed just now – our chief herdsman, who had taught me to ride with our beasts, when I was ten – Christophe told me that he was descended from a yellow cow of those days that had chased us once into the marshes. "He kicks just like her," said Christophe. "He can side-kick as he jumps. Have you seen, too, that he is not deceived by the jacket when a boy waves it? He uses it to find the boy. They think they are feeling him. He is feeling them always. He thinks, that one." I had come to the same conclusion. Yes – the creature was a thinker along the lines necessary to his sport; and he was a humorist also, like so many natural murderers. One knows the type among beasts as well as among men. It possesses a curious truculent mirth – almost indecent but infallibly significant——'

Monsieur Voïron replenished our glasses with the great wine that went better at each descent.

'They kept him for some time in the yards to practise upon. Naturally he became a little brutal; so Christophe turned him out to learn manners among his equals in the grazing lands, where the Camargue joins the Crau. How old was he then? About eight or nine months, I think. We met again a few months later – he and I. I was riding one of our little half-wild horses, along a road of the Crau, when I found myself almost unseated. It was he! He had hidden himself behind a wind-break till we passed, and had then charged my horse from behind. Yes, he had deceived even my little horse! But I recognised him. I gave him the whip across the nose, and I said: "Apis, for this thou goest to Arles! It was unworthy of thee, between us two." But that creature had no shame. He went away laughing, like an Apache. If he had dismounted me, I do not think it is I who would have laughed – yearling as he was.'

'Why did you want to send him to Arles?' I asked.

'For the bull-ring. When your charming tourists leave us, we institute our little amusements there. Not a real bull-fight, you understand, but young bulls with padded horns, and our boys from hereabouts and in the city go to play with them. Naturally, before we send them we try them in our yards at home. So we brought up Apis from his pastures. He knew at once that he was among the friends of his youth – he almost shook hands with them – and he submitted like an angel to padding his horns. He investigated the carts and tractors in the yards, to choose his lines of defence and attack. And then – he attacked with an *élan*, and he defended with a tenacity and forethought that delighted us. In truth, we were so pleased that I fear we trespassed upon his patience. We desired him to repeat himself, which no true artist will tolerate. But he gave us fair warning. He went out to the centre of the yard, where there was some dry earth; he kneeled down and – you have seen a calf whose horns fret him thrusting and rooting into a bank? He did just that, very deliberately, till he had rubbed the pads off his horns. Then he rose, dancing on those wonderful feet that twinkled, and he said: "Now, my friends, the buttons are off the foils. Who begins?" We understood. We finished at once. He was turned out again on the pastures till it should be time to amuse them at our little metropolis. But, some time before he went to Arles – yes, I think I have it correctly – Christophe, who had been out on the Crau, informed me that Apis had assassinated a young bull who had given signs of developing into a rival. That happens, of course, and our herdsmen should prevent it. But Apis had killed in his own style – at dusk, from the ambush of a wind-break – by an oblique charge from behind which knocked the other over. He had then disembowelled him. All very possible, *but* – the murder accomplished – Apis went to the bank of a wind-break, knelt, and carefully, as he had in our yard, cleaned his horns in the earth. Christophe, who had never seen such a thing, at once borrowed (do you know, it is most efficacious when taken that way?) some Holy Water from our little chapel in those pastures, sprinkled Apis (whom it did not affect), and rode in to tell me. It was obvious that a thinker of that bull's type would also be meticulous in his toilette; so, when he was sent to Arles, I warned our consignees to exercise caution with him. Happily, the change of scene, the music, the general attention, and the meeting again with old friends – all our bad boys attended – agreeably distracted him. He became for the time a pure *farceur* again; but his wheelings, his rushes, his rat-huntings were more superb than ever. There was in them now, you understand, a breadth of technique that comes of reasoned art, and, above all, the passion that arrives after experience. Oh, he had learned, out there on the Crau! At the end of his little turn, he was, according to local rules, to be handled in all respects except for the sword, which was a stick, as a professional bull who must die. He was manœuvred into, or he posed himself in, the proper attitude; made his rush; received the point on his shoulder and then – turned about and cantered toward the door by which he had entered the arena. He said to the world: "My friends, the representation is ended. I thank you for your applause. I go to repose myself." But our Arlesians, who are – not so clever as some, demanded as encore, and Apis was headed back again. We others from his country, we knew what would happen. He went to the centre of the ring, kneeled, and, slowly, with full parade, plunged his horns alternately in the dirt till the pads came off. Christophe shouts: "Leave him alone, you straight-nosed imbeciles! Leave him before you must." But they required emotion; for Rome has always debauched her loved Provincia with bread and circuses. It was given. Have you, Monsieur, ever seen a servant, with pan and broom, sweeping round the base-board of a room? In a half-minute Apis has them all swept out and over the barrier. Then he demands once more that the door shall be opened to him. It is opened and he retires as though – which, truly, is the case – loaded with laurels.'

Monsieur Voiron refilled the glasses, and allowed himself a cigarette, which he puffed for some time.

'And afterwards?' I said.

'I am arranging it in my mind. It is difficult to do it justice. Afterwards – yes, afterwards – Apis returned to his pastures and his mistresses and I to my business. I am no longer a scandalous old "sportif" in shirt-sleeves howling encouragement to the yellow son of a cow. I revert to Voiron Frères – wines, chemical manures, *et cetera*. And next year, through some chicane which I have not the leisure to unravel, and also, thanks to our patriarchal system of paying our older men out of the increase of the herds, old Christophe possesses himself of Apis. Oh, yes, he proves it through descent from a certain cow that my father had given his father before the Republic. Beware, Monsieur, of the memory of the illiterate man! An ancestor of Christophe had been a soldier under our Soult against your Beresford, near Bayonne. He fell into the hands of Spanish guerrillas. Christophe and his wife used to tell me the details on certain Saints' Days when I was a child. Now, as compared with our recent war, Soult's campaign and retreat across the Bidassoa——'

'But did you allow Christophe just to annex the bull?' I demanded.

'You do not know Christophe. He had sold him to the Spaniards before he informed me. The Spaniards pay in coin – douros of very pure silver. Our peasants mistrust our paper. You know the saying: "A thousand francs paper; eight hundred metal, and the cow is yours." Yes, Christophe sold Apis, who was then two and a half years old, and to Christophe's knowledge thrice at least an assassin.'

'How was that?' I said.

'Oh, his own kind only; and always, Christophe told me, by the same oblique rush from behind, the same sideways overthrow, and the same swift disembowelment, followed by this levitical cleaning of the horns. In human life he would have kept a manicurist – this Minotaur. And so, Apis disappears from our country. That does not trouble me. I know in due time I shall be advised. Why? Because, in this land, Monsieur, not a hoof moves between Berre and the Saintes Maries without the knowledge of specialists such as Christophe. The beasts are the substance and the drama of their lives to them. So when Christophe tells me, a little before Easter Sunday, that Apis makes his début in the bull-ring of a small Catalan town on the road to Barcelona, it is only to pack my car and trundle there across the frontier with him. The place lacked importance and manufactures, but it had produced a matador of some reputation, who was condescending to show his art in his native town. They were even running one special train to the place. Now our French railway system is only execrable, but the Spanish——'

'You went down by road, didn't you?' said I.

'Naturally. It was not too good. Villamarti was the matador's name. He proposed to kill two bulls for the honour of his birthplace. Apis, Christophe told me, would be his second. It was an interesting trip, and that little city by the sea was ravishing. Their bull-ring dates from the middle of the seventeenth century. It is full of feeling. The ceremonial too – when the horsemen enter and ask the Mayor in his box to throw down the keys of the bull-ring – that was exquisitely conceived. You know, if the keys are caught in the horseman's hat, it is considered a good omen. They were perfectly caught. Our seats were in the front row beside the gates where the bulls enter, so we saw everything.

'Villamarti's first bull was not too badly killed. The second matador, whose name escapes me, killed his without distinction – a foil to Villamarti. And the third, Chisto, a laborious, middle-aged professional who had never risen beyond a certain dull competence, was equally of the background. Oh, they are as jealous as the girls of the Comédie Française, these matadors! Villamarti's troupe stood ready for his second bull. The gates opened, and we saw Apis, beautifully balanced on his feet, peer coquettishly round the corner, as though he were at home. A picador – a mounted man with the long lance-goad – stood near the barrier on his right. He had not even troubled to turn his horse, for the capeadors – the men with the cloaks – were advancing to play Apis – to feel his psychology and intentions, according to the rules that are made for bulls who do not think. . . . I did not realise the murder before it was accomplished! The wheel, the rush, the oblique charge from behind, the fall of horse and man were simultaneous. Apis leaped the horse, with whom he had no quarrel, and alighted, all four feet together (it was enough), between the man's shoulders, changed his beautiful feet on the carcass, and was away, pretending to fall nearly on his nose. Do you follow me? In that instant, by that stumble, he produced the impression that his adorable assassination was a mere bestial blunder. Then, Monsieur, I began to comprehend that it was an artist we had to deal with. He did not stand over the body to draw the rest of the troupe. He chose to reserve that trick. He let the attendants bear out the dead, and went on to amuse himself among the capeadors. Now to Apis, trained among our children in the yards, the cloak was simply a guide to the boy behind it. He pursued, you understand, the person, not the propaganda – the proprietor, not the journal. If a third of our electors of France were as wise, my friend! . . . But it was done leisurely, with humour and a touch of truculence. He romped after one man's cloak as a clumsy dog might do, but I observed that he kept the man on his terrible left side. Christophe whispered to me: "Wait for his mother's kick. When he has made the fellow confident it will arrive." It arrived in the middle of a gambol. My God! He lashed out in the air as he frisked. The man dropped like a sack, lifted one hand a little towards his head, and – that was all. So you see, a body was again at his disposition; a second time the cloaks ran up to draw him off, but, a second time, Apis refused his grand scene. A second time he acted that his murder was accident and – he convinced his audience! It was as though he had knocked over a bridge-gate in the marshes by mistake. Unbelievable? I saw it.'

The memory sent Monsieur Voiron again to the champagne, and I accompanied him.

'But Apis was not the sole artist present. They say Villamarti comes of a family of actors. I saw him regard Apis with a new eye. He, too, began to understand. He took his cloak and moved out to play him before they should bring on another picador. He had his reputation. Perhaps Apis knew it. Perhaps Villamarti reminded him of some boy with whom he had practised at home. At any rate Apis permitted it – up to a certain point; but he did not allow Villamarti the stage. He cramped him throughout. He dived and plunged clumsily and slowly, but always with menace and always closing in. We could see that the man was conforming to the bull – not the bull to the man; for Apis was playing him towards the centre of the ring, and, in a little while – I watched his face – Villamarti knew it. But I could not fathom the creature's motive. "Wait," said old Christophe. "He wants that picador on the white horse yonder. When he reaches his proper distance he will get him. Villamarti is his cover. He used me once that way." And so it was, my friend! With the clang of one of our own Seventy-fives, Apis dismissed Villamarti with his chest – breasted him over – and had arrived at his objective near the barrier. The same oblique charge; the head carried low for the sweep of the horns; the immense sideways fall of the horse, broken-legged and half-paralysed; the senseless man on the ground, and – behold Apis between them, backed against the barrier – his right covered by the horse; his left by the body of the man at his feet. The simplicity of it! Lacking the carts and tractors of his early parade-grounds he, being a genius, had extemporised with the materials at hand, and dug himself in. The troupe closed up again, their left wing broken by the kicking horse, their right immobilised by the man's body which Apis bestrode with significance. Villamarti almost threw himself between the horns, but – it was more an appeal than an attack. Apis refused him. He held his base. A picador was sent at him – necessarily from the front, which alone was open. Apis charged – he who, till then, you realise, had not used the horn! The horse went over backwards, the man half beneath him. Apis halted, hooked him under the heart, and threw him to the barrier. We heard his head crack, but he was dead before he hit the wood. There was no demonstration from the audience. They, also, had begun to realise this Foch among bulls! The arena occupied itself again with the dead. Two of the troupe irresolutely tried to play him – God knows in what hope! – but he moved out to the centre of the ring. "Look!" said Christophe. "Now he goes to clean himself. That always frightened me." He knelt down; he began to clean his horns. The earth was hard. He worried at it in an ecstasy of absorption. As he laid his head along and rattled his ears, it was as though he were interrogating the Devils themselves upon their secrets, and always saying impatiently: "Yes, I know that – and *that* – and *that*! Tell me more – *more*!" In the silence that covered us, a woman cried: "He digs a grave! Oh, Saints, he digs a grave!" Some others echoed this – not loudly – as a wave echoes in a grotto of the sea.

'And when his horns were cleaned, he rose up and studied poor Villamarti's troupe, eyes in eyes, one by one, with the gravity of an equal in intellect and the remote and merciless resolution of a master in his art. This was more terrifying than his toilette.'

'And they – Villamarti's men?' I asked.

'Like the audience, were dominated. They had ceased to posture, or stamp, or address insults to him. They conformed to him. The two other matadors stared. Only Chisto, the oldest, broke silence with some call or other, and Apis turned his head towards him. Otherwise he was isolated, immobile – sombre – meditating on those at his mercy. Ah!

'For some reason the trumpet sounded for the *bandilleras* –

those gay hooked darts that are planted in the shoulders of bulls who do not think, after their neck-muscles are tired by lifting horses. When such bulls feel the pain, they check for an instant, and, in that instant, the men step gracefully aside. Villamarti's bandillero answered the trumpet mechanically – like one condemned. He stood out, poised the darts and stammered the usual patter of invitation. . . . And after? I do not assert that Apis shrugged his shoulders, but he reduced the episode to its lowest elements, as could only a bull of Gaul. With his truculence was mingled always – owing to the shortness of his tail – a certain Rabelaisian abandon, especially when viewed from the rear. Christophe had often commented upon it. Now, Apis brought that quality into play. He circulated round that boy, forcing him to break up his beautiful poses. He studied him from various angles, like an incompetent photographer. He presented to him every portion of his anatomy except his shoulders. At intervals he feigned to run in upon him. My God, he was cruel! But his motive was obvious. He was playing for a laugh from the spectators which should synchronise with the fracture of the human morale. It was achieved. The boy turned and ran towards the barrier. Apis was on him before the laugh ceased; passed him; headed him – what do I say? – herded him off to the left, his horns beside and a little in front of his chest: he did not intend him to escape into a refuge. Some of the troupe would have closed in, but Villamarti cried: "If he wants him he will take him. Stand!" They stood. Whether the boy slipped or Apis nosed him over I could not see. But he dropped, sobbing. Apis halted like a car with four brakes, struck a pose, smelt him very completely and turned away. It was dismissal more ignominious than degradation at the head of one's battalion. The representation was finished. Remained only for Apis to clear his stage of the subordinate characters.

'Ah! His gesture then! He gave a dramatic start – this Cyrano of the Camargue – as though he was aware of them for the first time. He moved. All their beautiful breeches twinkled for an instant along the top of the barrier. He held the stage alone! But Christophe and I, we trembled! For, observe, he had now involved himself in a stupendous drama of which he only could supply the third act. And, except for an audience on the razor-edge of emotion, he had exhausted his material. Molière himself – we have forgotten, my friend, to drink to the health of that great soul – might have been at a loss. And Tragedy is but a step behind Failure. We could see the four or five Civil Guards, who are sent always to keep order, fingering the breeches of their rifles. They were but waiting a word from the Mayor to fire on him, as they do sometimes at a bull who leaps the barrier among the spectators. They would, of course, have killed or wounded several people – but that would not have saved Apis.'

Monsieur Voiron drowned the thought at once, and wiped his beard.

'At that moment Fate – the Genius of France, if you will – sent to assist in the incomparable finale, none other than Chisto, the eldest, and I should have said (but never again will I judge!) the least inspired of all; mediocrity itself but, at heart – and it is the heart that conquers always, my friend – at heart an artist. He descended stiffly into the arena, alone and assured. Apis regarded him, his eyes in his eyes. The man took stance, with his cloak, and called to the bull as to an equal: "Now, Señor, we will show these honourable caballeros something together." He advanced thus against this thinker who at a plunge – a kick – a thrust – could, we all knew, have extinguished him. My dear friend, I wish I could convey to you something of the unaffected bonhomie, the humour, the delicacy, the consideration bordering on respect even, with which Apis, the supreme artist, responded to this invitation. It was the Master, wearied after a strenuous hour in the atelier, unbuttoned and at ease with some not inexpert but limited disciple. The telepathy was instantaneous between them. And for good reason! Christophe said to me: "All's well. That Chisto began among the bulls. I was sure of it when I heard him call just now. He has been a herdsman. He'll pull it off." There was a little feeling and adjustment, at first, for mutual distances and allowances.

'Oh, yes! And here occurred a gross impertinence of Villamarti. He had, after an interval, followed Chisto – to retrieve his reputation. My Faith! I can conceive the elder Dumas slamming his door on an intruder precisely as Apis did. He raced Villamarti into the nearest refuge at once. He stamped his feet outside it, and he snorted: "Go! I am engaged with an artist." Villamarti went – his reputation left behind for ever.

'Apis returned to Chisto saying: "Forgive the interruption. I am not always master of my time, but you were about to observe, my dear confrère . . .?" Then the play began. Out of compliment to Chisto, Apis chose as his objective (every bull varies in this respect) the inner edge of the cloak – that nearest to the man's body. This allows but a few millimetres clearance in charging. But Apis trusted himself as Chisto trusted him, and, this time, he conformed to the man, with inimitable judgment and temper. He allowed himself to be played into the shadow or the sun, as the delighted audience demanded. He raged enormously; he feigned defeat; he despaired in statuesque abandon, and thence flashed into fresh paroxysms of wrath – but always with the detachment of the true artist who knows he is but the vessel of an emotion whence others, not he, must drink. And never once did he forget that honest Chisto's cloak was to him the gauge by which to spare even a hair on the skin. He inspired Chisto too. My God! His youth returned to that meritorious beef-sticker – the desire, the grace, and the beauty of his early dreams. One could almost see that girl of the past for whom he was rising, rising to these present heights of skill and daring. It was his hour too – a miraculous hour of dawn returned to gild the sunset. All he knew was at Apis's disposition. Apis acknowledged it with all that he had learned at home, at Arles and in his lonely murders on our grazing-grounds. He flowed round Chisto like a river of death – round his knees, leaping at his shoulders, kicking just clear of one side or the other of his head; behind his back hissing as he shaved by; and once or twice – inimitable! – he reared wholly up before him while Chisto slipped back from beneath the avalanche of that instructed body. Those two, my dear friend, held five thousand people dumb with no sound but of their breathings – regular as pumps. It was unbearable. Beast and man realised together that we needed a change of note – a *détente*. They relaxed to pure buffoonery. Chisto fell back and talked to him outrageously. Apis pretended he had never heard such language. The audience howled with delight. Chisto slapped him; he took liberties with his short tail, to the end of which he clung while Apis pirouetted;

he played about him in all postures; he had become the herdsman again – gross, careless, brutal, but comprehending. Yet Apis was always the more consummate clown. All that time (Christophe and I saw it) Apis drew off towards the gates of the *toril* where so many bulls enter but – have you ever heard of one that returned? *We* knew that Apis knew that as he had saved Chisto, so Chisto would save him. Life is sweet to us all; to the artist who lives many lives in one, sweetest. Chisto did not fail him. At the last, when none could laugh any longer, the man threw his cape across the bull's back, his arm round his neck. He flung up a hand at the gate, as Villamarti, young and commanding but *not* a herdsman, might have raised it, and he cried: "Gentlemen, open to me and my honourable little donkey." They opened – I have misjudged Spaniards in my time! – those gates opened to the man and the bull together, and closed behind them. And then? From the Mayor to the Guarda Civile they went mad for five minutes, till the trumpets blew and the fifth bull rushed out – an unthinking black Andalusian. I suppose someone killed him. My friend, my very dear friend, to whom I have opened my heart, I confess that I did not watch. Christophe and I, we were weeping together like children of the same Mother. Shall we drink to Her?'

ALNASCHAR AND THE OXEN

There's a pasture in a valley where the hanging
    woods divide,
  And a Herd lies down and ruminates in peace;
Where the pheasant rules the nooning, and the
    owl the twilight tide,
  And the war-cries of our world die out and
    cease.
Here I cast aside the burden that each weary
    week-day brings
  And, delivered from the shadows I pursue,
On peaceful, postless Sabbaths I consider Weighty
    Things –
  Such as Sussex Cattle feeding in the dew!

At the gate beside the river where the trouty
shallows brawl,
I know the pride that Lobengula felt,
When he bade the bars be lowered of the Royal
Cattle Kraal,
And fifteen mile of oxen took the veldt.
From the walls of Bulawayo in unbroken file
they came
To where the Mount of Council cuts the blue . . .
I have only six and twenty, but the principle's the
same
With my Sussex Cattle feeding in the dew!

To a luscious sound of tearing, where the clovered
herbage rips,
Level-backed and level-bellied watch 'em move –
See those shoulders, guess that heart-girth, praise
those loins, admire those hips,
And the tail set low for flesh to make above!
Count the broad unblemished muzzles, test the
kindly mellow skin
And, where yon heifer lifts her head at call,
Mark the bosom's just abundance 'neath the gay
and clean-cut chin,
And those eyes of Juno, overlooking all!

Here is colour, form and substance! I will put it
to the proof
And, next season, in my lodges shall be born
Some very Bull of Mithras, flawless from his
agate hoof
To his even-branching, ivory, dusk-tipped horn.
He shall mate with block-square virgins – kings
shall seek his like in vain,
While I multiply his stock a thousandfold,
Till an hungry world extol me, builder of a lofty
strain
That turns one standard ton at two years old!

There's a valley, under oakwood, where a man may
dream his dream,
In the milky breath of cattle laid at ease,
Till the moon o'ertops the alders, and her image chills
the stream
And the river-mist runs silver round their knees!
Now the footpaths fade and vanish; now the ferny
clumps deceive;
Now the hedgerow-folk possess their fields anew;
Now the Herd is lost in darkness, and I bless them as
I leave,
My Sussex Cattle feeding in the dew!

The Wish House

'LATE CAME THE GOD'

Late came the God, having sent his forerunners
who were not regarded –
Late, but in wrath;
Saying: 'The wrong shall be paid, the contempt
be rewarded
On all that she hath.'
He poisoned the blade and struck home, the full
bosom receiving
The wound and the venom in one, past cure or
relieving.

He made treaty with Time to stand still that the
grief might be fresh –
Daily renewed and nightly pursued through her
soul to her flesh –
Mornings of memory, noontides of agony, mid-
nights unslaked for her,
Till the stones of the streets of her Hells and her
Paradise ached for her.

So she lived while her body corrupted upon her.
And she called on the Night for a sign, and a
Sign was allowed,
And she builded an Altar and served by the light
of her Vision –
Alone, without hope of regard or reward, but
uncowed,
Resolute, selfless, divine.
These things she did in Love's honour . . .
What is a God beside Woman? Dust and
derision!

The new Church Visitor had just left after a twenty minutes' call. During that time, Mrs Ashcroft had used such English as an elderly, experienced, and pensioned cook should, who had seen life in London. She was the readier, therefore, to slip back into easy, ancient Sussex ('t's softening to 'd's as one warmed) when the 'bus brought Mrs Fettley from thirty miles away for a visit, that pleasant March Saturday. The two had been friends since childhood; but, of late, destiny had separated their meetings by long intervals.

Much was to be said, and many ends, loose since last time, to be ravelled up on both sides, before Mrs Fettley, with her bag of quilt-patches, took the couch beneath the window commanding the garden, and the football-ground in the valley below.

'Most folk got out at Bush Tye for the match there,' she explained, 'so there weren't no one for me to cushion agin, the last five mile. An' she *do* just-about bounce ye.'

'You've took no hurt,' said her hostess. 'You don't brittle by agein', Liz.'

Mrs Fettley chuckled and made to match a couple of patches to her liking. 'No, or I'd ha' broke twenty year back. You can't ever mind when I was so's to be called round, can ye?'

Mrs Ashcroft shook her head slowly – she never hurried – and went on stitching a sack-cloth lining into a list-bound rush tool-basket. Mrs Fettley laid out more patches in the Spring light through the geraniums on the window-sill, and they were silent awhile.

'What like's this new Visitor o' yourn?' Mrs Fettley inquired, with a nod towards the door. Being very short-sighted, she had, on her entrance, almost bumped into the lady.

Mrs Ashcroft suspended the big packing-needle judicially on high, ere she stabbed home. 'Settin' aside she don't bring much news with her yet, I dunno as I've anythin' special agin her.'

'Ourn, at Keyneslade,' said Mrs Fettley, 'she's full o' words an' pity, but she don't stay for answers. Ye can get on with your thoughts while she clacks.'

'This 'un don't clack. She's aimin' to be one o' those High Church nuns, like.'

'Ourn's married, but, by what they say, she've made no great gains of it . . .' Mrs Fettley threw up her sharp chin. 'Lord! How they dam' cherubim do shake the very bones o' the place!'

The tile-sided cottage trembled at the passage of two specially chartered forty-seat charabancs on their way to the Bush Tye match; a regular Saturday 'shopping' 'bus, for the county's capital, fumed behind them; while, from one of the crowded inns, a fourth car backed out to join the procession, and held up the stream of through pleasure-traffic.

'You're as free-tongued as ever, Liz,' Mrs Ashcroft observed.

'Only when I'm with you. Otherwhiles, I'm Granny – three times over. I lay that basket's for one o' your gran'chiller – ain't it?'

''Tis for Arthur – my Jane's eldest.'

'But he ain't workin' nowheres, is he?'

'No. 'Tis a picnic-basket.'

'You're let off light. My Willie, he's allus at me for money for them aireated wash-poles folk puts up in their gardens to draw the music from Lunnon, like. An' I give it 'im – pore fool me!'

'An' he forgets to give you the promise-kiss after, don't he?' Mrs Ashcroft's heavy smile seemed to strike inwards.

'He do. 'No odds 'twixt boys now an' forty year back. 'Take all an' give naught – an' we to put up with it! Pore fool we! Three shillin' at a time Willie'll ask me for!'

'They don't make nothin' o' money these days,' Mrs Ashcroft said.

'An' on'y last week,' the other went on, 'me daughter, she ordered a quarter pound suet at the butchers's; an' she sent it back to 'im to be chopped. She said she couldn't bother with choppin' it.'

'I lay he charged her, then.'

'I lay he did. She told me there was a whisk-drive that afternoon at the Institute, an' she couldn't bother to do the choppin'.'

'Tck!'

Mrs Ashcroft put the last firm touches to the basket-lining. She had scarcely finished when her sixteen-year-old grandson, a maiden of the moment in attendance, hurried up the garden-path shouting to know if the thing were ready, snatched it, and made off without acknowledgment. Mrs Fettley peered at him closely.

'They're goin' picnickin' somewheres,' Mrs Ashcroft explained.

'Ah,' said the other, with narrowed eyes. 'I lay *he* won't show much mercy to any he comes across, either. Now 'oo the dooce do he remind me of, all of a sudden?'

'They must look ârter theirselves – 'same as we did.' Mrs Ashcroft began to set out the tea.

'No denyin' *you* could, Gracie,' said Mrs Fettley.

'What's in your head now?'

'Dunno . . . But it come over me, sudden-like – about dat woman from Rye – I've slipped the name – Barnsley, wadn't it?'

'Batten – Polly Batten, you're thinkin' of.'

'That's it – Polly Batten. That day she had it in for you with a hay-fork – 'time we was all hayin' at Smalldene – for stealin' her man.'

'But you heered me tell her she had my leave to keep him?' Mrs Ashcroft's voice and smile were smoother than ever.

'I did – an' we was all looking that she'd prod the fork spang through your breastes when you said it.'

'No-oo. She'd never go beyond bounds – Polly. She shruck too much for reel doin's.'

'Allus seems to *me*,' Mrs Fettley said after a pause, 'that a man 'twixt two fightin' women is the foolishest thing on earth. 'Like a dog bein' called two ways.'

'Mebbe. But what set ye off on those times, Liz?'

'That boy's fashion o' carryin' his head an' arms. I haven't rightly looked at him since he's growed. Your Jane never showed it, but – *him*! Why, 'tis Jim Batten and his tricks come to life again! . . . Eh?'

'Mebbe. There's some that would ha' made it out so – bein' barren-like, themselves.'

'Oho! Ah well! Dearie, dearie me, now! . . . An' Jim Batten's been dead this——'

'Seven and twenty year,' Mrs Ashcroft answered briefly. 'Won't ye draw up, Liz?'

Mrs Fettley drew up to buttered toast, currant bread, stewed tea, bitter as leather, some home-preserved pears, and a cold boiled pig's tail to help down the muffins. She paid all the proper compliments.

'Yes. I dunno as I've ever owed me belly much,' said Mrs Ashcroft thoughtfully. 'We only go through this world once.'

'But don't it lay heavy on ye, sometimes?' her guest suggested.

'Nurse says I'm a sight liker to die o' me indigestion than me leg.' For Mrs Ashcroft had a long-standing ulcer on her shin, which needed regular care from the Village Nurse, who boasted (or others did, for her) that she had dressed it one hundred and three times already during her term of office.

'An' you that *was* so able, too! It's all come on ye before your full time, like. *I*'ve watched ye goin'.' Mrs Fettley spoke with real affection.

'Somethin's bound to find ye sometime. I've me 'eart left me still,' Mrs Ashcroft returned.

'You was always big-hearted enough for three. That's somethin' to look back on at the day's eend.'

'I reckon you've *your* back-lookin's, too,' was Mrs Ashcroft's answer.

'You know it. But I don't think much regardin' such matters excep' when I'm along with you, Gra'. 'Takes two sticks to make a fire.'

Mrs Fettley stared, with jaw half-dropped, at the grocer's bright calendar on the wall. The cottage shook again to the roar of the motor-traffic, and the crowded football-ground below the garden roared almost as loudly; for the village was well set to its Saturday leisure.

Mrs Fettley had spoken very precisely for some time without interruption, before she wiped her eyes. 'And,' she concluded, 'they read 'is death-notice to me, out o' the paper last month. O' course it wadn't any o' *my* becomin'' concerns – let be I 'adn't set eyes on him for so long. O' course *I* couldn't say nor show nothin'. Nor I've no rightful call to go to Eastbourne to see 'is grave, either. I've been schemin' to slip over there by the 'bus some day; but they'd ask questions at 'ome past endurance. So I 'aven't even *that* to stay me.'

'But you've 'ad your satisfactions?'

'Godd! Yess! Those four years 'e was workin' on the rail near us. An' the other drivers they gave him a brave funeral, too.'

'Then you've naught to cast-up about. 'Nother cup o' tea?'

The light and air had changed a little with the sun's descent, and the two elderly ladies closed the kitchen-door against chill. A couple of jays squealed and skirmished through the undraped apple-trees in the garden. This time, the word was with Mrs

Ashcroft, her elbows on the tea-table, and her sick leg propped on a stool. . . .

'Well I never! But what did your 'usband say to that?' Mrs Fettley asked, when the deep-toned recital halted.

''E said I might go where I pleased for all of 'im. But seein' 'e was bedrid, I said I'd 'tend 'im out. 'E knowed I wouldn't take no advantage of 'im in that state. 'E lasted eight or nine week. Then he was took with a seizure-like; an' laid stone-still for days. Then 'e propped 'imself up abed an' says: "You pray no man'll ever deal with you like you've dealed with some." "An' you?" I says, for *you* know, Liz, what a rover 'e was. "It cuts both ways," says 'e, "but *I*'m death-wise, an' I can see what's comin' to you." He died a-Sunday an' was buried a-Thursday . . . An' yet I'd set a heap by him – one time or – did I ever?'

'You never told me that before,' Mrs Fettley ventured.

'I'm payin' ye for what ye told me just now. Him bein' dead, I wrote up, sayin' I was free for good, to that Mrs Marshall in Lunnon – which gave me my first place as kitchen-maid – Lord, how long ago! She was well pleased, for they two was both gettin' on, an' I knowed their ways. You remember, Liz, I used to go to 'em in service between whiles, for years – when we wanted money, or – or my 'usband was away – on occasion.'

''E *did* get that six months at Chichester, didn't 'e?' Mrs Fettley whispered. 'We never rightly won to the bottom of it.'

''E'd ha' got more, but the man didn't die.'

''None o' your doin's, was it, Gra'?'

'No! 'Twas the woman's husband this time. An' so, my man bein' dead, I went back to them Marshalls as cook, to get me legs under a gentleman's table again, and be called with a handle to me name. That was the year you shifted to Portsmouth.'

'Cosham,' Mrs Fettley corrected. 'There was a middlin' lot o' new buildin' bein' done there. My man went first, an' got the room, an' I follered.'

'Well, then, I was a year-abouts in Lunnon, all at a breath, like, four meals a day an' livin' easy. Then, 'long towards autumn, they two went travellin', like, to France; keepin' me on, for they couldn't do without me. I put the house to rights for the caretaker, an' then I slipped down 'ere to me sister Bessie – me wages in me pockets, an' all 'ands glad to be'old of me.'

'That would be when I was at Cosham,' said Mrs Fettley.

'*You* know, Liz, there wasn't no cheap-dog pride to folk, those days, no more than there was cinemas nor whisk-drives. Man or woman 'ud lay hold o' any job that promised a shillin' to the backside of it, didn't they? I was all peaked up after Lunnon, an' I thought the fresh airs 'ud serve me. So I took on at Smalldene, obligin' with a hand at the early potato-liftin', stubbin' hens, an' such-like. They'd ha' mocked me sore in my kitchen in Lunnon, to see me in men's boots, an' me petticoats all shorted.'

'Did it bring ye any good?' Mrs Fettley asked.

''Twadn't for that I went. You know, 's'well's me, that na'un happens to ye till it *'as* 'appened. Your mind don't warn ye before'and of the road ye've took, till you're at the far eend of it. We've only a backwent view of our proceedin's.'

''Oo was it?'

''Arry Mockler.' Mrs Ashcroft's face puckered to the pain of her sick leg.

Mrs Fettley gasped. ''Arry? Bert Mockler's son! An' *I* never guessed!'

Mrs Ashcroft nodded. 'An' I told myself – *an'* I beleft it – that I wanted field-work.'

'What did ye get out of it?'

'The usuals. Everythin' at first – worse than naught after. I had signs an' warnings a-plenty, but I took no heed of 'em. For we was burnin' rubbish one day, just when we'd come to know how 'twas with – with both of us. 'Twas early in the year for burnin', an' I said so. "No!" says he. "The sooner dat old stuff's off an' done with," 'e says, "the better." 'Is face was harder'n rocks when he spoke. Then it come over me that I'd found me master, which I 'adn't ever before. I'd allus owned 'em, like.'

'Yes! Yes! They're yourn or you're theirn,' the other sighed. 'I like the right way best.'

'I didn't. But 'Arry did . . . 'Long then, it come time for me to go back to Lunnon. I couldn't. I clean couldn't! So, I took an' tipped a dollop o' scaldin' water out o' the copper one

Monday mornin' over me left 'and and arm. Dat stayed me where I was for another fortnight.'

'Was it worth it?' said Mrs Fettley, looking at the silvery scar on the wrinkled forearm.

Mrs Ashcroft nodded. 'An' after that, we two made it up 'twixt us so's 'e could come to Lunnon for a job in a liv'ry-stable not far from me. 'E got it. *I* 'tended to that. There wadn't no talk nowhere. His own mother never suspicioned how 'twas. He just slipped up to Lunnon, an' there we abode that winter, not 'alf a mile 'tother from each.'

'Ye paid 'is fare an' all, though'; Mrs Fettley spoke convincedly.

Again Mrs Ashcroft nodded. 'Dere wadn't much I didn't do for him. 'E was me master, an' – O God, help us! – we'd laugh over it walkin' together after dark in them paved streets, an' me corns fair wrenchin' in me boots! I'd never been like that before. Ner he! Ner he!'

Mrs Fettley clucked sympathetically.

'An' when did ye come to the eend?' she asked.

'When 'e paid it all back again, every penny. Then I knowed, but I wouldn't *suffer* meself to know. "You've been mortal kind to me," he says. "Kind!" I said. "'Twixt *us*?" But 'e kep' all on tellin' me 'ow kind I'd been an' 'e'd never forget it all his days. I held it from off o' me for three evenin's, because I would *not* believe. Then 'e talked about not bein' satisfied with 'is job in the stables, an' the men there puttin' tricks on 'im, an' all they lies which a man tells when 'e's leavin' ye. I heard 'im out, neither 'elpin' nor 'inderin'. At the last, I took off a liddle brooch which he'd give me an' I says: "Dat'll do. *I* ain't askin' na'un'." An' I turned me round an' walked off to me own sufferin's. 'E didn't make 'em worse. 'E didn't come nor write after that. 'E slipped off 'ere back 'ome to 'is mother again.'

'An' 'ow often did ye look for 'en to come back?' Mrs Fettley demanded mercilessly.

'More'n once – more'n once! Goin' over the streets we'd used, I thought de very pave-stones 'ud shruck out under me feet.'

'Yes,' said Mrs Fettley. 'I dunno but dat don't 'urt as much as aught else. An' dat was all ye got?'

'No. 'Twadn't. That's the curious part, if you'll believe it, Liz.'

'I do. I lay you're further off lyin' now than in all your life, Gra'.'

'I am . . . An' I suffered, like I'd not wish my most arrantest enemies to. God's Own Name! I went through the hoop that spring! One part of it was headaches which I'd never known all me days before. Think o' *me* with an 'eddick! But I come to be grateful for 'em. They kep' me from thinkin' . . .'

''Tis like a tooth,' Mrs Fettley commented. 'It must rage an' rugg till it tortures itself quiet on ye; an' then – then there's na'un left.'

'*I* got enough lef' to last me all *my* days on earth. It come about through our charwoman's liddle girl – Sophy Ellis was 'er name – all eyes an' elbers an' hunger. I used to give 'er vittles. Otherwhiles, I took no special notice of 'er, an' a sight less, o' course, when me trouble about 'Arry was on me. But – you know how liddle maids first feel it sometimes – she come to be crazy-fond o' me, pawin' an' cuddlin' all whiles; an' I 'adn't the 'eart to beat 'er off . . . One afternoon, early in spring 'twas, 'er mother 'ad sent 'er round to scutchel up what vittles she could off of us. I was settin' by the fire, me apern over me head, half-mad with the 'eddick, when she slips in. I reckon I was middlin' short with 'er. "Lor'!" she says. "Is *that* all? I'll take it off you in two-twos!" I told her not to lay a finger on me, for I thought she'd want to stroke my forehead; an' – I ain't that make. "*I* won't tech ye," she says, an' slips out again. She 'adn't been gone ten minutes 'fore me old 'eddick took off quick as bein' kicked. So I went about my work. Prasin'ly, Sophy comes back, an' creeps into my chair quiet as a mouse. 'Er eyes was deep in 'er 'ead an' 'er face all drawed. I asked 'er what 'ad 'appened. "Nothin'," she says. "On'y *I*'ve got it now." "Got what?" I says. "Your 'eddick," she says, all hoarse an' sticky-lipped. "I've took it on me." "Nonsense," I says, "it went of itself when you was out. Lay still an' I'll make ye a cup o' tea." " 'Twon't do no good," she says, "till your time's up. 'Ow long do *your* 'eddicks last?" "Don't talk silly," I says, "or I'll send for the Doctor." It looked to me like she might be hatchin' de measles. "Oh, Mrs Ashcroft," she says, stretchin' out 'er liddle thin arms. "I *do* love ye." There wasn't any holdin' agin that. I took 'er into me lap an' made much of 'er. "Is it truly gone?" she says. "Yes," I says, "an' if 'twas you took it away, I'm truly grateful." "'*Twas* me," she says, layin' 'er cheek to mine. "No one but me knows how." An' then she said she'd changed me 'eddick for me at a Wish 'Ouse.'

'What?' Mrs Fettley spoke sharply.

'A Wish House. No! *I* 'adn't 'eard o' such things, either. I couldn't get it straight at first, but, puttin' all together, I made out that a Wish 'Ouse 'ad to be a house which 'ad stood unlet an' empty long enough for Some One, like, to come an' in'abit there. She said, a liddle girl that she'd played with in the livery-stables where 'Arry worked 'ad told 'er so. She said the girl 'ad belonged in a caravan that laid up, o' winters, in Lunnon. Gipsy, I judge.'

'Ooh! There's no sayin' what Gippos know, but *I*'ve never 'eard of a Wish 'Ouse, an' I know – some things,' said Mrs Fettley.

'Sophy said there was a Wish 'Ouse in Wadloes Road – just a few streets off, on the way to our greengrocer's. All you 'ad to do, she said, was to ring the bell an' wish your wish through the slit o' the letter-box. I asked 'er if the fairies give it 'er? "Don't ye know," she says, "there's no fairies in a Wish 'Ouse? There's on'y a Token." '

'Goo' Lord A'mighty! Where did she come by *that* word?' cried Mrs Fettley; for a Token is a wraith of the dead or, worse still, of the living.

'The caravan-girl 'ad told 'er, she said. Well, Liz, it troubled me to 'ear 'er, an' lyin' in me arms she must ha' felt it. "That's very kind o' you," I says, holdin' 'er tight, "to wish me 'eddick away. But why didn't ye ask somethin' nice for yourself?" "You can't do that," she says. "All you'll get at a Wish 'Ouse is leave to take someone else's trouble. I've took Ma's 'eadaches, when she's been kind to me; but this is the first time I've been able to do aught for you. Oh, Mrs Ashcroft, I *do* just-about love you." An' she goes on all like that. Liz, I tell you my 'air e'en a'most stood on end to 'ear 'er. I asked 'er what like a Token was. "I dunno," she says, "but after you've ringed the bell, you'll 'ear it run up from the basement, to the front door. Then say your wish," she says, "an' go away." "The Token don't open de door to ye, then?" I says. "Oh no," she says. "You on'y 'ear gigglin', like, be'ind the front door. Then you say you'll take the trouble off of 'oo ever 'tis you've chose for your love; an' ye'll get it," she says. I didn't ask no more – she was too 'ot an' fevered. I made much of 'er till it come time to light de gas, an' a liddle after that, 'er 'eddick – mine, I suppose – took off, an' she got down an' played with the cat.'

'Well, I never!' said Mrs Fettley. 'Did – did ye foller it up, anyways?'

'She askt me to, but I wouldn't 'ave no such dealin's with a child.'

'What *did* ye do, then?'

''Sat in me own room 'stid o' the kitchen when me 'eddicks come on. But it lay at de back o' me mind.'

''Twould. Did she tell ye more, ever?'

'No. Besides what the Gippo girl 'ad told 'er, she knew naught, 'cept that the charm worked. An', next after that – in May 'twas – I suffered the summer out in Lunnon. 'Twas hot an' windy for weeks, an' the streets stinkin' o' dried 'orse-dung blowin' from side to side an' lyin' level with the kerb. We don't get that nowadays. I 'ad my 'ol'day just before hoppin', an' come down 'ere to stay with Bessie again. She noticed I'd lost flesh, an' was all poochy under the eyes.'

'Did ye see 'Arry?'

Mrs Ashcroft nodded. 'The fourth – no, the fifth day. Wednesday 'twas. I knowed 'e was workin' at Smalldene again. I asked 'is mother in the street, bold as brass. She 'adn't room to say much, for Bessie – you know 'er tongue – was talkin' full-clack. But that Wednesday, I was walkin' with one o' Bessie's chillern hangin' on me skirts, at de back o' Chanter's Tot. Prasin'ly, I felt 'e was be'ind me on the footpath, an' I knowed by 'is tread 'e'd changed 'is nature. I slowed, an' I heard 'im slow. Then I fussed a piece with the child, to force him past me, like. So 'e '*ad* to come past. 'E just says "Good-evenin'," and goes on, tryin' to pull 'isself together.'

'Drunk, was he?' Mrs Fettley asked.

'Never! S'runk an' wizen; 'is clothes 'angin' on 'im like bags, an' the back of 'is neck whiter'n chalk. 'Twas all I could do not to oppen my arms an' cry after him. But I swallered me spittle till I was back 'ome again an' the chillern abed. Then I says to Bessie, after supper, "What in de world's come to 'Arry Mockler?" Bessie told me 'e'd been a-Hospital for two months, 'long o' cuttin' 'is foot wid a spade, muckin' out the old pond at Smalldene. There was poison in de dirt, an' it rooshed up 'is leg, like, an' come out all over him. 'E 'adn't been back to 'is job – carterin' at Smalldene – more'n a fortnight. She told me the Doctor said he'd go off, likely, with the November frostes; an' 'is mother 'ad told 'er that 'e didn't rightly eat nor sleep, an' sweated 'imself into pools, no odds 'ow chill 'e lay. An' spit terrible o' mornin's. "Dearie me," I says. "But, mebbe, hoppin' 'll set 'im right again," an' I licked me thread-point an' I fetched me needle's eye up to it an' I threads me needle under de lamp, steady as rocks. An' dat night (me bed was in de wash-house) I cried an' I cried. An' *you* know, Liz – for you've been with me in my throes – it takes summat to make me cry.'

'Yes; but chile-bearin' is on'y just pain,' said Mrs Fettley.

'I come round by cock-crow, an' dabbed cold tea on me eyes to take away the signs. Long towards nex' evenin' – I was settin' out to lay some flowers on me 'usband's grave, for the look o' the thing – I met 'Arry over against where the War Memorial is now. 'E was comin' back from 'is 'orses, so 'e couldn't *not* see me. I looked 'im all over, an' " 'Arry," I says twix' me teeth, "come back an' rest-up in Lunnon." "I won't take it," he says, "for I can give ye naught." "I don't ask it," I says. "By God's Own Name, I don't ask na'un! On'y come up an' see a Lunnon doctor." 'E lifts 'is two 'eavy eyes at me: " 'Tis past that, Gra'," 'e says. "I've but a few months left." " 'Arry!" I says. "*My* man!" I says. I couldn't say no more. 'Twas all up in me throat. "Thank ye kindly, Gra'," 'e says (but 'e never says "my woman"), an' 'e went on up-street an' 'is mother – Oh, damn 'er! – she was watchin' for 'im, an' she shut de door be'ind 'im.'

Mrs Fettley stretched an arm across the table, and made to finger Mrs Ashcroft's sleeve at the wrist, but the other moved it out of reach.

'So I went on to the churchyard with my flowers, an' I remembered my 'usband's warnin' that night he spoke. 'E *was* deathwise, an' it '*ad* 'appened as 'e said. But as I was settin' down de jam-pot on the grave-mound, it come over me there was one thing I *could* do for 'Arry. Doctor or no Doctor, I thought I'd make a trial of it. So I did. Nex' mornin', a bill came down from our Lunnon greengrocer. Mrs Marshall, she'd lef' me petty cash for suchlike – o' course – but I tole Bess 'twas for me to come an' open the 'ouse. So I went up, afternoon train.'

'An' – but I know you 'adn't – 'adn't you no fear?'

'What for? There was nothin' front o' me but my own shame an' God's croolty. I couldn't ever get 'Arry – 'ow *could* I? I knowed it must go on burnin' till it burned me out.'

'Aie!' said Mrs Fettley, reaching for the wrist again, and this time Mrs Ashcroft permitted it.

'Yit 'twas a comfort to know I could try *this* for 'im. So I went an' I paid the greengrocer's bill, an' put 'is receipt in me hand-bag, an' then I stepped round to Mrs Ellis – our char – an' got the 'ouse-keys an' opened the 'ouse. First, I made me bed to come back to (God's Own Name! Me bed to lie upon!). Nex' I made me a cup o' tea an' sat down in the kitchen thinkin', till 'long towards dusk. Terrible close, 'twas. Then I dressed me an' went out with the receipt in me 'and-bag, feignin' to study it for an address, like. Fourteen, Wadloes Road, was the place – a liddle basement-kitchen 'ouse, in a row of twenty-thirty such, an' tiddy strips o' walled garden in front – the paint off the front doors, an' na'un done to na'un since ever so long. There wasn't 'ardly no one in the streets 'cept the cats. '*Twas* 'ot, too! I turned into the gate bold as brass; up de steps I went an' I ringed the front-door bell. She pealed loud, like it do in an empty house. When she'd all ceased, I 'eard a cheer, like, pushed back on de floor o' the kitchen. Then I 'eard feet on de kitchen-stairs, like it might ha' been a heavy woman in slippers. They come up to de stair-head, acrost the hall – I 'eard the bare boards creak under 'em – an' at de front door dey stopped. I stooped me to the letter-box slit, an' I says: "Let me take everythin' bad that's in store for my man, 'Arry Mockler, for love's sake." Then, whatever it was 'tother side de door let its breath out, like, as if it 'ad been holdin' it for to 'ear better.'

'Nothin' was *said* to ye?' Mrs Fettley demanded.

'Na'un. She just breathed out – sort of *A-ah*, like. Then the steps went back an' downstairs to the kitchen – all draggy – an' I heard the cheer drawed up again.'

'An' you abode on de doorstep, throughout all, Gra'?'

Mrs Ashcroft nodded.

'Then I went away, an' a man passin' says to me: "Didn't you know that house was empty?" "No," I says. "I must ha' been give the wrong number." An' I went back to our 'ouse, an' I went to bed; for I was fair flogged out. 'Twas too 'ot to sleep more'n snatches, so I walked me about, lyin' down betweens, till crack o' dawn. Then I went to the kitchen to make me a cup o' tea, an' I hitted meself just above the ankle on an old roastin'-jack o' mine that Mrs Ellis had moved out from the corner, her last cleanin'. An' so – nex' after that – I waited till the Marshalls come back o' their holiday.'

'Alone there? I'd ha' thought you'd 'ad enough of empty houses,' said Mrs Fettley, horrified.

'Oh, Mrs Ellis an' Sophy was runnin' in an' out soon's I was back, an' 'twixt us we cleaned de house again top-to-bottom. There's allus a hand's turn more to do in every house. An' that's 'ow 'twas with me that autumn an' winter, in Lunnon.'

'Then na'un hap – overtook ye for your doin's?'

Mrs Ashcroft smiled. 'No. Not then. 'Long in November I sent Bessie ten shillin's.'

'You was allus free-'anded,' Mrs Fettley interrupted.

'An' I got what I paid for, with the rest o' the news. She said the hoppin' 'ad set 'im up wonderful. 'E'd 'ad six weeks of it, and now 'e was back again carterin' at Smalldene. No odds to me *'ow* it 'ad 'appened – 'slong's it *'ad*. But I dunno as my ten shillin's eased me much. 'Arry bein' *dead*, like, 'e'd ha' been mine, till Judgment. 'Arry bein' alive, 'e'd like as not pick up with some woman middlin' quick. I raged over that. Come spring, I 'ad somethin' else to rage for. I'd growed a nasty little weepin' boil, like, on me shin, just above the boot-top, that wouldn't heal no shape. It made me sick to look at it, for I'm clean-fleshed by nature. Chop me all over with a spade, an' I'd heal like turf. Then Mrs Marshall she set 'er own doctor at me. 'E said I ought to ha' come to him at first go-off, 'stead o' drawin' all manner o' dyed stockin's over it for months. 'E said I'd stood up too much to me work, for it was settin' very close atop of a big swelled vein, like, behither the small o' me ankle. "Slow come, slow go," 'e says. "Lay your leg up on high an' rest it," he says, "an' 'twill ease off. Don't let it close up too soon. You've got a very fine leg, Mrs Ashcroft," 'e says. An' he put wet dressin's on it.'

' 'E done right.' Mrs Fettley spoke firmly. 'Wet dressin's to wet wounds. They draw de humours, same's a lamp-wick draws de oil.'

'That's true. An' Mrs Marshall was allus at me to make me set down more, an' dat nigh healed it up. An' then after a while they packed me off down to Bessie's to finish the cure; for I ain't the sort to sit down when I ought to stand up. You was back in the village then, Liz.'

'I was. I was, but – never did I guess!'

'I didn't desire ye to.' Mrs Ashcroft smiled. 'I saw 'Arry once or twice in de street, wonnerful fleshed up an' restored back. Then, one day I didn't see 'im, an' 'is mother told me one of 'is 'orses 'ad lashed out an' caught 'im on the 'ip. So 'e was abed an' middlin' painful. An' Bessie, she says to his mother, 'twas a pity 'Arry 'adn't a woman of 'is own to take the nursin' off 'er. And the old lady *was* mad! She told us that 'Arry 'ad never looked after any woman in 'is born days, an' as long as she was atop the mowlds, she'd contrive for 'im till 'er two 'ands dropped off. So I knowed she'd do watch-dog for me, 'thout askin' for bones.'

Mrs Fettley rocked with small laughter.

'That day,' Mrs Ashcroft went on, 'I'd stood on me feet nigh all the time, watchin' the doctor go in an' out; for they thought it might be 'is ribs, too. That made my boil break again, issuin' an' weepin'. But it turned out 'twadn't ribs at all, an' 'Arry 'ad a good night. When I heard that, nex' mornin', I says to meself, "I won't lay two an' two together *yit*. I'll keep me leg down a week, an' see what comes of it." It didn't hurt me that day, to speak of – 'seemed more to draw the strength out o' me like – an' 'Arry 'ad another good night. That made me persevere; but I didn't dare lay two an' two together till the week-end, an' then, 'Arry come forth e'en a'most 'imself again – na'un hurt outside ner in of him. I nigh fell on me knees in de wash-house when Bessie was up-street. "I've got ye now, my man," I says.

"You'll take your good from me 'thout knowin' it till my life's end. O God send me long to live for 'Arry's sake!" I says. An' I dunno that didn't still me ragin's.'

'For good?' Mrs Fettley asked.

'They come back, plenty times, but, let be how 'twould, I knowed I was doin' for 'im. I *knowed* it. I took an' worked me pains on an' off, like regulatin' my own range, till I learned to 'ave 'em at my commandments. An' that was funny, too. There was times, Liz, when my trouble 'ud all s'rink an' dry up, like. First, I used to try an' fetch it on again; bein' fearful to leave 'Arry alone too long for anythin' to lay 'old of. Prasin'ly I come to see that was a sign he'd do all right awhile, an' so I saved myself.'

' 'Ow long for?' Mrs Fettley asked, with deepest interest.

'I've gone de better part of a year onct or twice with na'un more to show than the liddle weepin' core of it, like. *All* s'rinked up an' dried off. Then he'd inflame up – for a warnin' – an' I'd suffer it. When I couldn't no more – an' I *'ad* to keep on goin' with my Lunnon work – I'd lay me leg high on a cheer till it eased. Not too quick. I knowed by the feel of it, those times, dat 'Arry was in need. Then I'd send another five shillin's to Bess, or somethin' for the chillern, to find out if, mebbe, 'e'd took any hurt through my neglects. 'Twas *so*! Year in, year out, I worked it dat way, Liz, an' 'e got 'is good from me 'thout knowin' – for years and years.'

'But what did *you* get out of it, Gra'?' Mrs Fettley almost wailed. 'Did ye see 'im reg'lar?'

'Times – when I was 'ere on me 'ol'days. An' more, now that I'm 'ere for good. But 'e's never looked at me, ner any other woman 'cept 'is mother. 'Ow I used to watch an' listen! So did she.'

'Years an' years!' Mrs Fettley repeated. 'An' where's 'e workin' at now?'

'Oh, 'e's give up carterin' quite a while. He's workin' for one o' them big tractorisin' firms – plowin' sometimes, an' sometimes off with lorries – fur as Wales, I've 'eard. He comes 'ome to 'is mother 'tween whiles; but I don't set eyes on him now, fer weeks on end. No odds! 'Is job keeps 'im from continuin' in one stay anywheres.'

'But – just for de sake o' sayin' somethin' – s'pose 'Arry *did* get married?' said Mrs Fettley.

Mrs Ashcroft drew her breath sharply between her still even and natural teeth. '*Dat* ain't been required of me,' she answered. 'I reckon my pains 'ull be counted agin that. Don't *you*, Liz?'

'It ought to be, dearie. It ought to be.'

'It *do* 'urt sometimes. You shall see it when Nurse comes. She thinks I don't know it's turned.'

Mrs Fettley understood. Human nature seldom walks up to the word 'cancer'.

'Be ye certain sure, Gra'?' she asked.

'I was sure of it when old Mr Marshall 'ad me up to 'is study an' spoke a long piece about my faithful service. I've obliged 'em on an' off for a goodish time, but not enough for a pension. But they give me a weekly 'lowance for life. I knew what *that* sinnified – as long as three years ago.'

'Dat don't *prove* it, Gra'.'

'To give fifteen bob a week to a woman 'oo'd live twenty year in the course o' nature? It *do*!'

'You're mistook! You're mistook!' Mrs Fettley insisted.

'Liz, there's *no* mistakin' when the edges are all heaped up, like – same as a collar. You'll see it. An' I laid out Dora Wickwood, too. *She* 'ad it under the armpit, like.'

Mrs Fettley considered awhile, and bowed her head in finality.

''Ow long d'you reckon 'twill allow ye, countin' from now, dearie?'

'Slow come, slow go. But if I don't set eyes on ye 'fore next hoppin', this'll be goodbye, Liz.'

'Dunno as I'll be able to manage by then – not 'thout I have a liddle dog to lead me. For de chillern, dey won't be troubled, an' – O Gra'! – I'm blindin' up – I'm blindin' up!'

'Oh, *dat* was why you didn't more'n finger with your quilt-patches all this while! I was wonderin' . . . But the pain *do* count, don't ye think, Liz? The pain *do* count to keep 'Arry – where I want 'im. Say it can't be wasted, like.'

'I'm sure of it – sure of it, dearie. You'll 'ave your reward.'

'I don't want no more'n this – *if* de pain is taken into de reckonin'.'

‘ ’Twill be – ’twill be, Gra’.’

There was a knock on the door.

‘That’s Nurse. She’s before ’er time,’ said Mrs Ashcroft. ‘Open to ’er.’

The young lady entered briskly, all the bottles in her bag clicking. ‘Evenin’, Mrs Ashcroft,’ she began. ‘I’ve come raound a little earlier than usual because of the Institute dance to-naite. You won’t ma-ind, will you?’

‘Oh, no. Me dancin’ days are over.’ Mrs Ashcroft was the self-contained domestic at once. ‘My old friend, Mrs Fettley ’ere, has been settin’ talkin’ with me a while.’

‘I hope she ’asn’t been fatiguing you?’ said the Nurse a little frostily.

‘Quite the contrary. It ’as been a pleasure. Only – only – just at the end I felt a bit – a bit flogged out like.’

‘Yes, yes.’ The Nurse was on her knees already, with the washes to hand. ‘When old ladies get together they talk a deal too much, I’ve noticed.’

‘Mebbe we do,’ said Mrs Fettley, rising. ‘So, now, I’ll make myself scarce.’

‘Look at it first, though,’ said Mrs Ashcroft feebly. ‘I’d like ye to look at it.’

Mrs Fettley looked, and shivered. Then she leaned over, and kissed Mrs Ashcroft once on the waxy yellow forehead, and again on the faded grey eyes.

‘It *do* count, don’t it – de pain?’ The lips that still kept trace of their original moulding hardly more than breathed the words.

Mrs Fettley kissed them and moved towards the door.

RAHERE

Rahere, King Henry's Jester, feared by all the
Norman Lords
For his eye that pierced their bosoms, for his
tongue that shamed their swords;
Feed and flattered by the Churchmen – well they
knew how deep he stood
In dark Henry's crooked counsels – fell upon an
evil mood.

Suddenly, his days before him and behind him
seemed to stand
Stripped and barren, fixed and fruitless, as those
leagues of naked sand
When St Michael's ebb slinks outward to the
bleak horizon-bound,
And the trampling wide-mouthed waters are
withdrawn from sight and sound.

Then a Horror of Great Darkness sunk his spirit
and, anon,
(Who had seen him wince and whiten as he turned
to walk alone)
Followed Gilbert the Physician, and muttered in
his ear,
'Thou hast it, O my brother?' 'Yea, I have it,'
said Rahere.

'So it comes,' said Gilbert smoothly, 'man's most
immanent distress.
'Tis a humour of the Spirit which abhorreth all
excess;
And, whatever breed the surfeit – Wealth, or
Wit, or Power, or Fame
(And thou hast each) the Spirit laboureth to
expel the same.

'Hence the dulled eye's deep self-loathing –
hence the loaded leaden brow;
Hence the burden of Wanhope that aches thy
soul and body now.
Ay, the merriest fool must face it, and the wisest
Doctor learn;
For it comes – it comes,' said Gilbert, 'as it
passes – to return.'

But Rahere was in his torment, and he wandered,
dumb and far,
Till he came to reeking Smithfield where the
crowded gallows are.
(Followed Gilbert the Physician) and beneath the
wry-necked dead,
Sat a leper and his woman, very merry, breaking
bread.

He was cloaked from chin to ankle – faceless,
fingerless, obscene –
Mere corruption swaddled man-wise, but the
woman whole and clean;
And she waited on him crooning, and Rahere
beheld the twain,
Each delighting in the other, and he checked and
groaned again.

'So it comes, – it comes,' said Gilbert, 'as it came
when Life began.
'Tis a motion of the Spirit that revealeth God to
man
In the shape of Love exceeding, which regards
not taint or fall,
Since in perfect Love, saith Scripture, can be no
excess at all.

'Hence the eye that sees no blemish – hence the
hour that holds no shame.
Hence the Soul assured the Essence and the
Substance are the same.
Nay, the meanest need not miss it, though the
mightier pass it by;
For it comes – it comes,' said Gilbert, 'and, thou
seest, it does not die!'

The Gardener

One grave to me was given,
  One watch till Judgment Day;
And God looked down from Heaven
  And rolled the stone away.

One day in all the years,
  One hour in that one day,
His Angel saw my tears,
  And rolled the stone away!

Everyone in the village knew that Helen Turrell did her duty by all her world, and by none more honourably than by her only brother's unfortunate child. The village knew, too, that George Turrell had tried his family severely since early youth, and were not surprised to be told that, after many fresh starts given and thrown away, he, an Inspector of Indian Police, had entangled himself with the daughter of a retired non-commissioned officer, and had died of a fall from a horse a few weeks before his child was born. Mercifully, George's father and mother were both dead, and though Helen, thirty-five and independent, might well have washed her hands of the whole disgraceful affair, she most nobly took charge, though she was, at the time, under threat of lung trouble which had driven her to the South of France. She arranged for the passage of the child and a nurse from Bombay, met them at Marseilles, nursed the baby through an attack of infantile dysentery due to the carelessness of the nurse, whom she had had to dismiss, and at last, thin and worn but triumphant, brought the boy late in the autumn, wholly restored, to her Hampshire home.

All these details were public property, for Helen was as open as the day, and held that scandals are only increased by hushing them up. She admitted that George had always been rather a black sheep, but things might have been much worse if the mother had insisted on her right to keep the boy. Luckily, it seemed that people of that class would do almost anything for money, and, as George had always turned to her in his scrapes, she felt herself justified – her friends agreed with her – in cutting the whole non-commissioned officer connection, and giving the child every advantage. A christening, by the Rector, under the name of Michael, was the first step. So far as she knew herself, she was not, she said, a child-lover, but, for all his faults, she had been very fond of George, and she pointed out that little Michael had his father's mouth to a line; which made something to build upon.

As a matter of fact, it was the Turrell forehead, broad, low, and well-shaped, with the widely spaced eyes beneath it, that Michael had most faithfully reproduced. His mouth was somewhat better cut than the family type. But Helen, who would concede nothing good to his mother's side, vowed he was a Turrell all over, and, there being no one to contradict, the likeness was established.

In a few years Michael took his place, as accepted as Helen had always been – fearless, philosophical, and fairly good-looking. At six, he wished to know why he could not call her 'Mummy', as other boys called their mothers. She explained that she was only his auntie, and that aunties were not quite the same as mummies, but that, if it gave him pleasure, he might call her 'Mummy' at bedtime, for a pet-name between themselves.

Michael kept his secret most loyally, but Helen, as usual, explained the fact to her friends; which when Michael heard, he raged.

'Why did you tell? *Why* did you tell?' came at the end of the storm.

'Because it's always best to tell the truth,' Helen answered, her arm round him as he shook in his cot.

'All right, but when the troof's ugly I don't think it's nice.'

'Don't you, dear?'

'No, I don't, and' – she felt the small body stiffen – 'now you've told, I won't call you "Mummy" any more – not even at bedtimes.'

'But isn't that rather unkind?' said Helen softly.

'I don't care! I don't care! You've hurted me in my insides and I'll hurt you back. I'll hurt you as long as I live!'

'Don't, oh, don't talk like that, dear! You don't know what——'

'I will! And when I'm dead I'll hurt you worse!'

'Thank goodness, I shall be dead long before you, darling.'

'Huh! Emma says, " 'Never know your luck." ' (Michael had been talking to Helen's elderly, flat-faced maid.) 'Lots of little boys die quite soon. So'll I. *Then* you'll see!'

Helen caught her breath and moved towards the door, but the wail of 'Mummy! Mummy!' drew her back again, and the two wept together.

At ten years old, after two terms at a prep. school, something or somebody gave him the idea that his civil status was not quite regular. He attacked Helen on the subject, breaking down her stammered defences with the family directness.

' 'Don't believe a word of it,' he said, cheerily, at the end. 'People wouldn't have talked like they did if my people had been married. But don't you bother, Auntie. I've found out all about my sort in English Hist'ry and the Shakespeare bits. There was William the Conqueror to begin with, and – oh, heaps more, and they all got on first-rate. 'Twon't make any difference to you, my being *that* – will it?'

'As if anything could——' she began.

'All right. We won't talk about it any more if it makes you cry.' He never mentioned the thing again of his own will, but when, two years later, he skilfully managed to have measles in the holidays, as his temperature went up to the appointed one hundred and four he muttered of nothing else, till Helen's voice, piercing at last his delirium, reached him with assurance that nothing on earth or beyond could make any difference between them.

The terms at his public school and the wonderful Christmas, Easter, and Summer holidays followed each other, variegated and glorious as jewels on a string; and as jewels Helen treasured them. In due time Michael developed his own interests, which ran their courses and gave way to others; but his interest in Helen was constant and increasing throughout. She repaid it with all that she had of affection or could command of counsel and money; and since Michael was no fool, the War took him just before what was like to have been a most promising career.

He was to have gone up to Oxford, with a scholarship, in

October. At the end of August he was on the edge of joining the first holocaust of public-school boys who threw themselves into the Line; but the captain of his OTC, where he had been sergeant for nearly a year, headed him off and steered him directly to a commission in a battalion so new that half of it still wore the old Army red, and the other half was breeding meningitis through living overcrowdedly in damp tents. Helen had been shocked at the idea of direct enlistment.

'But it's in the family,' Michael laughed.

'You don't mean to tell me that you believed that old story all this time?' said Helen. (Emma, her maid, had been dead now several years.) 'I gave you my word of honour – and I give it again – that – that it's all right. It is indeed.'

'Oh, *that* doesn't worry me. It never did,' he replied valiantly. 'What I meant was, I should have got into the show earlier if I'd enlisted – like my grandfather.'

'Don't talk like that! Are you afraid of its ending so soon, then?'

'No such luck. You know what K. says.'

'Yes. But my banker told me last Monday it couldn't *possibly* last beyond Christmas – for financial reasons.'

' 'Hope he's right, but our Colonel – and he's a Regular – says it's going to be a long job.'

Michael's battalion was fortunate in that, by some chance which meant several 'leaves', it was used for coast-defence among shallow trenches on the Norfolk coast; thence sent north to watch the mouth of a Scotch estuary, and, lastly, held for weeks on a baseless rumour of distant service. But, the very day that Michael was to have met Helen for four whole hours at a railway-junction up the line, it was hurled out, to help make good the wastage of Loos, and he had only just time to send her a wire of farewell.

In France luck again helped the battalion. It was put down near the Salient, where it led a meritorious and unexacting life, while the Somme was being manufactured; and enjoyed the peace of the Armentières and Laventie sectors when that battle began. Finding that it had sound views on protecting its own flanks and could dig, a prudent Commander stole it out of its own Division, under pretence of helping to lay telegraphs, and used it round Ypres at large.

A month later, and just after Michael had written Helen that there was nothing special doing and therefore no need to worry, a shell-splinter dropping out of a wet dawn killed him at once. The next shell uprooted and laid down over the body what had been the foundation of a barn wall, so neatly that none but an expert would have guessed that anything unpleasant had happened.

By this time the village was old in experience of war, and, English fashion, had evolved a ritual to meet it. When the postmistress handed her seven-year-old daughter the official telegram to take to Miss Turrell, she observed to the Rector's gardener: 'It's Miss Helen's turn now.' He replied, thinking of his own son: 'Well, he's lasted longer than some.' The child herself came to the front-door weeping aloud, because Master Michael had often given her sweets. Helen, presently, found herself pulling down the house-blinds one after one with great care, and saying earnestly to each: 'Missing *always* means dead.' Then she took her place in the dreary procession that was impelled to go through an inevitable series of unprofitable emotions. The Rector, of course, preached hope and prophesied word, very soon, from a prison camp. Several friends, too, told her perfectly truthful tales, but always about other women, to whom, after months and months of silence, their missing had been miraculously restored. Other people urged her to communicate with infallible Secretaries of organisations who could communicate with benevolent neutrals, who could extract accurate information from the most secretive of Hun prison commandants. Helen did and wrote and signed everything that was suggested or put before her.

Once, on one of Michael's leaves, he had taken her over a munition factory, where she saw the progress of a shell from blank-iron to the all but finished article. It struck her at the time that the wretched thing was never left alone for a single second; and 'I'm being manufactured into a bereaved next of kin,' she told herself, as she prepared her documents.

In due course, when all the organisations had deeply or

sincerely regretted their inability to trace, etc., something gave way within her and all sensation – save of thankfulness for the release – came to an end in blessed passivity. Michael had died and her world had stood still and she had been one with the full shock of that arrest. Now she was standing still and the world was going forward, but it did not concern her – in no way or relation did it touch her. She knew this by the ease with which she could slip Michael's name into talk and incline her head to the proper angle, at the proper murmur of sympathy.

In the blessed realisation of that relief, the Armistice with all its bells broke over her and passed unheeded. At the end of another year she had overcome her physical loathing of the living and returned young, so that she could take them by the hand and almost sincerely wish them well. She had no interest in any aftermath, national or personal, of the war, but, moving at an immense distance, she sat on various relief committees and held strong views – she heard herself delivering them – about the site of the proposed village War Memorial.

Then there came to her, as next of kin, an official intimation, backed by a page of a letter to her in indelible pencil, a silver identity-disc, and a watch, to the effect that the body of Lieutenant Michael Turrell had been found, identified, and re-interred in Hagenzeele Third Military Cemetery – the letter of the row and the grave's number in that row duly given.

So Helen found herself moved on to another process of the manufacture – to a world full of exultant or broken relatives, now strong in the certainty that there was an altar upon earth where they might lay their love. These soon told her, and by means of time-tables made clear, how easy it was and how little it interfered with life's affairs to go and see one's grave.

'*So* different,' as the Rector's wife said, 'if he'd been killed in Mesopotamia, or even Gallipoli.'

The agony of being waked up to some sort of second life drove Helen across the Channel, where, in a new world of abbreviated titles, she learnt that Hagenzeele Third could be comfortably reached by an afternoon train which fitted in with the morning boat, and that there was a comfortable little hotel not three kilometres from Hagenzeele itself, where one could spend quite a comfortable night and see one's grave next morning. All this she had from a Central Authority who lived in a board and tar-paper shed on the skirts of a razed city full of whirling lime-dust and blown papers.

'By the way,' said he, 'you know your grave, of course?'

'Yes, thank you,' said Helen, and showed its row and number typed on Michael's own little typewriter. The officer would have checked it, out of one of his many books; but a large Lancashire woman thrust between them and bade him tell her where she might find her son, who had been corporal in the ASC. His proper name, she sobbed, was Anderson, but, coming of respectable folk, he had of course enlisted under the name of Smith; and had been killed at Dickie-bush, in early 'Fifteen. She had not his number nor did she know which of his two Christian names he might have used with his alias; but her Cook's tourist ticket expired at the end of Easter week, and if by then she could not find her child she should go mad. Whereupon she fell forward on Helen's breast; but the officer's wife came out quickly from a little bedroom behind the office, and the three of them lifted the woman on to the cot.

'They are often like this,' said the officer's wife, loosening the tight bonnet-strings. 'Yesterday she said he'd been killed at Hooge. Are you sure you know your grave? It makes such a difference.'

'Yes, thank you,' said Helen, and hurried out before the woman on the bed should begin to lament again.

Tea in a crowded mauve and blue striped wooden structure, with a false front, carried her still further into the nightmare. She paid her bill beside a stolid, plain-featured Englishwoman, who, hearing her inquire about the train to Hagenzeele, volunteered to come with her.

'I'm going to Hagenzeele myself,' she explained. 'Not to Hagenzeele Third; mine is Sugar Factory, but they call it La Rosière now. It's just south of Hagenzeele Three. Have you got your room at the hotel there?'

'Oh yes, thank you. I've wired.'

'That's better. Sometimes the place is quite full, and at others there's hardly a soul. But they've put bathrooms into the old

Lion d'Or – that's the hotel on the west side of Sugar Factory – and it draws off a lot of people, luckily.'

'It's all new to me. This is the first time I've been over.'

'Indeed! This is my ninth time since the Armistice. Not on my own account. *I* haven't lost anyone, thank God – but, like everyone else, I've a lot of friends at home who have. Coming over as often as I do, I find it helps them to have someone just look at the – the place and tell them about it afterwards. And one can take photos for them, too. I get quite a list of commissions to execute.' She laughed nervously and tapped her slung Kodak. 'There are two or three to see at Sugar Factory this time, and plenty of others in the cemeteries all about. My system is to save them up, and arrange them, you know. And when I've got enough commissions for one area to make it worth while, I pop over and execute them. It *does* comfort people.'

'I suppose so,' Helen answered, shivering as they entered the little train.

'Of course it does. (Isn't it lucky we've got window-seats?) It must do or they wouldn't ask one to do it, would they? I've a list of quite twelve or fifteen commissions here' – she tapped the Kodak again – 'I must sort them out tonight. Oh, I forgot to ask you. What's yours?'

'My nephew,' said Helen. 'But I was very fond of him.'

'Ah, yes! I sometimes wonder whether *they* know after death? What do you think?'

'Oh, I don't – I haven't dared to think much about that sort of thing,' said Helen, almost lifting her hands to keep her off.

'Perhaps that's better,' the woman answered. 'The sense of loss must be enough, I expect. Well, I won't worry you any more.'

Helen was grateful, but when they reached the hotel Mrs Scarsworth (they had exchanged names) insisted on dining at the same table with her, and after the meal, in the little, hideous salon full of low-voiced relatives, took Helen through her 'commissions' with biographies of the dead, where she happened to know them, and sketches of their next of kin. Helen endured till nearly half-past nine, ere she fled to her room.

Almost at once there was a knock at her door and Mrs

Scarsworth entered; her hands, holding the dreadful list, clasped before her.

'Yes – yes – *I* know,' she began. 'You're sick of me, but I want to tell you something. You – you aren't married, are you? Then perhaps you won't . . . But it doesn't matter. I've *got* to tell someone. I can't go on any longer like this.'

'But please——' Mrs Scarsworth had backed against the shut door, and her mouth worked dryly.

'In a minute,' she said. 'You – you know about these graves of mine I was telling you about downstairs, just now? They really *are* commissions. At least several of them are.' Her eye wandered round the room. 'What extraordinary wall-papers they have in Belgium, don't you think? . . . Yes. I swear they are commissions. But there's *one*, d'you see, and – and he was more to me than anything else in the world. Do you understand?'

Helen nodded.

'More than anyone else. And, of course, he oughtn't to have been. He ought to have been nothing to me. But he *was*. He *is*. That's why I do the commissions, you see. That's all.'

'But why do you tell me?' Helen asked desperately.

'Because I'm *so* tired of lying. Tired of lying – always lying – year in and year out. When I don't tell lies I've got to act 'em and I've got to think 'em, always. *You* don't know what that means. He was everything to me that he oughtn't to have been – the one real thing – the only thing that ever happened to me in all my life; and I've had to pretend he wasn't. I've had to watch every word I said, and think out what lie I'd tell next, for years and years!'

'How many years?' Helen asked.

'Six years and four months before, and two and three-quarters after. I've gone to him eight times, since. Tomorrow'll make the ninth, and – and I can't – I *can't* go to him again with nobody in the world knowing. I want to be honest with someone before I go. Do you understand? It doesn't matter about *me*. I was never truthful, even as a girl. But it isn't worthy of *him*. So – so I – I had to tell you. I can't keep it up any longer. Oh, I can't!'

She lifted her joined hands almost to the level of her mouth, and brought them down sharply, still joined, to full arms' length below her waist. Helen reached forward, caught them, bowed her head over them, and murmured: 'Oh, my dear! My dear!' Mrs Scarsworth stepped back, her face all mottled.

'My God!' said she. 'Is *that* how you take it?'

Helen could not speak, and the woman went out; but it was a long while before Helen was able to sleep.

Next morning Mrs Scarsworth left early on her round of commissions, and Helen walked alone to Hagenzeele Third. The place was still in the making, and stood some five or six feet above the metalled road, which it flanked for hundreds of yards. Culverts across a deep ditch served for entrances through the unfinished boundary wall. She climbed a few wooden-faced earthen steps and then met the entire crowded level of the thing in one held breath. She did not know that Hagenzeele Third counted twenty-one thousand dead already. All she saw was a merciless sea of black crosses, bearing little strips of stamped tin at all angles across their faces. She could distinguish no order or arrangement in their mass; nothing but a waist-high wilderness as of weeds stricken dead, rushing at her. She went forward, moved to the left and the right hopelessly, wondering by what guidance she should ever come to her own. A great distance away there was a line of whiteness. It proved to be a block of some two or three hundred graves whose headstones had already been set, whose flowers were planted out, and whose new-sown grass showed green. Here she could see clear-cut letters at the ends of the rows, and referring to her slip, realised that it was not here she must look.

A man knelt behind a line of headstones – evidently a gardener, for he was firming a young plant in the soft earth. She went towards him, her paper in her hand. He rose at her approach and without prelude or salutation asked: 'Who are you looking for?'

'Lieutenant Michael Turrell – my nephew,' said Helen slowly and word for word, as she had many thousands of times in her life.

The man lifted his eyes and looked at her with infinite

compassion before he turned from the fresh-sown grass toward the naked black crosses.

'Come with me,' he said, 'and I will show you where your son lies.'

When Helen left the Cemetery she turned for a last look. In the distance she saw the man bending over his young plants; and she went away, supposing him to be the gardener.

THE BURDEN

One grief on me is laid
  Each day of every year,
Wherein no soul can aid,
  Whereof no soul can hear:
Whereto no end is seen
  Except to grieve again –
Ah, Mary Magdalene,
  Where is there greater pain?

To dream on dear disgrace
  Each hour of every day –
To bring no honest face
  To aught I do or say:
To lie from morn till e'en –
  To know my lies are vain –
Ah, Mary Magdalene,
  Where can be greater pain?

To watch my steadfast fear
  Attend my every way
Each day of every year –
  Each hour of every day:
To burn, and chill between –
  To quake and rage again –
Ah, Mary Magdalene,
  Where shall be greater pain?

One grave to me was given –
  To guard till Judgment Day –
But God looked down from Heaven
  And rolled the Stone away!
One day of all my years –
  One hour of that one day –
His Angel saw my tears
  And rolled the Stone away!